"We're hoping to start just such a crackdown as you suggest. It's with the Politburo now, waiting their final assent. . . . This clandestine group is obviously one of long standing, well entrenched, extremely carefully organized and run; it has all the marks, in fact, of a bona fide KGB operation. . . . Our man has chosen well: he has chosen to infiltrate the KGB because we alone can offer him the unique lever which could bring about this political change. . . . We hold the political direction of the country in our hands. Our man is in this organization quite simply because he knows where the reins are. . . . We have to imagine a man who is among us."

COLLIER SPYMASTERS SERIES

Consulting Editor: Saul A. Katz,
Founder, 999 Bookshop, New York City

THE SIXTH DIRECTORATE

Also by Joseph Hone

The Private Sector
The Oxford Gambit
The Valley of the Fox
The Paris Trap

THE
SIXTH DIRECTORATE

JOSEPH HONE

COLLIER BOOKS
Macmillan Publishing Company
New York

For S M B *and* H M B

Collier Books
Macmillan Publishing Company
866 Third Avenue, New York, NY 10022

Library of Congress Cataloging-in-Publication Data
Hone, Joseph, 1937–
The sixth directorate / Joseph Hone.—1st Collier Books ed.
p.   cm.
Reprint. Originally published: New York : Dutton, 1975.
ISBN 0-02-012613-1
I. Title.
[PR6058.049S59   1990]
823'.914—dc20   89-25218   CIP

First Collier Books Edition 1990

10 9 8 7 6 5 4 3 2 1

Printed in the United States of America

I sent a letter to my love
    and on the way I dropped it.
And one of you has picked it up
    and put it in your pocket.
It wasn't you, it wasn't you,
    it wasn't you,
But it was YOU! . . .

Child's game

Book One

1

The comedian left the stage, the long applause died, and a balalaika ensemble took over, starting on a softly held high chord, a minute vivid fingering on all the dozen instruments, which rose gradually in volume into a long, trembling vibrato before the key was released suddenly, the tune emerged, and a sad and restless music spread over the hall.

In one of the boxes where two couples sat above the audience, Mrs. Andropov turned to her husband with an uncertain smile. "He's good, Yuri, isn't he?"

The two families had come that evening for the gala opening of Arkadi Raikin's new show at the Rossiya Hotel in Moscow.

"Yes, maybe." Her husband spoke without looking round at her. "The disguises certainly are good." Yuri Andropov was gazing intently at the stage where a few minutes before the comedian had undergone one of his instant character transformations, and he seemed to be still trying to fathom the trick, the mechanics behind the comedian's sudden and complete changes of identity. "Yes," he went on, "Arkadi Raikin—he's not bad at all. But doesn't he sometimes overdo it a bit? No? What the Americans would call an 'old Vaudeville Ham'?"

Yuri Andropov took off his spectacles, blinked, rubbed the corners of his eyes vigorously between thumb and forefinger. He was a tall, heavily built man with a generous flow of lightly silvered hair going straight back from his forehead, an equally straight and forceful nose, a perfectly bowed upper lip matched by a lower one that turned outward gently, invitingly, like a sensualist's. Only his eyes betrayed his substantial bearing: they were very small, the lids narrowed together—almost a deformity in the generally expansive context. There was nothing generous here: care and suspicion were the only spectators at these windows of the soul.

"What do you know about American vaudeville, Tata?" his daughter, Yelena, said. "Why should there be anything American about Arkadi Raikin?" She laughed.

Yet Yuri Andropov did know about such things. Long before, he had hoped for a theatrical career and later for something technical with Mosfilm. But neither idea had borne fruit. Instead, at fifty-seven, he had done well elsewhere. He was head of the KGB.

He was therefore one of the very few people in Moscow who could afford to openly criticize Arkadi Raikin by comparing him to an "old American Vaudeville Ham." If Arkadi Raikin had put himself beyond reproach through laughter, so too had Yuri Andropov through fear.

"What do you think?" Yuri Andropov turned to his son-in-law. "Do you really think he's as good as all that? You ought to know in your job—you were in America last year. Of course you're aware of his background, aren't you?"

It was a leading question, among a million others that had come from the same source over the years. The wrong answer could mean nothing more than a delayed promotion, a drop in salary, a change of job, a smaller apartment, a move to a provincial town. But it could lead to worse: a labor camp, a hospital ward, an asylum for the sane; the wrong grammar here could make you a nonperson overnight. All this change of fortune lay within Yuri Andropov's gift, and he was a generous man. His son-in-law knew these things well and he was relieved in the end that he did not have to give a full reply, for just then an aide came in behind them, reminding Yuri Andropov of some pressing business elsewhere in the huge hotel.

"My appointment. You'll forgive me." Andropov stood up and bowed around at his family as though he were a courtier and not a husband and a father. "I'll probably be back late. Don't wait up."

Accompanied by two aides, his personal assistant and a bodyguard, Yuri Andropov walked briskly along a deserted corridor leading from the hall toward the central courtyard of the hotel. It was a few minutes to nine. For the moment everyone in the hotel was either trying to eat or watching Arkadi Raikin. There were more than 5,000 people in the huge building, but here in this long corridor there was nobody and no sound.

At the end of the passageway one of the many KGB men permanently attached to the hotel opened the door out into the courtyard for them. The group passed through into the chilling April cold, the air lying brutally about their faces for a moment before they entered the Presidential Wing, the twenty-three-story tower that rose from the middle of the hotel. This building had been made to accommodate important state guests in a number of exclusively furnished suites. But even now, nearly twenty years after the construction of the Rossiya had begun, not all of these luxurious apartments had been finally completed.

The suite on the nineteenth floor where they met that night was one such. It had never been completed at all. The rooms were nude: the walls and ceilings were completely bare; the central conference table was enclosed by a membrane of soundproofing material, like a huge barrage balloon. There were no telephones, light fixtures, or power points, illumination being supplied by a series of free-standing battery lamps. The floor had never been laid and was raised up now, on open joists, in a series of wooden duckboards a foot above its true level. The furnishings were minimal and spartan, without drawers or any other appendages, and cast in solid steel. Nothing could be concealed here anywhere.

This suite—one of two in the tower (the other was for guests, when they had such)—was permanently reserved by the KGB as office space outside their various official headquarters where unacknowledged business might be conducted. And tonight was just such a case—a meeting between Andropov and the heads of his five Chief Directorates. It was, quite simply, the only single area in the hotel where no electronic eavesdropping equipment had been installed and, just as importantly, where it could literally be seen that none ever was.

The reasons for this isolated choice were several. Here the heads of the five KGB Directorates, each intensely jealous of the other's place and power in the overall hierarchy of the organization, could meet secretly and speak openly; for there were no minutes kept, no records of any sort. The suite was a clearing house for misunderstandings, budding antagonisms, bureaucratic rivalries—far from the centers of that bureaucracy in Dzerzinsky Square and elsewhere. It was also a place to discuss future policy and for Andropov to try and glean some true measure of past mistakes from his five chiefs. It was a think tank, completely isolated, lurking high in the freezing weather above Red Square, where the behavior of the more than 300,000 KGB employees could be studied in the long term, without any one of those people having an opportunity to study their masters in return.

And that was the most important point in the present circumstances. Yuri Andropov and his five directors had come to this place at the start of 1971 in order to discuss, and be able to continue to discuss in the utmost privacy, the most serious ideological threat to the Soviet Union since Trotsky's deviations nearly fifty years before.

In November of the previous year, the KGB Resident at the Embassy in London had given Andropov a confidential report on the matter—mere outlines, but with some quite conclusive, though impersonal evidence. The Resident had returned to London charged with pursuing the matter, but the few trails by then had gone quite cold: a hotel porter had disappeared; the address on a piece of paper had become an empty apartment, the tenants so far untraced. The real trail, through which the whole thing had come to light, was impossible to resuscitate: crossed lines one evening on the Resident's home telephone in Highgate when he had broken in on a long conversation in Russian. Immediately afterward, through a further astounding electronic and professional error, he had found himself listening to the technical staff of a British counterespionage section, incarcerated in some basement telephone exchange, reflecting on the strange dialogue they had all of them just heard: the British had been monitoring the same mysterious source.

But the Resident had clearly established one fact, given actual foundation at last to rumors that had come and thankfully gone over the years. He had confirmed now, without question, one of the worst and oldest fears of the KGB, and before that the NKVD and GPU, something that went back, indeed, to the earliest days of the revolution in 1917: there was within their organization another and far more secret group, the nucleus of an alternative KGB, and therefore, potentially, of alternative government in the Soviet Union. As Yuri Andropov had come to see it, this clandestine Directorate must logically then be complete with its own Chief, deputies, foreign Residents, couriers, counterintelligence, and internal security operatives; its own impenetrable cells and communication arrangements; its own fanatic loyalties and carefully prepared objectives. And this was the worst thing to emerge from the evidence: although they had no precise knowledge of what its objectives were, it was quite clear from the overheard telephone conversation in London that the group was politically orientated toward democratic rather than dictatorial socialism. Thus further supposition was not difficult: "Communism with a human face," as the journalists had it. Yuri Andropov could almost exactly visualize *Time* magazine's descriptions of this counterrevolution if it ever came to light: "It was a move in the direction of a more human brand of Marxism, toward one of its happier variants, that had in the past found favor among so many deviants in the movement, from Rosa Luxemburg to those who perished in the Prague spring...."

There had been a hundred different interpretations of the true faith over the years, Andropov thought, and none of them had really mattered; they could be identified, isolated, and crushed, as had happened so many times before: with Trotsky, with Hungary in 1956, and in Czechoslovakia twelve years later. But here was one Marxist deviation that mattered a great deal, for it had taken root in the heart of the citadel: a flower that had bloomed ferociously in secret; a drug of liberal dissidence that had seeded itself who knew how far about the organization; a belief that could not be identified, isolated, and therefore could not be crushed. It was a threat that could only, as yet, be smelled, elusive and frightening as the sweet smell of a ghost passing from room to room in a charnel house.

When and where would it rise up and take form?

Somewhere, hidden in the vast ramifications of the KGB, totally integrated in the huge secret machine, trained from youth, and now paid by the organization, was a group of people—ten, a hundred, or a thousand, who could say?—more dangerous to the Soviet Union than any outside threat. For what might come from east or west had for long been a known quantity; the KGB had been responsible for the information. But the nature of this force was quite unknown. It fed and had its being at the magnetic center of the State and to look for it was to reverse the whole natural process of the KGB, to turn the organization in upon itself, toward an unmapped territory of vast treason where they had no guides. Here the compasses which before had led unerringly to secret dissension everywhere else spun wildly. So it was that these men had set themselves and this suite aside to take new bearings, to identify this disease at the heart of their lives, to isolate the canker and cut it out.

They were all there when Andropov arrived, the heads of the five Chief Directorates, some already seated at a table in the main room, two others who had been talking by the window quickly joining them: the old man Alexander Sakharovsky, Chief of the KGB's foreign intelligence operation, the First Directorate; Alexei Flitlianov, the youngest of them, a bachelor of forty-nine, head of the Second Directorate responsible for all security matters within the State; Vasilly Chechulian, Third Directorate, counterespionage, a muscular, hearty man; Gregori Rahv, impeccably dressed, the cartoon image of a capitalist banker, in charge of the KGB's scientific arm—electronics, communications, their laboratories; and the Chief of the Fifth Directorate—Management, Personnel, and Finance—Viktor Savitsky, an anonymous figure, member of the Party's Central Committee, an accountant by early profession, whose only noticeable characteristic was that he still took immense pains to look and behave like one.

Andropov bowed quickly around the table, exchanged brief and formal greetings, and then sat down. He lifted both hands to his face, shaped them as for prayer, brought them to either side of his nose, and rubbed it for a second. Then, closing his eyes, he clasped his fingers beneath his chin and was quite silent. Finally, as though he had completed grace before a meal, he spoke.

"I take it we have no further news." He didn't bother to look around for confirmation, but instead let another silence grow on the air, allowing it unnecessary age, so that it became a herald of mysterious change. Then he continued suddenly and brightly: "Very well, then. Since we've got nowhere with the facts, let's try using our imagination. Put ourselves in the position of this group, or more precisely let *one* of us do that. There are five of you here. We will create a Sixth Directorate and thus try and establish its composition and purposes—and a head of that Directorate. And we'll put him sitting in that chair—a man that has come here, just as each of you has, to discuss the problems of his section. Alexei, you start it off. You're transferred from the Second to the Sixth Directorate as of now. Let me start by asking you a few questions. First of all, some background. What are your objectives?"

Alexei Flitlianov smiled and moved easily in his seat. He was a compact, intelligent-faced man, like an energetic academic, full but prematurely graying hair sweeping sideways across his head into white tufts above his ears, and front teeth just slightly out of true; his eyes were dark and set well back in his skull and in the winter pallor of his face they glittered like candles inside a Halloween pumpkin: an awkward face with several bad lapses in the design, but for all that, as so often in such cases, attractive in a way not immediately decipherable.

"I'm honored." Flitlianov's smile ended and he leaned forward earnestly, shoulders hunched, concentrating on a spot somewhere in the middle of the table. "Objectives. Well, to begin with, control of the KGB."

"You want my job."

"Yes. But not for reasons of mere power play. The motives are political.

"Do they originate from the Politburo, the Central Committee, or the Army?"

"No. My origins lie entirely within the KGB."

"Do you have contacts, support in government or the Army?"

"Yes, I think I must have, after so long. Let's say I have my men marked outside. I know who to approach when the moment is ripe."

"And these political objectives—they are toward 'Open Socialism,' democratic alternatives?"

"Yes. The provenance here would be Trotsky, Luxemburg, Dubček—among others. Particularly Dubček, I should say; 'The Prague Spring' that would be the line. Marxist, certainly, but without a dictatorial, monolithic structure." Flitlianov emerged briefly from his role and looked around the table. "In fact we know the nature of these inappropriate objectives very well indeed. We have successfully inhibited them for many years, within the Union and more particularly outside it."

"The counterrevolution then? At last . . ." Andropov smiled.

"Not in any overtly violent terms. A bloodless coup. It would depend on timing—on choosing the right moment to support and promote a group of people in the Central Committee and one or two others in the Politburo."

"The new leaders?"

"Yes."

"So you must have the support, I think, of one or two of these political figures already. You would surely not have gone ahead for so long on your scheme without it."

"Yes, I must have such support. Thus there must be a political arm to this Sixth Directorate. It would have been quite unrealistic of me to have continued such a scheme without that."

"What would the 'right moment' be in all this? What would induce you to move? What are you waiting for?"

"Some moment of crucial dissent within the Central Committee or the Politburo."

"What might give rise to that?"

"China, perhaps? If the proposed escalation of the present border war goes through, for example; if the Kosygin faction bows under current Army pressure, the Politburo could easily divide itself. As you know, there is strong political opposition to any escalation. And that could be the moment for this

Sixth Directorate to move. That's one scenario. There are others."

Andropov said nothing, thinking for half a minute. His expression, with that of the others around the table, had become more than serious; it was numb. "Could any of this really be so?" they all seemed to be asking. "Have we taken this charade too far?"

"Aren't we taking this game a little too far?" Vasilly Chechulian said. "It seems to me we are presupposing something too clever by half." He turned to Flitlianov. "Much as I acknowledge and admire your skills, Alexei, I doubt if even you could pull such a scheme off. The profile you're drawing here, the head of this Sixth Directorate—he must be either a fool or a superman; the vast hazards you've contrived for him in your projections could make him no less than one or the other. There's too much—far too much—that could go wrong. I may believe in the existence of some sort of 'Directorate,' as you've outlined it, but I don't believe for a second that it has a chance of ever getting to the starting gate. Principally because your own Directorate, Alexei—the *real* Second Directorate—would find out about it long before that. Your internal security hasn't been exactly lax recently, Alexei. You've clearly marked out and curtailed every other dissident movement. Why should you fail with this one?"

No one spoke. Then Flitlianov said slowly and good naturedly: "Those are all fair points, Vasilly. I agree with you. I hope I do get this group. I'm sure I will. But for the moment I haven't."

Andropov nodded in agreement. "That's why we're *making* these projections, Vasilly, to give us something to aim at. And we should always allow for the most unlikely targets."

Gregori Rahv, the engineer, had been anxious to prove his worth for some time. Now he leaned forward, settling the folds of his fine new suit. "I tend to agree with Vasilly. I think we may be getting off the track. The center of this clandestine operation may not be in the KGB—or in the Politburo. Let's take a look at some *likely* targets." He turned to Andropov. "This typewritten newsletter that's been causing so much trouble recently, *The Chronicle of Current Events,* surely someone connected with that is the man we want, someone you've not caught up with yet—head of an outside group that has *contacts*, merely, inside the KGB—the voices our man in London heard being some of them, or *all* of them. Shouldn't we simply intensify our crackdown on these dissident movements, this newsletter?"

Andropov sighed quietly. But Alexei was brightly placatory. "I think you might be right, Gregori. But I have had no authorization to raise the pressure on these dissident movements. My directive," he looked at Andropov, "has been to handle them very carefully during the current rapprochement with the U.S."

"Surely that can now be changed—if the security of the State is at risk—as I assume it is?" Rahv asked quickly.

"Yes, Gregori," Andropov replied. "That *can* be changed. We're hoping to start just such a crackdown as you suggest. It's with the Politburo now, waiting their final assent. Suslov will get that for us. Unfortunately I can't agree that the *center* of this group lies outside the KGB, in any dissident intellectual movement. The reason is simple: this clandestine group is obviously one of long standing, well entrenched, extremely carefully organized and run; it has all the marks, in fact, of a bona fide KGB operation. Now, no outside organization could have successfully maintained such an operation for so long—they would have been discovered long ago. Yet as part of the KGB they could remain undetectable, as they have done. Our man has chosen well: he has chosen to infiltrate the KGB because we alone can offer him the unique lever which could bring about this political change. Tacitly, we hold the political direction of the country in our hands. Our man is in this organization quite simply because he knows where the reins are. The actual power for political change behind *The Chronicle of Current Events*—for all that it may worry us in other ways—wouldn't light a flashlight bulb. No, we have to imagine a man who is among us. Let's continue with our profile of him. Right, Alexei, you want my job. You're capable of doing it?"

"Yes. I must assume so."

"At the moment, therefore, you hold some considerably senior rank?"

"Yes."

Andropov was much encouraged. "Good." He turned, looking around the table. "We are beginning to see something now, a senior man, bringing outsiders into the KGB, a careful, difficult job, time consuming. So I think we can assume—if they have men in London—that this Directorate started some time ago; ten, more like twenty years ago. Or even before that. During the war perhaps. And this may give us the reasons which started it. We're somewhere in the early forties or late thirties. We're at the end of the Moscow trials, gentlemen, the Stalin-Hitler pact. Those events could well encourage dissention in the mind of some young NKVD recruit of the time. So what do we see? A dissenter, therefore an intellectual in his student days during the late thirties; good army career, almost certainly as an intelligence officer; joined us sometime between 1945 and 1950, at the very latest. Well, we shall have the files on all such recruits—Savitsky? Will you make a note?"

The head of Personnel, Management, and Finance nodded. "I had already thought along such lines, sir. The files reflecting such a profile are ready."

Andropov made no acknowledgment of this initiative, continuing instead in his enthusiastic chase with Flitlianov: "Now how many people do you have with you in your Sixth Directorate, Alexei?"

"Well, if I've been recruiting for, say, twenty years, but having to be extremely careful over who I choose, I'd say I'd picked up someone about once a month. Say—around two hundred people now."

"What sort of people, Alexei? What jobs are you placing them in? Which Directorate would it be most to your advantage to control—when the 'moment' came?"

"Obviously my own, the Second Directorate—internal security through the Union, on the spot, ready, as you say, for the 'moment.'"

"Yes, of course." Andropov thought once more. "Except they'd lack mobility in the Second Directorate and be highly exposed to any investigation. And I don't think you'd keep all your eggs in one basket, Alexei. You'd have some of your men overseas, I think, as an alternative group, men who could start the whole thing again. That would be the normal procedure, wouldn't it?"

"Yes. The group would be in the usual cell form, each one self-contained, with complete cutouts between them—no —links, each one headed by a deputy."

"You'd use the block cutout—that's to say you know each of your deputies—"

"No, I'd use the other process: the chain cutout. I would know my *first* deputy; he would have recruited the next and so on. And each deputy would have recruited his own staff. Thus I would know, by name, only a very small proportion of the entire group: this would give us a chance to regroup in the event of myself or any deputy being caught."

"That first deputy is an important figure then, isn't he, Alexei? If we took you, we'd have to be sure we could get him too. If he went to ground properly we'd be no further on at all in the affair. We'd have to be certain that he never had any warning that you'd been cracked, for example, or that we were on to you."

"Yes. That first deputy would have to have his ear very much to the ground, ready to bury himself the moment anything started to give at the top. Ideally he would have direct access to all top policy movement in the KGB—to this committee here, in fact."

Flitlianov had at last voiced something which had gradually been forming in the minds of all present at the table. Vasilly Chechulian was the first to speak, a harshness, almost an anger in his normally easy voice. "Look—what have we imagined? A very senior man in the Second Directorate, stationed in Moscow, ex-army intelligence officer, joined us immediately after the war, a particularly able man, an intellectual among other things, and quite a young man, in his late forties now perhaps. Well, it must be clear to all of us here—and most of all to you, Alexei—that this background is very similar to your own." Vasilly Chechulian turned to Andropov. "I'm curious to know why the Chief of the Second Directorate, in response to your queries, has almost exactly described himself in this role of counterrevolutionary. What are we meant to deduce from this?"

Chechulian lit a cigarette, the first man at the meeting

to do so. Tilting his head, he blew a stream of smoke almost straight upward where the burned tobacco formed a small wispy cloud under the soundproofing membrane. There was a sudden smell of life in the arid room.

"Ask him yourself, Vasilly," Yuri Andropov said. "We're all supposed to be asking questions here."

"Well, Alexei—what are you condemning yourself out of your own mouth for?"

"Not at all, Vasilly. I was asked to *imagine* myself as head of this mysterious Sixth Directorate. That's how *I* would have gone about organizing it. You would have done it differently, I'm sure—yet not, I think, so very differently. There are constants in the formation of any clandestine group. You formed just such a group yourself in West Germany just before the war. We know that. I might also add that the background I've given this man could, at a stretch, fit you as well as me."

"Oh, I'm no intellectual, Alexei. You've a degree. You were even a professor once, as your cover overseas. Besides, I'm older than you."

"Yes, but the rest stands, or near enough. Indeed your counterespionage directorate might be the expected place to look for this sort of conspiracy. Your Third Directorate, necessarily, of course, is the most secretive part of our organization. By comparison my Second Directorate is an open book, and I'm hardly more than a traffic policeman."

Flitlianov smiled briefly. Chechulian said nothing. Andropov broke the moment's unease that had suddenly sprung up.

"Gentlemen, I didn't come here—nor, I hope, any of you —to conduct a purge. That was not the purpose of my questions to Alexei. I wanted a picture of the *type* of man we're after. And I think Alexei has given us that. I think probably, too, the man is in Alexei's Directorate. But that, as we've shown, is to be expected. His is by far the largest, more than 20,000 fully established staff, at least 200 of which occupy senior rank, and some of these must share some or all of the characteristics we've established. We'll go through all these men very carefully now, take them apart. And I'd like each of you to do the same within your own Directorate. We have a rough picture, a profile. It may be the wrong one, but for the moment we've nothing else to go on. Let's see if we can find the body that fits it." He looked around at the five men. "And kill that body quickly."

Andropov paused, consulting some notes in front of him. The others relaxed. Chechulian poured himself a glass of mineral water from a bottle in front of him, tasted some of it and then puckered his lips. He looked at the contents of the glass sadly and pushed it away. Andropov had found his place. "Gentlemen, our second consideration this evening, normally our first: next year's budget. As you know, our allocations are to be cut, by up to 18 percent over three years, starting January 1972. We must continue to mark out areas of economy. However, we may be able to limit this to one area and Gregori Rahv will brief you on this in a moment. In outline, what it amounts to is this: I believe we may be able to make substantial reductions in our scientific budget, particularly in the area of communications and in future capital development in that field. You'll remember our discussion at the last meeting; since then we've established beyond doubt that the British have now successfully developed their new code transmission system and will shortly be introducing it into all their diplomatic and intelligence traffic; as far as we can tell, it's a form of electronic one-time pad. There's no doubt that if we can obtain the precise technical data on how this system operates—which we can only do *at source*, on site—this information alone should enable us to reduce our expenditure by the required 18 percent over three years. Gregori, would you give us the present position in more detail?"

Gregori Rahv broached these electronic mysteries very carefully and clearly, like a teacher among witless, rascally children. Chechulian hunched his great farmer's shoulders and let his head sink on his chest. Andropov removed his spectacles and pinched the bridge of his nose. Flitlianov closed his eyes. Sakharovsky studied the label on the mineral water bottle in front of him, massaging his old hands. Savitsky remained obviously alert; a saving of 18 percent over three years would bring more credit to him than to anyone else in the room.

Technical data filled the air for the next fifteen minutes. Sakharovsky had to force himself to attend, for he knew that his First Directorate would be made responsible for obtaining this information in England. And so it was later agreed. After ten minutes on other business, the meeting broke up.

"Come, Alexander," Andropov turned to the old man. "We must welcome our guests. Alexei? Are you coming to meet our Czech colleagues? No? Well, see you on Sunday then. You too, Vasilly; you're with us on the hunt as well, aren't you?" Remember it's a five o'clock start. Unless you want to sleep at the lodge overnight? No one else coming downstairs with us?" Andropov looked around the room. "Very well, then. I thank you for your attention. Gentlemen: I bid you a 'happy weekend.' "

Andropov sometimes introduced odd, English phrases into his conversation: "Vaudeville Ham," "happy weekend," "the more the merrier." The colloquialisms were always there, waiting rudely to emerge, often in the most inappropriate circumstances. And this was one of them, Alexei Flitlianov thought. "Happy weekend?" Certainly Andropov's professional outlook at that moment did not warrant any such *jeux d'esprit*, the weather around him seemed threatening indeed. There was some contradiction here, these happy words in a time of vast conspiracy. Flitlianov could not account for this good humor. It was as though he had stumbled for the first time on an untranslatable idiom in Andropov's commonplace phrase book.

"Good. I didn't think he'd come with us. We can talk after we've seen our Czech friends." Andropov spoke to Sakharovsky quietly as they walked down one flight of stairs to the eighteenth floor to the second KGB suite (reserved for their visitors) in the Presidential Tower. There they welcomed their guests who had arrived earlier in the evening on the last flight of the day from Prague: the head of the Czech Internal Security police, Colonel Hartep, and Andropov's Russian liaison officer in Prague, Chief of the KGB bureau there, together with assorted deputies, assistants, and bodyguards. But the little social reunion between the two security organizations didn't last long.

Andropov brought it quickly to a close. "Gentlemen, you've had a long day. Tomorrow, our first meeting. Comrade Sakharovsky will be in the chair. I will be with you for the afternoon session. On Sunday, as last year, our hunting party." He turned to the Colonel. "I trust your aim remains true, Colonel? The quarry, I gather, is as lively as ever. I believe we shall have some 'good hunting.'" But Colonel Hartep was not a linguist and Andropov's sally died at once in the rigid atmosphere.

But for Andropov and Sakharovsky the meeting had served its purpose: it had delayed their departure from the hotel; they had not had to leave with the other chiefs and could thus travel back home together, undetected in the same car.

"Well?" Andropov spoke as soon as the big Volga limousine began to gather speed through the freezing empty streets of the city, moving out of Red Square toward the northern suburbs. "What do you think?"

Sakharovsky rubbed his hands busily again, though the car was warm enough against the bitter night.

"I don't know. I'm not sure now. He handled it perfectly. A great actor—or else he's nothing to do with it."

"Yes. I had the same feeling for a while. But I'm sure it's him."

"I don't know. It *looks* very possible, I agree," Sakharovsky went on. "But that's my worry; it's too obvious. What Flitlianov did in his imaginary profile of the Sixth Directorate was to outline almost exactly the real subsidiary group—which he controls, which your predecessor appointed him to, which you and I know about. The Sixth Directorate he suggested—almost everything about it, its formation, composition, and so on—corresponds with our own internal security division, which he heads: an equally 'clandestine' directorate. Are we to suppose that this is the basis of the whole conspiracy, that the men Flitlianov has recruited over the years are not there to ensure the security of the KGB but its destruction?"

"That seems to me very probable," Andropov replied. "You say it's too obvious. But look at it another way: it was also a unique opportunity for anyone with this sort of long-term conspiracy in mind: Flitlianov has had the entire responsibility for forming this security division, with very little reference to the top. He had his own budget, which always included a large floating allocation, including hard currency overseas. He kept everything to himself. That was the whole point of the operation originally, which I don't think I would ever have sanctioned; he was to recruit and train a special corps of men, here and abroad, quite *outside* the regular KGB channels, and to place these men among KGB operatives whose loyalty or performance we had doubts about. His division is an early warning system throughout the KGB. And all right, I'll admit it has worked extraordinarily well. We've suffered very few lapses. But you can see the unique lever it's given him: none of the other Directorates know of the existence of this group. And how much do you and I really know of it? That again was part of the original plan: that the names of Flitlianov's little army of *agents provocateurs* should be kept on single file, with *him*. There was, of course, to be no general access to them, no possibility of crossed lines, of anyone in the official KGB ever knowing the names, or anything about the members of this unofficial group."

"You have access to those files, if you want it. You could open the whole thing up."

"Yes, I have. But the birds would fly before I got anywhere with an investigation. Besides, it is likely that most of the names he has on file in Moscow are bona fide members of security group. And the rest, the real members of his conspiracy, won't be on any list at all. No, when we move, we must hit *everyone* in this, not only the leader. That's essential. Otherwise it is just killing part of a worm; the rest lives on and reproduces itself. And remember this is not merely one or two defectors or double agents—or someone working for the CIA or the British SIS or the Germans, just out to get a few secrets from us. This is a group of men, a disciplined intelligence corps—there could be hundreds of them—dedicated to throwing over the KGB and after that the Soviet State. Unless we get all the leaders of this group we might as well not bother at all."

"You'd have to track these people down almost simultaneously then, if you want them all. Flitlianov pointed that out. An almost impossible task."

"We'll see. But whatever we have to do this is the time to keep Flitlianov in the dark, keeping him guessing, undermine his confidence. That's why I gave him the opportunity of describing his own security division at the meeting; I put the words into his mouth. He must have been surprised: he can have no idea what I'm up to—*whether* I know and if so *what* and *how much* I know. Prepare him psychologically. It's the only way we can ever hope to get anything out of him when the time comes. Meanwhile, we keep the pressure on him. Sunday will give us another occasion for that. It's an invitation, in the present circumstances, he can't refuse."

"But what if he does refuse it?" Sakharovsky asked. "What if Alexei is the leader of this group, realizes he's a marked man, and decides to break now—before Sunday? In his position, even under the closest possible surveillance, he mightn't find it impossible to get out of the country."

Andropov was suddenly happy in the warmth, looking out on the bitter, empty streets, happy as the man who has the final ace up his sleeve.

"Well that, as I see it, is the whole point of this psychological pressure: to *make* him run. That would be the beginning of the end of our troubles, I think, one sure way of getting a lead on the other ringleaders. Those are the people he'd make for. Or person. That's the one thing he'd have to do at some point outside—make contact with his deputies— or deputy—and start reactivating his group from outside the Union."

"You see, as you pointed out just now, the strange thing is that almost everything Alexei said about the formation of this imaginary Sixth Directorate is true of his own clandestine group. He went out of his way to make the point—an extraordinary risk which nearly came off, an immense double bluff: telling the *truth* about his own group in order to put us off his trail entirely. You remember what he said, what he *insisted*, that he would use the chain and not the block cutout system with his men? He would know the name of his first deputy, who in turn would have recruited the second, and so on; each deputy recruiting his own men? Well, if that's true, and I think it is, then his immediate contact overseas would be this first deputy. And that's someone we want as much as Alexei himself. Through him we start to eat our way along the chain to all the others. So I'm hoping he *will* run."

"Good. Good." Sakharovsky nodded, following the line of thought. "On the other hand, if he does run in order to make this vital contact he's going to be looking over his shoulder."

"Certainly. That's why I have in mind two things: I want to make him think it's time to run, yet without allowing him to think that we know for certain he's our man. He's given us an opening on this with Vasilly Chechulian: he's suggested him as an alternative suspect. Well, we'll go along with that. We'll take Vasilly. And afterward keep Alexei moving in his real job, take the heat off him, put him back on an even keel with some genuine priority business in his own Second Directorate. And that's the moment I think he'll choose to run. It was always catching people that mattered in our job." Andropov ruminated. "Now it's just the opposite; making sure they get away."

There was silence as the car glided along toward the slopes of the Moscow hills, approaching an exclusive suburb, a parkway with villas along either side and a guard post at one end of it.

"You're putting a lot of strain on my surveillance here," Sakharovsky thought aloud. "And most of it overseas. A small mistake by one of my men—a one-way street he doesn't know about, a metro system which Alexei knows backward —and you've lost him as well as all your leads. Why not just take Alexei in Moscow—and screw it out of him here? Keep it simple. Shouldn't that be the essence of it all?"

Yuri Andropov leaned across and put his hand on Sakharovsky's knee.

"Yes, Alexander, but remember something else: we're

almost certain it's Flitlianov. Not absolutely. We could still be wrong. If he runs we'll have conclusive proof. And we still need that. Look, what's the use of cutting the wrong man's leg off? Of course we could get a confession out of him—to anything we wanted. But what would be the point? This isn't a show trial. We want the truth. And therefore we have to have the right man to begin with before we can think of extracting confessions. We can't put every senior KGB officer who *might* be guilty into the wind tunnel. No, if Alexei runs, then we'll know who it is. And that's half the battle. We can take him overseas and interrogate him there if necessary, or wait and see what contacts he makes. We can do any number of things. But we get nowhere by leaving things as they stand. We must make the running, induce the action—*that* is of the essence."

"Very well then. I'll make the arrangements. Increase his surveillance. But remember, I'm stretched on that, using my own men in Moscow who are normally overseas operators. I can't of course use anybody from Alexei's own Second Directorate."

"I know. But there won't be long to wait, I think, before he goes over to your side of the fence. Not long."

It was nearly midnight when he dropped Sakharovsky at his villa. Andropov wondered if his daughter, Yelena, might still be up when he got home himself. He hoped she would be. He wanted to see as much of her as possible before she went back to Leningrad after the weekend.

Yelena was in the kitchen, dressed for bed, making a hot drink, when Yuri Andropov arrived home at his villa further up the parkway.

"For you, Tata?" she asked. "It's English cocoa from the dollar shop. Shall I make you a cup?"

"Please. A half cup. I don't know if I like it."

He didn't like it at all. But he wanted an excuse to be with her, any reason; to talk with her, just gossip; to look at her, this tall daughter of his with a round soft face like her mother's, but with sharper eyes, blackberry dark and quick, and a mind far sharper still; her fine hair severely flat now over her head, and tied up at the back ready for the pillow—the single bed next to the other in the spare room. Did she bring them close together for the night, he wondered? Closer to that dull husband of hers? Did she make that kind of gesture with him? What sort of relationship did they have that way? How did they manage in bed?

He thought about these things now. For now he knew that she shared these things about and inside her body with another man, that she had not given herself up for good to the worthy jailer who lay upstairs. She lived in other, secret ways. It had started a month before with a rumor which he had checked on, arranging for one of his personal assistants to carry out the surveillance. A report confirming it had been given to him that morning: for more than a year his daughter had been having an affair with Alexei Flitlianov.

They had met ten years before, when Yelena had been at university in Moscow, almost a child. But the liaison had only begun recently, had flourished in Leningrad where Flitlianov, with his interest in painting, had gone to see exhibitions at the Hermitage museum where she worked, and had continued intermittently and discreetly whenever she had come down to Moscow to see her old friends and family. He should, he knew, have been shocked by her behavior, and vastly alarmed by the threat their association presented to him in the current circumstances. But he was not; rather the risks they had run, and his vision of those risks, appealed to him in a strange way, just as Arkadi Raikin's many disguises had done.

Yuri Andropov had various official appointments in the Kremlin the next morning, a Saturday. But one in the late morning before he left was unofficial, unknown and unseen.

Andrei Suslov, First Deputy Premier, Senior Politburo Member, and intellectual conscience of all the hardliners and Stalinists in the Party, met him in the empty conference room next to his office. He was a tall, emaciated figure, bald patches in his wispy, plucked-out hair, and a jaw that narrowed fearfully into a foreshortened chin in an egglike skull.

He had the air of a mystic, of some old anchorite on a hill, birdlike above the storms, observing with distant relish the turmoil which his teachings had brought about.

"Sakharovsky will take it," Andropov said as soon as they were alone. "But he's no fool as you well know. He'll report my plan for Flitlianov to your security committee. You can only try and ride it out with them."

"Leave that to me. To us. Your plans for rounding up Flitlianov's aides can be made to seem perfectly appropriate to the Politburo. The important thing is that Flitlianov should be made to run. Is that going ahead?"

"Halfway. There's more to come. But I think he'll run."

"He'd better. Because unless he does we really can't move at all. We've no hard evidence. But once he's out of the country, known to be in the clear, then we can hit all the softliners here, in the Politburo and Central Committee, crack down on the new men, put them through the hoop one by one. Kosygin will not be able to prevent it: the security of the State will be in obvious jeopardy."

Suslov lit another cigarette, chain-smoking.

"Remember, we *want* some real conspiracy to show its head clearly: that would be the supreme justification for the new regime. We need some *real* opposition to make a proper change, an end to the Ostpolitik and the U.S. détente. Flitlianov *must* run; that is the first thing. We can't take him here. Any confession extracted from him by us would be mistrusted completely: our faction would be at a disadvantage from the outset. We must, when we move, be seen to be working quite naturally in response to a genuine threat to the State, which this is. We shall have ample grounds for starting our operation by the very fact of his escape. After that of course you must make every effort to get the names of the others in his group. But the crux of our whole plan is that Flitlianov should get safely out of the country and that his escape should be confirmed without question. What will he do, do you think? Where will he go? How will he do it?"

"London perhaps. Where the telephone call originated. But how? I've no idea. He'll have thought up something pretty good. He's had the time, the position, the contacts. We may lose him from the very beginning."

But as he said this Andropov felt the nervous reaction of a lie that had moved deep within him. For he thought he knew how Flitlianov would leave the country: he would leave it with or through his daughter. And he felt completely paralyzed by this intuition, unable to prevent it or even investigate it. For this was precisely his and Suslov's intention: as long as Flitlianov left the country, it didn't matter how he did it. And Yuri Andropov saw his daughter for a moment floating away in the air, as in a fairy tale, escaping to a happy kingdom in the arms of another man—who was himself.

2

They drove almost two hundred kilometers northeast of Moscow, to the village of Orlyoni, in the darkness of Sunday morning. Turning off the main road here, passing a police checkpoint, they traveled another ten kilometers due east along what had once been little more than a winding cart track but now was a narrow paved road, with huge banks of frozen snow pushed into both ditches by plows. The country here was heavily wooded, undulating, without habitation. The trees were fir, cut fifty yards back from either side of the road, but from then on rising steeply and thickly in long avenues over the many small hills that dotted the area. It was part of a huge forestry development covering thousands of acres of what had once been a great estate before the revolution. Now it had been sealed off and, with the Lodge at its center, made over to the KGB. It was their country seat, as it were, used to entertain guests and for training seminars and conferences.

The sky had just started to lighten as the half-dozen cars drew up in front of the hunting lodge. It was on a hill which sloped gently away over open parkland down a long valley toward the forest, and its tall chimneys and decorated gables caught the first thin rays of the sun while the men beneath stamped their feet about in the half light of the forecourt. In the folds of the valley itself, below them to the west, there were still pools of complete darkness, broken here and there with haloes of mist, the tops of a few trees just visible, sticking up through these ponds of milk as though flooded in white water. The weather was gray, indeterminate, and the temperature well below freezing. But the message in this early dawn was clear: quite soon the sharpness would catch fire and the sun would explode all over the short day.

In the long hall of the Lodge the men gathered round a huge mahogany table where breakfast had been prepared: there was vodka, and two silver samovars of burbling tea. The service was solicitous, the fare more ample. The house and all its period furnishings had been preserved meticulously. There was an air of old bounty and tradition everywhere. Indeed apart from the electric grill for the cutlets and other burning meats there was nothing in the hall which might not have passed there at a hunting breakfast a hundred years before.

The men, numbed after their drive, spoke little at first. But soon, with plates in their hands, tentatively fingering the hot meat, gathering around the two log stoves at either side of the hall, they began to take on the lineaments of a mild humanity. And later they were further encouraged by small, quick draughts of vodka and hot tea. That and the smell of wood smoke, warm leather, and gun oil drew about and stirred within the men a mood of expectant euphoria they could not resist.

The atmosphere in the hall, which had at first gradually relaxed, now quickly tightened. And by the time cigarette smoke drifted upward past the boars' heads and other trophies which ringed the walls, there was a clear sense of impending, irresistible release over the whole party.

The big hall doors were opened. A wall of air moved in over the company, crisp and cold as broken ice. The stoves roared quickly in the sudden draft; the waiters shivered; the men moved out into the forecourt—putting on their greatcoats, fur helmets, and gathering up their guns—with happy fortitude. And the sun, for that moment, perched in the mists of the eastern horizon, an orange bird held briefly in a cage of hills and trees before flight.

They set off westward in a group down across the open parkland toward the forest. Here, at the lowest part of the valley, where the line of trees began sloping upward for miles ahead of them, they were briefed by the head gamekeeper. The hunting block they were taking for the wild boar, he explained, would follow the oldest part of the plantation in the shape of a huge inverted L: a four-mile long first leg, bordered on the left by the road and guard fence of the estate, and then a shorter leg, starting with a clearing of rough underbrush turning northward. For the first part of the hunt they would spread out along the mile width of the block, in line abreast, each of the dozen or so hunters accompanied by a gamekeeper. Shortly after they started, beaters would gradually move toward them from the northern extremity of the block so that, ideally, in this pincers movement, their quarry would be pushed toward the junction of the two arms by both parties and trapped in the clearing of the woods four miles ahead of them.

Outside a gamekeeper's hut at the edge of the trees, they drew lots for position in the line. The head keeper checked the slips of paper. Yuri Andropov found himself at the extreme right-hand end of the line, the Czech Colonel was in the middle, with Alexei Flitlianov and Vasilly Chechulian at two points in between them. The group broke up and moved along the line of trees toward numbered posts which had been set up several hundred yards apart as starting markers.

It was just after eight o'clock when a whistle pierced the woods and the men left the trampled snow at the bottom of the valley and began to move upward through the light, clean white carpets that lay between the long avenues of fir.

Two grouse exploded just in front of Alexei Flitlianov before he'd gone many steps into the forest, their wings beating sharply in alarm, squawking, as they skimmed along beneath the branches further into the woods. He stopped, shaken for a moment. His keeper joined him, a small, wizened-faced man in an old fur cap with ear flaps and rather dirty, oily hands. He looked more like a garage mechanic than a sportsman.

"Those are easier shooting," he said, trying to establish too immediate a comradery, Flitlianov thought. "With shotguns. These boar are difficult animals. You were here last year weren't you, sir? I remember you got a big tusker then."

"No. That was Comrade Chechulian."

"Oh yes, of course. You're right. It's hard sometimes to tell people apart—all in the same kind of hunting clothes."

"Yes, indeed." The man had put his finger on it at once, Flitlianov thought: everyone in more or less the same kind of clothes, this shooting while moving forward in a line, the chance of a stray boar running back between two positions, a rifle swinging around in a ninety degree arc. An accident in these circumstances could be made to seem the most natural thing in the world. He had realized this from the beginning, of course, two days before at their meeting in the Rossiya Hotel. But he had long before agreed to go on this hunting expedition—he went every year—and could not therefore have avoided the occasion today: in Andropov's present surprising mood he might fall upon anything as evidence of guilt.

He had been puzzled by Andropov's behavior at the meeting: he'd said there had been no intention of conducting a purge among his deputies, but this was exactly what seemed to be happening. Was he trying to raise Chechulian from some cover? Was Vasilly, who shared some of his own background, the man he suspected of this conspiracy? He seemed an unlikely candidate. But anything was possible. And it was in this vague cloud of suspicion and invention which Andropov now held over his deputies that Flitlianov saw the answer to the mystery: Andropov was not sure of anything. He was simply intent on creating a mood of alarm, of psychological unease, by suggesting that he had complete knowledge of the conspiracy so that the man or men involved would become unnerved, make a mistake, break cover. Andropov was in the middle of an elaborate bluff and this day's hunting, Flitlianov felt sure, was a potentially dangerous part of it. Anything might happen. And thus he had laid his plans accordingly: he would move himself, long before anything *could* happen. The garage mechanic was not to be trusted of course. He would have to be the first to go.

Flitlianov moved forward again into the tunnel of heavy branches, bright sunlight breaking through them here and there on the snow in front of him, speckling the dark arcade with small patches of brillant tinsel. After ten minutes' walk he saw a small clearing ahead with a pile of fir trunks stacked in a large pyramid waiting to be taken away.

Further along the line to the right, Vasilly Chechulian checked his rifle. He removed the ammunition, shot the bolt back and forth quickly several times, depressed the magazine spring up and down violently with his huge thumb, and then reloaded it again carefully with a different supply from an inner pocket. For him this gun was what would get him safely through the day. It was a Mauser .375 attached to a Winchester sporting stock and he was remarkably well able to use it. He too had been worried by Andropov's recent behavior, his untypical flights of fancy over this imaginary Sixth Directorate, and he had come up with no good answer for it. He only knew, with the sure intuition born of many years experience of cover in the field, that he was exposed, at risk. From what quarter he had no idea, no more than he knew when or where the boar would run. And so the nerve of action was sharp in him that morning, all his senses resting on a hair trigger: if there were to be any untoward accidents in the coming hours he was determined to be the cause and not the result of them. He lit a cigarette and watched where the breeze would take the smoke: it drifted southward along the line. He threw the cigarette away, washed the oil from his hands in a fistful of snow, dried them carefully in a fresh chamois cloth, and then drew a long breath, drinking the keen air several times deeply into his lungs. He waited another minute with his keeper, listening intently all around him, trying to fathom the silences that ran away from him in every direction, peering intently down all the long green tunnels. He saw that there was only a properly clear field of fire directly ahead or behind him, if he stayed in the track between the long straight rows of trees. So he moved forward in a zigzag pattern, changing the angle of his walk by ninety degrees every forty yards or so, always moving diagonally across the lines of trees and thus, from any distance away, almost completely covered by them.

Half a mile away, to Chechulian's right, at the edge of the line, Yuri Andropov walked along between the head gamekeeper and another man. The line of trees ended fifty yards away. There was a logger's track along the side of the wood and beyond that two hundred yards of open ground rising steeply to the brow of a hill where the forest began again in a younger plantation. Behind him, out of sight in the distance, a forester's jeep followed them along the rough track. He could just hear the engine on the wind as it climbed the steeper gradients, turning back toward it every so often, as though he was being pursued and not protected by it. His fingers were numb on the weapon; he did not know really how to use it. The spectacles he wore bit painfully into the bridge of his nose. His eyes had begun to water in the sharp air, blurring his sight. He could feel the drops running down his cheek; warm at first, like blood, but icy pellets by the time they reached his chin. He stumbled over some dead branches, making hard going in the thicker drifts of snow that had blown in from the edge of the wood. He seemed generally ill at ease.

Alexei Flitlianov stopped by the large pile of fir trunks, leaned his rifle against them and glanced up at the circle of brillant blue morning sky above the small clearing. He took his gloves off, blew on his hands, and rubbed them together vigorously. They had been walking for almost half an hour. His keeper joined him, keeping his rifle in his hand.

"Just the weather, isn't it?"

The man nodded. "We had such snow this winter. The road out was blocked for weeks."

"You're from these parts are you?"

"No. From Leningrad. I'm stationed at the village. Two weeks duty up here, then four days off."

"I know. You're under Rakovsky aren't you, at Orlyoni? Second Directorate, Leningrad southeast division."

"Yes, sir."

Flitlianov thought then that the man must have been a plant put up to him by Andropov. Hadn't Rakovsky been moved from that Leningrad area command six months before? But he couldn't remember precisely.

"Married?"

"Two boys. Twelve and fourteen."

"Is your family with you here?"

The man hesitated. "No, they've not joined me yet, They're still in Leningrad."

"Pity. I expect they'd like the hunting."

"Yes, sir, the younger one, Pytor, is very keen. It's more the guns than the animals, I'm afraid: he's very keen on guns. Youngsters are!" The man laughed quickly, easing the rifle strap on to his shoulder.

"Indeed, I know." Flitlianov chuckled, and then belched hugely. "God, I ate too well this morning. I must get it out. Will you wait for me?"

Flitlianov walked around toward the other side of the stack of logs, unbuttoning his coat. But the moment he was out of sight, he climbed quickly up the slope of trunks and found himself a niche between two of them at the top. He squeezed down, lying out full length, and waited. He must have been at least fifteen feet up, so that unless the keeper went looking for him up the hill, and then turned round, he could not be seen from beneath. Besides, in his fur helmet, brown leather overcoat, and tan boots, he knew he must look something like a log.

Several minutes passed in silence. The sun beat down thawing the frozen drops of moisture on his sleeves. Already it had warmed the resin that seeped from the gashed trunks, so that with his face buried among the logs, he felt himself beginning to suffocate in the strong smell of rising pine. Then he heard a sound, like a knuckle cracking, a rifle bolt breaking and then the bullet being rammed home. The man had come around to the far side of the logs. Another minute passed.

"Comrade Flitlianov—are you all right?"

From somewhere away to their left a branch cracked, the sound running clearly down the light wind. Flitlianov raised his head a fraction. The man was just below, his back toward him. He turned his head in the direction of the sound.

"Comrade Flitlianov?"

The gamekeeper's voice was thin this time, as if he expected no response. The man looked at the confused footprints in the snow and then started to follow them backward down the hill into the trees. After a hundred yards he turned back and retraced his steps to the clearing. Then he started to climb the pyramid of logs. At the top he stood up and looked all around him, shading his eyes from the hard sun. There was nothing to see anywhere—nobody, no sound, an empty world.

Flitlianov by now was well away from the clearing and running hard up the hill between the thickly arched trees. Then he turned sharply, at right angles, moving northward across the plantation lines. He would have to be careful; this path would cross that of two or three other hunters, including Chechulian, before he came to Andropov's beat at the end of the line. He had suspected from the beginning that somehow Andropov might be the real target of the day. Now he needed confirmation of this and of the marksman, if possible.

He had crossed two sets of tracks and must have been close to Chechulian's path. But there was no sign of him or of his footprints. Chechulian must have slowed or been delayed in his walk. Flitlianov would have to wait until he passed. He stood quite still for a moment, listening, his eyes probing the dark corridors. There were footsteps somewhere, faint, but coming toward him, rising up the hill to his right. Then, a stone's throw in the same direction, the undergrowth crackled and a brown shape exploded from it. The boar stood an instant in its tracks, then came for him, head down, moving fast, kicking up a flurry of snow behind it.

Chechulian raised his rifle to the animal and fired in one movement. Then he fired again at the receding form. The second shot had winged it, he thought, somewhere in the shoulder. The beast's head had reared violently, it had stumbled, but had then charged away across the line of trees to the right. Chechulian reloaded and moved after it, running.

After the first shot the boar had veered away from Flitlianov just as he'd thrown himself to one side, finding cover among some brush at the base of a large fir trunk. The second shot had hit the animal, ripping through the top of his shoulder, and a moment later he saw Chechulian and his man hurrying after it not five yards away from him. Flitlianov waited until the two of them were out of sight before getting up and moving quietly on across the line of trees.

Yuri Andropov heard the two shots to his left, and thirty seconds later the sound of underbrush and dead branches splintering violently, this new noise approaching him like an arrow. He gripped his rifle, half raising it—an involuntary, useless gesture, he knew, for the ammunition it contained was blank. And then the boar was upon them through the nearest line of trees. The group had no time to scatter. The keepers fired almost simultaneously. But for the first of them it was too late: the animal rammed him viciously about the legs and then started to gore his midriff. The second keeper threw himself forward, trying to kick the beast away, unable to get another shot in.

A rifle had fallen to the ground. Andropov picked it up and ran. He was fifty yards away from the struggling keepers, zigzagging through the trees before a first shot followed him; then came a ragged volley, the bullets slapping into tree trunks, kicking up little gobbets of snow about his feet. But it was useless. Andropov was running southward, against the grain of the wood, the trees masking him more and more completely at every step. The forester's jeep drew up at the edge of the trees. Two men got out and, leaving the keeper to tend his wounded colleague, they set off in pursuit.

Alexei Flitlianov kept his head well down among the bushes while this new shooting raged invisibly in front of him. When it had stopped he raised his head an instant and then ducked again. A man was running wildly toward him— a tall, burly figure, with a light silver fox-fur helmet and rimless spectacles: Yuri Andropov. But as he passed a few yards away from him Flitlianov recognized something else about the man: it was not Yuri Andropov but someone dressed and made up to look very like him.

Vasilly Chechulian had stopped in his pursuit of the wounded animal when he heard the shooting. It could only mean one thing: Andropov, or some other party to his right, had sighted the boar, missed it, and succeeded only in heading it back toward him. It was coming for him now, the undergrowth rattling fifty yards ahead. He raised his rifle but the noise suddenly stopped. Something moved in a patch of dark scrub beneath the trees. He would have to flush the animal out. He fired once, and then a second time, the shots ringing violently in the silence. Then he moved carefully toward the patch of scrub. Halfway there he stopped. Two men were facing him from the other side of the bushes, their rifles covering him. And in the bushes lay the body of a man: Yuri Andropov.

Flitlianov worked his way across the edge of the forest and paused, crouching down behind the last line of trees. A covered forester's jeep was parked on a logger's track, its back toward him. There was no one around. He walked up behind it slowly. The front seats were empty. He put his head in through the driver's window. Yuri Andropov and Alexander Sakharovsky were sitting quietly in the back seat. They started forward in alarm.

Flitlianov looked at them easily, "I heard all the shooting. What's happened?"

The two men said nothing, looking at him in dulled astonishment.

"What's going on?" Flitlianov put his rifle on the bonnet of the jeep and opened the driver's door.

"We don't know yet. The men have gone to see," Andropov said at last. And then the two-way radio started to crackle beneath the dashboard. Flitlianov picked up the receiver and handed it over to Andropov.

"Yes?" he said listening. "Who? What happened?" His voice rose in genuine surprise. "Yes, all right. Get them all back here as soon as possible. Yes, we'll carry on with the hunt." He handed the receiver back. "An accident, Alexei. They've shot me." He looked at Sakharovsky, smiled, and began to clamber out of the jeep, brushing himself off, stretching and stamping his legs in the snow. "Yes, they got me in the end." He looked up at the marvelous sky, blinking, his face bright now, satisfied, enjoying the crisp air. "And I thought it might have been you, Alexei." He smiled again, breathing deeply.

"I don't quite follow."

"Well—it did look just possible, no? This conspiracy, your background. I had to take everyone into consideration, even my deputies. But it wasn't you of course, Alexei. I did you an injustice. It was Vasilly Chechulian. Who would have thought it? Yes, Vasilly has just shot me."

"I'm sorry," Flitlianov said in real astonishment.

"A tragedy, Alexei," Andropov came forward, wiping his spectacles, then pinching the bridge of his nose. "You were right at our last meeting. All we need do now is chase the rest of the group up. I think we have our conspirator. Our liberal, our counterrevolutionary." He put his hand on Flitlianov's shoulder. "Thank you, Alexei."

Andropov took his rifle from Sakharovsky, shot the bolt several times, loaded it, checked the safety catch, and finally made some imaginary passing shots in the air. Then he turned and swung the rifle down toward Flitlianov. Sakharovsky, standing behind him, made an involuntary movement to one side.

"Oh, and by the way, Alexei," Andropov checked his rifle again, crooked it under his arm like a shotgun and walked casually toward him. "Now that we're all three alone together, we can get on with some other important business that's come up: your internal security division. We need some work done in America. I'd like you to get one of your men to New York to check out one of our circles there. Do you have anyone you can send at once? You normally have someone in the pipeline ready for these occasions—a completely fresh face."

"Yes, I have someone—due to go over to America quite soon in any case. Part of a routine replacement. He's ready."

"A good man?"

"Yes."

"I mean, you're sure of him? He's clear. No one has any tail on him?"

"Absolutely. As you know, we keep these men completely clear of any contact at their base before sending them into a target area. He's done some work before for us in Africa, years ago. But he's completely unmarked now."

"Fine, I'll give you the details tomorrow. Let's get on with the hunting."

The three men walked away from the jeep, up the hill, Andropov still brushing himself off, almost frisking about, as though he had been in a cardboard box all morning. His driver and his bodyguard emerged from the woods with the body of a man. The two groups stood together a moment in the dazzling light, Andropov giving directions like a stage producer, before they separated and the three hunters disappeared into the dark green tunnel of trees.

Alexei Flitlianov shot nothing at the hunt, and on the drive back to Moscow that afternoon he looked out at the dull landscape, the bright day gone, remarking on the weather and the traffic to his Czech colleague who traveled back with him. But he disliked this flat countryside—a muddy April thaw edging the road, beginning to creep in over the immense fields; a landscape so drab and featureless by comparison with the sharp mountains and tangy springs of his own Georgian background in the south. And thus he politely lied about the beauties of the Moscow plain to the man beside him: he lied as he had done for most of his life, while thinking of other things that were true.

So they believed it was Chechulian, who had been quietly arrested midway through the hunt, or did they? Did Yuri Andropov really think that or was he pretending just as he'd had another man pretend to be him, and had Chechulian conveniently shoot the imposter? Or had the shooting been pure chance, an accident as Chechulian, he'd heard, had protested? Questions one could never ask. But whatever the reasons behind Andropov's behavior, whatever his real motive in arresting Chechulian, there was no doubt that Andropov, in his charade at the hunt, had been putting the pressure on him as well.

Chechulian's arrest could have been a blind, so that he should feel himself in the clear—clear to make the one mistake which would completely convict him, which would be indisputable evidence of his guilt. And that mistake would be to run now.

Yet, on the other hand, if one took the arrest to be genuine, as it might well be, there was an inevitable progression to it: Chechulian, Flitlianov knew, was innocent; he himself was the man they wanted. And Andropov must soon discover Chechulian's innocence: then the lamps would move brightly onto him. And then he would wish he'd run when there was the chance.

The English had a phrase for it—he could hear Andropov himself using it, happy in his sudden bizarre colloquialism—"six of one; half a dozen of the other." There was nothing in it. He had a few days. He had to run.

They had come to the outer suburbs of the capital now, an expanse of identical high-rise apartment buildings that stretched away far beyond his vision. A People's Park lay beside the roadway. And that too had been completely laid out in concrete. Yet Alexei looked now on these drab emblems of his nation's progress with regret, and even spoke enthusiastically of the new development to his companion. He would have to go.

And so this brutal urban sprawl took on a precious form. A time had come that he'd hoped would never come again, for he'd always imagined that he would have been able to see his work through without another exile like the first—his years as a KGB officer in Beirut, West Berlin, New York, London, preparing the way meticulously for his eventual return to Moscow and his present position within the organization.

It was a game of snakes-and-ladders, and he had hit the

square high up on ninety-nine just before the end of the game that sent you tumbling right back to the beginning.

Yet not quite the beginning, he reflected. He wasn't running away; he was running back into it all over again from the outside, fulfilling one of many contingency plans that had been arranged long before. He was leaving in order to build his group up again inside the citadel of Dzerzinsky Square. There were men at this moment—he didn't know their names or how many, some of them quite possibly colleagues of his, and other senior KGB officers in Moscow and elsewhere in Russia—who were members of his group, who had been recruited over the years by his various deputies overseas and at headquarters. And the only way he could make contact with these people, and reactivate the group at the center, was to get out and contact his first deputy, and with him set the whole business in motion again. This man was his link with all the others, and thus with his whole political and personal future.

There was also the list, held in safety overseas by a person whose real name and whereabouts only he knew of, and which he might now familiarize himself with for the first time. This was a complete register of all the members in his clandestine group—their names, positions within the KGB and elsewhere in the Soviet establishment, and all other relevant data: their "file." One more reason for leaving—for the identity of the first deputy was the most crucial information of all, and it was at risk now and would continue to be for as long as he remained in Russia.

There were as well a number of key figures in Moscow— four in the army, two in both the navy and the air force, three senior officers with the KGB, six on the Central Committee, and two in the Politburo—with whom he had made common cause over the years. They were his "recruits"; and this had been his main activity during his years in Moscow— searching out these men of new government in the Union, these men of goodwill who, for the moment, were behaving just like all the others, as bureaucratic robots who had for so long denied all the human values of Marxism. They had worked well at the mechanics of government, these people, at industrial, of course military, and now even consumer development. But they had left Russia barren of individual spirits, of singular idiosyncracy and choice, of all inventive and exuberant life. And these qualities, Flitlianov believed, had been among the essential purposes of the revolution. They had been consistently and intentionally betrayed by all but a very few in power over the years, and of those who had supported these ideals nearly all were now in exile or long dead; apart from Flitlianov's contacts, the very few in government who were still there were like cocoons buried deep in rotten wood, waiting for the spring.

But of course he could make no use of such people now. It was impossible to risk their cover simply in order to save his own skin. They would soon find out that he was gone, keeping their heads down until the storm blew over, and wait developments from abroad. All the more important that he should get out now, he knew, for these were names he might well disclose under torture.

How closely were they watching him, he wondered, when he got back to his apartment in the center of the city that evening? He looked out at the dark street: a few people hurrying by, fewer cars, a thin snow falling. There was no one around, no stationary vehicles. One of his own personal security guards in the ground-floor apartment would probably have been made responsible for the surveillance. Very well, then, he would make use of him. It didn't matter for the first part of the journey. It would only count when he made the switch. He telephoned downstairs, speaking to the duty officer of the guard.

"My appointments are in Leningrad this week—I'll travel overnight on the sleeper. Reserve me a front compartment and whatever you need for yourself. No, tonight. Now. Yes, I'll be going alone. Warn the Leningrad bureau. Have them pick me up first thing when I get there."

He went through some papers on his desk, putting a few of them in a brief case. There was nothing to destroy. There never had been. He had always kept himself ready for immediate retreat. His housekeeper, a silent Eskimo-faced woman from the north, busied herself about the place, making up a suitcase for him. There was nothing else he needed to take. Everything would be ready for him in Leningrad. There were only the photographs which he would have to leave: his mother not long before she died, so young looking it seemed she had years of life in her; and his father, the railway engineer, stout with moustaches in the Georgian manner, quite old, taken at a holiday camp for retired staff on the Caspian. And there was his younger brother and sister, their families, his nephews and nieces. Would they suffer? *How* would they suffer? Long experience of his own work so quickly led him to an actual vision of that possible suffering, the mechanics of it.

He had not married so that there should not be that tie to deal with if the occasion ever arose, as it had now. But there were all these others, suddenly frail and exposed with his leaving. He felt for a moment that he should stay in Russia—simply go to Leningrad, return, and accept the consequences. But just as he had made every physical preparation for sudden departure so he had long before anticipated exactly this emotional hurdle and the attitude he would take to it: the answer, he knew, was that they might well suffer, be used as hostages to try and bring him back to Russia. And he would do nothing about it. It wasn't selfishness. He had staked his life on his political beliefs. Once you did that there was nothing you could do about the others. You had condemned them, in a society such as his, from the first moment of deviation—a contrary thought thirty years before, a morning at the university when a professor had presented as fact something you knew to be a lie: and that sudden moment's consciousness of truth and difference was as dangerous as a bullet, a gun pointing at you and your friends and family for ever afterward.

He didn't look around the apartment. Yet he was suddenly aware of the deep silence of the rooms, a quality of abandoned space, a prefiguration of his departure. He said good-bye to the housekeeper, counting out her money for her, exactly.

Then he went.

But she called to him when he was halfway down the corridor, and came to him, the money in her hand. He knew what it was at once. She never spoke of these things in the apartment itself.

"Would you?" she said, handing him some of the money. "If you had the chance. From the dollar shop—lipstick, hair spray, toothpaste, anything like that. My daughter—"

"Fine, I'll see to it. Next time my secretary goes there. Keep the money."

He turned away and now for the first time his leaving became real to him.

There was a smell of burned flint in the station—dead sparks from the overhead cables, the leaking discharge of dynamos, the peppery smell of recent fireworks. The big engine throbbed at the end of the shallow platform. Just beyond it, outside the canopy, the snow fell brightly in the light. But a yard beyond this glittering curtain there was a deep darkness and a silence, so that the noise and illumination inside made the terminus a stage for a huge party, the guests taking frenzied last drinks and saying good-bye before embarking for an uncertain destination. The heavy sleeper carriages waited for them, curtains drawn, like the vehicles of a cortege.

Flitlianov's compartment was near the head of the train and as he walked toward it, his two security men behind him, he saw Yelena Andropova and her husband climbing up the steps of the same carriage. The three of them met in the corridor while the attendant was showing them to their separate quarters.

"Hello!" She shouted to him loudly, still half the length of the corridor away, so that his security men turned questioningly behind them. Even a greeting from her, he thought, had all the brazen quality of a revolutionary manifesto, a call from the beginning for the truth. He feared for her, more than for himself. His world of deceit wasn't hers after all. And though she shared his beliefs he was amazed each time she publicly confirmed her association with him. When he left, what would happen to her, even with her father's influence? A woman whom some would so sharply remember had been a friend of his.

But she had always told him not to fear. So often she had

said that when he'd spoken to her about the risks she took.

"I'd rather die laughing than crying. . . . What other way is there? . . . Discretion is the worst means of concealment." And there were other phrases of the same sort, brisk affidavits of her faith which were a continual absolution for him—outspoken, serious words, but never given seriously. In her fearlessness and free intelligence she had the quality of some prerevolutionary aristocrat, he thought. Yet she had been born after that time. And this brought him great warmth, for sometimes he felt his ambitions were unique, that individual spirit had disappeared completely in Russia. Yet now, in her greeting alone, he sensed the existence of irony, knowledge, and laughter hidden everywhere in the land.

He had tea with them in their compartment, the three of them crowded slightly among the bunks; the train was pulling out of the station and beginning to sway very slightly, a boat moving into the current of twisting rails, the drive of wind and snow. Her husband talked to him formally about nothing, drinking nervously, so that soon she took the conversation up herself.

"We saw Arkadi Raikin's new show at the Rossiya on Friday night. Did you go? It was fine."

"Not yet. I've been busy. An official visit—a Czech delegation."

"Yes, Father told me. You were hunting on Sunday. I suppose you never missed once. What's it like up there where you go? Near the Morivinian forests isn't it? I've never been there."

"Very wild, isolated. Swamps, bogs, and of course forests." He smiled at her.

"It's where all the labor camps are, yes? 'Prison Province.' "

The train lurched over points, going through a junction some miles north of Moscow, keeping left on the main Leningrad line.

"Yes," he said. "This is the junction here. They go off that way." He pointed eastward through the curtains.

" 'They.' " Yelena considered the word carefully. "What do they do up there?"

"Logging mostly. Timber felling and carting. And they

make furniture. And television cabinets. They do fairly well. It's not too bad. Short-term and first offenders."

"The others go further away?"

"Yes. The serious cases. Persistent offenders. They go all the way. The Ukraine, Siberia, the Arctic Islands."

"Really to another country?"

"Yes." He nodded, looking closely at Yelena now. "Another country altogether."

The attendant came to the door. His compartment was ready. He stood up, wondering if she had understood anything of his plans, his predicament, from this exchange.

"Oh, by the way," she said, returning his look just as carefully, "talking about other countries, you should take a look at the London exhibition we have at the Hermitage now: 'Two Centuries of European Baroque.' Paintings, metalwork, porcelain, jewelry. Mostly from the Wallace Collection. It's the last few days before we send them back, if you think you *need* to see them?" She emphasized the word, questioningly.

"Yes—if I have time." And then more urgently: "Yes, I'd like to," and then softly, as her husband was speaking to the attendant, "as soon as I can. Tomorrow."

She nodded and looked quickly away and he thought now that she had understood everything, that his message had got through to her. For in their affair, publicly and alone, they had long become accustomed to just such unspoken communication, adept in transmitting their needs as well as their affection through parables or by an expressive silence.

Flitlianov went to his compartment, checking with his two security men in the adjoining one on the way, then he locked the door, and, with much bumping and clattering of shoes went through the motion of settling down for the night.

At two o'clock in the morning the train pulled into Morivinia station, the halfway point on the journey. Here it would wait for the arrival of the Leningrad-Moscow sleeper, due at any moment on the down platform. The snow had stopped. Odd strong gusts of wind whipped a thin covering of white along the roofs and across the platforms. The sky was clear, all the stars perfectly ordered and visible. The huge train slept. A lone official walked along the platform past its curtained windows. The guard stepped down from his van at the end. Two militiamen, heavily clothed in fur coats and helmets, machine pistols slung from their shoulders, stood silently by the exit at the middle of the platform. Behind them in the shadow of the station canopy, two plain-clothes men from Sakharovsky's special task force looked on.

Inside the train, Flitlianov's two security men were awake—looking and listening, plumbing the silence for the slightest sound or movement: one in the corridor standing next to Flitlianov's locked compartment; the other scanning the deserted platform on the other side of the tracks.

A minute passed. The militiamen shifted their feet discreetly. The guard checked his watch with the official at the far end of the platform. At the opposite end, in the cabin of the leading engine, a man was talking easily to the driver.

"Of course, Comrade," the driver said, "I knew your father. When I worked the Southern Region—the Yalta-Moscow line—he was engineer-in-charge, a very fine man, a great man."

In front of them as they spoke, half a mile away, the engine lights of the Moscow sleeper appeared, two long brilliant beams, fanning out over a carpet of snow, rounding a curve. It glided toward them against the wind without a sound.

"It's an honor to meet you, Comrade," the driver went on as the express passed their cab, drawing into the station. "I've greatly enjoyed our talk. Though you know as much about the railways as I do myself, if I may say so."

"My father taught me everything, never stopped talking about it. I take no credit for it. He was the real railway man."

"Indeed, indeed." They shook hands firmly, warmly, full of old memory. Then Alexei Flitlianov took his brief case and climbed down onto the tracks between the two trains. He rounded the last carriage of the Moscow-bound sleeper and confronted the guard who had just got down from it, showing him his identity card. The man saluted promptly.

"My reservation please. For Moscow. It was booked last night—joining the train at Morivinia."

"This way, sir. I'll get the attendant at once."

Flitlianov climbed up into the last carriage where a compartment had been reserved for him. The attendant opened the door.

"Some tea, sir. Or some coffee? We have some coffee."

"Something stronger, please. If you have any. It's cold."

"Certainly, sir. At once. Do you have anyone traveling with you?"

"No, no one."

Flitlianov turned toward the curtained window. The wheels of the Leningrad sleeper moaned briefly as the brakes were released and the train began to draw out of the station. Two minutes later his own train left and the attendant arrived with a half bottle of export vodka and a glass on a little tray.

By eight o'clock he was back at the Moscow terminus—just in time to catch the morning express to Leningrad. And by five that afternoon he had crossed the bridge onto Nevsky Prospect and was walking toward the Hermitage museum.

Posing as the curator of a distant museum come to the Hermitage to choose some paintings for a provincial exhibition, he met Yelena in her office of the Exhibition and Loans Department in the basement of the building. They walked along the basement to the new storage room, a long, specially lit and heated chamber. Here they inspected various paintings from the several thousand available, stored in lines, each canvas suspended over the floor in a sliding rack, marked alphabetically after the artist, so that any work could be reached almost immediately by pulling the open crates out on their runners into the wide central aisle. The room was empty, smelling slightly of warm turpentine, and there was the vague sound of machinery somewhere. But nonetheless, Yelena spoke briskly and officially.

"All the same, it seems to me, for a proper balance, you need some of the moderns, even if you're not going beyond 1900. You should perhaps acknowledge the beginnings of the movement. . . . The Impressionists, of course. But none

of our major examples is available, I'm afraid. A Manet perhaps. We have a sequence of his *Seine at Marly* paintings—
one of those we could spare."

"Yes," Flitlianov said uneasily. "And what about Modigliani?"

"Really outside your period altogether. Though we
have some exceptional examples."

They moved half down the chamber to the racks of the
middle letters: "Manet, Matisse, Modigliani, Murat."

"Let me show you some in any case."

She pulled a rack out gently, the first open crate sliding
forward, a canvas stored on either side. And then another
one. And a third, so that the central aisle was now partly
blocked and they were hidden from the doorway. They stood
facing a large Modigliani nude.

"Well?" Yelena inquired in a true voice, turning away
from the dark glamour of the picture, the rose thighs, the
incisive outlines of body and crotch.

"Yes," he said simply, suddenly tired, gazing at the
nude, a weary businessman in a strip club. "Yes, it's now."

"Everything is ready. A few details, that's all."

"Passports, exit visa, money?"

"You prepared it all yourself, Alexei. It's all here. All
you have to do is sign and predate your own authority for
this man."

"And the London paintings will be the first trip out
of here—the Baroque exhibition?"

"Yes, you're lucky. Thursday morning. The exhibition
ends today. There'll be two days packing. Then they go
direct to London, part of the weekly cargo flight, an Ilyushin
62."

She pulled the Modigliani over to one side and replaced
it with another canvas, an early Matisse.

"Cubist. Not for you at all." She changed her tone again.
It was formal, almost scolding. "But effective. I like his invention—and his restraint. They balance out. With Picasso the
same thing gets out of hand—too wild and no control."

"Stop it, for God's sake."

They looked at each other, both suddenly angry: tongue-
tied, so much to say, and no time now, or place, to say it;

resenting their shared experience because they could no longer acknowledge it. So they felt guilty as if they had carelessly broken their affair themselves sometime before and had met now with only the blame to apportion.

"You'll have two days to wait. The room is ready."

Two men appeared at the far end of the aisle, a young man and someone much older, balding with glasses. The young man had a clipboard and pencil in his hand.

"The deputy curator. They're preparing an old master exhibition—Titian, Tiepolo, Vermeer, Velasquez: they'll be coming past us. Let me do the talking if they stop."

But they stopped some distance in front of them, pulling a rack out early in the alphabet.

"Boucher, Botticelli," Yelena said brightly. "We're all right. Yes, the room: you know it. The old varnishing room. There's food. And water from the sink. It's kept locked, used as a paint and chemical storeroom now. They have to come to my office for the key. And there's still an internal telephone, so I can warn you. Everything is there, as we arranged: the suitcase on top of the cupboard on the left. The suit is inside, hanging with a lot of old overalls. And the papers are taped underneath the cupboard: two passports, the Russian and the Lebanese, your new KGB identity card, and the money, $25,000 in traveler's checks. I have your exit visa here, stamped last week and dated for travel on Thursday. All you do is sign it."

The two men had finished with Botticelli and had now begun to move down the aisle toward them.

"Hello Vladimir." Yelena turned to the balding man.

"Can't wean you off the moderns, can we Yelena? All that bourgeois decadence."

With any encouragement he might have stopped and talked. But she looked at him quickly, a finger to her lips, gesturing over her shoulder at Alexei. The deputy curator moved away.

"How many will there be?" Alexei asked when they had gone.

"Two porters and an assistant curator from the museum and a fourth man, one of our security staff. You'll be the fifth in the party—the additional KGB security officer, as we arranged. Loading starts first thing Thursday; I'll phone down, let yourself out and come up to the packing room. Introduce yourself, hang around. The flight leaves at midday. There'll be some of our Embassy staff in London to meet it. But you should get clear away at the cargo terminal before they know who you are. The cargo manifest which they'll have beforehand only names the four museum staff as accompanying personnel. They won't know anything about you. Come on." She pushed all the M's—the Modiglianis and Matisses—gently back into position.

"I'm sorry, he said as they moved towards the entrance of the sweetly humming chamber.

"No. I'm not surprised. Once we started on this, put so much work into it, I was sure that one day you'd have to use it. The sorrow was there from the beginning. Will it be all right in London?" she went on in the same matter-of-fact voice. "You'll have someone there?"

"Yes, I'll be contacting a colleague. A close friend. I'll be all right."

They looked at each other once, walking slowly up the aisle, but said nothing more.

Book Two

1

McCoy had never hunted someone down before, least of all an Englishman, a major Soviet agent. Yet now, in these last moments, he found he hadn't much taste for the job. He surprised himself. After years of unrequited bullying, at school and from behind various desks in the Middle East section in Holborn, this should have been a crowning day: a day when he could lay the many ghosts that had possessed him since youth, a time at last when he could take the men —or man, at least—who would stand for all the others who had betrayed and scorned him.

Before, in his professional life, they had just vanished —from apartments in Beirut, or top security prisons in England—just as the day boys whom he had caught cheating and had beaten before lunch found sanctuary every afternoon at half-past three from the school where he had been a boarder. His life seemed to have been cruelly dictated by such people: boys who had known the exam questions beforehand; men who were far better up on borders, checkpoints, and night ferries than he was; men who, like the children in his junior school playing tag, not only made base before he did but when they got there would turn on their pinnacles and, pointing him out for the rest, would mock him with a special and happy impudence.

Nor had it been sufficient excuse that his had always been a desk job in British Intelligence, and that he had never been more than a *fonctionnaire* in espionage, even though he headed the Middle East section in Holborn now. Before this promotion he had been Control to a field section centered on Cairo. He processed their reports and had no business with timetables and guns. In any case, a chronic shortsightedness made variations in his physical routine a matter for careful thought, so that years before he had accepted certain limits of action. But in his heart he had always longed to play the puppet, not the master. For only there, he thought, among the men, might he find the nursery where these instabilities bloomed—might learn what it was that led these men astray, took them in giant strides clean out of one life, over a border, and into another. If he could be part of them for once, and not their master, he might at last make fair copy, among so many botched post mortems, of the original sin, trace it far back to some source which he knew lay beyond the political simplicities of a Cambridge student rally in the thirties.

After so many betrayals McCoy had a psychiatrist's hunger to lay bare the initial fault. He knew that the mechanics of frailty could be displayed, as under a surgeon's knife; that a dissembling nature could be opened up and the parts named like a chapter in Gray's *Anatomy*. And he nurtured this hope obsessively, like a longed-for doctorate, for only then, he thought, in this sure delineation of another's treachery, could his own sorrow and incomprehension be lifted.

Until now he had never had a specimen to work on. And now of all times, now that the net was closing at last, he felt the cowardice of first love come over him, as if in this longed-for, imminent penetration he would lose the puritanical strengths and flavors which had nurtured his obsession in the years of waiting. He had come so to expect unsuccess in his work that the scent of victory made him shudder. He had come now to the border for the first time himself—close to the wire that divided certainty from confusion, the sure from the frail, loyalty from dishonor.

Quite soon he would look into another country, poisoned lands that he had heard much of. In an hour or less he would face the reality of evil: a figure that would sum up dissolution. Their eyes would meet and he would be responsible for the future. A time had come when he could at last fall upon the object of his passion and yet he could find no virtue in the day.

The day was late in April, the sky above Marylebone faintly blue, the color scrubbed out of it by a long and rigorous winter. Clouds ran in from the west, pushed fiercely by a damp wind that had already brought two downpours before lunchtime. The last of these had driven McCoy and Croxley into Henekey's pub in the High Street next to the Greek restaurant.

"What will you have?" He turned to Croxley, head of the Special Branch team that lay all about them in the streets, waiting for the man.

"White Shield, if I may, sir."

The girl started to decant the beer slowly, tipping glass and bottle into gentle diagonals, so that a small froth bloomed and the sediment remained undisturbed. She knew her business. McCoy doubled the order.

"You've been here before then, Croxley? You know the beer."

They were in the corner of the room at the far end of the bar, drinking comfortably like good men, between one of the old mahogany arches. Two cut-glass decanters, one of port, the other claret, stood in front of them, undisturbed, while young lunchtimers pushed and shouted all over the rest of the room, anxious for runny shepherd's pie and thin sandwiches and draft beer that was so weak everywhere now that it was nothing more than a gesture. People didn't come to pubs just to drink at lunchtime in England any more. Both men, though so formal, felt awkward, even dissolute.

"Yes, indeed," Croxley replied. "We had a long surveillance up here once. Guy Burgess had a flat around the corner. Course we didn't know about him then. It was one of his friends we were after. Lived with him. That was during the war. We used to drop in here, changing shifts. Funny thing, you know—one night I was as near to Burgess as I am to you; just where you're standing. By himself, wasn't drinking. But he was drunk. There'd been a party at his flat, going on for two days, and he'd come out for a breather. Cornered me, he did, and of course you couldn't help liking him. I mean, he really was very funny; very good company. Witty."

Croxley drank the top off his beer and put the glass down carefully, thinking. A caricature of a man remembering: steady blue suit and quietly formal overcoat—going back to a time in the ranks in a distant war; gas masks in the cupboard under the stairs in Battersea and a conversation in the blackout with Burgess.

"Witty? Even in drink?"

"Oh yes. He had that ability—then. I don't know about afterward. I was on other work."

"He rather fell to pieces, I can tell you."

"Yes, but we never got him. He got away."

"He was just lucky."

"He had the confidence, though," Croxley insisted, that brings the luck."

"A certain juvenile insouciance, that's all."

"What?" Croxley sipped again, perplexed. He was a straightforward man. The room was loud with chat and clatter but McCoy knew he'd heard him.

"It wasn't based on anything," McCoy went on. "He had nothing else. Just that confident good-fellowship. So he had to push it like a lifeboat."

"Yes, certainly." Croxley thought again, as though pondering an exam question. Then he turned, with hope: "Yes, he offered to get me a proper bottle of Scotch, I remember, not knowing my job of course. Cost price. Couldn't be done with it. Said the black market was all wrong."

"I bet he did. Always had the right connections." McCoy paused, openly bitter. "A playboy. God knows even Moscow did their best to push him under the carpet when he got there."

"But he'd done his stuff by then. Covering for the others—Maclean, Philby. That was a certain skill. He knew we'd look right through a good-humored classy drunk like him, never see a thing. Knew we'd notice his boozing, though, which would take the pressure off his friends. His indiscretions saved them all."

McCoy turned away, curious at this sympathy. He felt a sudden unease standing next to this man who had once stood next to Burgess, in the very same spot. And though Croxley hadn't let Burgess go, had played no part in that disaster, McCoy felt that he was somehow guilty by association, as if he had picked up some infection in that innocent drink he'd had with Burgess twenty-five years before, a disability which would tell in the coming hours with another traitor fifty yards down the street. McCoy looked around at the unchanged, ancient bar with its dark woods and barrels, its crusted paneling and ports and crystal, and thought there might be something buried here, in the wood or forever in its air—some omen which favored only the bad fairies, some hidden order which might reach out again at any moment, to protect the chancy, the dishonest, the laughter-makers, against all the ploys of honest people.

In fact, it was Croxley's sympathy that had brought him to the top. He had a gentle fascination for the men he set out to trap. In another world they would have been among his closest friends at the Club. He appreciated their lying skills and secret humors, and failure to take them at the end had never soured his appetite, as it had McCoy's.

It was so obvious, Croxley had always thought: a man, traitor to one side, was all the more necessarily hero to the other. And you had to recognize the other side of the coin whether you liked it or not. Other people had a right to their heroes, even if, as he knew, such men everywhere died miserably for little good.

They sipped their drinks again. McCoy thought he had spotted some sediment rising in his glass. But it was a trick of the light, golden motes caught in a sunbeam. The shower was dying outside.

Once they were sure the man was with the KGB, having tapped his phone, they had watched him for nearly two months, hoping to trace his contacts—from the Embassy, some other deep cover "illegal," or someone in the British forces or Intelligence. But he met no one. And no one had come near him. At first they assumed the man was sleeping or that he reported in some other extremely intermittent manner. Then, when they discovered he was making preparations to go abroad, they realized he was on transfer, marking time before his next posting, keeping his tail clean. At least, everyone except McCoy believed this. McCoy was still certain that he would make some contact before he left. And so Croxley and the others waited for orders to take him. McCoy was running the show.

"Another week," McCoy had said. A fourth, then a fifth. This was the eighth week, close surveillance, around the clock, and Croxley had come to know their quarry in his sympathetic way, like a friend one remembered in every detail but hadn't spoken to for a long time—but a friend for all that, where the friendship would last no matter how long the parting. But he thought McCoy an optimistic fool who should have known better.

The man lived off Marylebone High Street, halfway up toward Regent's Park, in a small flat above a firm of medical suppliers, and until a week before had gone every day to his present work as a Senior Reports Officer at the Central Office of Information in Westminster. A week before, he'd finished his packing and there'd been a small party at his flat, saying good-bye to a few colleagues and friends. But he hadn't left. They'd learned that his booking on the New York boat wasn't until a week later, and they'd watched him all the harder then, for surely, McCoy thought, this would be the week for some last contact, for some final check. But nothing happened. Even Croxley was initially surprised at this hiatus, while McCoy was incensed by it.

The man spent the week like a tourist, walking endlessly about the city, but with aims of sheer pleasure: he went to art galleries and museums in the morning, cinemas in the afternoon, theaters and restaurants at night. He had even fitted in the Tower of London and the Bridge as well. Croxley's men had pursued him diligently, egged on by sighs of horror from McCoy. They skinned their eyes for a contact or a message drop. They had gone into public lavatories after him, rooting up tiles and destroying expensive flush systems. They had quizzed waiters, museum curators, and vehement little ladies in the box offices. They had stuck to him like clams, done everything but sleep with him, and had come up with absolutely nothing. He had spoken to no one, written nothing, dropped nothing, nor picked anything up. He had fallen out of his old life like a stone.

McCoy had been involved in the chase from the start. The man had at one time worked indirectly for his section while he was with the British Council in Beirut. Almost certainly, McCoy thought, the KGB had recruited him there at the same time. Probably Henry Edwards had done the work. For Edwards, they'd discovered—just before his death in Cairo in 1967—had been a senior KGB officer within British Intelligence for nearly twenty years.

And now, impossibly, like a bad joke long condemned, here was another man in that disastrous chain, one more character popping up in the big book of deceit, negligence, and snobbery that had for so long characterized British Intelligence. It had started with Burgess and Maclean, then Philby, Blake, and the others. And just when they'd thought it had finished four years previously with Edwards, here was another ghost that had quietly laid ruin all about them, and who, when caught, would cause them more trouble still. For to catch a man like this was to publicly compound the vast defeat. Better to leave him free, some thought, with tabs on, than to win Pyrrhic victories at the Old Bailey.

But McCoy didn't believe this. Retribution was his guiding principle. So when Croxley had come to him and told him of the chase, he had put on his riding boots and grabbed a whip, like the old stager he was, full of anger and discredit. McCoy thought he saw a chance of saving everything, never admitting that the battle had been well lost long ago and far from any fields that he, in his small way, patroled. Now he believed, with a flush of acid hope, that he could save the day by catching more than just this single traitor. Through him he would feel his way along a chain, find the initial contact, and take the rest one by one: deep cover illegals he hoped, as this man was, operating quite outside the Soviet Embassy or trade missions, a kind of agent seldom caught in Britain. That would be the saving grace. McCoy saw at last a golden page for himself in the unwritten history of the service.

So it was that the man's innocent behavior upset him intensely; his infuriating independence came to plague all his hopes. The man had said good-bye to everyone a week before but hadn't left and had done nothing since. Yet he must have stayed on for some clearly sinister reason, for what sane man, a Londoner from birth, could take pleasure from a constant wandering about a place he must know so well, through streets that had been always his, among parks and buildings and trees that had stood up on his horizon for half a lifetime? And the man had looked at all these famil-

iar shapes, and all the objects of the city, with such intensity and contentment, as a stranger might, come to a dying
Venice for the first time.

McCoy couldn't understand, but it hadn't taken Croxley long. For Croxley knew what could come over someone
before they left their country—the moods of an industrious
nostalgia, the need to imprint all the last reminders, fix the
solutions of a city—because you might not come back, or
would be prevented, or because everything was at risk in
any case: the buildings would be torn down, and the parks
and trees tidied up and put away. So you banked as much
pleasure as you could before you left and might take a week
off, alone, to do it. But McCoy couldn't accept such willful
license in a man. His character, as much as his profession,
condemned him to seek ulterior motives, and he had long
ago been taught that pleasure was a permit, not a liberty.

"I only hope you're right," he said to Croxley. "That
he's just been looking at the city."

"He's taken a week off, grubbing around, why not?"

"As if he knew it was his last chance."

"He doesn't. He just likes to do that sort of thing. He'd
do it anyway. Besides, it's always a last chance, when you
think of the buses. Or a slate from a roof. There was a job
I was on once, waiting outside a pub in a bit of a wind, and
this sign fell on me, bloody thing, 'The George and
Dragon.' "

"Yes, but why doesn't he see *anyone*, though? None of
his friends. Just picture galleries and matinees. And eating.
You'd think he was working his way through the Good Food
Guide."

"He's resting." Croxley looked at McCoy's puzzled face.
It was his turn to explain. "As actors say. Pity to take him
somehow."

"You've too much feeling for him, Croxley. Too much
altogether."

"If I didn't feel for him, sir," Croxley put in with real
and quiet concern, "if I didn't get into his skin with feeling, we'd never get him. It's the feeling that gets results you
know. That's how Philby and the others survived so long,

playing double. They had the feeling. We kept our heads in the sand."

McCoy looked displeased, as if the sediment had, after all, been lurking all the while in his ale, and had just then risen, souring his mouth. The big crevices in his face narrowed and his lips puckered.

"You still think he may make some contact?" Croxley asked with care but in an easy tone. "It's two months now. There's been nothing."

"One more afternoon. One never knows—some last minute instructions, a change of plan." McCoy was angered by the inevitable apology in his voice.

"I doubt it. As I've said before, they let a man sleep completely before a transfer. Give him an absolutely blank trail. It was only sheer luck we got into him in the first place with that phone call. He had his last instructions six months ago and more, I shouldn't be surprised. When he was accepted for this UN post. They've been preparing this move for years. With a deep cover chap like this they take the long view, you know."

"All right. We'll just see where he goes after lunch. A last shot. Then you can take him."

"The Wallace Collection."

"That's near here, isn't it?"

"Round the corner."

"He must have been to it before then."

"Usually not," Croxley was like a doctor with sad news. "One never seems to get around to the sights on your doorstep. Look at me, been living next to Clapham Junction for over thirty years, and never taken a train from there."

"Yes—but why the Wallace?"

"He usually does a gallery after lunch."

"And he's done all the others?" McCoy was as weary of the man's aesthetic proclivities as he was of Croxley's ability to forecast them. The two men seemed as master and student in a university where he had no arts.

"Most of them." Croxley took out a notebook and murmured the names quickly: "B.M., National, National Portrait, Tate, V. and A., Horniman, Thomas Sloane; then the private galleries: the Bond Street ones, most of them, and even the ones in the suburbs. Wimbledon—he was there yesterday. I don't expect he'd leave the Wallace out of that collection, do you? Stands to reason, sir, not feeling."

"A pound to a penny, Croxley."

"A pound to a penny it is, sir."

The two men looked at each other, their eyes meeting in grim measure for a second. Then they left the pub and walked down towards Hinde Street past the Greek restaurant.

2

They could see him now inside, sitting with his back toward them in the window seat. Nearly every day he had taken lunch there, before setting out on his odysseys, and each day there had been one or two of Croxley's men with him, at some other table, but he'd always been alone and had never spoken to any other guest. McCoy had gone there himself for lunch a few days before, just to be sure, sitting in a corner as far out of the way as possible.

It was an unpretentious Cypriot place, not a kebab shop. There was linen on the tables and Mediterranean fare of some variety, even originality. The man had used the place like a Continental, as a regular and concerned patron, knowing the waiters, speaking some of their language, savoring a decent but in no way elaborate meal: homous, sometimes a rice soup, warm pancakes of hollow bread, followed by a pork or lamb kebab spiced with an interesting chopped garnish, always a freshly dressed salad and a half bottle of some Attic burgundy, ending with a gritty Turkish coffee. And olives: big, puffed up black olives, glistening in their own clear oil. He never missed these, keeping a bowl of them by his plate throughout the meal, picking them out at odd moments, punctuating the other foods with them, biting the flesh decisively from between thumb and forefinger and letting the pips drop neatly in a line along another plate.

At the end of the meal he would smoke a pipe of some

mildly aromatic tobacco, Dutch perhaps, certainly not English. And the day McCoy had been there he had taken a glass of Metaxas brandy with it, though this was not a regular feature of his lunch. He left his serious drinking and eating for the evenings; nothing stupendous apparently, Croxley's men had reported: a succession of carefully chosen menus in small restaurants of repute about the city. And his other pleasures had been carefully listed too: *Monday*. Hayward Gallery: Art in Revolution—Soviet Art and Design after 1917. *Wednesday*. Marlborough: Sidney Nolan—Recent Graphics. *Thursday*. Mayfair Gallery—Andy Warhol: Graphics and Paintings. *Friday*. British Museum: Treasures from Romania: "4,000 Years of Art and Silver." His interest in the theater and the movies was fully represented as well, almost every decent thing that had been on in London that month.

These gastronomic and artistic concerns reinforced McCoy's unease tenfold, made him suppose that, just as the man visited so casually so many different restaurants and strange imaginations, so in the end he would give them the slip too and disappear forever into the world, where he seemed to have a season ticket; whereas a choice of sausages and suet puddings and smutty seaside postcards would inevitably have limited him, and McCoy would have slept easier.

They walked quickly past the window but McCoy had time to glance again at the tweed jacket, the broad back leaning forward at that moment as he reached for an olive or glass. He wasn't that tall but the face was like the back, McCoy remembered, a good square face, slightly leathery and tanned from years in the sun, relatively unlined for a man more than forty. He had the air of a sportsman. But not musclebound; his would have been the summer games, of rules born in fine weather, played on strings and wood, on beaches and underwater; the lightly coppered face, like the dust of travel; gestures so fluid that they seemed melted down by the years of sun and recast in a happier mold; sinews that had relaxed and lengthened with fulfilled pleasure.

The face was conventionally handsome in a lost way, as in some old advertisement for pipe tobacco in the thirties; the clear, open expression of a "good sort" in those times:

a casually tended but reliable face. There was nowhere about him clues to a contemporary life, nothing indoor or metropolitan, no smoky rooms or brandy or modern art—no suggestion anywhere of what McCoy had always seen as the epitome of dissolute bohemianism: an interest in graphics and oysters.

Above all there was nothing of Moscow in that quickly good-humored face, no trace of Beria, the Berlin Wall, and all the good men gone. But there it was, and McCoy realized he ought to have seen it sooner: trips to view the likes of Messrs. Warhol and Nolan were commensurate with the worst the KGB had to offer. There was no doubt they were clever people, fiends. . . .

They came to the end of the High Street to the great gray hulk of the Methodist Church on the corner, where they met Reilly, one of Croxley's men, who had just left the Greek restaurant. He was wiping his mouth surreptitiously, shamefacedly indeed. A streak of something, some foreign gravy, ran down his lapel.

"Nothing, sir," he reported. "Except—" he choked a little. "Except those wicked little starved sardines to begin with—" He stopped again, trying to batten down the hatches on some sickness within him.

"Anchovy, Reilly, anchovy."

"Sir! Well then that flour paste, four sticks of pig, most of a bottle of Greek red biddy, and a glass of that caramel water they call brandy. Quite a blowout in fact. Think it means anything?"

"You're getting quite expert, you lot, aren't you?" Croxley said. "In the Greek manner."

"I don't know about that, sir. I shouldn't like to be in the Greek Special Branch, I can tell you." Reilly smothered a belch.

"I expect not, Reilly. Though they do very well on it out there these days."

"Oh, and the olives. More than the usual quota I'd say. Pipping and poking at them all through the meal he was."

"Summers is still inside with him?"

"Frankly, sir, I came over a bit queasy after the meat. Needed a spot of air. Summers is looking after him."

"All those sheep's eyes rumbling about the belly a bit, eh Reilly? Have to get you an easier pitch next time. Surveillance from a cafe in the Mile End Road."

And then the man was sick. At first it seemed he had just turned away to cough, cupping his hand over his mouth. But the cough rapidly matured into a long groaning spurt, a violent eruption of purplish liquid which shot from his mouth like a hose, all over the one corner of the church steps. The two men jumped in surprise at the violence of the fit and then went for Reilly as he began to fold.

"I'm sorry, sir, I shouldn't—" Reilly erupted once more. "I shouldn't—"

"Well done, Croxley. *Well done!*" McCoy almost shouted. "If he sees us now—" McCoy danced around the steps in a wild fury. Croxley did no more than growl at him by way of reply. He was looking after one of his own men. "Give me a handkerchief," he said. Then he was on to Reilly again.

"Get right down, Reilly, *right* down. Get it out of you!"

Reilly had his hands to his throat, gasping. He was a wretched sight.

"It's all right now, sir," he murmured after a time. "I should have had an omelette."

"Don't worry." Croxley brushed him down with McCoy's handkerchief like a parent. "It doesn't matter. Probably better you had the Greek stuff, olives and all. He could well have been suspicious, seeing a man eating an omelette in that sort of restaurant. Get back to the van, take it easy. We have enough men. You know, back entrance to the Wigmore Hall, where they bring the pianos in."

Their backs were turned when the man came to the end of the street by the church. The man paused and glanced at the three waving figures, the most unsteady man in the middle, and reflected, not for the first time, on the British tendency to public drunkenness—squiffy at midday, staggering by early afternoon. But it was a form of release he understood well enough. He had used it himself in less happy times. It was a necessary tool of his trade. You had to know how to handle it, that was all.

He relit his pipe, savoring the burnt sweetness for a

moment, waiting for the traffic to pass. Then he crossed over, going in the opposite direction along Hinde Street, toward Manchester Square. It had been a good lunch, simple, yet full of precise flavors. And now what? Why not a glance at the Wallace Collection? How true it was, he reflected, that one never gets around to seeing the treasures on one's own doorstep.

Summers had walked after him to the corner and now he almost ran to where the three men were standing.

"He's moving, sir!" Croxley turned. "He's on his way now, toward Manchester Square."

"The Wallace Collection."

"I should think so," Summers said. "Bound to be."

Croxley turned to McCoy but didn't bother to take the advantage. He was serious now. In his book these games were coming to an end.

"All right. Let's take him." McCoy pruned the syllables viciously into sharp points. "Take him, Croxley." And now his words were harshly anguished like the pleas of Trojan women. "Take him—and let's be done with this tomfoolery. Stop this nonsense, almighty God. . . ."

McCoy had risen in anger, the fats about his body expanding like a cake. He looked up at the sooty portico of his church and at last cared nothing for blasphemy. He swore then that he would fall upon this man with venom, forget a lifetime's careful doubt. Within the hour he would make him pay for all the glitter, the sins and gifts of others.

"Bring them in, Summers. Call them in," Croxley said gently, as if his men were children who had strayed over the hill. "You know the routine. Back and front of the building. Keep the cars at a distance. When you're ready, give us the word." He turned to McCoy. "It should go like clockwork. We planned it all before, you see."

3

The man studied the group of Canalettos in the anteroom to the left of the hall. He had thought at first of leaving them to the end of his tour, but they had tempted him strongly, bright visions in the distance, and he was glad he'd given in. On closer inspection, he wondered if they might be deteriorating. There were cracks, minute hairline fractures, running like waves about the placid blue arcs of sky over the canals. He felt a quick sadness, a disappointment. These perfect memorials were as ephemeral as the perfect originals. Even art was not long. He stepped back for a larger view.

Then he heard the voices and had to force himself not to turn about and run.

Two voices, a man and a woman, talking in an unfamiliar Russian dialect. Estonia, Latvia, the Ukraine? He wasn't sure, except that it was Soviet. Then he recognized a sentence; they were speaking of Canaletto and the Doge's Palace. He relaxed and turned his head a fraction. One of the gallery attendants, a stocky fellow in his fifties with a face like a rock, was explaining Venice to a younger woman, toughly built like him, almost a gypsy woman in her rough, unfinished bearing, her fair hair streaked with carrot. And the man was able to place them immediately, these displaced people. There had been hundreds of thousands of them just after the war, POWs for the most part, Russians who had been in prison and then in refugee camps all over Germany for years after 1945; nationalist minorities who had never gone home to Mother Russia but had chosen to settle anywhere else, in countries the world over, without ever forgetting their homeland, their language, or their loss.

It ruined his afternoon. For months now, prior to his transfer, he had lived clear of all control and contact. He had been sleeping, without a trail, twenty-four hours a day, for many days. He had been nothing but George Graham, Senior Reports Officer at the COI in Westminster. There had been no other life but that of his cover and he had inhabited it guilelessly and completely so that he had come to forget, as was his purpose, that he was an officer with the KGB. Had he been interrogated, even tortured, during that time it is likely that he would have given nothing away. For he had, quite literally, put a curtain about his real past and future. He had been well trained in the craft—like Pelmanism or some other mnemonic game—to completely separate the real man from the false; to bury the first while the other went forth.

Yet some hazard or commonplace, like words in an empty gallery, could resurrect and reunite these halves long before their time and trigger the whole man into dangerous action. There had been no threat in the words of the old Russian exile, boring his daughter or his cousin, yet they had broken straight through into his secrets like the verbal shafts of a skilled prosecutor.

And now he saw nothing but the politics and dangers of his real commitment, his proper concern divested of all its pleasurable cover. He no longer saw the pictures, the Bouchers or Fragonards, or the green glaze, fathoms deep, or the Urbino porcelain, or the mineral wonders of the Louis Quinze mantel clocks. He looked on these marvelous gilded and enameled artifacts but saw nothing, they meant nothing. His critical perspective disappeared; his knack of enjoyment died. All the casual pleasures that he had taken in the past weeks were soured, faded into some dull place in his mind where they lay like old and unrewarding duties. His links with the world, which had been so firm in that April of easy strolling through the fortunate weather, had been cut off suddenly. Now, in the silence, the other man, whose only business was guile, alert and smelling the wind, reared in him, while the happy man cursed the hour.

So it was that he was not altogether surprised when he turned in the armory room at the end of the building and saw them. The innocuous words of the old man ten minutes before had led them to him as surely as a cord through a labyrinth: the disinherited man and the carroty woman had somehow advertised him as clearly as a shout all over the streets of Marylebone.

The two men stood in the doorway, in sensible coats and hats, behind the great medieval horseman, sword flourishing in the air above his tortuous Gothic armor. He had come into this room on a wrong turning, looking for the exit, straight into a cage of antique weaponry. An orchestra of gleaming metal lay everywhere about him. Blades from Damascus and Toledo, Italian pikes and tufted halberds, taut Bavarian crossbows, and small infernal devices from France— enough to nourish a new crusade. He put a hand out, touching the thick glass on a case of pearl-handled Arab daggers, then gently ran his fingers down the slope in the offhand gesture of some proud and fastidious collector. It is here, he seemed to say, all in one place. After a lifetime's pursuit I have gathered all this violence safely up, calmed this bloody provocation, resting quietly under my fingertips. It is here, I have tamed it all and have no need of it now.

The men walked toward them, past a silver inlaid Spanish cannon that said "Do Not Touch," and they took him quietly by a case of arquebuses and hatchets.

His pipe fell as they frisked him and the burnt grains of tobacco scattered on the shiny floor. Croxley bent down to pick the pipe up and thought of the blackened grain in the gut of a dead bird, shot violently out of a big sky. Summers went through his other pockets, but the man had no weapons.

"Nothing, sir. Except this bag of olives."

4

McCoy went around to see Croxley in his office by the Thames later next morning. He was impatient.

"He's in the basement. We're starting, but it will take some time. Do you want to go down?"

"How long?"

"They disorientate him first."

"A week?"

"Depends. It's an army speciality. We have one of their men on it now. Depends on how long the sounds take to sink in. And the darkness, as well as the other physical . . . awkwardness. It's cumulative, you know, forty-eight hours perhaps, at best."

Croxley was embarrassed even in hinting at this psychological violence, so that he turned away from McCoy and looked over the river as a precaution. He had realized long ago the disadvantages, among outsiders, of his sympathetic approach to security interrogations. They took it for weakness. Only other professionals recognized the skill that lay behind his gentle attitudes; the tools that Croxley masked with his diffidence were those of a great interrogator. And when the army had finished, the man downstairs would recognize this too, without knowing it, and by Croxley's sympathy be moved to bestow outrageous confidences, as many other men had been.

McCoy came down again three days later, sooner than expected, for Croxley had a preliminary report ready for him.

"So?" McCoy glanced rapidly through it. "How so soon?"

Croxley shrugged, drawing a blank over the whole procedure and McCoy looked at the opening paragraphs: *George Graham. Born Islington, Royal Free Hospital, July 14th, 1929. . . .* These were details they knew already. *Recruited by Alexei Flitlianov, KGB Resident in Beirut, in April 1952, while he was teaching there with the British Council.*

"Well, we practically knew that." McCoy flicked through the pages. "What's the rough outline of the rest? What's important? Who are his contacts here? Anyone else on our side?"

"No. Nothing of that sort, and no deep cover Soviet illegals either. His contacts, such as they were, were all with Embassy or trade mission staff. And they were practically nonexistent. No message drops or anything like that. Nothing. Very thin on the ground."

"But what is it all about? What was he *giving* them?" McCoy insisted. "It couldn't just have been COI stuff. There's hardly anything classified there—just a lot of Commonwealth public relations jaw."

"Well, that's the point of course. That's what I had to press him on. He seems to have passed on nothing at all. That wasn't his job. You see—"

"That couldn't have been all. They don't keep a man on ice for so many years doing nothing. There must have been something else."

McCoy's impatience rose again. After all this, he thought, nothing—the man was just a complete sleeper, a back marker, nothing more than a courier perhaps, just a weak queer in love with Marx. Croxley inclined his eyes sympathetically toward the unhappy McCoy. He was the doctor once more.

"They'll keep someone quiet for as long as they have to," he said. "If there's something else in mind. And there was. There was something else. They kept this man out of the way all these years on purpose, kept him clear—"

"Because he was a dolt, a back marker, no real use to them."

"On the contrary. He was highly skilled, a deep cover illegal, senior rank. They took a great deal of trouble over him. Initially in Beirut and subsequently when he taught in Cairo. He went back to Moscow during his holidays there, said he was looking around the Middle East, Petra, and such like, long hikes. In face he was doing their advanced training, what they call the 'Silent School'—individual tuition, you might say, where he'd meet no other KGB men except one or two at the top. They took a lot of trouble."

"For what?"

"For the job he was *going* to do. In the future. Always in the future. The job that was to start next week in New York."

McCoy had taken out a pipe but quite forgot about it now. It stuck out of his puffy white face, clenched in his teeth, giving him the startled immobility of a snowman.

"He was going to start an alternative KGB circle in America. A new network, a satellite circle. These are completely unknown to the local KGB Resident, and quite separate from any other espionage network in the country. They report only, and directly to Moscow, almost as a freelance might do. There's never more than, at most, half a dozen people involved. And sometimes just one person. The point of these circles is to keep tabs on the official espionage groups. They're set up, very quietly, with that express purpose—to spy on the spies. That's what they've been holding Graham for all these years—to head one of these circles."

Croxley paused, wondering if McCoy had really followed the implications. But he had.

"So, Graham would know the identity of the people in the other official groups?"

"Not before he went there, he wouldn't. Too risky."

"What happens?"

"Well, he told me," Croxley said quietly, as though the man had given him the information over a cucumber sandwich tea, "he picks up the information on this when he gets there. When he gets into his new cover."

"How?"

"There's always one crucial contact in the designate circle area. Either someone sent specially from Moscow, or more often what they call a 'stayer,' someone already there who has absolutely no activity other than that of passing on the names that Moscow wants a check on."

"Who would that be?"

"Graham wouldn't know that either. The contact would be completely one-sided. The Stayer makes it. And he'd know very little about the new man. All he would know would be his name, real or assumed, what his cover was, where he worked."

"Then he'd make the contact?"

"Yes. In this case all he'd have been told was that a George Graham, from London, was joining the UN as a Reports Officer in their information department round about a certain date. He'd check him over carefully beforehand, then make an approach."

"Check him? He'd have a photograph? Exchange a code? How would he be sure of him. That would surely be crucial."

A plan was straining in the depths of McCoy's mind, something which might save the day in this disappointing affair.

"No photographs. There'd be nothing documentary, nothing on paper. If anything, it would be verbal. So, yes, there could be an exchange code."

"What they used to call a 'password,' " McCoy sighed for *Kim* and *The Jungle Books*.

"Yes." Croxley looked at McCoy, his face full of understanding as usual, but not caring this time whether McCoy took offense or not. "It's a risk you'd have to take."

"What do you mean?"

"You could replace this man Graham, couldn't you? Have someone else go to New York in his place."

"It wouldn't work." McCoy refused to admit the possibility, for it had been exactly his own thought.

"Perhaps. On the other hand you'd really be on to something then, if you could break the Stayer. You could work your way through an entire deep cover network, for example, just with the Stayer's name, if you handled it properly.

"They must take very considerable pains to prevent that happening," McCoy said sharply.

"They have. They have indeed. They've done just that. They've kept Graham clean as a whistle for years. It was sheer chance we got on to him in the first place. Absolute chance. No one's been near him, possibly for years, until they told him he was on for this job they'd trained him for. He's a loner. He had to be, at this juncture especially. Everything depended on Moscow's keeping completely clear of him, keeping him clear, so that there could be no trail and therefore no chance of any substitution. That's the way it works. As far as they're concerned he'll be on the boat to New York next week. You see, the essence of the matter is that for him to be effective in his future role, no one must know about him in the past. He's completely unknown to any KGB Resident here or anywhere else. That's the beauty of it: the man had no previous form. Among his own, he had no identity. So you can create that for him—in the shape of another man. You have a chance in a million."

"That's the odds against it, I'd say, Croxley. Not the chances. I'll read your report. Is he downstairs now?"

"There is just one other thing, before you go," Croxley said. Again the deprecatory tone, as though the matter were of no real importance. "Graham spoke of something else— after he'd told me about his real work for the KGB."

" 'Spoke'—willingly?"

"Well, not exactly. No, not willingly. Not at first. It was about his communicating with his chiefs, making his reports in America. I asked him how he did it—what the form was. I, er, pressed him on that. He eventually became—incoherent, yes—"

"Delirious?" McCoy asked, suddenly interested.

"He was, well, babbling rather. Yes."

"Goodness me!" McCoy was thoroughly aroused. "How did you manage that?"

"I'd rather not, if you don't mind. The point was he mentioned a letter drop in New York, a private mailbox at Grand Central Post Office, when he was cloudy, so to speak. Afterward we—we, er, taxed him on that, when he was clearer in the head. And he denied having ever mentioned such a thing. But we had a recording. And eventually the whole thing came out: what he said was this, and I think he must have been inventing it all, as a blind, but he said he was a member of a dissident liberal group within the KGB. Gave us details—which we couldn't possibly check. Then he came on to our side about it all. It's in my report. He pleaded with me to let him go, to carry on with this work saying that the West should help support this group, that it was a vital lever for change in the Soviet Union. Well, you'll have to pass the stuff on to your political experts. It's my view that it was sheer bluff. I can't see the KGB riddled with dissidents. Least of all with this man Flitlianov heading them."

"He said that did he? Flitlianov's head of their Second Directorate, in charge of all internal security. Unlikely, to say the least. And this letter drop in New York—this was to communicate with the other dissidents in the group?"

"Yes."

"You have the number of it?"

"Yes."

"Well, we can put tabs on it through the FBI. See who goes there, who took the box out. That won't be difficult. And I'll pass that part of your report on to the politicals. But I agree—it seems a complete blind. That box was surely there for him to report on his activities against the official

KGB networks in America. And that's the horse we should ride, if we ride anything."

Croxley nodded. "I should have thought so."

"Come on then—let's take a look at him."

Graham was in one of the special cells with a one-way observation glass let into the top half of the door. McCoy was surprised at his demeanor. He was sitting at a small table, pen in hand over some scribbled paper. But he was writing nothing now. The pen jumped every so often, involuntarily. His eyelids flickered continously, twitching in awful duet with his eyebrows. A lot of his hair had come away from the top of his head, so that he now had the air of some badly eccentric academic, ten years older, a scalp ravaged like a bird's nest after a hawk, the hairline shrunk all about his head. He still wore his tweed jacket. But there were purple stains down its back which McCoy couldn't understand. It was as if something entirely unnatural, some terrible physical mutation, had overcome the man, enabling him to twist his head around by 180 degrees, to be violently sick in reverse. There was the remains of some uneaten or picked at or vomited food by a plastic bowl on the floor. One couldn't tell what process it had undergone. A dog, it seemed, was occupying the room.

Three days ago he had been a quiet man-about-town. But those few days had done ten years' damage to him. He was like someone who had been abroad for a long time, in a hard country; someone who one had remembered leaving with hope and vigor and who had returned unexpectedly damaged beyond repair.

"What's he writing?"

"He insisted on it. His 'confession.' But there's nothing there. Nothing to confess. He gave it all before. He can't write. Can't really even think now. Do you want to see him? I'm afraid—"

"No. No, there's nothing I can do. Nothing." McCoy spoke quickly, like a doctor surprised in a morgue. He had thought for so long that when you caught a traitor, he would remain more or less the same man; there would still be the evidence of his treachery in him. He believed that deceit had an ineradicable lineage, and was now vastly surprised by his mistake. This man was so changed he might have been born anew. The footsteps where he had come through life had been completely erased.

Yet McCoy had thought that Graham, when caught, would release the mysteries, explain the hidden trails, give him a fair picture at last of those border lands, all the exact colors of his temptation and betrayal. Instead, he saw just a shape now, not a man, something quite mutilated which could now never be repaired, only replaced.

"It's not pleasant." Croxley looked through the one-way glass.

"It's what happens. I've no doubt it would be a lot more unpleasant elsewhere," McCoy said unctuously.

"New for us, though. They developed it in Aden. And Belfast. Black bags and wind machines. We can still beat the world in some developments. Some development this. . . ."

"It must make your work a lot easier."

"Takes all the skill out of it. Like taking sweets off a seven year old."

"What do you expect? Development. You said it yourself. He's alive, after all."

"Of course."

"He's breathing. Plenty of places where he wouldn't be."

"No, he's not dead."

"No. No, indeed. So?"

"Well, I wouldn't call it progress. Sounds more like redundancy to me."

"I'll read your report."

McCoy took a last look at the man. A collection of broken pieces. What had he ever looked like originally? McCoy could barely remember now. Yet he wanted to remember, for he wanted someone very soon to look like him, wanted a replica of that happy man who had strolled around the galleries and restaurants with a sweet tobacco drifting in his trail.

McCoy left Croxley and walked up Whitehall. The principal outlines were clear: someone around forty, well-built, with fluent Arabic; someone who had known Beirut and

Cairo well, who had lived there; someone with experience, yet who had worked out of any limelight; someone not currently in the field, even if there was time, for Moscow could well have tabs on such a person. Someone at home then, with Arabic and therefore from his own section; skilled, but at the same time relatively dispensable, for the chances of success were less than fifty-fifty. It was more than a difficult combination; such a man was a contradiction in terms.

He talked the whole matter over with his deputy, John Harper, showing him Croxley's report, when he got back to Holborn, in the front office of the new building with the Hepworth abstract in the forecourt. And they seemed to have got nowhere by the time his secretary brought them a second coffee by midday.

Harper had stood up and gone to the window, looking down on the stream of secretaries fluttering out into the sun, leaving for an early lunch from the front entrance. Harper seemed to be picking up each of the figures with his eyes, examining them closely, turning them over in his mind, before replacing them gently on the pavement all unawares. Among other things, Harper was responsible for security within the building. Then he turned and with unnecessary, heavy elaboration picked up his coffee cup and drew it slowly toward his lips. McCoy hated these silent dramatics that Harper went in for, hated his meddlesome, pugnacious, Australian face. Harper had the querulous, unsatisfied expression of a vet who has been struck off the register for unnatural practice.

"Marlow," Harper said at last. "Peter Marlow. He has all those qualifications. Every one, except experience in the field. But then Graham doesn't seem to have had much of that either."

McCoy narrowed his eyes, as if about to start a difficult position in yoga.

"Marlow. You remember. The Scapegoat. Three years ago, or was it longer? The man Williams insisted on sending down for that Cairo business. The Cairo-Albert circle. The fellow Moscow framed, using his ex-wife—got a bag over her head, put her in a plane out of Cairo, and let *Der Spiegel* photograph her outside GUM next day. Marlow got twenty-eight years for it as I remember. A costly affair. . . ."

"I remember."

"You were his Control then, weren't you?"

"No, that was Edwards. Marlow was in Information and Library."

"Of course, Reports Officer, wasn't he?"

"Yes." McCoy looked up. "Yes, he culled all the stuff from the Arabic press—*Al Ahram* and all the other socialist rags they deliver free all over Africa."

"And Graham, what was he?"

"Reports Officer," McCoy said reluctantly, looking down again, going sour. Another hand lost.

"Well?" Harper moved in for the kill.

"Would he play though?"

Harper put his hands in his pockets and started flapping them about inside a bit, beating his thighs. Then he started to put his papers together.

" 'Would he play?' I should think so. Wouldn't you? With twenty years ahead of you if you didn't. On a spike, by the short and curlies."

"And reliable, of course?" McCoy was grasping at straws.

"He used to be. As I remember. Faithful as a dog. Stayed at his post till the last, went down with all hands. Though God knows what—where did he go? Durham wasn't it? God knows they may have knocked the reliability out of him. You'd have to see."

"It's awfully good of you, Harper. Very good of you." McCoy couldn't help commenting out loud. Nor could he bother to disguise the cynical tones of his commendation.

"Nothing at all. Just picked it out of a hat." Harper stared at him.

"Get Marlow's file out, will you?" McCoy called through to Rosalie. Then to Harper: "I'll look at it on the way up in the train."

Harper smiled, his face hunching up into lumps and valleys, the pockmarks of some old disease expanding into little craters. When he smiled, it was no more than a short break in the gray weather over the stumps and mud of no man's land. "Lunch?" he said. "Let's have some lunch. You're onto a good thing, sir. No doubt about it. Subtle. Simple."

"He's dispensable, too, of course," McCoy said as they left the building.

"My goodness yes. If it misfired no one at this end would be any the worse off. No one at all."

"Exactly."

"Couldn't be more so."

" 'The George?' Half a pint?" Harper said, raising the ghost of a thirst.

"Why not? Why not indeed? Have to be a quick one though."

5

It was afternoon in Moscow, faintly sunny through a darkening mist, late April, the bitter weather still more than a match against the odd incursions of spring—the small midday thaws on high roofs and small puddles, the few liquid hours, minute victories, which would soon stiffen up again like a corpse in the huge grip of the night.

The nearly old Englishman stamped his feet on the steps of the building in Dzerzinsky Square, as he'd been doing outside doors and buildings in the city all winter, not so much to loose the slush from his boots, for he always traveled by car on duty, but as part of a winter habit of warmth he'd picked up years before he'd come to Moscow. In the temperate climate of England, even during the mildest winters, he'd stamped his feet. It was something you did at that season before coming indoors; it went with Christmas and mulled wine from silver punch bowls and expensive cards of stage-coaches lost in snow drifts. He was a man of habits; he tended them carefully, even when they had lost all meaning, as others will retain precious but empty photographs of their youth or marriage and keep them prominently on desks or mantelpieces. He went inside and was escorted upstairs into Yuri Andropov's office.

The visitor had an intelligent, convivial face—dark hair, just a hint overgrown at the back, and sad, bedroom eyes. Fat had come to it suddenly in his middle years and, finding no support in his cheekbones, had seeped down into small rolls beneath his jaw and about his neck. And the same had found an even more abundant refuge about his waist.

The eyes were the only contradiction in this well-set figure: "I've lost something," they seemed to say, "and I can't for the life of me forget it"; while the rest of his body, in its freshly chubby content, suggested just the opposite: "I had nothing, but now I have come into my due reward." For the moment, however, he was neither sad nor confident: he was simply a little on edge. He played nervously with his fingers, and his eyebrows fidgeted as though he was anxious for a drink in company he knew to be strictly temperate. He stammered a greeting in Russian. But Yuri Andropov made a point of welcoming him in courteous, rather archaic English, as though their meeting had been in the Reform Club and not Dzerzinsky Square.

"Comrade Philby, how good of you to come. How are you?" Andropov then lapsed into Russian. "Come, let's sit down." They moved away from the desk to a small conference table by the window.

"Sakharovsky has already outlined our problem to you, and I'd be most grateful if you could listen to my thoughts on it and give me your opinion on them. As you know, Harper—one of our men with the British SIS, I believe you knew him slightly?—has now been able to confirm to us that a very senior man in the KGB is the chief figure in some sort of conspiracy against us. A number of other KGB officers are with him in it—we don't know who. However, we do know the name of one of them: an Englishman working for us in London, attached to the British government's Information Service, called George Graham. British Security picked him up a week ago, interrogated him, and found out not only that he was with us but who his boss is—this senior figure we're after."

Philby was still fidgeting, slightly mystified. He reached for some cigarettes. "May I?"

"Certainly, certainly." Andropov hurried on. "Now Harper tells us that George Graham also gave the names of a number of other KGB operatives overseas that he had contacts with—bona fide contacts, not necessarily part of the conspiracy, though of course we don't know that yet for sure. However, one thing was clear, Graham was part of it, an important part of it, one of this man's deputies in fact. Now the chief—let's call him that for the moment—we think he must have been working a chain cutout system in his clandestine group, not a block cutout: he recruited all his deputies, who in turn recruited their own men. The chief knew the names of his immediate deputies but not the rest of the staff as it were."

"So to get the *whole* group you need only put the pressure on this top man? That was rather foolish of him." Philby puffed at his cigarette unsuccessfully. It had gone very damp at the mouth end. He lit a fresh one.

"Possibly. But on the other hand, it means that if we *fail* to get anything out of him, we get nowhere. The rest of his group will be blocked to us. And this is the problem: if this man chose the chain system, keeping all the links in his group to himself, it means that he thinks he can keep those secrets, under whatever pressure. Now this is where George Graham comes in: the British managed to get an extraordinary amount of information out of him. And remember he was a senior operative with us, specially trained, he'd lived successfully as a deep cover illegal for nearly twenty years—a man who knew every counterploy under interrogation, who'd lived his cover in the British Information Service as successfully as you did in British Intelligence. And yet what happened? He broke in less than a week, with no circumstantial evidence against him; they found nothing on him or in his apartment. The only lead they had was a telephone conversation they broke in on quite by chance. And they nailed him on that—a few vague hints on the telephone. Now what does all this suggest to you?"

Philby smiled. "Who was the interrogator?"

Andropov smiled with him. "That's why I asked you

here this afternoon; his name was Croxley, from the British Special Branch."

"Detective Inspector—probably Superintendent by now—Croxley. I knew him by reputation. MI5 wanted him put on to me but there was so much interdepartmental jealousy around Whitehall ten years ago it wasn't difficult for my section to head him off. Besides he was junior then to the man I got—Skardon. Skardon was the man everyone feared and of course he was good. But Croxley was thought to be just as good, and he was younger. And stamina plays a big part in these question-and-answer games."

"Of course, the point struck me, Philby, if Croxley got this man Graham to break, why not the head of this conspiracy? What do you think of that?"

"Yes, possibly. How would you get this chief to England?"

"He travels abroad from time to time. And if not, I'm sure we could find ways of getting him there and them breaking him to the authorities. He'd be taken to Croxley, wouldn't he?"

"Almost certainly. He must be the number one by now. The trouble is if Croxley failed to get anything out of him you'd lose your trail to the rest of the group. They'd just bang your key figure in jail for twenty years."

"Yes. Now what could you do to prevent that? Or rather, what precautionary steps would you take, as another string to the plan? So that you still had a chance of following the rest of the group up?"

Philby answered almost immediately. "What about this man George Graham? Could you replace him? Have Harper put someone else in his shoes and wait and see what messages, if any, were passed to him from above or beneath. Send him off to do whatever assignment Graham had been given—and see where it led him to. Use him as a stalking horse."

"That's a daring idea." Andropov considered it as if for the first time. Then he added sagely: "But I think you're right. That's exactly what the British are going to do. Harper has suggested it already—since, of course, they're just as anxious as we are to try and follow this trail down the line, to pick up the rest of Graham's KGB contacts. Our interests here coincide precisely: we want to find out who these men are just as much as they do. British intelligence may in fact be able to do most of this job for us. There's just one more point, Philby: a possible problem. The man they've chosen to replace George Graham: he's an ex-British SIS officer, used to work in their Middle East section, Peter Marlow. Did you know him?"

"Marlow?" Philby was surprised. "Hardly an 'officer.' More a clerk. He was in Information and Library. And he's in jail now isn't he? A long sentence. We used him to get Williams clear three or four years back."

"Yes, but they're going to spring him quickly. Point is, he doesn't seem the best choice for this sort of job."

"A complete amateur—from the little I know of him."

"That's the problem. A weak link. You have a phrase for it, don't you?"—and he went on in English—" 'Fools jump in when angels go to bed.' "

Philby looked at Andropov with some embarrassment. "Yes, well, er—perhaps. On the other hand, look on the bright side: he's served us far better than he had the British in the past, as regards Williams, for example. He's natural fall-guy material—I suppose that's why they thought of him. After all, replacing a KGB officer in this way, if the contacts he's after discover the deception, that's not a healthy future."

The two men nodded in agreement. The afternoon had died outside the window. The dark had run in over the city like an accident.

Book Three

1

The heavy prison buildings had ceased to interest me some while back. Before, during the first months—first couple of years indeed—I'd struggled against the bar as it were, knowing it was quite the wrong thing to do, that survival came from blocking out all the terrible minutiae of the place, all the insulting brick, and thinking of anything else.

Originally, there had been twenty or so other prisoners in the new security wing, who, even if one saw them rarely, one could occupy one's thoughts with. At exercise or in chapel—my goodness, how we all believed then—there was little opportunity for talk, but one soon got around that. The trick was to memorize the odd words, particular faces, momentary vignettes: how one man held his dinner knife like a penholder, another lifted a cup like a duchess, a third spoke in the purest tones of Stockbroker Surrey. And then one would take this visual and aural booty back to one's cell, to feed on it, rationing it out, during the eighteen hours solitary we did every day then. One's company, in those few moments out of solitary, became transfers which one took back and colored in one's mind, vehemently, with daring strokes and bright hues, giving those train robbers and rapists a brilliance which, despite their previous activities, they never possessed inside. Men who had hiked a million from a mail train and had had the imagination to invest most of it in Post Office bonds before they were caught, here became monumental nonentities, empty spirits, razed tablets. So that afterwards, at the end of table tennis or "Steptoe and Son" in the hall, I would bring these skeletons back with me to my cell and put flesh on them bit by bit, and then set them moving as bearable, even interesting companions. I would take a single characteristic of a man I'd exchanged no more than a few words with at exercise, a child murderer perhaps—a habit, say, of rocking on the balls of his feet, hands dug deep into his jacket pockets—and from this isolated trait I would form a whole new character and set him free in some happy context.

From such unpromising material one formed a whole repertory of imagined characters and serial dramas, and I eventually learned to occupy myself continuously with my unknown friends about the building in this way. All one needed, like a sleeping pill, was that one initial character-istic, some dull reality—a certain hair style or an extended ear lobe—which then became a talisman for all sorts of high and quiet adventure. Some people, I learned—often those of an academic or artistic bent—think of nothing but vio-lent sport in prison, motor racing and such like, pursuits which they had no interest in whatsoever when they were free. I, on the other hand, who had once been fond of such athletic activities, would create fantasies of leisured, rather donnish talk in musty circumstances, a recreation I should have loathed in the real world.

A long prison sentence, inexorably, invents and opens up all the possibilities of the world for you: a lifetime's sub-scription to the *National Geographic* magazine running through one's head night after night. That, indeed, is the punishment. One creates the Monaco Grand Prix or the easy chat at the high table with a sharpness and reality which is matched only by the subsequent realization that such things can never be part of your future. Thus one comes to regret one's imagination. And the hours that you had looked forward to, alone with it, building the world, become hours dogged with the knowledge of a sour end—like evenings with a girl that you enjoy as much as ever in an affair that she has told you has no future.

So it had been for me in Durham. In the first two years there had been my anger; anger at being framed by Wil-liams to save his skin, an anger so fierce that for days on end I thought it would literally eat me away with its vio-lence, an anger that was absolutely isolated, a monument on an empty plain. And because of it I couldn't talk or eat or sleep then. Later, when I had come more to "accept mat-ters" (yes, learning to live in prison is like coming to terms with the loss of someone loved, even though it was oneself), there had been the brief company of the others, and, for all its dying falls, there were the invented odysseys and conversations I'd made with them. But then Mountbatten's "top security" reforms were questioned; his idea of corralling so many dangerous louts together seemed an increased risk, and one by one my library of characters was dispersed to other jails so that eventually, by the spring of 1971, there were only half a dozen of us left in "E" wing and finally only one other man, one of the train robbers, whom I barely saw at all.

I ceased to care then.

I learned the final trick of prison life: how to sleep twelve or fifteen hours a day. I became a vegetable, without pain, and had to be literally forced to my feet by warders with cold sponges, waking into the terror which every moment of consciousness had become, to defecate, to eat, to prove to the prison commissioners and the taxpayers that there was life yet, one live prisoner present and accounted for. To live was the only pain then; to get through those few waking hours was like living an imminent death, due at any moment, which one loathed yet longed for. And they realized this, of course, so that it became far more important that I should stay alive than that they should prevent my escaping. Gradually my cell and everything I might use in it turned softer, was padded in foam rubber, while implements of every kind turned to wood or polyethylene. The fibrous grit, the hardness, was taken out of everything, so that in keeping me alive they sent me back to the womb; finally I was sleeping nearly all the time on a rubber sheet, half drugged under a quilted Swedish duvet. Even the moody, inventive Swedes, they knew, hadn't yet learned how to strangle themselves with an eiderdown.

Later they had moved me from my cell in the middle of "E" wing to an improvised hospital ward at the end of the corridor—two cells with the wall between bashed out, and two beds, one for me and the other, empty, for the train robber, who had kept his mind intact with purposeful dreams of escape and the money somewhere under a stone in the Surrey woods. This fellow, with fourteen years in front of him, lived at the far end of the corridor, taking adult education courses in Spanish and business management and beating off offers from the *News of the World* to do a weekly column of investment advice. I suppose he'd already bought a suite of offices in the big new Alcoa building on Copacabana Beach and was considering copper futures in the light of Allende's recent victory on the other coast. While for my part, when I was not asleep, my only thought was to get to sleep.

I lay on my stomach and face, struggling in various positions, legs straddling imaginary fences, trying to ease the permanent feeling of cramp and strain in every muscle, arms crabbed over my head, sweating and shivering, like a man locked in a permanent hangover, longing for oblivion. For exercise I was forced up and held by two warders and frog marched up and down the corridor while the train robber played bar-football with another warden at one end, the two of them looking at me with real horror as I came toward them and left again, a Lazarus, a perpetual yo-yo.

I remember from that time, really the only clear thing, the viscous metallic clamor of the football machine and the invigorating cries of the two men, the displaced Cockney warder and the train robber, so that when my back was turned, going away from them, I was easily carried into the frenzied world of a real game, the swaying mass of red and white Arsenal hats and scarves, like curling surf, when there were near goals. The robber was a Londoner, too, from Islington. And warders are human enough, especially on a basic of £21 a week with six children and the mother-in-law in the back room. And their charge must often have seemed to them a living proof of the chance of eight home draws on next week's pools. He had half a million under a stone somewhere outside, all the fun of the world in six years' time, with remission, and good luck to him.

I, on the other hand, was a "traitor," which was something they didn't really follow. My "crimes"—the political charges, giving "succour and support to Her Majesty's enemies," like a cow, the clause in the Official Secrets Act under which I'd been sent down for twenty-eight years three years before—all this was gobbledegook to them. I'd been a spy, a double agent with the KGB, I'd betrayed the Queen. These bare bones, which they knew of, meant nothing to them, since there'd been no sex or guns, or champagne or swimming pools, involved. I was a contradiction in terms for them: a dull spy, as far removed from their routine as an atomic scientist might have been. Thus the only badge they could pin on me was that of confidence trickster and intellectual from a class way above them. I was someone— a real rogue, top of the ladder—in that criminal category of fraudulent stockbrokers and crooked captains of industry; old school tie boys, class enemies, and remittance men from the home counties Jaguar-and-pine belt; cads whose richly deserved comeuppance was appropriately equaled only by the length and severity of their punishment.

2

When he came he said "good morning."

It sounded like an old radio comic ("Goodmorning— *Goodmorning!*") until I realized he'd simply been repeating the phrase over and over, leaning across my bed, trying to wake me; I'd been deeply asleep.

"Good morning, Marlow. How are things? How are you?"

What a grandmother of a man McCoy had always been. The more he observed the proprieties the more dangerously stupid one knew he was being, or going to be. In those days, when he planned things for Williams in Holborn, how well I had come to know his hopeless foolishness, his sycophantic flourishes, his disdain for people in the field.

"Hello, Marlow. I've come to see you—if I may. . . ."

I thought I was dreaming, and it was this that woke me, startled.

"Mr. *Marlow*. . . ."

A face. Round. A chin too many. Older than the bland doctor who came to see me most days, talking behind the screen about sugar content and drip feeds. A tightly knotted, striped old boy's tie; white detached collar, dark suit; austerity in everything, except the face, which rose up from the tight neck like a pastry—puffy, substantial, but without any definition.

"I'm Donald McCoy. You remember—your ACO in Holborn. You were in Library and Information. My office was on the floor below, next to the annex. You remember...."

I remembered the accents then. It was the only thing McCoy remained true to in the constant temporizing and prevarication which were his life—the tough and broad, yet often elusive north country tones. McCoy the scholarship boy, Belfast man, and hard-line Protestant; of course I remembered him.

He sat on a chair now, next to the bed, seeming perplexed; a traveler who had come home to find a relative far worse than he expected, having to think of undertakers instead of grapes.

"I'm sorry to wake you. But it's important. Would you like to sit up? Have some coffee? You used to smoke didn't you? Can I get you some cigarettes?"

I hadn't smoked for a year either; taste had gone as well as dreams; all the interpretative senses. But he got up and went outside, returning with the doctor and a warder with a trolley of coffee, biscuits, and two packets of Players. They must have been waiting outside, on cue. The trolley interested me, more than any of the people. It was new, lacquered in dull gold with a handled tray on top, like nothing we'd ever had in Durham. And I thought—he's brought the lot up with him from Holborn, the ten o'clock coffee ritual, the trolleys in the corridors, the tough little Irish and Jamaican ladies hovering outside the senior offices waiting for the disdainful Tumbridge Wells secretaries to make an order. Again, I'd not thought about Holborn in a long while, and now each moment of McCoy's presence brought something of it back. He was picking up the bits of a puzzle I'd once been part of and had then been smashed and thrown away years before; picking them up and offering them to me. A messenger would come in through the cell door at any moment with a pile of "Extras" and "Ordinaries," the flimsy internal memos with the different security ratings, and by midmorning my copy of last Saturday's *Al Ahram* would arrive with Heykal's weekly message for the whole world.

The doctor said to McCoy: "Here you are, Mr. Hewlett. Let me know if there's anything else." And then to me, leaning down as though to a child: "This is Mr. Hewlett. Come all the way from London to see you. So do be a bit bright about it. We're doing our best." He fixed a brief smile onto his face, as quick as a franking machine running over an envelope with the message "So much for humanity," and he was gone.

Hewlett? I pushed myself up and got the pillow behind me, sensing a return of all the old anger in me, bitter ironies forming again: Hewlett. They couldn't ever let up, could they? Couldn't go ten miles out of London without aliases, subterfuges, games, letter drops, cutouts, surveillances.

McCoy got up, meticulously, as if on cue for a master shot in a film, and walked over to the trolley. And his words came as if from a script too—well-worn, tired, the twelfth take of the same scene that morning in a B movie.

"Hewlett, yes." He paused and poured. "Yes, indeed." He licked his top lip judiciously. As far as they're concerned I'm your accountant, come about your financial affairs. Hewlett, of Carter, Hewlett, and Bagshawe, Red Lion Square." He was pleased with the conceit, isolating the idea to himself, like a stage-struck juvenile pondering a great character role. "They don't know. About Holborn and that, except the governor."

"You are a fool, McCoy. A bloody fool. Besides, I've got no accountant."

I hadn't voiced such a direct opinion in years and my throat felt cracked and dry as though I'd made a long speech. I'd shocked myself far more than him. He put a cup of coffee on the table next to me and I wanted it now, like iced water, but didn't dare, knowing I'd spill the thing in physical confusion. Thought had come again, a creaking process, unearthed feeling groping for words and finding true sentences first time round. I might not be so lucky again and feeling was still miles away from action.

"They tell me you've been getting pretty low here, Marlow. Not—facing up, eh?"

"Not," I'd wanted to say, "not taking it like a man," but couldn't. The "t" in "taking" threw me completely.

"No need to force it, Marlow. I know what it must feel like. Just listen for a minute. I'm Hewlett because what I've got to suggest is just between you and I; no one else. So don't rush it. I'll be here overnight. We'll be seeing as much of each other as *you* need. You see, they may have made a mistake, you see. All of them, I mean. About you, about your trial. And I want you to help us put it right."

McCoy was a great believer in self-help. For him the sin would always remain, indelibly struck on the man, even if he were later proved guiltless. Even then, four years later, in the matter of my trial, it wasn't a question of my having been right and everyone else wrong. His Puritanism demanded that he excuse his own mistakes in the matter by spreading the fault equally amongst everyone involved. No one could ever be free of blame in McCoy's Old Testament canon; except himself, for he had seen the light and had a permanent message for all the fallen men of his department. McCoy believed deeply in other people's original sin. How he must sometimes have longed for the original faith itself, where, bleeding, he could have put himself upon a cross.

"You remember, at the trial? Your defense tried to show that Williams had been a double, a KGB man for years—how, when you learned this in Egypt, Williams framed you by getting Moscow to abduct your wife and then display her in Moscow. At the time it all added up perfectly. Your guilt, I mean."

"Yes. Perfectly."

McCoy ran on, encouraged. I stretched out a hand for the coffee. "Here, let me help."

"I'll do it myself." And I did.

"Well, we lost the whole Cairo-Albert circle out there. And only you had been in touch with them all. Then you
 ̄ ̄ed up back in England—remarkably, in the circum-
 ̄ ̄es. How could the Egyptians have missed you, we

thought, when they got everyone else? Because the Russians organized your escape, you were one of them, being sent home to roost again. We couldn't really come to any other conclusion. You were the deep cover man in our section, not Williams."

"Cairo-Albert circle": the ridiculous code designation rang out for me that morning like a distant "Tally-ho!" I was grateful that morning for anything that linked me indubitably to a past existence, which proved I had lived once, however badly. And that must have been exactly McCoy's intention: the thought behind his precis, with which he had to jog my heart. I would be no use to him, I was dead unless he could reinvest me with my previous identity, tempt me with the evidence of an old role. He knew the rot, the pretense, of offering anybody the chance of "turning over a new leaf." He knew that what we really want is a future in old and rash ways, subtle approval of a lost excess; knew, with the perception of a psychiatrist, that if we are all prisoners (and there could be no doubt about that in my case) the grudge we bear for this insists that, for release, we must take up where we left off, not start afresh. And so that morning he called up for me my old self, the men, and all the details of the Cairo-Albert circle four years before, all the shabby folly of those times, as one drags a rotten carcass across the land to stir a fox.

"What could we do? The evidence seemed. . . ."

He shook his pulpy head in amazement as if the evidence had been as awful and incontrovertible as a quartered body in the well of the court. Whereas it had been as thin as paper, as insubstantial as the blurred photograph of a woman in Moscow in one of Springer's scandal rags.

"How could we have seen it?"

"By looking beyond your nose. If you could." McCoy was prodding me, tempting me, searching out the vengeance, blowing the embers. And they were there, too. He knew that. I'd begun to feel the little heats myself.

"There are mistakes. People—"

"Lucky they've done with the rope then."

"People can be wrong. People—"

"The law is an ass."

"One can be made a fool of; I don't deny it. The Russians, the Americans too—"

"Twenty-eight years is quite a price to pay, even for a fool."

"The evidence—" he said. I interrupted him. Now I had suddenly found my stride in fury.

"*Fuck the evidence*. And four years locked up alone in this place is quite a payment on account. What would you say the interest was on that—my interest? The compensation?"

"Be reasonable, Marlow. Rationally—"

"Where's the application form, McCoy? One of those chits Miss Charlbury dealt with in the annex? What's owing this time? 'Out-of-pocket expenses?' Right then. Item: to four years wait, sixteen seasons. How many holidays would that make in Normandy? How many lobsters in season with Muscadet? Or even the odd bottle of Guinness in Brighton? Anyway, item: missing the rain, drying in the sun, drinking myself silly—oh yes, McCoy; item: How much will you pay for a thousand opening times and friends in the evening? And how many women, McCoy, could you fit in afterward, three long winters lying in different beds? Item: to a dozen casual girls—or perhaps one or two real ones—missing. And sometimes, McCoy, oh yes indeed, I used to watch cricket in the summer, tumbling out of bed with someone before lunch on Saturdays. Lords, and even the Oval. And there were the papers on Sundays. You'd have been surprised with my Sundays, McCoy, how little I did with them. But they were mine to lose. Item: To how many lost weekends? How many items for Miss Charlbury, McCoy? *How many, how many?*"

And then I was at him, uncontrollably, with what I thought was all the precisely dictated fury of an animal. I was standing over him, squeezing his throat dry, my fingers crushing the old starched-white collar. I expected his eyes to bulge, and choking noises, but there was nothing. He sat on the chair impassively, his suit smelling of too much dry cleaning, his torso shaking gently under what I felt was a barrage of force. When he started to push me away I thought grip unbreakable so that I was amazed to see my hands slip from his neck, lightly and easily, as though they were oiled. When the warder came in I was lying on the floor, shouting. "When will I be *paid*, McCoy, for all that, *all that? . . .*"

And McCoy was happy, helping me back into bed. There was lightness in his face, a relief, the expression he'd assumed in the old days when some bureaucratic ploy of his had come off, when some pawn of his had just left his office and had started on his long journey down the river. His face reflected a professional's joy in a point well taken; he had discovered my enmity again, accepted in my lifeless fists the crucial transference which signals a cure. He had wound me up secretly, compressing the vehemence, like a toy. Then he had slipped the catch.

We were alone again. I was cold. Suddenly the quilt had no warmth in it and I wanted sheets and blankets. I drank the coffee and it had a taste. The cigarette seemed fragrant as woodsmoke.

"What were we fighting about, McCoy? I don't remember. Except that you realize I was framed. You've found out about Williams. So now what do you want? I'm free."

"Yes, we've found out—*something*. Not about Williams. So don't jump too soon. That depends about your being free. Depends on you in fact."

I could see it already. Another plan, no doubt as careful as the one that had sent me after Henry had given me a life sentence. But in this case it would take me out into a world whose flavors I had just begun to sense again, and I had to remember not to snatch at it, not to seem too willing. The truth was that I'd have done anything to have been in London that weekend, to book a hotel room there and disappear into life.

"Listen, Marlow, just listen. Then you can take it—or leave it." McCoy looked about the cell and up at the small window with its view over the roof of the old laundry if you stood on tiptoe. The day was gray and wet, a smell of sodden ashes coming on the wind from the garbage dumps on the other side of town. I knew what he meant. He went on confidently now, as though recounting an old chestnut that never yet failed to please. "A week ago we took a man in London, fellow called George Graham, deep cover KGB. An illegal. He was on his way to start a satellite circle in the United States, one they have to spy on the spies there. Just a lucky chance, one in a million, that we got on to him. He used to be involved with our circle in Beirut and afterwards in Cairo, but before your time there. His cover till now has been as a Senior Reports Officer with the COI, advising on overseas propaganda, doing radio and television programs and such like. He's forty, dark hair, pretty well built, fluent Arabic, few connections; he's been out of the light for a long time, but he knows the ropes all right. He's quite a bit like you in fact, Marlow. And he's going to New York next week. . . ."

"And he's dispensable, just like me," I said when McCoy had finished outlining his "suggestion," as he put it. "The old story, I've heard it before. It's what put me here."

"And it will take you out. Dispensable, yes. But that will be up to you. If you survive, you'll stay out. All this—will be forgotten." He looked around him again.

"I'll get a medal."

"None of us are indispensable," McCoy said quickly, as if to forestall an accusation of cheating. And for that moment I believed him, sensed that, at heart, he recognized his own failures intimately.

"Besides, you'll survive. You're just as much an unknown quantity as this other man. Most of your trial was in camera. The photographs the press dug up on you were from five and ten years before. And no one will know you from Adam in the United Nations. Point is, Marlow, we're going to turn you into a completely new man—new name, new background, new future. That should be your cue, a real chance to start over again."

"Jesus, you like the games, don't you?"

"You tell me a better way of setting you on your feet? Ten years as Reports Officer with us, Arabic, the right accents—you'll pass as someone born to the job in the UN. And the Third World they're always talking about: you know about that too, don't you? All those grubby back

streets in Cairo and bilharzia in the canals." McCoy raised
his eyes again to the high window and the dark gray clouds
like smog rolling over the city. "That's what should worry
you, Marlow." He nodded sagely at the bruised view, curling his lips a fraction, like a picture restorer contemplating
a hopeless canvas. "That should be your first concern. Fresh
fields and that. Isolation kills more than anything. You'll
be doing yourself the favor."

"And you."

"And *us*, Marlow. All of us are going to be happy. I've
thought a lot about it."

"I'll bet you have. Another plan up your sleeve for
dumping me somewhere worse than this."

"What could be worse than this, Marlow?"

The main door into "E" wing opened and slammed. I
heard the milk lorry leaving, the churns bouncing over the
little concrete ridges they had before Main Gate to slow the
traffic down. Then the train robber's doors opened down
at the end of the corridor. He was going out for exercise.
The dogs had been shut in between the new electric fence
and the east wall. A siren shrieked, then died, in the town.
Automatically I knew the time, the date, the day. The governor's twelve o'clock lunch, lamb chops and HP sauce, the
tin canteens that would come up from the main kitchen to
our wing, to be left untouched. Then the doctor's orders,
the hospital food that was just as unpalatable. I'd come to
live on crackers and honey at that time, listening to the
talk of drip feeds behind the screen.

The only thing I really doubted then was my strength
to play the role McCoy had offered me. I had already accepted it, there was no doubt about that, listening to the
robber's footsteps, his high-pitched laugh with the warder,
as they went out to walk those concrete circles in the gloom.
He would always be stuck with the man he had been, the
failure of his past. Even if he reached Copacabana Beach
he would never throw off his grubby identity; he would always inhabit the same devious turns of mind, trying to
swindle Allende now, instead of the Postmaster General.
But I was being offered a whole fresh personality, a cure
which would really make a new man of me. It would be a

matter of survival to forget my own past, not to look backward, to live in a new present: rehabilitation in the grand manner. I might learn to forget vengeance, too, and the other acids that eat up time, forget disenchantment in the swirls of another man's future. This was the theory anyway.

"Yes," I said. "All right then. You'd better give me the details."

The rain started in earnest. All morning it had fluttered minutely on the window pane, spotting the glass in odd hurried squalls before dying. But now when it came the sky was so black and full and close that it was hard even to imagine fair weather. McCoy's face darkened in the gloom but the features were clear enough, those of a smiling conspirator, of a boy who sets out happily once more from the softly lit stairhead into the darkest recesses of the house, hiding from nanny before bedtime.

McCoy got up and switched on the light.

"You'll be out of here by morning. We'll do the rest in London. You're being transferred, Marlow. Another jail. Place isn't safe enough to hold you. They're dispersing all the dangerous fellows, you know. Sending them all over England. Into the wide world."

I spent a long time that night taking McCoy's plan apart, isolating the pieces, looking for the flaw, the other plan he had for me behind the first. There were a dozen awful possibilities, besides the one of twenty years more inside, and before I slept I was sick of thinking of them, knowing, as McCoy had, that I'd risk anything to live again with alternatives, whatever they were, for that was the world.

3

Alexei Flitlianov—now Timor Grigorian, an Armenian businessman from Beirut—looked out from the bedroom window of his hotel just off Marylebone High Street, gazing at the doorway of the apartment building to his right some way down on the other side of the street. It was his third day in London and his second morning's vigil. The man he was looking for had neither left the building at breakfast time nor returned there in the evening, and the lights in the front room in the apartment had never been switched on.

George Graham had disappeared. Perhaps he'd simply left town to say good-bye to a friend or relative in the provinces. But more likely he'd been caught. Flitlianov had always feared that it had been Graham's voice which their KGB London Resident had originally picked up on the telephone that British security had been tapping. But Flitlianov had no way of finding out now. All he could do was wait and watch until the day Graham had been due to leave for New York and hope that he'd turn up.

Flitlianov started to move away from the window but just as he did so he noticed a very muddy car drawing up at an apartment doorway twenty yards down from the hotel on the same side of the street. There was something official about the large new sedan, he thought vaguely, something institutional in its dark blue paint, its small two-way radio aerial on the roof. Three men got out. And now Flitlianov was sure there was something unusual about the vehicle. For two of the men had the knowing solidity of plainclothes police everywhere in the world, while the third, a taller, younger man, had all the marks of a prisoner—weak, unsteady, at a loss in the strong light, noise, and bustle of the city. After more than twenty-five years close observation of the clandestine, Flitlianov recognized these characteristics almost automatically. The party disappeared into the doorway of the building. It was almost opposite Graham's block on the corner of the High Street. Was there any connection between them, Flitlianov wondered? He settled down again by the window to wait and see.

4

"We've just three days before your boat goes," someone called Harper said to me, with a face like a piece of bad carpentry, looking at me unhopefully. We were in the front room of a third-floor apartment next door to an hotel just off Marylebone High Street, where I'd been taken direct from Durham that morning. The furniture was covered in dust sheets and there was a faint smell of gas in the rooms. Harper opened a window and I noticed the weather in the south had taken a turn for the better, brisk and cold, and bright—big-city weather with the houses like white cliffs and the sun as sharp as silver paper. Footsteps shot up from the pavement below with a metallic clatter which was quite unreal to me. Now that I was face to face with it I had no conception of people walking freely in a street and felt the need to keep away from the windows, as though crippled with vertigo.

Harper went over to the window. "His apartment is there, opposite us on the corner. You'll be moving in tonight. This meanwhile will be H.Q. Ops. as it were. We've rigged up some data for you next door." We walked through into what had been a dining room but was now cleared of most furniture. Instead there were photographs of Graham and other blowups, of his handwriting, letters he'd written and received, and such like, fixed into a row of insulating boards which had been set up about the room. The dining table had been left and on it were Graham's personal effects, the last known bits of his life: a tweed jacket, flannels; latch keys; wallet; a square-faced, gold-cased Hamilton watch; an old Mentmore fountain pen; long-stemmed briar pipe, roll of Dutch aromatic tobacco; a catalogue of Warhol's graphics from the Mayfair Gallery; some restaurant bills and two paid accounts, one from the Express Dairies and the other from a car hire service which had taken him to Wimbledon for some reason a week previously. The room was like the remains of a bad accident in which the body had disappeared completely, shattered by the force and thrown in pieces to the four winds. Harper bent down, turning on a radiator.

"Tailor fellow'll be coming later for any alterations. Bringing shoes too. We don't seem to have had the shoes. Try the jacket on for size. Just been cleaned. Had any experience of this sort of doubling?"

"Who has?"

"No. I suppose not." I put the coat on. "Not bad. Sleeves could come out an inch. You're about that much taller than he was."

"Was?"

"To all intents and purposes. Don't worry. You're not going to bump into him in the street." Harper laughed, "Used to do it at school—the dressing up bit. Every Christmas. Midsummer for us actually in Australia. Lots of horseplay. Well, then. Let's take a look. The face is a more difficult business." We moved toward a series of enlarged full-face and profile shots of Graham. Harper looked from me to them. "Nothing much there I'm afraid. A fuller face altogether. And more hair. Prison doesn't help, of course, with you. And Graham was leading the good life by all accounts. Eating in all the best places in town; cinemas, theaters, museums, art galleries—the lot. You've seen the details already, haven't you? The Special Branch reports?"

"Yes. But you're not going to try and fake my face, are you?"

"We thought of it. But there's no point. No, the point of all this is that we have to make *you* feel completely in his shoes. Confidence in that is everything. Second skin— and you've got to really feel at home in it. Now, to do that you've somehow got to get to *like* this man. Then you'll come to *look* like him. To all intents and purposes. Sympathy is the second thing, Marlow. And let's hope that's not too difficult. He seems to have been quite a likeable fellow, by all accounts. Apart from his politics, of course."

I looked into the large eyes, the curiously circular, rather than oval, lids in the photograph, the police measurements graded off round the edge of the print. Other than being a necessary part of the many parts that go toward making up something called a face, Graham's eyes expressed nothing; nor did the other parts. He looked straight through the lens toward me with all the expression of a painted balloon. Yet a pinprick would prove this bag less than insubstantial; it had no existence. This man had already destroyed his identity and I felt angry at the mechanisms in the world that had brought this about. Graham had nothing left to leave anyone. If I stepped into his shoes there would be nothing there: no one would be forced out, for he had released himself forever sometime before, from every pleasure and pain.

Harper bent down to pick up another photograph that had fallen, pinning it back on the board. I thought for a second that it was a different man. But it was Graham, talking to a turbaned Sikh, standing up in the corridor of a train.

"A year ago. Some COI work with Indian railways. Reporting on the new Delhi-Calcutta Express. Can you imagine? Never at a loss for good cover, this fellow."

Here the skin had every natural ornament. By comparison with the first photograph this one was a moving picture; one felt all the mobility that had gone into his life before and after the captured instant: gestures, words, the hard bright light through the window, the folds in the turban; each was part of a continuing fabric, and in Graham's face one clearly saw all the happy marks of a long endearment with these moments, a firmly held commitment to the briefest values. His whole bearing, somewhere in India, was a forward position in a world where others often turned and ran, his expression an exposed asset in the general conspiracy, so much so that through his smile at that moment one could almost hear the words coming out of the two mouths that hot afternoon:

"Only thing you don't have on the train is a bar."

"Well, that's why we're going to Calcutta."

It was a good photograph. In the other a whole life style had leaked away. And in the comparison all Graham's politics slipped away for me too.

I didn't care how many manifestoes he'd swallowed. I saw him now as one of those few expatriate communists who don't give the movement a bad name, deviant because he was a person concerned with people, not committees, a character out of a lost book on the faith. I wondered only where his blindness lay that had allowed him to permanently compromise his intelligence and affection, for he must have known the communist reality bettter than most, known that, before the millennium, his men would ruin man in getting there, just as the other men would.

Perhaps it wasn't blindness, but a sad knowledge of this that made him smile for the moment, flashing through the famine lands of Bihar state, and the same true sense of the priorities that took him in search of Romanian art at the British Museum, Bratby in Wimbledon, and perfect meals in small restaurants. Perhaps he had seen the bitter cul-de-sacs a long way off, the horrors that are due to great ideas, and had quietly resigned his politics over the years. Instead, long before, he had launched himself on the little roads that went somewhere—to museums in the London suburbs, to the restaurants in Charlotte Street.

It wasn't a question, I felt then, of replacing him, of copying his guile, for that had only been his cover in life. Instead I would pick up his life, where he had dropped it, and live it for him, like a memorial. I would continue something, replace nothing. Now I had no real need of Harper and McCoy; I was no longer on their side, I was on Graham's. And I knew, in those terms, I could make myself indistinguishable from him though physically we so little resembled each other. It was an idea that I had to take over, not a body. What I needed now were the real details of this man's life, the clear shapes of his affection, not this cold data that Harper had put about the room like a black museum.

"Have to put a bit of weight on," Harper said. "You'll have time on the boat. Graham was partial to good food. You look as if you'd spent a year in bed."

"I have." We'd moved over to another board, headed "Eating Habits."

"It's all here. Born with a silver fork in his mouth."

"Olives?" I said, looking at one of the first items.

"Yes," Harper said slowly. "Little bastard always went Continental. You don't have to."

"I like olives."

A cloud ran across the silly shapes of Harper's face.

"You're welcome to them," he snapped.

"You said I ought to try and like him. 'Sympathy,' you said."

"That was my advice to you. I don't have to take it

myself." Harper moved off round the room pointing out the other boards.

"Physical characteristics, family background, education, career, personal habits, hobbies, peculiarities—some sound tracks, even a film show—the lot. You and I will take a rough look at it now. Then this evening we'll break each classification down with the experts, McCoy and the man who took him, fellow from Special Branch."

We'd stopped by the board marked "Peculiarities."

"No. Not queer," Harper said, as if some axiomatic law of nature had been detonated. "On the other hand, very few women. And then only casuals. Hardly more than tarts."

"Perhaps he was Irish. Or Australian."

Harper scowled against my smile.

Under "Peculiarities" I read off the names of the various art galleries and museums I'd heard about from McCoy. And at the end was the fact that he subscribed to *Country Life*.

"Now that was peculiar," Harper said.

"Must have been for the saleroom notes at the end," I said. And the pictures of antiques in country museums. *Country Life* had been one of the most popular magazines among the old lags in Durham.

"Wrong. He got it for his mother in South Africa. Sends it to her every week. You'll be writing to her. Let's go back to the beginning."

We moved up to "Background, Education, and Career" at the end of the room where the sideboard would have been.

George Graham. Born 14 July 1931. Royal Free Hospital, Islington, of Mary and John Graham, 32 Canonbury Sq., W.C. 1. Father was Master Printer with Seale & Co., small firm of fine art printers in South Kensington. John Graham enlisted with Argyll and Sutherland Highlanders as an N.C.O. in 1939. Served with them in North Africa, Lybia, and Egypt and was killed in action, Western Desert, May 1943. With the help of a grant from the Worshipful Guild of Master Printers, George Graham attended St. Paul's Boys' School, Westminster, taking a scholarship from there to St.

*Andrew's University in 1948, reading English and Modern
Languages. Graduated in 1952. Joined British Council in
same year and was posted to Beirut where he spent one year
teaching English in the British School. In September 1953
was transferred to the British School, Heliopolis, Cairo,
where he taught for two years. From September 1955 until
he left Egypt during the Suez campaign of November 1956,
he was Senior English Master at Victoria College, Cairo.
Subsequently he worked as a teacher and university professor
in East Africa attached to the British Council: at Nairobi,
Markarere College, Uganda, and finally at colleges in what
was then Nyasaland and Northern Rhodesia. At the break
up of the Federation of these countries in 1961 he returned
to London where he took up work as a Junior Reports
Officer at the Central Office of Information attached to their
East African section, where he was responsible, among other
things, for various TV and radio documentaries. Since 1968
he had been responsible for advising Information Controller,
COI, on general policy matters relating to British propaganda in the Middle East, Africa, and India. In this capacity
he was away from London for several long periods. . . .*

"Never trust these schoolteacher fellows, can you?"
Harper said to himself, running his eye down the paper.
"Always something wacky there." He paused. "But of course
that was your stamping ground, wasn't it? I forgot. Anyway,
as regards his 'career' we've got quite a few papers on that.
And there's bound to be more in his flat and his luggage.
You can bone up on it on the boat."

"What about his flat?"

"He's packed nearly everything. What he isn't taking is
being stored. Pickford's are coming tomorrow. The only
people you should be meeting. You're off the day after."

"The keys and so on. The rent?"

"All paid up. Keys go back to the Traherne estate office
in Welbeck Street. It's not a service flat. No porter."

"And what about all his friends?"

"Think he left last week. Didn't McCoy tell you?"

"They may write to him. Or visiting firemen. They
know he's gone to the UN."

"Have to make sure you don't give them a bed then."

"Relations?"

"Really only his mother. In Durban. He typed most of his few letters to her, and you'll have his signature off pat when you start."

"And nobody else?"

"Yes, his father's family. Scottish, from outside Aberdeen. An uncle and cousins. The uncle comes down every second year to London for the Calcutta Cup. So you're all right there. Two years to go till the next one."

"Must have been someone he was closer to. At the office."

"Oh yes. He had a lot of friends. But he was British, you know—*colleagues*, you understand. Kept his distance. Gave a drinks party for them all before he left. They'll have forgotten all about him in a week."

"And no women. You really think that's likely?"

"Not *no* women, Marlow. I didn't say that. None we've traced, that's all. You may be luckier, what with all these new singles bars I hear about in New York. The point is, Marlow, this fellow didn't cultivate close friendships. For the job in New York he had to keep himself as clean as a whistle. Then he could start living. Now let's see the film and recordings." Harper drew the curtains and started to fiddle incompetently with a projector at the end of the table. "Give you some idea of the living man."

They were all street shots, mostly in the Marylebone area: coming out of his apartment, going into restaurants, walking in the little park behind the ugly Kellogg building in Baker Street, where the film car couldn't follow him. He disappeared among a crowd of old pensioners sitting in the sun on benches and one could just see his head bobbing away behind the shelter in the middle. Another sequence followed him down the High Street in a shower. A girl came toward him, trying vainly to open an umbrella. They nearly collided. Then he helped her with it.

"Gallant," Harper said. "Thought she might have been a contact."

Once Graham seemed to look straight into the camera for a long moment, standing at the curb, about to cross.

"They always do that some time or other. Can't see a

thing of course. Gives you the creeps though. Notice the way he walks?"

"How?"

"He doesn't hang about, looking for green stamps, bargains in the windows, and so on. Not even in the antique shops. Always seems to know exactly where he's going."

"Unusual?"

"It can be. We thought at first he knew he was being followed. You don't slow down then." Harper was depressed at the man's decisiveness. "It's as if he'd mapped every pace down to the last foot before he left home."

"Why not? You said he was out to enjoy himself. Why waste time?"

There was another shot of him now, coming out of a Sicilian restaurant in Frith Street.

"Mafia I suppose. He's with the mob, not the KGB."

Harper was disgusted. "I don't know what they were paying him for."

"Not your typical rat, is he? Crawling along alleyways in dark glasses with a .38, moseying around Wimbledon common looking for letter drops. It's upsetting."

They'd collected some of Graham's radio tapes and documentary films from the COI and, more daringly, a recording of him ordering dinner in Chez Victor.

The voice wasn't like his walk. I was surprised. There was no speech hesitancy, but it ambled rather, tended to double back; it seemed intentionally oblique and diffident, rushing into high notes over the contents of an hors d'oeuvre; slumbering, almost dead, in its comments on a beef casserole. I wondered what gave it this vivid yet indecisive character before deciding that Graham had all the varied tones and rhythms of a natural actor yet who loathed self-advertisement.

One felt, in his accents, some huge sense of excitement within him which he wished to restrain, as a liability in dull times and as a danger to his work. The little dramas in his voice had been put there as an eccentric diversion, which, because they so nearly mirrored his obsessive taste for life, would all the more certainly put people off the track of this, his real nature. Graham's mild histrionics was a role indeed, covering all his real history. He knew what he wanted on the menu all right, but he wasn't going to let anyone know of his enthusiasm.

"So?" Harper drew back the curtains.

"He's nothing much like me."

"Apart from all his Mid East experience. And being a teacher and a Reports Officer—like you. And the coat, Marlow. If the coat fits . . . and it fits you pretty well."

I stood up. I had forgotten I was still wearing it.

"There's food in the kitchen. And the bed's in the usual place. The others will be here in the evening."

Harper went out and locked the door. I watched him from the window, crossing the road, going down toward Oxford Street. He stopped and talked to a man on the opposite pavement.

McCoy arrived with a small man called Croxley just after six o'clock. McCoy was impatient. The small man behaved as if he'd been sniffing gas leaks and looking around such dust-covered apartments all his life.

"Had a good run-through with Harper?" McCoy's dramatics were so thin.

I said, "Yes. We couldn't find the fellow's shoes though."

"What do you want his shoes for?"

"I'm getting everything else about him, why not his shoes? Somebody who knew him—first thing they'll notice: I've got the wrong feet on. It's a point."

"You're beginning to enjoy it all, are you Marlow?"

"I know. You'd like to put the smile the other side of my face."

McCoy left shortly after. "*I'll* give you his shoes," he muttered. I think he felt he was slipping.

"How do you feel about the man?" Croxley said when we had got into the dining room. The light was still bright and slanting with long shadows outside. We'd had an extra hour of daylight all winter, on European time, and now it was really beginning to tell. I wished I'd been able to make better use of it.

"He seems to have been a likeable fellow."

I was fed up with McCoy and Harper, but Croxley seemed to have wider sympathies.

"Yes. Yes, he was. All this"—he looked around the line of boards—"can't give more than a trace of him. But we like it, thinking of people as bits of paper. Photographs."

"It's the curse of the age." And Croxley sighed too for bureaucracy.

"All you need from these are the factual details, or as much as you can absorb. In case there are queries. But the real business, you'll have to create that yourself."

"Queries?"

"Yes. I imagine McCoy only touched on it. The Stayer. The man who contacts you. He may have some way of making sure of your identity."

"He may have seen 'me' before. Awkward."

"No. Not on the job you're doing. Won't know you from Adam. That's absolutely the point. He'll just give you the names Moscow wants a check on, potential 'unreliables.' And we know from Graham that most of these KGB people, not necessarily all Soviet nationals, are currently placed in the UN, either in the Secretariat or in one of the delegations in New York. That's why Graham was aimed for the job. The Stayer will probably be in the UN too. So he'll have time to check up on you before he makes an approach."

Croxley sat at one end of the table thumbing through some notes.

"These transcripts aren't of much use. What checks this contact may make I can't say. Graham didn't know, *wouldn't* know. So it could go wrong from the first; he may never make a contact. On the other hand, in the nature of your KGB job, the Stayer should know nothing about you or your past. Graham was let lie fallow for years precisely in order to avoid the chances of any substitution, so they won't suspect that, nor will the Stayer. He'll just have been told your name and number in the UN. You see, Graham had no identity among his own, so you too should be safe enough."

"Who does Graham report to? And how?"

"A senior KGB officer stationed in Beirut who recruited Graham in 1952 is the crucial figure," Croxley said. "He runs Graham, though Graham said he hadn't seen him for more than ten years. A man named Alexei Flitlianov. He has some mild cover job with the Soviet Foreign Ministry in Moscow. Allows him to travel about. In fact he heads the KGB's Second Directorate, their internal security division, as well as a satellite security bureau, which Graham was working for—quite outside the main organization, reporting only to Flitlianov. This fellow comes to America from time to time. He'd be coming to hear from you, probably a couple of months after you get there. Graham didn't know exactly when. Let's hope we can get the word to you when he does. In fact though, with any luck, you should be out of it all by then. And we should have the name we want."

"Not names?"

"Well, yes, the names he gives you. But the Stayer—that's the man we really want. That man will have more names in him than any Resident. He'll have been passing names for years, dealing out the execution cards, never playing the game himself. And that's what makes it practically impossible ever to get such a man. He's never involved in any action. He's just a walking list of KGB operatives."

"But he's never going to *give* me his name. I won't even see him. I'll just get a message. Over the phone."

"Maybe. And in that case we'll just have to settle for putting the squeeze on the people he gives you. On the other hand I have a feeling you will meet him. He'll certainly come face to face with you, without your knowing it. Besides, where can he phone you? Only at your UN office, since he won't know your home number. Those are practically open lines for the KGB—and for the CIA. He's not going to risk it."

"Just give me an outside number to contact him, then. A call box between certain times."

"And risk being picked up at that number, between those certain times? No, I think you'll see him. I don't think he's going to risk phoning you, or writing anything down on paper. But if he does, well, we'll just settle for the names."

"You call these KGB men they want checks on 'potential unreliables.' When we get their names, are they going to be all that useful to anybody? Surely we want the names of the reliable men?"

"Just the opposite. You think it out. The KGB is doing half our work for us, pinpointing their weak links, the people in their networks open to pressure. Now your contact with us, when you get any names, is through Guy Jackson, one of our men, already in the UN Secretariat. He works in the Secretary-General's political department, African section. And you should be able to meet him quite openly: informally, since you're both on the British quota to the UN; and professionally, since your reports work can easily be made to coincide with his interests at certain points. He's been briefed on all this. You'll have no trouble there. And he's your link in New York if anything else untoward happens."

"Now, let's go through the details of your UN posting. I have all Graham's papers here on that—seems like a good job, lot of money, tax free, and a lot of allowances. Even without a family."

"I hope I won't be there long enough to have time to enjoy it. And—my wife won't need it."

A little nervousness moved over Croxley's face.

"Yes. I remember. Your wife. You were with Skardon four years ago, weren't you? Got you twenty-eight years. I thought it might have been a frame-up, that. I think he did too. But the Crown insisted. Rotten business."

"My *department* insisted."

"Comes to the same thing."

"Yes. I don't suppose the Queen was consulted."

Croxley opened a folder and drew out a large printed sheet headed "UN Secretariat: Salary, Grade, and Allowances."

"And I don't suppose this will sweeten things that much either."

"Better than a poke in the eye with a sharp stick."

"They'd have left you in Durham, wouldn't they?"

"Yes."

Croxley looked sad again. He had a facility that way. But it was a true gift. The light was dying now outside, even with the extra hour, and I felt sleepy again. The room was hot, I'd eaten nothing, and the whole long day had done nothing but repeat the promise of summer, full of the free, fine weather I'd thought never to know again. I felt all Graham's appetites now, and more.

"Listen, Croxley," I said. "I'm finished with being locked up. I'm doing the job, so let's stop this zoo nonsense. I want some air, a drink. I'll even settle for some olives."

"Why not?"

Croxley was like an absent-minded aunt being at last reminded of the real interest of her visit for her schoolboy nephew: a ten-shilling note to blow in the tuck shop. "I can tell you about the job when we're outside. There's a pub around the corner. Wine bar, too, if you like that sort of thing. And a good Greek restaurant next door."

5

Graham's apartment was at the top of a narrow, ill-lit, almost grubby staircase, on the first floor. One long front room looked over the street, with a large floppy sofa and two armchairs on an old but genuine Persian carpet. Three small rooms, kitchen, bedroom, and bathroom, gave off this to the back, their doors, together with the hall door, in a line along the wall like the set for a bedroom farce. At one end of the living room half a dozen tea chests had been filled with books and papers and with small domestic objects—from the kitchen, the walls, shelves, and tables. At the other end, a cabin trunk and three suitcases lay open and half packed with clothes. On a table next to the window were a duplicate set of keys and a note from Pickford's confirming their arrival the next morning to remove the furniture and chests.

I turned the light on in the bedroom, which was in the same confusion. The kitchen, on the other hand, was conspicuously clean and tidy. But then, of course, he had rarely used it.

The place had about it all the mundane doom of departure. Graham had lived here for nearly ten years. It was hard to credit this in any measure of personal time. His jumbled possessions had reasserted all the predominance which they had had on Graham's first confused day here, a decade ago, which they would always have in the end. They had been kept at bay by the force of his life in the place. Each moment he had spent there—active or even in sleep—the pots and pans, the furniture, the dirty shirts, and the toothbrush had cowered from him, camouflaged in unwilling order. Now, as if sensing his demise, they had bloomed about the apartment with the speed and rapacity of weeds on a ruined estate. The armchair was an ambush, finally, that had once held him comfortably with a gin, thinking of the evening; the sofa a booby trap for many of his girls in all those ordered years.

Then the voice rose from the bedroom next door, suddenly and sharply, a man angry in a hard north country way:

"Tell her I've left the country!"

It was one of those few moments in my life that I wished I'd had a gun. I looked around for something.

"Leave it," the man shouted again. "Keep away from the window. And stay there. If anyone comes, tell them to get out."

What a fool I'd been—going straight into it again, the oldest trick in the world, taking you at the last moment, just when you felt in the clear. The voice was McCoy's of course. He'd left the other apartment hours before and had hidden in Graham's bedroom. Now his real plan for me would emerge.

"The windows were closed," the voice said heavily. "The heat struck up at them from the linoleum. There was a stink of rubber and wax. One curtain was slightly drawn."

I looked around the kitchen. Everything was almost exactly as he said. I wondered how on earth he could see me through the wall.

"All right, McCoy," I said, hoping to calm him. "Take it easy. I'm here. Come on out and tell me all about it."

But instead he continued: "Gaunt reached out to pull it." I was sure now McCoy had lost his head, become the mad paranoiac that I'd always felt had lain at the bottom of his character.

"The calendar on the wall advertised a firm of Dutch diplomatic importers. . . ."

I moved my head a fraction. The calendar in Graham's kitchen was by courtesy of a local delicatessen. I stole toward the living room and stopped just outside the bedroom door.

". . . it's like a prison cell, he thought; the smell was foreign but he couldn't place it."

I swung the bedroom door open softly with my foot.

"Well I *am* surprised," Gaunt was saying. "This is Mr. Harting's room. Very gadget-minded, Mr. Harting is."

I went in and saw the radio next to Graham's bed. It was a powerful mains receiver connected to the light switch which I had turned on at the door. BBC Radio 4: "A Book at Bedtime." The announcer came in: "You can hear the next episode of John le Carré's *A Small Town in Germany* tomorrow evening at eleven o'clock: episode three— 'The Memory Man.' "

And I was sorry then, for a moment, that it hadn't been McCoy, that I hadn't come back among him and Harper and Croxley, into a world of devious ploys. For Graham's apartment was appallingly arid, so empty of everything, that one might even have welcomed McCoy's deceits into its vacuum as evidence, at least, of life. The place badly needed people, arguments, chatter, even lies. Now it was just four walls where all the clues, like Graham, had been packed up and put away.

I spent most of the next thirty-six hours unpacking them, looking for some real leads to the previous man. In the tea chests there were a great many papers, mostly copies of his African reports, but not many letters, apart from those from his mother and one or two other people.

There were some yellow Kodak folders with a collection of rather uninteresting photographs of Graham and his family, together with the original negatives. They seemed not to have been touched since they'd come back from the chemist's thirty years before: childhood cameos for the most part—Graham at the zoo, the boy and the monkeys both grinning badly; Graham shivering on a Scottish lake, a boy from one of Arthur Ransome's stories.

There were other folders, too, packed tight with the detritus of life, odds and ends that are kept in the hope of a fascinating maturity: copies of his school magazine, a refer-

ence to his tennis skills in the junior championships, his
university notes, and the beginnings of a diary he'd kept on
his first arrival in Beirut as a teacher. I thought this might
prove significant, but it stopped after the first few pages,
which included nothing but the usual traveler's notes on the
more obvious aspects of the city and its history. His university papers, too, suggested an intellectual approach which
was traditional, even dull: a model student marking time.

Graham from the first seemed intent on creating a very
different image: something at once more formal and less
true to himself, the image of a man with safe, unambitious
appetites. He must, in fact, have entered his cover in boy-
hood, prolonged the natural adolescent differences with his
parents in his hidden profession. And there were, of course,
no documents on this lifelong disguise, no clues which suggested Graham's real animation. He must have intentionally
destroyed everything, the smallest item, which could give a
lead to his real political character. The image here was of
the completely reliable civil servant, the hack without inspi-
ration or any other deviant quality. And yet one knew that
he had been otherwise, that beyond his real politics he had
been a happy man; a man sure in his own small pleasures,
certain of the wider folly, and frail in any other belief. And
of this creed I could find nothing either, as though Graham
had looked on such optimistic evidence as damning as the
phone number of the Russian Embassy found in his notebook.

I had my answer next morning. That day a two-month
national postal strike ended, and a collection of delayed
letters came for Graham, business letters and bills for the
most part, and one from his mother in South Africa. But
three of the letters—or rather one long letter in three separate parts—were quite different, from a woman, without signature or address, postmarked Uxbridge, the large sprawling
handwriting falling over the pages in a long hurry. These
were real clues I'd been waiting for—something no one could
have foreseen. As I began to read them I realized I had left
Harper and McCoy well behind now, feeling Graham's real
identity coming over me properly for the first time.

Dear darling—he didn't find out, he doesn't know. I'll write and even if this strike comes on it doesn't matter—you'll just have to read these letters like a book later, whenever you get them. I won't say anything rash—just I must, I want to, write. I'll have to put up with him for the moment, that's all.

It's as it was before we met—a terrible depression, living in a continuous drizzle from one day to the next, when I thought it would never happen again—you know, being excited—not knowing that there were ever going to be good days again whenever I saw you. And when we loved each other, that it was going to be so easy, willing a thing—that it had nothing to do with disguise and cheating, I mean with hotel bedrooms and porters in the middle of the night and all that. It wasn't being in a strange place at all. We made up everything—absolutely—between ourselves.

The point is I won't be with him forever, not for any longer than can be helped, he knows that. And that length is for the children, as soon as I can be sure of a proper settlement over them. I hate all this legal business. But having gone through with it in the first place legally I'm determined to get out of it properly in the same way. That's a habit.

It's a habit too, the remnants of a stiff background as much as other needs, that makes me write to you in this almost indecipherable way, not giving a name or address and so on. I don't want you to get involved in some boring divorce case with adultery as the reason. I want the grounds to remain "incompatability" or whatever—the *truth* just, of a bad marriage, and not the fact that I met you halfway through it. The facts of *us* should have no bearing on my failure with *him*: that you and I were so quickly together in hotels, that shouldn't come into it legally, or in any way except for us. It was dead with him long before you arrived. I'll go on with this later.

Who was this woman? How long had she known George Graham? There were no answers to this. One could only imagine. How many months or years had they been slipping in and out of back doors and hotel beds, phoning on the dot at midday, two rings and the next one is from me? How long had there been the business of code words on the telephone, poste restante addresses, and slipping her letters into the box next to MacFisheries in Uxbridge on soaking Monday mornings?

A married woman, husband, children: Graham hadn't had much luck—fighting and losing on two fronts, the personal and the professional. And these letters were the only clues to the affair, the only lifelines left, written to a man who was another man now. It was beyond irony.

Wednesday
It's now six years since that party for the Africans in your office when we met. That man you brought back with you from Kenya working on the film with you, the one who was so keen at being at ease with whites that he did his best to get off with me, while you just stood there. He nearly succeeded too, one of those Belafonte men in a Nehru jacket, you know, without a collar, edged with gilt braid. Pretty handsome. Your secretary, Sarah something who had such dark eyes and spoke French, brought him over. And I thought, I was *sure*, when they came across to us, that she was yours—you know, in that way. And that was the first time, the sense of disappointment. I felt it then before I ever thought of wanting you: a sudden guilty feeling that I'd been caught doing something wrong, I didn't know what. And then I knew what it was: I wanted to be with you and not Belafonte.

I looked up Graham's curriculum vitae. He had come back from East Africa in the spring of 1965: six years of clandestine effort, emotional and sexual. I wondered if the woman was really being true in thinking that hotel bedrooms and hall porters had added nothing to their relationship. Deceit will lend all the more impetus to an affair when we openly admit and discount this element in it from the start, for what we do then is to indulge in a stronger excitement than simply the illicit, which is to anticipate, to visualize, the strange wallpaper above the bed rather than waiting to be surprised by it.

But certainly there was nothing casually indiscreet about it all. Six years of such dissembling was proof of gravity and application at least, and these are real attributes of passion. Graham, of course, hadn't ever risked a note to her, I thought. It wouldn't have been in character. But I was wrong: these letters were where his real character lay, reflected back at me now in the daring intimacies of remembered affection. These were Graham's proper secrets beside which my own and Harper's inventions paled.

Saturday

. . . "Thank you for your letter"—I feel like a secretary—"of the 17th inst." I picked it up OK. Yes, Africa. Of course it was mostly South Africa for me—he and his parents and the high plainsland before the children came. The Kruger National Park. And the elephants did all the nutty things then that they did with us on that trip we managed to East Africa—waddling across the road that evening with their great wrinkled backsides, our hearts stopped, the car inches away from them; the leopard with its eyes in the headlights for a second before it disappeared into the long grass; the snake we crunched over later on outside the game lodge—stomach turning—and the three lionesses creeping around the waterbuck in the mists by the river next morning. . . .

I was reminded of all that, and of some of the happy early years I had with him when we were a good deal more merry than we are now. He was someone in the country then, not just something in this city. He and I so nearly stayed out in Rhodesia there, farming and shooting, an animal life in every sense. And there are regrets, I'd be pretending otherwise—not for the better, because more simple life; it was a pretty mindless sort of existence we had—but regrets for all the horizons of the time. That was ten, fifteen years ago, of course, before Sharpeville, before Vorster and the concrete mixers took over, before we knew much about Africa, knew or cared anything about the dark side of it, as we have to now.

We had an unreasoning Arcadia: for you Africa is a laboratory where the whole future of the continent has to be displayed, tested, catalogued. But in fact what you propagandists are doing there is making up the gunpowder, preparing the blood baths. I'm not running away from what will happen in Africa as a result of the old comfortable colonial paternalism and your new "development." Just the opposite. I *know* what will happen: that when they have finished killing themselves out there as a result of both our efforts whoever is left afterward will really start concreting the grass. That's what "progress" will have amounted to, democracy or whatever other name you give the lie: some-body will be "free" all right: the wrong people, in a world not worth living in.

I was surprised at this ideology. The affair seemed to have had far wider dimensions than those of a double bed. I had pictured a woman formidable in desire, perhaps, but not in political spirit. It seemed an unlikely relationship, this between a Marxist and an old-fashioned colonial. Yet was she that? She seemed to be correcting my thoughts on her even as I read her letter, as though she were close to me, as though I were hearing her voice in the next room:

Thursday
I am not afraid of the future. I am not the "Natural Tory" you once called me. It's simply a determination to be happy, and having come halfway through life, I've proved certain ways to this end, traveled some of them, and don't believe I've got anywhere near the end yet. And those ways, that map, is for me most often in the past; in things half done then, not in new shapes and forms. We think we have ex-perienced the past just because, willy nilly, we have lived through it, we have completed it. But we haven't. There were hundreds of turnings off the main street which we knew about then and never took. I want to take them now, not to *re*live anything—this has nothing to do with nostalgia—but to live now all that was unlived then.

Pickford's removal men interrupted me later that after-noon, clearing the place out, leaving only the basic furniture that had come with the flat. Afterward I didn't feel like going on with the letters. I packed them up in his suitcase, along with the rest of Graham's data. There was a last meeting with McCoy and Croxley at the end of the day and the Southampton boat train first thing next morning.

"Well," McCoy said pompously in the fading light, "anything new in your researches?"

We were sitting at the dining room table again, sur-rounded by Graham's shadowy remains. Croxley got up and turned the light on. Graham's shoes were on the table.

"Nothing," I lied. "But I see you've filled in a missing piece."

"But you are getting the hang of the man?" McCoy said abruptly.

"Oh yes. I'm beginning to see him very well."

We went over all my routines again, checking everything once more. It was Croxley who nearly upset things at the end. "The postman," he said. "What did he bring Graham this morning? The strike's finished. We saw him come."

"Yes. A lot of bills." I reached inside my coat. "I nearly forgot. And a letter from his mother."

"We'll settle those." I handed the envelopes over, and Croxley looked through them.

"Not much in eight weeks' post," I said. But I didn't press my luck.

"He wasn't the writing type," Croxley said. "In his position you don't commit yourself, least of all to written confidences."

"No, of course not."

"Just bills from the Gas Board."

"And his old mother in Durban."

I was sorry to deceive Croxley.

"Come on," McCoy broke in, "you're not writing an obituary of Graham. Get into his shoes, Marlow. And go!"

The ship left at midday. Yachts were far out in front of us, colored triangles heeling right over in a sharp wind and spray of Southampton waters that did nothing to us at all. We had gone far beyond the natural elements in our steel hulk, were already a world within a world.

For me the huge ship was a prison again, of another sort, and I gazed as longingly at the sea that morning as I'd watched the sky move past my Durham window. It was one of those moments when, in middle life, one makes a promise to renew the buried athlete in oneself, swears brief fealty to some natural order, thinking, just for a few minutes or so before sleep, that tomorrow one will break the cage of self, leap out of it at a bound—into falconry, mountain climbing, yachting, or even golf. So, even in escape, in gliding down the water, feeling the first small butts and tremors of the channel, I wanted some other and greater escape.

I didn't bother with lunch that day. I was so tired. Instead I lay down in my cabin amidships and took out the woman's letters again.

. . . we walked to the top of a hill in Tsavo Park, with the warden and his stories about hippos on the banks of the Nile, where he used to be. Do you remember? How he and his wife met one walking by the river and hit it with his walking stick on the nose, and then hit it a second time: "Now I'm absolutely certain," he said, "that if you stand up and face these animals, nine times out of ten they'll break." A Jack Hawkins figure in an old bush hat and with a Landrover. The air was so crisp in the evenings, when it got cold and dark within half an hour, as the cedar roared in the grate, the Tilley lamps hissed and people chatted and laughed over their beers before dinner. . . .

I couldn't quite make it out—the writer's style, the knowledge; this recurrent African theme. There were the obvious images of space and freedom and something lost. But that wasn't all. What had they been up to? A shooting safari? Who was this woman, what was she like? What else had happened in Tsavo National Park, and what, precisely, had happened at all the other times they'd spent together which I didn't know about? I was already beginning to suffer the onset of that blatant curiosity that comes with shipboard, or any other enclosed life, though it might have been nothing more than the dregs of my profession stirring again, the never dying taste for the curious that is the essence of the trade.

Falling in and out of sleep as the ship slid down the channel, the waves starting to boom gently on its flanks, I tried to fill in the gaps in her letters and in Graham's notes and memos, trying to properly compose their affair like a Maupassant story or a new *Brief Encounter*.

I had to complete Graham's reality in myself, polish it, make it shine perfectly. I had so far an unformed part, handed out by the script editor, the lines of character briefly drawn, and for my own survival I had to research the role to its limits.

Very well, then. I would start by inhabiting Graham's most intimate secrets—by imagining, inventing them.

We had met that spring six years ago just after I'd come back from a trip to Kenya: under the chandeliers in the huge salon on the first floor in Whitehall: glasses falling about the place, the long table at one end littered with bottles, half a curtain drawn against the glare of evening light from the river; Africans standing up everywhere through the day chatter, as significant on the horizons of the room as baobab trees on their own plainsland: the rich African's Africa; the shapely, dusky confidence. And this woman had somehow stood out from all this, talking to Belafonte, from the Voice of Kenya Radio, who was doing a script with me. She had risen above this expensive gathering so that I had noticed her as easily as I would a potentate on a throne as I walked toward her. . . .

At what point had I realized that she was married, that her husband wasn't with her? When she had said something and looked at me candidly, pushing her hair backward over each ear in the quick movements I was afterward to become so familiar with, fingers moving from the parting in the middle of her forehead, raking the dark strands sharply several times on either side as though seeking a way through undergrowth, looking for a path which she had to follow urgently. There was something of a hurry in her. The eyes always moved, were always swinging or lifting, like a commander at the head of an armored brigade pressing into new country. She was commanding, then? Yes, but with a deprecation, almost an apology, as though she had taken over the lead perforce, simply because the other officers had fallen by the way. Something around five feet nine inches, in a red and gilt brocade Kashmiri waistcoat, a smock dress with a lace bodice. Why not?

In the days that followed, in the empty spaces of gray and uneventful ocean, in the short times between one meal and another, in the good moments after dinner when I was by myself in one of the six bars, I passed the time by living the on-and-off incidents of the affair, building detailed pictures of the abrupt times we had spent together. This after all, I thought, was a story I had been licensed to invent. Luckily she and I had never managed to spend long in each other's company—I should have needed a world trip to deliberate that—so there was no need to construct a continuous tale, with its flats and soggy shallows. I need invest only in

quick and startling snapshots of desire, swinging the glass
hurriedly over the bad times, quickly isolating the heart
that mattered. I could indulge the slender moments, the
thefts from ordinary time, which are the flavor of such secret
appetites. I didn't bother with the corollary: the husband
rifling through her desk and laundry, the detective lurking
in the laurel driveway. I contrived a properly salty and reck-
less scenario, such as any proper affair demands.

> . . . We were eating together, somewhere outside London, at
> an inn not far from the river which we'd been out on in a
> boat that afternoon. She had grazed her finger on the gun-
> wale, or a splinter from the oar had pierced it just below the
> knuckle, and she'd bandaged the cut from the hotel's first-
> aid kit, wrapping up the fine bone of her long middle finger
> in a neat cocoon. And that night, lying on her back, hands
> raised across the pillow, the white cotton roll stood out
> awkwardly, temptingly, the last piece of clothing in a long
> desired nakedness.

For most of the first two days at sea I played with this
woman, trying to piece together her relationship with Graham, with me, unwilling to free her from my imagination
until I had properly completed her, fulfilled her destiny as
a real person. Her reality had come to obsess me.

But then on the third evening, with more wine for dinner than I needed, I realized it was pointless, useless. I could
invent only her physical traits, and some few imagined circumstances in which she had her being—nothing more. She
was as void of any actual character as Graham was of his own
identity. Only I was real. I had spent so long inventing affection and involvement in the isolation of Durham jail that I
had been unable to stop the process in my first days outside.

Blue weather came halfway across the ocean as we cut
through the Gulf Stream on the southerly route. I spent the
first part of the morning walking the deserted decks and
reading some of the books Graham had packed for his journey on a deck chair. Anthony Burgess's Malayan trilogy,
The Long Day Wanes, proved rewarding; Joyce Cary's *The
Case for African Freedom* I found less easy going. I kept well
clear of organized "games" in the afternoon and the casino
in the evening. Instead I visited the cinema, the swimming

pool, and the sauna, and rode much on a mechanical bicycle in the gym.

And I realized that the first few days out from Durham had been the dangerous time, when the sense of freedom had almost overcome me, inducing impossible visions, of falconry and bright women. I had gone on, as I had done in prison, imagining life, reaching out for it in pieces where it could not have existed: I had let my imagination run away with me, as they say. Now, gently, I was learning to see and take things as they were, to be happy in reality—alone, slipping off the skin of the past as we sighted land and glided through the Narrows toward Manhattan, a free man for the moment on the ship; unattached, unencumbered, and unobserved.

Alexei Flitlianov had watched the man carefully, from a distance, during his last days in London, when he had seen him taking over Graham's identity, and throughout the voyage across the Atlantic. He could see him again now, standing up with a crowd of other passengers by the port rail as the huge ship slid beneath the Verrazzano Bridge, the city rising brilliantly in the distance.

Who was he? What was he up to? What would his contacts be? He would go on following him very carefully until he found out. For in him now, not in George Graham, lay all the keys to his dangerous future.

Book Four

1

The city had climbed up in front of us long before, when we'd passed under the Verrazzano Bridge eight miles out; the towers, the points, all the steps and cliffs of Manhattan growing up on the horizon, poking gradually into the sun. One had seen those towers so often in so many images—in polychrome and black and white, moving or with music—that all of us standing on the forward deck that morning had the expression of picture dealers scrutinizing a proffered masterpiece, leaving a polite interval before crying "Fake!"

Yet, from a distance, in the sharp light over a gently slapping metal-blue sea, the place looked better than any of its pictures. Wind had rubbed the skyline clean, light glittered on the edges of the buildings, and all I saw was a place where I was unknown, where unknown people bore ceaselessly up and down those cavernous alleys, between bars and restaurants and offices, all busy with an intent that had nothing to do with me.

The city stood up like a rich menu I could afford at last after a long denial.

The first feeling in the streets was like meeting a girl somewhere, in a group, swapping something, giving and taking, creating an appetite, sharing a look and a mood which you know will take you together before nightfall. There was something inevitable and long expected, something one had missed, in New York. The noise and rush from the cab, the filth of the dockside streets, were words quickly spoken, suddenly desired intimacies, saying it was right, and right, we wanted it now. The clatter was like whispers, the flashing signs sure signals of an impending affair. It was the true excitement of coming to a new land.

We had been sailing for many days about an unchartered sea when on the feast of St. Brendan, toward noon, an island appeared set in a calm bay. We found it to be a place of the carob tree, with vines and sweet water, a land different from all our knowledge. And being soured in the known world, and anxious in our time, and fraught with journeying, we took rest in this new place. . . .

The island was an empty map as I crossed it that afternoon. All I had heard or learned about Manhattan, everything I had imagined, all these received notions disappeared at the cross-park exit above the Plaza Hotel, waiting for the lights to change. I was looking at two men in homburgs and thick-soled brogues talking on the sidewalk. The collars of their straight black coats were turned up under their ears, their faces almost completely hidden from the wind. They stood there quietly, firmly, communicating: two slabs of black marble. And I realized I couldn't imagine what they were saying, couldn't invent a language for them, couldn't invest any of my experience of mankind in them to tell me what their business might have been, or anything of the fabric of their lives. It was as if an anthropologist had been given the opportunity of observing the nature, the language, the social rites of a tribe so far removed from his own experience, and all the learning of the world, that he was forced to conclude that their society was not only unique but also linked directly with prehistory.

Out of all mankind I couldn't place these two men at all. Nothing I had taken up in forty years through the world had prepared me for them. The basic usages and assumptions which linked men—even savage with literate men—were absent here. Yet I was not gazing at robots; these two had life.

And then I knew what it was. There was nothing absent in them; they were as ordinary as any men. It was I who had lost something at last: a received vision of mankind. For so long in life, in my job, I had been taught to categorize and define, to value or hate something only when I could name it, to fear always the unknowable and unnameable. And these two men had sprung up at me from the sidewalk without definition, identity. I feared them. There was no meaning I could attach to them, as when one gazes so long at an

object that the language we have ceases to justify it, as a fork
will lose its forkness and the world itself become mysterious
and chaotic once we have broken through the barriers of
common usage. In just the same way I had looked so long,
so casually, at men that they had lost their true capacity and
potential. I had come to assume simply their existence and
death, and had forgotten that one is obliged to them in other
ways, that they themselves have other moments.

And then, that afternoon in the city, from having been
wraiths and carcasses, these two people stood up in front of
me as freshly and sharply as parents must when a child can
first name them, and place them in a common territory. And
it was then too, I think, in that moment of new recognition
that I finally passed from the world of Marlow with all its
distortion and disaster into that of George Graham—a world
which I could now make over completely in a new shape.

2

"I'm Wheel of Reports," the man said, snuffling and choking
from a terrible cold on the thirty-third floor of the UN
Building. "Adam Wheel. Pleased to meet you." I took a step
towards a big gray metal desk done in a curvilinear style of
the early fifties.

"Don't touch—for Christ's sake!" the man cried hoarsely.
He gestured toward two huge wobbly piles of mimeographed
paper on his desk and then to similar stacks which reared up
all over his office. "Committee Reports," Wheel advised.
"Six thousand tons of paper a year. The UN and its agencies
must be one of the biggest despoilers of woodlands anywhere.
The 24th Committee on Namibia—South-West Africa to
you; the 6th on St. Kitts and the Windward Islands; report,
on the 1,038th session on the Decolonization Committee,
19th session on pollution in the atmosphere, the 7th on
underwater pollution, the 122nd Committee on the implementation of the 1947 Kashmiri Treaty. . . ." Wheel padded
around his office, touching and naming the piles like a

commander, remembering famous regiments and their battle honors. "You'll get the hang of it pretty soon. It's good to have you with us, Graham. Welcome to the glass house."

Wheel was a big man, balding, with a loping, easy-going confident American manner. There was a heavy jaw and a wide, beaming, friendly face with long bones in the right places, yet there was nothing clumsy about him. He seemed neither diffident nor pushy—seemed to lack all the labels of contemporary American malaise, to be a middle American in a forgotten sense, neither a smart East Coast liberal nor a California conservative nor a hick from the grass roots; not a Nixon man nor a Kennedy one either. The only real bias he showed lay in the unfashionable impression he gave of being at ease in his own country.

Wheel's department—a new flower in the wildly blooming bureaucracy of the place—was dedicated to reporting on the reports. It was his job to study the need and efficacy of the tons of paper that rolled from the basement printed every day in three languages; the often illiterate reflections of general, plenary, ad hoc, and other committees—reports in hundreds of copies that were usually only read by two people: the author and the translator. But of this I learned later. For the moment the talk was of my own future contribution to this babel: "On the Improvement and Co-ordination of the UN Information Services, with particular reference to the broadcasting media," to give my projected work its full title. Wheel handed me over a copy of the "Projected Preliminaries" on this scheme, a dull and lengthy document which I had tried to read on the way over. Everything was "projected" or "preliminary" in the UN; it was safer that way; action or completion were horrifying thoughts.

"I suggest you just read up on things for a week or two. Look around. Listen to some tapes. See some film. Meet the people. You can't rush this sort of thing. Reporting on the reports, sort of spying on the spies, right?"

I nodded to each of his suggestions except the last.

Wheel gestured around his office again hopelessly, then took another momentous puff into his hanky.

"What you'll have to realize here, Graham, is that the swords have been beaten into Xerox machines, not plowshares. That's all we really do here: a living memorial to memoranda. That's all. I don't know how that plowshare business ever came into it. This is the real 3M organization: "Memoranda, Mediocrity, and Money." There are men in this building—farmers, even goatherds—who never saw this side of the Mexican High Sierras until ten years ago, who are pulling down $25,000 a year now, with fourteen dependent children at $700 a throw, three wives at double that, no tax, and a big pension. How can you beat that?"

I looked at Wheel with intent. These homespun truths were not expected. I wondered for a moment if Wheel might be my "contact."

His bald pate shone in the sunlight that came in off the East River. The whole morning was lit up with a fine sharp blaze—water, air, and sky as crisp as broken ice, special weather everywhere. Isolated at this height over the river, in a silent room, there was the ridiculous sense of being in a magic machine, a personal airship. There was the sure sense that one could detach the glass cubicle from the rest of the building and float over the Erie and Pennsylvania Railroad barges that swung awkwardly in the stream, saunter in the air above Welfare Island before drifting down with a Circle Line ferry toward Chinatown and Battery Park.

We went next door to my office and Wheel introduced me to my secretary. She was a well-proportioned Latin-American lady of middle years whose minimal though enthusiastic greetings suggested that her working English would be likewise, a guess she was later to confirm many times. Wheel called her Mrs. Antonio, which seemed to surprise her, as though this was not her name, and this too I afterward found to be the case. Her name was Fernandez—*Miss* Fernandez. She was a newcomer to the organization and, like myself, still capable of surprise.

Outside our offices was a large, windowless secretarial pool, lined with filing cabinets and filled with an assortment of strange and tongue-tied women, silent and unusual because they shared no common national identity or language and were thus forced into a quite unnatural abstinence of gossip and chitchat. Due to the unique nature of their employer, these ladies were a more than usually divided lot.

They sat about the area at various haphazardly placed desks, some with small partitions round them, some nude to the view, some in groups, and others distantly isolated, as though the women had been attempting to repeat the geographical dispositions and political alliances of the countries which they came from.

There were small, china-boned Asiatic girls with widespread blackberry eyes like islands in faces that were othewise quite blank maps; and bigger, older women from the more developed lands, who had missed affection many years before, whose eyes spoke loudly of that loss but were still full of dangerous hope, beacons of long and sharply drawn desire, waiting, each one, for their Captain Cook.

Afterward Wheel introduced me to the rest of his department, the monklike occupants of many other small steel cubbyholes whose windows gave out on either side of the narrow building. They were a forbiddingly dull lot, except for the last of them.

"Let's end up with Mrs. Soheir Taufiq, who covers our Arabic interests," Wheel had said brightly, anxious as I was, it seemed, for some vision of life in the building.

Mrs. Soheir Taufiq was straight from the Great Earth Mother department; an overflowing Egyptian of indefinable years, hair built up at the back of her head in a huge bun. Her face was leathered and deeply grooved, forceful, competent. She had two girls with shorthand notebooks beside her, and was ministering to them alternatively with words and figures which they stumbled over and which she clarified with powerful and forebearing accents.

I had assumed that she was conducting UN business in her dictation. But Wheel told me later that she was most often to be found at her own correspondence, a matter which she needed considerable assistance with, since she wrote at length and had a wide circle of friends.

"Yes, I know," Wheel had continued afterwards, "but she's invaluable to us here. Such a diplomat. And she's got contacts all over the Middle East which even the S-G couldn't easily make. They consult," he added, in as dark a manner as he could muster, "whenever he wants another angle on Sadat and the rest of his pals. A real diplomat."

And indeed, for me, she had been just that. Of all the staff I met that morning, apart from Wheel, she was the only one who showed any real interest in my arrival, an uncomfortable interest almost. She must have studied Graham's UN application and curriculum vitae fairly closely and as a result of this I had, for the first time, to properly inhabit the man and his past, to go back over his career, right back to the time when he had taught in Cairo in the mid-fifties, before I'd ever gone there myself.

And she spoke to me in Arabic, not English. Mrs. Taufiq suddenly moved from a relaxed Anglo-American idiom to an equally colloquial argot of Cairo, full of those awkward vowels, sudden elisions and clamorous consonants that I'd not heard in four years but which drew me back to the city as ineluctably as if she'd taken a blindfold from my eyes and plugs from my ears and placed me squarely at the pastry counter at Groppis and Soliman Pasha in the middle of that dirty, blazing, busy city. She led me back there so surely in her words. Were they part of an innocent inquiry or an interrogation with a special motive? The curtain had gone up at last, and I was linked with her in the first words of that long dialogue I was to play with her and with others, rewriting and acting the words simultaneously, enacting a drama that a week before had actually been a man's life.

Graham was dead; long live George Graham. I had been handed a few props—some of his tattered belongings in a sack, an old Hamilton square-faced watch, a pair of flannels, and a Mentmore fountain pen—along with some papers of a prompt copy from the original production. Yet the dry bones would have to move again and the words flow, for McCoy and Harper, I remembered, had never stopped impressing upon me how Graham, in his time, had taken life and its pleasures with the confidence of a king.

"You were at the British school in Heliopolis, then?" Mrs. Taufiq seemed anxious to confirm a point in Graham's past which I had not mentioned.

"Briefly. Just for two terms. Before I went on to Victoria College."

"You were with Pendlebury in Heliopolis—no? And the Frenchman. What was his name? Jabovitch. Well, Franco-Russian. *White* Russian," Mrs. Taufiq added as if the man had been a bad wine. "With a monocle."

"Pendlebury, yes. He was the head in my time. But the other fellow—with a *monocle*?"

I'd known about Pendlebury from the files McCoy had got together. But the Franco-Russian was outside my area completely. There'd been nothing on him. I couldn't therefore risk any flat confirmation or denial.

"You must have known him." Mrs. Taufiq went on. "I had a daughter there at the time who used to give imitations of him when she came home. Quite shocking."

If this was a test I had to accept it full face. I smiled at Mrs. Taufiq, almost lovingly, taking her eye to eye, letting the creases gather sagely all over my face.

"You know, it's such a long while ago. And there were so many odd foreigners about in Cairo then. Monocles were the least of it. Did you ever come across Malt? Did English in Heliopolis for a while. Used to come to class in a dressing gown and throw books at the dunderheads from the gallery in assembly hall. Brilliant man, a fine scholar, quite out of his depth with children. Fell under a train at Bab-el-Luk on Black Saturday in fifty-two. Remember—when they burned Shepheard's? There was so much going on then I've really forgotten Jabovitch."

She tried to come in again but I didn't let her.

"I was on the terrace of Shepheard's that morning, in fact. With one of the British Council men. Man named Beresford, small fellow with red hair. You must have come across him. Lived in Garden City, always giving parties."

The trick was to turn the questions back to her, allowing only the facts I knew about Graham to emerge, embellished by my own later knowledge of the city; to pour out the authorized version of my tale, leaving no moment for her to get a finger in a crack and pry open the invention. Wheel stood by as audience for the performance.

"I loved Egypt, you know. I was able to get around quite a bit with the Council, used to give lectures—in Tanta, Zagazig, Alex. Doing the Lake Poets in some stuffy upstairs room looking over the tram terminus to a lot of dazed old ladies and young nationalists who stood up at the back and wanted to know what Wordsworth had to do with the liberation of the Egyptian people—there were no daffodils in Egypt, of course—and when we were getting out of the Canal Zone."

Mrs. Taufiq shared some mild laughter with Wheel. I felt I'd passed. I didn't expect any more questions. And there were none. Instead Mrs. Taufiq started to speak of the city of Cairo and its people in the same tones of affectionate remembrance as I myself had used.

"Yes, I must have been at some of your lectures. I used to go quite often to the Council." She looked at me carefully, with appreciation or irony I couldn't say. "You know, it's funny, because although I don't remember you, Mr. Graham, I remember someone very like you in Cairo. Not in the mid-fifties, but a few years later. A teacher at Victoria College in Maadi where my son was. I saw him once or twice at the school and at the Sporting Club there. An Irishman, I think. I don't remember his name. Not you, of course, because this was after Suez. But *like* you. Tall, chatty, rather liked jokes."

Mrs. Taufiq drew out each of these last descriptions slowly, as though in doing so, she could the better resurrect the total memory of this person, give the cloudy mixtures time to coagulate and take a shape. I waited, petrified. She was looking for myself, trying to disinter something as deeply buried as anything Graham possessed in the same place and time.

"Quite a good-looking fellow," she went on, distantly.

"Oh yes?" I said lightly.

"Yes. I remember he married the daughter of some friends of mine. The Girgises in Maadi. It came to a bad end I seem to remember."

I took out Graham's pipe with its chipped bowl and filled it with the aromatic Dutch tobacco he used.

Mrs. Taufiq paused, thinking. I lit a match and the little steel room was filled with sweetness. She seemed to have given herself over to the memory of it all, completely —to someone, to something that had happened on an evening long ago on a terrace in Maadi, as if the tobacco had become a little madeleine for her and through its aroma she was just on the point of breaking into time and recapturing the past. I felt her thoughts brush past and around me, lightly but insistently, searching for the key, disembodied characteristics looking for a name.

But she failed in her mental arithmetic, or seemed to have. She looked at me again, making a last attempt, wrinkling her eyes up quizzically, then giving the blurred negative up for lost. Yet even if she had failed to identify me, I wasn't sure at all of the innocence of her attempt.

"Well, that's a coincidence," I said, to fill the silence.

"Come on, Soheir," Wheel broke in lightly. "You're always seeing ghosts—"

"Oh yes, always," she interrupted. "Farouk, Nasser, the Maadi Sporting Club—all ghosts—"

"And now you're seeing Graham here, who's from Scotland, as an Irishman on the hard courts in Maadi and holding the bar up afterwards with a gin sling. You know, Soheir, you'll have to write your memoirs. I've always told you. She's full of coincidences." Wheel turned to me. "Everything hooks up in the end, isn't that right, Soheir? Full circle, in the Eastern mythology. The Wheel of Karma, you used to call me. Graham was a handsome dragon in a previous incarnation. She goes big on all that sort of thing, Graham," Wheel added, gently ribbing her. "I was a Manhattan Indian—remember Soheir?—before the Dutch bought me out for twenty-four dollars and a string of beads. Don't pay any attention to her, Graham, or she'll have you in on one of her table-tapping sessions. Talk about coincidences: if Graham looks like your friend in Maadi, then you're Golda Meir. I've always told you. Sitting down—couldn't tell you apart."

This must have been an old joke between them and indeed there was a distinct resemblance. But at the moment Mrs. Taufiq wasn't in a mood for jokes. She was still thinking.

"No, Adam. It's got nothing to do with mysticism. It's just a likeness that's all. A nice likeness." She looked up at me again. "What *was* that Irishman's name?"

*   *   *

"That's the only thing with Soheir," Wheel said, chatting to me on the way back to his office. "She has this spiritual kick, a little of the crystal ball. Take no notice. It doesn't mean a thing."

"I'm sure," I lied. "Of course." And I drew hard on Graham's pipe, like a lifeline.

"Come on. I'll introduce you to the Delegates' Lounge. You could use a beer, I'll bet. Cultural shock—arrival in the New World, tall buildings, going round in circles. I don't want you jumping out a window on your first day."

I nodded. I could use a beer.

"You know, there was a family that arrived here a few months ago, from Ceylon. The wife had never been much further than a paddy field, up country somewhere. He was an agricultural specialist. They put them in the UN Plaza building, up the road, and up thirty floors. Well, after a month or so being locked up in the clouds, the wife tried to take herself and her two children back home—out of the apartment window. Defenestration. Funny word. Sounds as if it had something to do with sex. They landed on East River Drive in the middle of rush hour. Cultural shock. It was an awful tragedy."

I nodded again. I could use a second beer already. We walked toward the first of the three lift banks, each of which served a third of the building. We were on the top third, the twenty-second to thirty-eighth floors.

"What about here?" I asked. "Do you have much trouble with that sort of thing—the windows?"

"Well, *they* have the trouble. We just pick up the bits afterward in a red blanket. But, now and again. Yes, it happens. And more often than it should. There's a lot of subdued temperament around here. It's the nature of the business."

"How do they get out? None of the windows open I notice. They're all sealed."

"Ah, but the Directors—the D 1s and 2s—they have keys."

"So it's only the senior staff that do themselves in? I'd have thought they might be the least frustrated."

"You have a point there. I hadn't thought of that. Well, maybe it's the guilt that makes the Directors jump. That would fit. It's got to be one or the other, doesn't it? Either you tell yourself you've got to go, the bad faith becomes unsupportable, or else it's just plain insanity—disorientation: not knowing who you are, what you're doing, or why. There's a lot of both around here. Especially the bit with the compass spinning around like a top. You'll see. It takes most people quite a while to find their feet here, their 'role,' as they like to call it. And some never do. My God, they head straight for the rocks."

We got off at the third-floor staff concourse, just next to the main staff cafeteria, the news and candy stand, and the shoeshine man. Wheel immediately decided on an appointment with this fellow, and I waited behind him while he put his boots up.

People streamed around us, queuing up for early lunch. There was a strong smell of some foreign gravy and a warm blast of scented air from secret whirring machinery. To our left at the end of a long corridor a barbershop advertised itself discreetly; to our right was a branch office of the New York Chemical Bank with a train of grave people fiddling with their wallets making their way politely to and fro; the whole area was remarkably like the first-class passenger concourse of a big tin liner, moored disconsolately and permanently beyond territorial waters, going nowhere.

Only the shoeshine man seemed real—a middle-aged, balding New Yorker, in a short-sleeved tartan shirt, bent permanently forward on a little wooden chair over his work, head bobbing furiously, his hands and forearms a dusty brown with the years of his trade. He was like a stowaway on this listless ship full of impeccable people, someone from a ghetto that had shinned up the anchor on our last night in port and had now been set to work his passage by the captain.

Wheel and he exchanged staccato pleasantries for a while. Then they both fell silent. The sun swept off the East River through a huge glass window, baking us all, exotic but tasteless cakes in a perfumed oven.

The shoeshine man started to hum and sing in an abrupt and inexact high tenor, some pop song from years before:

Winchester Ca-thed-draall . . .
. . . hum dum de de dum . . .
You stood and you watched
As my baby left town . . .

When he was finished with Wheel he suddenly thumped
the shoe box with his palm: "Next *please*. Step right up."

"Tap, tap, tap," the man went now, using both hands
on the box. "Tapety, tap; tapety, tap, tap, tap," as though
beginning something stylish on drums or sending a Morse
code message.

I suddenly thought I felt the first intimations of Wheel's
warning: cultural shock, the compass spinning madly. The
sun seemed to rip through the glass, lashing at all of us with
the intensity of a flamethrower.

"Tapety, tap, tap, tap, . . ."

The building had swelled all morning with echoes,
something straining behind all the appearances, an indecipherable message trying to get through—something trying
desperately to be known, but which one could never quite
get hold of.

"Winchester Ca-thed-drall. . . ."

The man had started up again, the inane tune cutting
through the busy noise of the concourse in its high register,
like a clue so obvious that no one notices it.

We passed through the double swing doors at the end
of the concourse and the sounds were all suddenly turned
out behind us like a light. The long corridor beyond, which
bordered the Security Council and other committee cham-
bers, led to the Delegates' North Lounge over a carpet so
soft and dark that it turned its travelers into skiers. Everyone cut their pace here, hovered like birds, the better to
fall on the right man or group, exchanging diplomatic
words, before passing back to committee or on to the lounge.

This long dark anteroom was full of precisely inten-
tioned messages; a slip of the tongue here could ruin the
false consensus; here were endless coincidental but contrived
meetings. But who might approach me in this place with
whispers, I wondered, linking arms over the deep carpet?
And would the message be for Graham, or one that would
not come at all, the messenger having seen me for the man

I was, not Graham, but the figure Mrs. Taufiq had partly
resurrected earlier that morning. Mrs. Taufiq had raised me
up again, the man of Cairo and of Durham jail whom I had
thought well lost. If the place was full of echoes, I realized
it was because I was listening now to everything with the
ears of two people, Graham and myself, moving from person to person in unnerving stereophony.

There were more than a hundred or so delegates dotted
about in groups and armchairs in the huge lounge at the
end of the building but not more than half a dozen people
were standing at the bar down by the river end of the great
football field. Journalists, Wheel told me, UN correspon-
dents for the most part, their backs firmly to the delegates,
arms and elbows against the counter, pondering the bottles
with all the wan humanity of drinkers.

When we got down to this distant fountain, Wheel put
a finger into his collar and pulled. It was hotter in the
lounge than anywhere else I'd been in the building. The
delegates, lightly inspired by this warmth and by coffee, released a mild euphoria on the air, like the end of an unimportant embargo. For once, these devious men were obvious
in their games. They lost their public timidity; here they
could lie unequivocally.

In such a place, this hypocritical Purgatory, Wheel was
in his element. We twirled our glasses. Wheel had introduced me to a strong Canadian ale. We watched the dark
foam ripple around the edges, smelling the sudden release
of hops and barley that pricked our noses. Then he lifted
his eyes to the moving scene in front of us like an old race-
goer, weighing form.

"That Russian there," he said, pointing to a peasant
eminence who had stood up near us, "is known as the 'Russian who said Yes.' Years ago—this is his second time here
—he once said 'Yes' by mistake at some unimportant committee on agricultural tariffs. He was sent home for a year.
When he came back the same committee cheered him. It
was hilarious. And that's Omar Feki. The Banker. He won't
sit down. When he first got here, twenty years ago, on his
first day, he sat down—there, on one of those sofas—and had
his pocket picked by another Arab. It turned out the robber

had been one of his customers in Beirut, some old disagreement about his account. So Feki's been on his feet ever since. They call him 'Once Bitten.' "

It was only then that I noticed the couple at a table opposite the bar, their backs to the sunny view, the rose gardens, and the statue of Peace beyond. The bright light had shielded them from me until that moment, keeping them more or less in silhouette, so that I had to put my hand over my eyes briefly, pretending to look out on the river, before I could make them out clearly.

The man had his legs crossed, so that one foot swayed dangerously in the path of diplomats on their way to the coffee shop beyond the bar: a long, thin foot, protruding from a fine dark worsted cloth and bound in a traditional, handmade English laced shoe. He was conspicuously lean and tall, even while seated, and just as obviously English in a way—though he couldn't have been more than forty—that was as old-fashioned and correct as his dress. A thin, firm face; something a little pinched about the lips; careful eyes and long flat ears; a certain chiseled hollowness touched up by a confident weariness: he might have taken drugs or been the last son of a profligate earl; chances very much favored the latter.

But it wasn't a wooden face by any means. Only its present outlines were fixed. For the moment it had simply withdrawn the currency of expression; it was resting, as if inwardly reflecting on its assets, leaving only a rough estimate of its worth on view, so that passers-by might be warned of the stakes involved before making an investment.

The woman was a little younger, halfway through her thirties perhaps, and where he was a little wan and fluted, she had the bearing of someone likely to be generous to a fault. But with her height, for she was tall as well, this fractional plumpness about the hips and chest, far from being a disadvantage, gave her the virtues of a classical anatomy, contours which artists used to attempt but human beings rarely achieve.

The two of them sat there, both with tubby crystals of light Scotch, with a confidence and ease that made everyone else in the long room seem misplaced.

Wheel noticed them just after I did and raised his hand. The man stood up in answer and, leaning over the woman, took her glass. Her eyes followed him as he came toward us. "The Jacksons," Wheel said. "They're compatriots of yours, Mr. Graham. Guy is with the politicals, on the floor above us."

When her husband was being introduced to me, the woman's eyes met mine in a brief gaze, smiling a little social message, as if to say: "I'm glad you've met him, for now so much the more easily will you meet me."

The three of us went back to join her at their table, our glasses refilled.

"Helen, this is George Graham," Wheel said. "He just came in from London. George, this is Helen Jackson. George is going to report on our reports—a new spy in the nest." Wheel looked at both of them and laughed, but got little response. Both of the Jacksons were looking at me intently, as if I was an expected guest.

And of course I was expected, by him at least. I realized that at once: Guy Jackson was my SIS contact with London, with McCoy and Harper. They had briefed me about him. As for Helen Jackson, her name rang out for me with an echo I couldn't catch, until suddenly I saw how it summed up her classic proportions. But at that moment, just after we had been introduced, she reflected her Trojan namesake like a statue. The warmth of her overture was still there, brightly on her face, but it had developed no further. The expression of welcome had frozen everywhere on her skin, startled to death.

Wheel set her animation going again with some sly remark about her presence in the building. And then her husband took me up with an interest he tried to conceal, as though he were trying to get me to sell him something he wanted badly without my realizing this and putting too high a price on it.

"Wheel told me you were coming over," he said agreeably. "With the COI, weren't you?"

"Yes, Reports Officer. East Africa mainly."

Jackson lifted his glass and I noticed a brassily gold signet ring on the marriage finger. It struck one as glaringly out of place with the rest of his restrained decor, like a dropped "h" in the middle of a speech from the throne. It seemed precisely intended as a vulgar flourish, calling attention to itself; an obscenity in the middle of the general refinement which he had purposefully isolated.

"God knows what you'll make of our UN reports," he went on, and I could hear Wheel's inquiries of Helen Jackson from the other side of the table. ". . . and the kids?" Guy Jackson's voice was soft, I realized now, like an old man's; his words spaced out too, as though he was anxious to give himself the maximum amount of time for thought without being obvious about it.

"I'm above you—the S-G's political department. Very few reports come out of us, thank God. We keep it to ourselves. But the rest of the building is an absolute snowfall. No doubt Wheel has told you. You were on the Africa desk in London, weren't you?"

"Latterly, yes. East Africa, Malawi, a bit of Rhodesia."

"I know that part myself. I farmed there for a while. In the south. Where are you staying?"

"They've put me up temporarily at the Tudor Hotel around the corner. Till I get an apartment."

I was still considering the problems of accommodation ahead, the dull business of phone calls, arguments, and too much money, when I stopped thinking of everything, as if I'd been shot, all the senses shocked out of me, and I was still running like a chicken without a head.

Africa. It was Africa again. *I farmed there for a while.* I fell on Jackson's casual words like a man in a music quiz trying vainly to complete a verse in a popular song. ". . . *farmed there for a while. In the south*"? The south. Farming up country? In the old Rhodesias or South Africa? And then the answer flew at me, the corresponding phrase, the next line of music: *"Once he was someone in the country; now, just something in the city"*—the words of some married woman (*"He doesn't know"*) in letters to George Graham. The letters I had read in Marylebone and on the boat over.

This was the message, I was sure, that had cheated me, lain in wait for me, all morning, the echoes of something unrevealed searching everywhere in the building for expression; a secret in the dry atmosphere, hidden in the shoeshine man's harsh singing, which only I could interpret, which was for me alone.

And now it had come clear, in Jackson's polite responses: "*I used to farm there for a while. In the south.*" He had given me a phrase in a vital lost language through which I could now elucidate a whole civilization's hieroglyphics. The puzzle resolved itself so simply and clearly that, before I thought of the long academic journey ahead toward full interpretation, I rushed headlong, an exultant scholar, into translating the first sentence of the mysterious text: I could suddenly see this thin, amused man—Guy Jackson—and his wife, Helen, standing outside a colonial farmstead on the uplands, the huge skies reaching down over them. They had just come back from doing something active—were standing there by the porch in old clothes, sweating, welcoming the evening.

I looked quickly across at Helen Jackson deeply gossiping with Wheel. I had forgotten: there was one other person who must have drawn from the morning something quite buried and forbidden: an equal secret. If she was the woman in the letters, I was not the man she had written them to; her lovely messages had gone badly astray. Only she would know that, but she would know it well, too well, the memory spreading like a fire through so many hotel bedrooms. I was looking across at a woman who had been waiting for her lover, and he had turned up all right, bright and early, untrue in everything except in name.

Helen Jackson and George Graham: they had been the lovers in the story, in those letters, who had come to argue about the past and future of Africa and the same ruthless pendulum of happiness: "I am not afraid of the future . . ."; the "Natural Tory" whose confident politics had collapsed and the disappointed Marxist: it all fitted. I was sure of it. Her manner exactly reflected Graham's comments on her, while her suddenly frozen welcome after she heard my name confirmed all my own quick inventions.

Helen Jackson, the wife of my London contact, was my mistress. What was the rest of the question? Had she any idea, for example, who George Graham really was? Was their relationship the only illicit thing they shared? Had she been covertly bound to him, hidden with him, for six years, without knowing his final identity? She must have been blind to that, I thought. Yet how had it all come about? How had a deep cover KGB agent come to love the wife of a senior officer in British Intelligence? Initially one can think only of coincidence in such a strange meeting, but years in the same profession made me have my doubts.

Jackson and I chatted on about New York apartments, the relative merits and dangers of the East and West Sides. He said they had a place in a new block on the East Side, off Second Avenue in the Fifties. "Wretchedly expensive and only really half safe—with the children. But there's not much alternative. It's only ten minutes' walk here, which cuts out the transport business. You'll come round, come for drinks this evening if you're free. We've a few friends coming."

I thanked him without saying yes or not. Already I felt myself an interloper, the lover gliding easily into the circle of the husband's trust, the cheat who takes every liberty— another man's wife, his gin; who tells his children a bedtime story before dinner, and makes clandestine arrangements for tomorrow with his wife while she tidies up afterward in the kitchen.

Jackson was pushing me into a role I didn't want. Yet this woman had been part of George Graham, the deepest thing in his life possibly. I could not avoid the implications of this indefinitely. I saw at once that I should either have to sort things out with Helen Jackson or explain the whole matter to her husband. But this latter course never struck me seriously: I was not going to betray this confidence of Graham's no matter in how many other ways I was his stooge. She and I would speak about it by ourselves, I thought. I should tell her the position, she would have to accept it and keep her mouth shut about it, as she had done about Graham six years previously.

Wheel had gone on talking to her about her children, two girls, Sarah and Sheila, whose ages I couldn't determine from the odd snatches of conversation—some question of a nanny or a teacher, I couldn't make out which, so that they

might have been two years old or twelve. And from her expression it now seemed that Helen Jackson was as unin-
volved in her conversation with Wheel as we two were on
the other side of the table. The curious intensity had
dropped from her eyes, the invitation had all been withdrawn, her flourishing airs quite subsided. Before, though
cast in a classic mold, her buoyancy and vitality had lifted
her far above those confines into a sphere of lightness and
finesse. Now she seemed exhausted, a weight had fallen on
all her natural virtues; she was hesitant in everything, as
though quite overcome with mundane domestic worries.
She turned to her husband:

"Adam has the address of that nursery school on the
West Side. We should go take a look at it."

It was only then I realized she was American: the accents, the grammar, were faint but distinct. Could this
woman have lived in South Africa or the old Rhodesias?
Perhaps I was quite wrong about her. Then she took a notebook from her bag and started to write down the address,
and I had no more doubts; the handwriting was the same
as that in the letters—even the ink, a black ink—the same
slanting, hurried, rather immature scrawl. She was leaning
forward, using the space of table right in front of me, as
though anxious that I should see her writing clearly, be
able to compare the messages. She seemed willfully to be offering me conclusive proof of our previous association, of her
fidelity and my lies. When she had finished writing she
looked up at me, but spoke to her husband:

"Where's Mr. Graham staying?"

I repeated my piece about the Tudor Hotel, and she
said at once like an old friend: "Oh, you can't go on staying there. Friends of ours on the West Side have an apartment in an old block; it's a co-op; they know the super—
I'm sure you'd get something there. Wouldn't he, Guy?"

She looked down at the address she'd just taken from
Wheel. "Their block's not far from the nursery school—
Ninety-second on the park. Come with me tomorrow if you
like, Mr. Graham, while I take a look at the school.

"That's an idea," Guy Jackson said nicely. "You don't
want to wander too much around the West Nineties on

your own if you can help it. Even in daytime. Take him along, Helen."

He might have been a *mari complaisant* furthering the wife's cause. Yet I was sure it was a piece of genuine solicitude on his part, toward me at least. She alone was making the running, furthering her intended inquiries with me and wasting no time about it.

How much experience she must have had in that sort of thing, I thought: bluntly arranging meetings, deceiving her husband right under his nose with all the urgent rashness that love requires and forgives. And I didn't blame her. She had not loved casually, that I knew. All her blatant intensity—the full weight of her happy curiosity that had filled her face until a few minutes before—had once devolved over another man, and had done so completely, without deviation or restraint. One could see that too—she would not play with any man.

I thanked her for her offer and then turned away at something Wheel had started to propound about muggings on the West Side.

And then I looked back at her for a second, for no reason, and found her looking at me, quite openly, her face puzzled in a quiet way, the lines of interest reviving minutely, with sadness, looking at me as any woman might on a messenger who had come to tell her that her hopes were dead. There was no purpose behind her gaze, no future; it was nothing more than a brief query, the formalities of identity, a woman gazing on a body in a mortuary.

Yet it was a face I recognized now, shorn of all its happy drama: it was the one I had invented myself after reading her letters on the boat journey over, trying to invest Graham with a realistic sexuality: Helen Jackson was very nearly the woman I had walked toward at the crowded party in Westminster—that spring, six years ago when I'd just got back from Kenya.

I remembered my inventions on the boat: "She was tall and rounded in a way that could never for a moment be described as fat. . . ." Had I then, in some way, really come to inhabit the remains of George Graham without knowing it? He would have known exactly what she looked like: the dark hauteur; the brown eyes sprinkled, broken here and there, with some even darker element; her permanent forwardness and willingness. But I had no belief in transfiguration. I had walked straight into an ambush on my first morning ashore, and that new identity, that cover I had so carefully built up, was now all gone.

3

I didn't go to the Jackson's apartment that night for drinks, pleading tiredness after the long day. And that was true, at least. I would have postponed forever, if I had been able, this meeting alone with Helen Jackson. I had no taste for it and even less for its outcome. It could not be other than awkward, at the least, for both of us—for her in a personal way and for me professionally. At worst, it could have a disastrous end for both of us.

I had thought about it on and off, lying on my hotel bed that evening, thought of alternatives to seeing her, but had found none. And in any case, I wanted an end to running. I had come to realize that the whole point of my taking over Graham's identity was to stop the dissolution, the canker, the treachery, and all the other needless horror which are the usual ends to our silly profession. I had already decided to pick up the remnants of Graham's life and fulfill it for him, complete it—deny the forces that had ruined him and very nearly done the same for me. I should have, then, to meet Helen Jackson.

We met downstairs in the main lobby of the Secretariat building next morning. She and Guy had walked over from their apartment in the East Fifties and the three of us stood there, by the elevator banks, the Secretariat staff moving past us toward their allotted traps. Even on my second day in the building, I felt a sudden huge luck in not having to go with them all, upward into their dry, glass cells, these hopeless workers of the world. I could go out and spend the crisp morning flat-hunting with a woman in a suede over-coat and a long red and white woollen scarf whose tails fell down, one in front, one behind. It was like the start of a school reunion, when we are all older and richer and better dressed and can spend the day as we will, without orders or denials. Even the business ahead could not dampen the moment's happy expectation I felt then; Guy Jackson and the others disappearing into the air-conditioning, we into the real weather outside.

"Do you like walking?" she asked. I pushed the glass doors open for her, against the run of fretful people.

"Yes, I do. I used to walk a lot."

"Guy likes the office. He used not to. He likes to get to his office. He was more active once. Where did you do your walking? Around Westminster?"

We had stopped at the pedestrian crossing outside the UN entrance looking over First Avenue.

"I was in the field a lot—as well as a desk. In East Africa. Doing TV programs, compiling reports: that was the active part of the job."

"Yes, I know. Guy told me."

A roaring stream of cars and trucks sprang up from the underpass to our right, and we could hear each other no longer.

"You used to live in Africa, didn't you?" I said when we'd got to the far side of the avenue and had started to walk up Forty-second Street.

"Just after we were married. In Northern Rhodesia—now Zambia." She turned and looked back at the long line of national flags in front of the Secretariat. "I can't see the flag." She gazed at the colors cracking in the wind, shading her eyes from the sun coming off the river between the Con Ed chimneys. "Green and black and white—I think."

"It should be easy," I said. "Zed. It must be the last flag on the line."

"What about Zanzibar?"

"Part of the Republic of Tanzania."

"You know all about Africa."

"No. Just the alphabet."

She turned back and we went on. Yes, we might have been starting out on a school reunion; tempting and teasing each other, seeing where the ground lay after so many years.

"We call 'Zed' 'Zee' over here. Took me quite a while to learn your way."

"Why did you bother?"

"Oh, they were very particular—Guy's relations in Africa, his friends. They didn't know what he was doing marrying an American in the first place. The usual thing—he should have married a *Country Life* girl and taken her to live on a thousand acres in Gloucestershire."

The huge glass wall of a building loomed up on our right: thousands of square yards of glass set between dark stone pillars and copper casements. Inside I could see nothing but a dense greenery: tall flowering cherries, palmlike trees with falling rubbery leaves, ferns, a carpet of exotic shrubs and bushes, a hothouse jungle with pools of water and little streams a few feet from the street. I stopped to look at it.

"The Ford Foundation." She said. "Were you long in Africa?" We both gazed through the glass at this immense natural contrivance; even Arcadia was not beyond the concrete and glass ambitions of Manhattan. Had I been long in Africa? All right, I would play the game as long as she wanted; in any case, I wasn't going to have the whole business out with her in the middle of Forty-second Street.

"In East Africa, yes. I went there first after Suez in fifty-seven, taught for several years in Nairobi, then the University at Kampala, finally in Nyasaland, more or less in a sort of technical college in Blantyre. It's Malawi now. That was in the early sixties." I knew Graham's curriculum vitae off pat, and looking into all the rampant tropical greenery, I felt for a second as if I'd actually experienced Graham's Africa myself—instead of just once, in Nairobi at one of the near game parks, on holiday from Cairo in the fifties.

"Nyasaland was just next to us," she said. "I mean—about five hundred miles away. But that's next door in Africa. We left when the Federation broke up and went to Kenya with Jomo. Guy was always very multiracial." She smiled slightly.

"Yes, I left Malawi then, too. Came back to London."

It was a ridiculous charade. I couldn't look at her.

"With the British Council, weren't you?"

She could so easily have said "*were you?*" but she had to press it. I could so easily, so properly, have said "How do you know?" since I'd said nothing of this to her husband the previous day. All he knew was that I was an ex-COI man. But of course I knew how she knew, and I let her keep her games. I knew how she must feel—wanting quickly, desperately to hear all; what had happened to George Graham, and why. And I knew, for all her headlong questions, the restraints she must have been imposing on herself.

"Yes, I was with the British Council in Africa. What did you—he do in Rhodesia? Mining?"

She smiled properly now for a moment, for the first time that day.

"He *looks* like a miner, doesn't he?"

"Farming, then—tobacco or cattle. Up country. A colonial farmstead. Not posh, but quite old, with a long wooden veranda, and fever trees around the lawn. Orange blossom climbing the front wall and a big acacia tree outside the kitchen door." I gazed at the green jungle in front of me, all the rubbery paraphernalia of trees motionless beyond the glass. Moisture ran down the huge windows in small rivulets. "The garden must have smelled like a ladies' hairdressers on a hot evening." I turned and looked at her. The smile had been held but was now an expression of open-eyed surprise as well.

"Not quite. But almost. How do you know? You sound like a detective."

"Not really."

"Not even in the same line of work?"

"Anyone who imagines too much is a detective."

We walked on up Forty-second Street, through the canyon, gray and busy and useless, the bright light of the morning now almost defunct as if the street were a long way underground and the real land began at the top of the buildings. We took a bus up Madison Avenue to Fifty-ninth Street, walked west to the Grand Army Plaza, and entered Central Park. Within moments we came to a zoo, right in the middle of it. I hadn't expected it; there were no turnstiles, it was free: a small but well-organized zoo. Africa was waiting round every corner for us that morning.

We had stopped by a pool, edged all the way around by a happy crowd. I could hear huge wallops on the water, followed by fountains of spray rising above the spectators' heads. Black and shiny shapes like wet gumboots jumped about between the crush of people. "The sea lions are great," she called back to me from where she had pressed herself right up to the rails for a proper view. Then she came back to where I was hovering on the outskirts of the crowd, a vendor with a wagon beside me trying to sell me a pretzel. "You don't like them, then?"

"I've never liked the sea," I replied. "Too cold, too big. And slippery. And salt in your mouth. And rough."

"Perhaps you like lakes? Unless you don't like water at all. When were you born?"

The vendor finally managed to sell me a pretzel. Two pretzels. I gave her one. I felt like an uncle with a godchild.

"February."

"Water, then. A watery sign. You must like water."

"Yes, all right. I like lakes. They're quieter at least."

"Lake Nyasa?"

"Lake Malawi you mean."

"Yes, well you must have liked that when you were in Malawi. It was tremendous—all those blue mountains around it, like Scotland. Don't you remember? We used to go there for holidays. One couldn't swim in it, of course."

"No, of course not." I remembered that problem very well from my days in Egypt—the snail-infested waters of the canals and lakes there where the liver bugs thrived, common all over Africa in still water: bilharzia.

"Bilharzia," I said. "That was the trouble, I remember, in Lake Victoria too, in Uganda, couldn't swim, had to rub yourself all over in engine grease if you went out in a boat. Gets right through the skin."

"Yes," she said.

We walked on, into the lion house. She was silent now, throwing a tail of her scarf around her neck again in another loop as if a cold wind had come up and not the warm meaty aroma, the acid wafts of old urine, that now surrounded us.

We looked at one of the huge animals asleep under a dead tree trunk, dead like it. Then she spoke, neither of us looking at the other, our eyes fixed upon the tawny beast.

She said: "The only point about Lake Malawi—anyone who'd been in the country would know it—is that you *can* swim in it. That's why we went there for holidays. The current from the Shiré River keeps the water moving and the weeds away. It's practically the only lake in Africa that *is* bilharzia-free."

"Oh dear," I said. "Oh dear, I am sorry."

The animal stirred, flicked its tail an inch, looked at us for a dull moment, before dispensing with the view and turning over flat on its other side.

"George knew that lake in Malawi," she went on. "I met him there once. We swam in it. There was a scrubby sort of Holiday Inn place above Fort Johnston on the western shore. No one ever went there, not after the break up of the Federation. It was empty. We spent a week there doing nothing."

"How did you manage that? Graham left Africa in 1961, came back to London."

"He came back to Africa quite often afterward. I thought you'd done your homework."

"Yes, but you'd left Malawi by then, hadn't you?"

"Yes, we were in Nairobi. Guy had an attachment there from the Foreign Office—leased as an advisor to the Kenya government. He took up with Whitehall when he stopped farming. Though in fact he was always with the FO, in one way or another."

After the zoo we took a cab up to the Guggenheim Museum and went wandering around Frank Lloyd Wright's strange inverted cone, pacing his gentle ramps slowly upward and outward, looking half-heartedly at the paintings.

"So you went back to meet Graham in Malawi?" I said. "Long after you'd left that part of the world."

"Yes, I met him there. Among other places. I was going back to see friends in Zambia anyway. He was researching a program in Malawi. We met up. It wasn't difficult."

"No, of course not."

She had all of Africa to be unfaithful in: those huge spaces where two such white lovers would surely have stood out terribly clearly. It may not have been difficult, but it must have been risky with her husband in Jomo's government in Nairobi, a town that was the sounding drum for all the far-flung gossip of East Africa. But one took risks in that sort of situation. I had forgotten that. And in a strange way the closer you went to the fire in such circumstances the safer you were. That was an old saw, tribal or civilized. Compromise was the only really dangerous thing between lovers.

"I thought the long trip you made was in *East* Africa— Uganda, Kenya, Tsavo National Park, for example?" I looked at her with a notebook in my eyes, like a police constable, a bad replacement for a small part in *The Mousetrap*.

"There were several long trips."

"You walked to the top of a small hill, didn't you—in Tsavo?—near an old mining village, with a Jack Hawkins figure in a bush hat who talked about beating hippos on the nose with a walking stick on the banks of the Nile. . . ."

It was my turn to ask her if she remembered things properly. I started to push the matter myself now, feeling a need to display my "homework." But more, I think, I was experiencing the beginnings of a mild jealousy, the jealousy of a new lover, who, even at a first meeting, wants to possess all the knowledge, all the intimacies, of the woman's previous affairs. Even then I wanted the entire baggage of Helen Jackson's recollected experience.

"Yes, I thought you'd have gotten onto that last letter. That was stupid of me."

"You didn't say anything rash. No one could have identified you from it—no address, signature, nothing. You had someone post it in Uxbridge." Then it struck me. "London airport of course."

We had stopped by a group of Kandinskys; dark lines, blots, jagged edges, nightmares. She turned away from it, with relief. But it was because of what I'd just said.

"I knew Graham was coming over here; we were going to meet. But you mean you didn't know about me? Who I was, where I was?"

"How could I have? It was pure chance—my meeting you here on my first day."

"What about the others—the people—the people who sent you here?"

"They couldn't have known about you either. They never mentioned you in connection with Graham. And I didn't show them your letter. It struck me as something completely personal, nothing to do with what I was doing for them."

"*Was* doing?"

"*Am* doing."

"What are you doing then?"

"That's covered by the Official Secrets Act."

"I know. Guy is in the same business, the same games."

"I thought they never told their wives."

"You can't ever have had a wife, then."

"Oh, I did. She was in the same silly business too."

We'd moved off Kandinsky and on to some important looking groups by Chagall, Delaunay, Leger, and Jackson Pollock. She had unwound her red and white scarf completely now, taken it off, and was carrying it in her hand, all bunched up like a football. She opened the top of her suede coat.

"No, it's really quite simple," I said. Then I thought of Graham's shoes on the table in Marylebone. "Well, my part is fairly simple. It's just bad luck that I should bump into you like—"

"Listen," she put in quietly, but digging her fingers into the wool. "The only simple things are these: you're impersonating George Graham. You've done a lot of homework on it; you've been helped by experts. You're tied up with British Intelligence in some way; Guy is too. George and I are —well, how would you describe it? You've read the letters."

"Yes. An affair?" I paused. "What else could you call it? I don't like the word."

"I love him."

I let her keep the present tense. It did proper justice to all that I had learned of her and George Graham, everything that had passed between them, even though I was sure that, technically, the grammar was not quite incorrect; it had been overtaken by events, though she knew nothing of it then, willing as ever to live in the present to the very last.

We had moved into an annex off the second floor, the Tannhauser Collection, and were looking at a Manet: *Before the Mirror*.

"Anyway, these things are clear enough," she went on. "You've come to New York as George Graham and so you know all about—us."

"Yes."

"My 'infidelity.' That's the word I don't like. All the same, it would do me no good in most quarters—if people knew. But the real thing is this: you can't tell me about the real George Graham because he's with British Intelligence as well, and you've got to protect him and the 'organization.' "

I said nothing. We silently inspected a Pissarro—*Les Coteaux de l'Hermitage*—and then moved on to Manet's *Woman with Parrot*.

"What's happened to him?" she said suddenly. "Where is he?"

"In London. I should think he's all right. I never met him."

"And?"

"And nothing. I told you. I can't tell you."

Even Renoir couldn't hold her. She walked on. She tossed her hair.

"Why did you tell me anything to begin with, then?" she said at the next picture.

"To get the situation straight, if I could. You knew—you were the only person—to know about me. I had to talk to you. But what can you do? If you press the issue about my impersonation you'll explode your marriage and your husband's job, at the very least. And you'll be absolutely no nearer to George Graham. But what I really wanted to say to you was this: I'll say nothing at all about what I know about you and him, not to your husband, not to anyone in London. That's the bargain, if you let me finish my business here. And maybe when it's all over you can pick up things again, where you were with him—" I couldn't go on with the lie and I think she noticed.

"That's very likely, of course, isn't it?"

"I don't honestly know."

"Rather a one-sided bargain, isn't it? And nothing really at the end to keep it for, from my point of view. Just to keep you in one piece—while he ends up in pieces."

"I would tell you. If it didn't matter. I'd tell you about him. I know what you must feel. I'm sorry."

" 'If it didn't matter,' you say. Who do you think this matters so much to, this man—if not to me?"

We walked on, not seeing the pictures at all. She was glowering. Then she began to hang back, isolating herself, looking at odd pictures alone. Soon we were yards apart, so that eventually I turned and walked back, angry.

"Look," I said, "don't you think I've the right to try and get out of this in one piece too? I didn't propose myself for this job. Doesn't that strike you? I didn't fix up this stupid business in London—any of it. I meant I was sorry, for me as well, if you like. I hate all this just as much as you do; as much, I think, as Graham hated it all too."

"Hated?"

"Hates." How quickly one lied, saving myself, not him.

"And you think if we work together all of us might get out in one piece?" she said dully.

"Yes."

Her face brightened a bit. I'd struck something hopeful in her again, that optimism she was so ready with, the warm parts that went with all her forward bias. "That's quite possible," I said.

"All right. Let's do that. And thank you for the sorry."

We were conspirators, then. But I loathed the conspiracy. It would bring no new or happier state; it was a lie. She would play along with me only because I had offered her the chance of taking up with Graham at some future point, a point which I knew could have no existence. Graham had been a senior KGB officer and she didn't know it. If he survived at all he would be sent down for as many years as I had been. He was lost to her, I thought, as firmly as death. A marriage between them would never be arranged. That freedom together, which she had sought so carefully, so vehemently, with such secrecy in her letters to him—when she could leave Guy, the question of the children properly settled—had, for all her care and vivid imagination, no possible end in reality.

And one day she would find this out, sharply and conclusively, all within a minute. That would be the worst thing: the moment when she discovered that all her efforts, her love, had proved as useful as careless, spendthrift fancies, while the years of careful passage she had made about his body had the same value as a one-night stand.

An affair of her sort is like a revolution after a hundred years of repressive peace. The odds are all against it. It requires more organization than a marriage to achieve half the trust and only a fraction of the physical availability. And apart from the need, the belief, the resources are nonexistent. Such a liaison survives as a beleaguered force making odd successful forays but always threatened with retreat and rout. Its defeat is far more likely than the end of formal ties, where convention, habit, economics, and children form an often impregnable rear guard. An affair may thrive for a while on its implicit disadvantages, like a guerrilla army. But if it loses, it loses everything. Unlike a marriage, there are no reserve troops, no stores, no headquarters, and no constitution to fall back on. There are no long-held lies or truths. To survive, the people in this dream of a free country must keep constantly on the move, never two nights sleeping in the same place; must constantly disband and regroup and the password has to be changed at every meeting.

Strategy, persistence, imagination, patience, trust in absence—the ability to bring everything to bear in a sudden short moment of engagement, to slip away without loss, to lie up in the long intervals without complaint or murmur: this was the field manual she and Graham had shared, the handbook of their affection. And I praised her for that, for her skill in this campaign, for we must all hope for the success of passion, just as we must suffer its ruthless ways and means. To possess the quality at all is to possess it too abundantly, to willingly betray one person so to fulfill it with another.

She had had an affair. She had managed it well. It had begun quite simply, casually no doubt, in a room somewhere, a visit to someone or at a party. And once the mark had been made, a dam of mutual interest against the indifference of the world, love had grown and spread out behind them like a lake—over half a continent, through half a dozen years. So many women would have botched the whole thing long before, in a fraction of the space, would have turned the delicate business into a nightmare for everyone concerned. But she had pursued it tenaciously—sometimes, surely, recklessly—yet kept the balance perfectly. I was surprised that nothing had gone wrong until now, that so deep and passionate a layer of her personality had gone unnoticed for so long: by her husband, her friends, the gossips everywhere. It was almost as if, like Graham, like any of our sort who inhabit permanent cover, she had conducted this real business of her life with all the assiduity of a master spy, like an agent whose marriage is nothing more than a deep cover for his real activities.

We left the museum and crossed back into Central Park. We were still walking. She wound the red and white football scarf about herself again and we moved up a short wooded slope toward a high wire fence. Beyond it lay a reservoir, a large mirror dumped in the middle of the dirty city, ruffled in the clear, blowy weather, vibrating gently with skyscrapers, flocks of sea gulls far away patterning it like bits of torn paper as they floated and glided over it.

This woman with a boy's scarf and expensive suede coat, with an impeccable Foreign Office husband, just the right number of zero population children, an apartment in the East Fifties—all of it was so studiously correct, so much in the new convention. She had all the rare finesse of a Park Avenue debutante who has passed thirty without a sigh, the skin fed with expensive lotions, hunger pampered with the right foods, at the right time, in the best auberges; the body massaged, formally and at night, in all the right places. There was, too, the untended confidence, something she tidied up now and then, brought up to date like a passport, in the happy social toils she made about midtown Manhattan: a beautiful person, a genuine ornament among the fun people.

She gave at a glance all the evidence of a graceful shallowness, a sense of tinkering with life, a surface concern; of days made up of exclusive engagements arranged through long telephone calls, noted in gilt-edged diaries, and experienced precisely, thirty minutes past the hour, each hour, on most evenings: drinks in a penthouse garden overlooking the park, dinner at La Cote Basque, and dancing at Arthur's later. But never a drink too many, a row with the waiter, or music with the wrong man.

And yet none of this was true, not a moment of it; everything was different in her. All this sophistication was truly skin-deep. I knew this; I supposed Graham must have as well. But I doubted if anyone else did. Her real existence had been carried out far from these glittering props. Her thoughts, her whole being, began when she had finished balancing the invitations and place names for dinner in Manhattan, and began instead to balance airline flights from Nairobi and old friends in Zambia against a meeting with her lover on Lake Malawi. She had never properly lived in the smart places: their apartment in the East Fifties, somewhere exclusive in Wimbledon, or an old-fashioned farmstead in the Colonies. These had been no more than poste restante addresses, where her husband or friends might reach her between her real purpose in life: the odyssey she'd made through hotel bedrooms and national parks with another man.

But why had the other man been with the KGB?

"Graham, of course, didn't know what your husband did, what he really does?" I asked her. It was useful having the answers, the original source, so close to hand. An official investigation into the whole business, asking the same questions, would never have succeeded in a thousand years.

"He knew he was in government. Of course he did."

"But just as a civil servant?"

"You called it the 'classic position' didn't you? Well it was. He didn't tell me he was in British Intelligence. I didn't tell him my husband was."

"How did you first meet him? How did you come to be at that African party in Westminster in 1965?"

"Home leave in London. We'd come back from Nairobi that summer. Guy had connections with all the African desks in London—at the FO, the COI, with the embassies. We were invited. One's always meeting people at parties, I'm afraid. Isn't one?"

"I'm sorry to pry."

"Fine. Go ahead. Fill in the spaces. You can't imagine everything, can you. Even you?"

She was quizzical then, turning to look at me against the metal-blue water, a serious half-smile threatening the open American face. I noticed how completely she could change her expression, what a distance there was between her normally uncommitted, even naive looks—too beautiful to touch, like a toothpaste or Coke advertisement in an old *National Geographic* magazine—and the deep lines of knowledge and loss she could take on in an instant, as though a map of Europe had suddenly been overlaid on one of the New World.

"He was interested in paintings, wasn't he?"

"Yes," she said, "he is."

"Modern painting. I'm afraid I'm not much good at it."

"Well, come on, for God's sake. You can't double for him all the way. You're not even like him, physically I mean. I wonder why they ever chose you to impersonate him? Anyone who'd ever met Graham would know you were a phony straight away."

She had an uncomfortable ability with her innocuous banter, taking you straight from trivialities to a leading question. I had thought to quiz her, without her knowing. But she was doing the same thing, more successfully, with me.

She said, "It can't be anything very serious, whatever your London people are up to, if they chose you for the job. The only thing you have in common with George Graham is his name. *Who* are you, Mr. Graham?"

Two policemen rode past us on two big chestnut mares. All four of them looked Irish. She turned and stared back at them, over her shoulder. "Someone in London must have thought you had a lot in common with George," she went on, "mustn't they? If not in looks, then in something else, something more important, where looks didn't matter. Career, let's say. Maybe your curriculum vitae matches his in some way, your personal background. Why choose you otherwise? There's nothing in a name. But shared experiences—

that's another thing. Suppose you and he had done some of the same kinds of things, lived in the same places, knew the same people: then someone who didn't know what George looked like, but knew his background, would take you for him, as soon as you confirmed all the other details."

"I can't stop your imagination. You're becoming a detective as well."

"George's main career was in the Middle East, not Africa, you know. He had fluent Arabic but not much Swahili. He was teaching with the British Council—in Beirut, Cairo, Alexandria—all through the fifties, before I met him. But you've never been within a million miles of those places, have you?"

Again, the suddenly overlaid smile that was not a smile but the shadow of knowledge—as though, without my saying a word, I had confirmed something for her which she had long suspected.

"No, not within a million miles," I said.

But it was no use. She could spot a lie at the same distance.

We walked all the way around the reservoir, coming out of the park somewhere in the West Nineties. A few blocks up, a small Protestant church, wedged long ago between huge high-rise apartment buildings, looked out over the trees and grass, its nineteenth-century steeple insignificant in the deep crevasse. The play-school was in the basement, through some heavy oak doors, down cold steps. The church above seemed to have forgotten its function long ago. Prayer books lay on the pews, as if they'd been left there by mistake, the only objects not sold in an auction a year before. But downstairs it was bright and warm, the area partitioned with long colored curtains which ran about on overhead runners, displaying one group of infants, hiding another, like Chinese boxes.

"Mrs. Jackson, Mr. Jackson, Hi! Nice to see you." a young woman said in too affable a tone, I thought, until I remembered she was American. I was in America. Good humor was the premier badge of citizenship here. No matter what disasters happened elsewhere—in bed, in Vietnam, with the blacks, or whatever—a smile was the steeply inflated currency of the country, a cure for every ill.

"You didn't bring the children?" the pert little woman asked too curiously, looking up at us, wide-eyed through saucer-size smoked glasses. Children, she seemed to suggest, would have committed us, like a prepayment, and as it was we might have been about to waste her time.

"No," Helen Jackson said, not rudely, but saying no more, so that the effect was almost the same. She could disrupt an untoward enquiry in an instant, I realized, and I wondered at my own good fortune earlier.

We wandered around, through the curtains and partitions, gazing at mysterious colored designs on the walls, puzzling educational shapes, and strange toys which the children played with confidently.

"What should I call you then?" Helen said, when we were by ourselves, looking at a little girl massaging her face with a bright poster paint, like soap. "You're not George Graham. Or Guy Jackson."

"The Third Man?"

"Yes. The whole thing is nonsense enough." The child came toward us with the pot of paint, holding it as an offering in both hands above her face, looking up at us silently. It seemed she was intent on sharing the mess with us. We went on again, behind another curtain like a maze, to a group playing with a basket full of fancy clothes, dressing up and discarding them carefully, like fastidious actors.

"You said you were married. Weren't there children?"

"No. We never got that far."

"She was in the same business, you told me—never time to get to bed?"

"Oh, we managed that all right. We did that."

"It's over now, I take it?"

"Yes. You can take it."

"A 'husband and wife' team, isn't it called. That must have been something. I didn't think such things really existed."

"Oh yes—the Krogers. . . ." But I couldn't think of anyone else.

"You must believe a lot in what you do. Mixing work and play like that—for the 'cause.' "

"Dedicated, you mean."

"Yes. You don't look the sort that's just in it for the money."

"What's your husband in it for? Not the money, I'm sure. But money for others. He believes in the West, doesn't he? A million dollars a minute for everyone who can grab it."

"No, he's just an intelligence officer. A professional. You'll see. You're the one who really believes in it all, or who doesn't believe a damn. I'm not sure which yet."

"I'm just a professional too. Doing a job that I don't much like. But do well enough."

"No, you don't do it well enough, that's the whole point. You're only doing it because you coincide with Graham in some way."

"If I told you all about myself would that make you feel better? If I told you how different I'was from him?"

"It might. But that wouldn't be altogether true either. Because you aren't that different from him. Oh, I don't mean physically; you're nothing like him in that way. But you share a sense of folly with him—treating the world as a spectator sport, booing and cat-calling everybody from your small corner."

She annoyed me with her insight. "Expectations lying in the gutter, you mean? A wrong turning taken long ago? I've heard that before. A lot of people feel that these days: a sense of folly. Liberals without a belief in progress. We're common as clay. That means nothing, sharing that with Graham."

Luckily the little woman came back at that moment and started lecturing us on how their approach at the nursery differed from Spock's: "You know, I think it's that we're much more tidy here, not that awful running around the place, doing what they want, allowing them to make a mess of everything. . . ."

She hadn't seen the child with the poster paint.

A sense of folly, indeed. How right Helen Jackson was. I thought of Harper's silly, unformed Colonial face, never

grown beyond pint pots with the rest of the Earl's Court
Australians; and McCoy's Northern disappointment, his
maiden aunt profundities. The hale-fellow-well-met and the
forgotten Puritan. What a duo they made, two St. Georges
in dark glasses, holding up all the values of the West. Yes, it
had been a spectator sport for me, as I'd expected it had been
for Graham with the Russians. But there was a difference,
though. For both of us it was a game where the players
would suddenly spring up from the arena, find you out from
all the others, and savage you. That was in the rules as well.
Graham had been caught when he must have thought himself forever free, like a Fenian traitor murdered in America
years afterwards, a world away from Dublin. And I was waiting now, a clear target on the skyline, waiting for this Stayer,
who might approach me amicably as arranged—or kill me.
One could laugh at the folly but one was part of it; that was
the snag. The fools had no manners; for them the end would
always justify the means. They had no inhibitions.

"Yes," the woman chattered on obsessively, "some people feel Dr. Spock may be to *blame* for the drug scene, for
Vietnam, by encouraging too permissive an attitude toward
the young over the past generation. . . ."

I thought again of running, before the Stayer had time
to fix me in his sights, for good or ill—run with the few dollars I had, out of the firing line and into the anonymous
multiplicity of life. Perhaps I could take up teaching somewhere again. Nothing could be more anonymous than that,
an usher in some backward place in an even more backward
school.

But I felt the heat of the basement just as I touched on
thoughts of escape; the long morning's walk began to tell,
the legs already feeling wasted, strong with the rumor of
coming weakness after the years of inactivity in Durham.

"Discipline, organization," the bossy woman went on,
pulling on the words like a harsh bell, "not through force,
but by firmness and example. We try to let them see that
there is a *limitation*—from the beginning."

She pulled back a long curtain without warning, displaying all one end of the basement. The rollers on the ceil-

ing shrieked briefly, ringing as though bones were being cut behind my eardrums.

And then I was falling into the open space, as if a wall had given way in a tall building. I put my arms up to ward off the blow, my wrists trembling against my eyes. There were some old pews lined up against the end wall, children playing among them, and either they were coming closer to me or I was walking toward them. I couldn't tell. Then both movements were happening together so that we seemed to converge.

The children were lined up in the pews now, staring at me silently, sitting properly in their desks. There was a blackboard just behind me. I had chalk in my hand and was laboriously explaining the implications of the three witches in *Macbeth*. The heat poured down into the room from above, from a sun that had perched for years just above the rafters, and the smell rose all about me—the dry dust of concrete and lime wash from long-burnt tropical buildings.

It was fifth-form English at the college in Cairo, fifteen years before. Samia, the bright girl in the front row, had her hand up—she always knew the answers; her mother was English, married to an Egyptian engineer from the refinery in Suez. Amin, in the back row, the tall twenty-five-year-old schoolboy, had his hand up as well, making faces, preparing to embark on one of his elaborately wearisome jokes. The headmaster, mad Dr. El Sayid, would be dictating the afternoon's business to us in the staff room in fifteen minutes: "Marlow: football for you, on the lower field. The junior houses, Port Tewfik and Suez. . . ." And at last, after school, the evening, the empty evening, with Bridget. The drive into the city along the Nile, the pyramids on the far side of the river cut out in soft charcoal against the huge orange tablecloth of falling light; meeting her beyond the pillars of the Semiramis lobby, in the bar there, over *sudanis* and gin, while the air-conditioning under the floorboards trembled in fits and starts, swaying the old room like mild water under a ship: meeting her, so quickly ruining the meeting, arguing with her. . . .

I must have fallen into the first row of pews. I remember the children scattering, some laughing, others cry-

ing. I felt like a bird swooping on them, falling out of a
huge blue sky, a kite over the Nile above Gezira Island,
attacking them. That was all.

I was sitting in one of the pews myself, collar opened,
the smoked saucer spectacles peering at me, handing me a
glass of water. Helen Jackson was behind her. They were
both talking, but I couldn't take in a word of what they said.
The vision of those years in Cairo was still there, astonishingly real, like a dream remembered immediately on waking.
I felt if I got up then and there and walked out of the room
my feet would immediately sink into the desert, the fields of
berseem clover around Maadi where the school had been,
the hard cracked earth of the football field. I would float
away down the feeder canal beyond the last goal post, past
the line of ragged Scots fir, sink happily into the murky
water where the bilharzia snails lurked, host to that small
fatiguing worm which could now freely feast on me as I
trailed away to join the river.

I was suddenly filled, completely inhabited, by this past
—these days of teaching and loving, before spying and marriage. I could feel the weight and texture of each of those
years, as if the years had been stones in my hand, each one
a clear representation of the pain, the pleasure, the ultimate
stupidity of that time.

I knew then I'd never teach again, never run back that
way. I wanted none of it, nothing, except one thing: the
chance now of making good these lost opportunities, the
wrong turnings taken long ago. And then, I thought, I've
heard this idea somewhere before, quite recently. Someone
had said it to me. Who? I drank the water.

"Are you all right?" Helen Jackson looked at me.

"Yes, yes. Just faint, that's all. The journey, culture
shock. Wheel said it might happen. Lucky I wasn't up at a
high window."

The curtains had been pulled across again, covering up
the rest of the basement, isolating us. One of the other
teachers had quickly taken charge of the children, distract-
ing them with a new game. I could hear them moving about,

enacting some nursery rhyme, with one child running around in a circle, chanting:

> I sent a letter to my love
> And on the way I dropped it,
> And one of you has picked it up
> And put it in your pocket.
> It wasn't you, it wasn't you, it wasn't you—
> But it was YOU!

Then there were the sounds of mad scampering around and around the room. "*I sent a letter to my love. . . .*" I remembered then. It had been in her letter to Graham, something about the past: 'We think we have experienced the past . . ." Yes, that was it. ". . . because, willy nilly, we have lived through it. But there were hundreds of turnings . . . which we knew about then but never took. I want to take them now." That was it, I. was sure; that was her real absorption, this cartography of previous time. And I wanted to ask her about it at once. Why did she want this? What was her old life? What had gone wrong in it? At that moment all this seemed the most relevant business in the world, against which our earlier preoccupations about Graham paled. I hadn't realized it until then, that this was what she and I really had in common: not just Graham, but a passionate attachment to an unfulfilled past.

We left the basement, moving past the suddenly quiet children, the little woman shepherding us like refugees being taken to a railhead. On the way out into the street I nearly fell again, into the arms of a man coming in the doorway, a tall fellow with a Pancho Villa moustache.

"Sorry," he said, "I am sorry," as though it had been his fault. He was English.

"People from everywhere. They must do well," I said to Helen, doing my collar up in the bright rushing air.

"They do. But I didn't. I'll find somewhere else. I'd sooner they didn't go to nursery school at all. All these theories. And tough madames. Hungry?"

"What?" I was still dazed, with the bright light now as much as anything.

"Eating. *Food*. Fainting like that. You know, you're thin as a rake."

"I should 'look after myself' you mean? That's very English. Like a landlady. What about my finding an apartment?"

"Okay, you don't have to eat. I should care."

"No. I'm sorry."

We stood on the sidewalk outside the church—arguing, the childless couple again, married too long. No, I thought, not that again, not that.

I said, "Yes, I'd like something. Maybe I could do the apartment business another day? I'm exhausted."

"There's a French place lower down on Columbus. Norman, or Breton. I'm not sure. It's supposed to be good. Shall we try it?"

The taxi cruised down Columbus. I'd not yet become used to the long straight avenues or the size of the huge cars that floated about the place, gliding in and out of lanes like boats. Everything I'd learned was so clearly from a smaller, more careful world. The huge heights, the long lengths and depths of Manhattan, the hard grid of the city —there was no subtlety but it spoke of things that I'd missed hearing in a long time. It said: "Things are as they seem here." It was blunt. There was no mystery, beauty, or imagination about it. And for once—that day, the light showering down and the huge tin cigars floating about around us—I liked that. The lines of shoddy buildings and transient, three-dollar hotels, shops with steel gratings over the windows, the taxi doors locked on the inside—one knew the risks here at least, the facts, knew where you stood. And it was almost a balm, this horror, this open wound of the island, after all the polite murder, the old-school-tie men in Whitehall, their graceful houses in S.W. 1. If you died here, I felt, it would be in open combat; if you were happy in the city it would be a condition truly earned, without provisos, conventions, compromises, traditions, a true state, free from the drag of the past.

"You're prickly. As well as thin," she said as though I was fruit for bottling.

"No. It's just the old clichés. They weary me."

"But you *are* thin as a rake. You don't look to have eaten properly in years."

She was onto me again, Sherlock Holmes inspecting the mud on my boots, seemingly caring only for the present, but anxious really for the past: who was I? What had happened to George Graham? But now I had the same ambitions. Not just "How had she met George Graham?" But, who was *she*?" I wanted to go right back. I was as anxious for her past as she was for mine. We'd become lovers in that respect.

"All right," I said. "Let's make up for it then. Let's make up for it."

4

The restaurant was small and crowded—the Brittany du Soir. There were coats of arms from the region and photographs of old Tour de France cyclists on the walls, and dark, diamond-paned, leaded windows which completely drowned the light from the street.

We had come to some happy spice island moored just off a barbarous shore. The air was warm with strange savories, something sharply burned, thyme crushed with lemon, the perfume of many freshly opened bottles. I thought of my four years on old mutton in Durham, and of that moment several weeks before when I had struggled with McCoy in "E" wing, yelling at him, trying to punish him for all the lost time. And I felt then that I'd been right to shout about it, to try and kill McCoy for it. Here it all was, at last the recompense.

We waited for a table at a small bar by the curtained doorway, almost a zinc *comptoir* in the old fashion, with the French girl who had managed the hats and coats now offering the drinks. The whole place was such a genuine import, with a signed photograph of Georges Carpentier behind the bar, that I thought when the girl came back she might say: "Monsieur, vous desirez . . . ?" But she didn't. She simply looked at me with a query in her awkward smile.

"What would you like while we wait," I said, "a Pernod or some other rash drink?"

Helen Jackson got a long thin cigarette out of her bag and fiddled with it. "Whiskey, please," she replied.

"It may not go with the wine, that's if you like wine. Grain and grape."

"So you have clichés too, do you?"

"I think I'll try a Pernod. It's years since I've had one."

"Whiskey, please—just with water. Does that make it any better?"

I lit her cigarette. "Fine."

The French girl turned away to arrange things. We stood there—she at an angle to the bar, elbow on the wood; I was facing it squarely, leaning against it, both arms outstretched. The drinks came and with them a plate of black olives. I raised my glass, but the word "cheers" seemed out of place. I'd denounced clichés.

"Cheers," she said in an English way, with that thought-reading ability of hers.

"All right. You win."

We drank, saying nothing. We had made a silence in the noisy place, intended and happy. Waiting. White clouds stormed slowly in my glass, the medicine of anis on my tongue. Zibib. Cairo on the hottest days when the coldest Stella beer did nothing but increase the sweat. I picked up an olive and bit into it decisively.

"Sorry." I pushed the saucer toward her and she took one without a word. The pips started to pile up on another dish. We drank. She smoked. I smoked too. It struck me suddenly that she liked smoking and drinking, as a man might—not as a necessary social attribute, to survive bores in smart drawing rooms, but as something genuinely enjoyed, for its own sake. Here was a minute crack, perhaps, in her surface perfection, a happy fault in the otherwise so carefully tended geography of her life. Of course, one might have said that she appealed to me because I shared these tastes, because she was simply a drinking man's woman, a half bottle girl. And perhaps there was some truth in that—sisters under the skin in a thirsty kingdom. Certainly her appeal had begun. It started just then, at the bar. I know, because of all the descriptions I must make here, I feel that the small business of her just standing there, carefully chewing olives before lunch, is the most important, the most necessary.

You will have to try and see what I saw—exactly. No other woman's face will do, or an approximation. It will have to be she alone; the easy bearing, the precise falls of flesh and cloth: the particular slope of shoulder, the sunflower-colored Donald Davis dress, the loose sleeves crushed against the counter, fingers resting on the glass. It will have to be that particular hand, fairly flat and wide with ordinary fingers. Yet the long wrist, longer than most, disappearing into the yellow tunnel of wool. And you may not have another face but this one—the one staring at me lightly now, this face that has aged without telling anybody, yet which is a curtain behind which some people have been told everything. A naive face that immediately takes on depth when you look at it properly, the large eyes gathering knowledge, the long cut of the mouth, sometimes so formless, becoming firm with intention—the whole expression grasping definition, meaning, purpose from nowhere, so that in the passage of a few seconds you have looked at two separate people.

You will have to see this warm envelope of skin, the stamp of bright colors, the lines of life all meeting eagerly on this one moment of time, a particular presence cutting deeply into present experience, giving herself to it, being carried along with it. And yet for all this happy commitment to the immediate, a mysteriously inhabited envelope as well, trailing long sheet anchors in the past—not the completely buoyant spirit but one which, as I had discovered from her letters, was as deeply linked with previous time as to any present moment of whiskey and olives.

I had been surprised initially by the force of her letters to Graham—as one must be by the intense fact, the unalterable evidence of another's passion—and surprised again by the glimpsed countries beyond, the times and places of its being.

And now, waiting for lunch, I was able to see in Helen Jackson the two people together properly—the innocent and the old—and feel their real weight for the first time, as through a stereoscopic device where a quite ordinary photograph, a landscape of hills, say, will take on completely new values, where it ceases to be a flat representation, one truth at one time, but becomes a succession of different truths going back over many different times.

She looked at me and I at her—just as the door opened and someone outside shouted "Hello," just as the girl left us for the coats and hats, just as the waiter came and told us our table was ready. And that is the moment you must see: a look where language is well lost; where one starts to live, feel life, under the impetus of another person's regard; after which, with such shared regard, two people must then live differently; where speech will be in a new tongue, the whole grammar of exchange made afresh.

We drank Sancerre to begin with, a year old. The smell of it was so fresh and rich that one feared to taste it and lose touch with a vineyard—the fruit-filled aroma of chalk soil and rain on some small hill that blew out of the glass, moist and chill. And at last we seemed to be able to talk of other things besides George Graham.

She must have noticed my unusual application to the food, sensed something of my four-year denials, for I could barely restrain myself over the menu nor moderate the attack I made on the meal when it came. She said, watching me: "Food is going back, isn't it? I mean, the basic reassurance—of one's right to greed and sympathy, like a baby. It's just a chore for most of us, most of the time, something to fill the day with. But you eat the other way, as if your whole life depended on the meal. As if it was your last."

"You mean 'Do this in memory of me'? Christ, I'm just eating." I looked at her, pausing over the blue point oysters.

"Yes, but not the gourmet or the gourmand, that's not you. You eat as if you were—as if the whole food thing was something you'd lost."

"Symbolic of good fellowship and warmth? That's a pretty common reason for going to restaurants."

"Have you lost that?"

"Maybe. Like Rip Van Winkle."

I let the oyster lie in my mouth for a moment, then

bit it gently before it slipped away. "Food is a homecoming, if that's what you meant when you said eating was 'going back.' A house that's always there, even when everything else has disappeared. A constant. It doesn't disappoint."

I sipped the sea water and lemon juice from the last oyster shell and the waiter took our plates away. We had ordered the plat du jour: gigot d'agneau de beaumaniere. I didn't know quite what it meant. But apparently it was the main smell in the room, the leg of lamb cooked in pastry somehow—with veal and herbs, the waiter had tried to explain—and the smell was good. The Sancerre was sharp and cold as ever but now its taste of vineyards was mixed with those of the sea and of the astringent lemon, and when you drank it, it was neither the sea nor the wine that was in your mouth but some new flavor, echoing down the throat, indeterminate and frail.

The waiter carved the gigot from a small table beside us. The beaumaniere consisted of a parcel of brown, eggbasted pastry which enclosed the leg of lamb which in turn —the bone removed—enclosed a black stuffing of mushrooms, pork, and veal. Each time he sliced it, the knife fell through it all without resistance. Afterward, he carefully spooned up the debris of herbs and stuffing and laid it over the slices of meat. Nice, but a fiddly way to cook a leg of lamb, I thought.

"You wrote about that to George Graham, didn't you?" I asked. "I'm sorry to drag it up again—but it seemed to absorb you."

"What?"

"This 'going back' thing. About not wanting to relive the past—that it had nothing to do with nostalgia—but to 'live now all that was unlived then.' I think you said, 'What was so *un*lived then?' You've lived pretty fully, surely?' Yet you seem to see yourself as somehow unawakened: the sleeping beauty, Rip Van Winkle."

"It's too long, that story."

"Of course it is. You're all of thirty-five."

"Well, if it's not nostalgic, it's unrealistic, isn't it?"

"Why? Wanting not to be unhappy with a man? That's not unrealistic. That's exactly what people mean when they want to change, to divorce: the chance to live what was unlived, to move away from an unlivable life. You wrote about that to Graham too!"

"It wasn't all that, not all to do with people. Not with living better or with living with one person rather than another. It was as much to do with a *generally* unlivable life. And that *was* unrealistic—to want to fix that. The general situation can't be changed so easily. There's no divorce from it, other than through madness perhaps."

"Not divorce—but you can change it, can't you? Change the 'generally unlivable.' That's not unrealistic." And then I suddenly thought: *"You're political, aren't you? I wouldn't have thought it."*

She ground some pepper on her gigot, strong though its flavors were already. "No, it's not that, nothing to do with Women's Lib."

"I didn't mean that, I meant—simply politics. How should we all be living, how to make that change."

She looked at me sharply, as though I was a child and had found something I didn't know was dangerous and was holding it toward her.

I thought of Graham's Marxism, and the image she had given him once of the old-fashioned colonial Tory—their arguments about the future of happiness and the future of Africa. Yes, it seemed as if it might be a long story, but not too long, not for me.

She said: "It's not only the poor who want to change the world, you know—or the intellectuals."

I looked at her dress, her make-up, her bearing, all the rich and careful choices about her person. "I know," I said, "It's just a surprise—finding the rich wanting revolution."

As soon as I'd said this, I didn't know quite what I meant. I couldn't follow the implications of it. She noticed this momentary confusion and stepped in before I could clarify the thought.

"I don't want revolution. My God, I wanted that old bore of a thing—to be at ease, happy. That's all. And I've spent time thinking of all the ways there are toward those ends. Some of the ways are political. Obviously. You don't just sit still crying 'poor little me.' You do something about it. You make the effort, you *give,* if you want any return.

Well, almost all that sort of outward effort is political in some degree, though it may not appear so. Your happiness, or at least mine, depends a lot on society's."

"The personal and the political, they must come together for you in some way? Like some people, they say, can only make love in moving vehicles. It's very difficult."

She laughed a little. "Why do you suddenly see me as a political animal, rather than as just . . . an animal? That's the way I'd like to come together. If you want to know."

"That passage in your letter to Graham about Africa, what else could one think? It's not an expected topic between lovers surely? The relative demerits of the old colonialism and the new imperialism in the Dark Continent. I was surprised by it in the letter, and even more so now, seeing you: rich Manhattan girl, apartment in the East Fifties, married to a diplomat. That's not the expected background for a person who suggests that every act has a political relevance, who feels that individual happiness must depend on the general well-being of society. That's not usual at all. I thought people like you rang the bell for a drink when they felt out of sorts."

The smile came again, the naive one, in which knowledge and experience had been dismantled and hidden.

"That's pretty old-fashioned of you. Where have you been locked up all these years—the Tower of London? You seem to have the old chivalrous idea of women: helpless creatures you have to lay down cloaks for. Does money mean you can't have a mind? Does sex—I mean the gender—debar me from political interest, or action for that matter? Come on. I'll really start to believe in Women's Lib if you go on like that. The world has changed since you put your head in the sand, wherever that was. I'm not trying to change it, I'm just part of the change." She looked at me closely. "You've been away somewhere a long while, that's the feeling you give me. The way you eat, as if you'd not eaten properly in years. And talking to me; and the way you look at me, as if you'd just emerged from a bout of some strange sleeping sickness and the last woman you'd seen was in corsets and curlers."

"Rip Van Winkle again, you mean? 'Change and decay

all around I see.' Or something. No, it's not that. I've just been in England. This is America; it's new to me. That's all. A little culture shock. I told you."

"Of course," she said suddenly, as though she had just then realized the sum of all our talk and was diagnosing an illness we both shared but refused to admit to, "the most tiresome thing about both of us is our indulgence in the past—and in the future. And the little action we give to now. We miss out on that vital link: the present, the here-and-now."

"Was George Graham like that too?"

"No. He was good at all three. He had hopes and memories everywhere, but he never let them slow him up."

"That's just temperament, isn't it? Other people can complete us. We may have something special for them. What do you think you had for him?"

We were halfway through a bottle of light Beaujolais. I poured her another glass and it bubbled slightly. The chatter in the dark room was dying about us as people moved out, back to work.

"I'm sure I just had all the ordinary things for him. We didn't have to talk about it. We had trust. We knew each other very well—and that didn't kill the other thing, you know, the excitement. Just saying that now, it sounds extraordinary, not ordinary. Of course affairs are far easier than most marriages, I know that. That's really the whole point of them. But this one lasted. It might just as well have been a marriage."

"Yes, six years. They don't usually last that long, I suppose. How was it your husband never came to find out about it, even suspect it? Or did he? Six years is a long time to pretend; and gallivanting around East Africa with Graham, how did you manage that without his knowing?"

"We separated for six months in the mid-sixties, a year after we moved to Nairobi. I went around East Africa with Graham then. Afterward my mother was ill before she died, upstate here, and I came back to help look after her."

"What brought you back to your husband? Why didn't you stay apart, get a divorce, marry Graham—or whatever you wanted to do together?"

"Back in your best Sherlock Holmes mood, aren't you?"

I thought I might have gone too far. But no, there came another of those easy smiles that she was so ready with, as if the worst of life could be dispelled by shining teeth.

"I was 'with child.' Two childs in fact," she said, lightly happily. "And they were his, not Graham's."

"Twins?"

"Yes. Sarah and Sheila. Twins. They're almost five. They brought us together again, like the good books say. But it wasn't really a happy ending. It began to die again, I'm afraid." She paused, almost visibly casting her mind back over the marriage. "Though there are many ways I'm perfectly fine with him, when he's at ease, and not trying to possess me like a life insurance policy."

"Your husband doesn't look the unconfident sort. Rather the opposite."

They'd brought some cheese, brie and Caprice des Dieux, and a big wicker basket of fruit. She chose brie and an apple.

"He's not. He has bouts of manic jealousy, that's all— when he wakes up out of his work. He's very English. He had to feel he owned me before he could love me, had to see me as a dependent relative before he could bed me. He's frightened of me, I think, but won't ever admit this. He never trusted me, because he didn't *dare* to know me, couldn't face what he might find. We were always that little bit off-beam with each other. And, of course, soon that means you're going in totally different directions, heading straight for two different sets of rocks."

"Yes, the oldest journey in the world."

Coffee came. She sniffed and then tasted some of my calvados, not wanting any herself. "Burnt apples," she said listlessly. She had tired of all her lighter moods, of all those airs of bright invitation when, before lunch with whiskey in her hand, she had seemed so at ease in the sway of the world. She had dragged herself back into her past, and I had helped her willingly, and I regretted it now, ashamed at my curiosity that had dulled her. At the same time, though, I felt just as clearly that somehow she needed that past, to explain it, relive it. She needed it more than drink; it was her drug, her tipple, and I had encouraged her, as she had wanted, in this real and secret excess.

She lit one of her long, thin cigarettes. "Now you know it all, really. Rather a sordid little tale. I should have left him—organized the whole thing better. There were the children, I know. But we could have arranged something before about them, if I'd really wanted. I was tired. And I shouldn't have been tired," she said with sudden energy. "I was tired of another change after moving around the place for ten years. And he's moving again now. Quite soon. Back to England, some new posting."

"London?"

"No. Something in the country. A Foreign Office job, to do with communications. In the Cotswolds, Cheltenham. Do you know it?"

"No."

"No. Anyway, there's no good reason for leaving him now. Our mutual friend, Mr. Graham—he's disappeared. Dead for all I know. Or dead for me, at any rate. I'm not likely to find him."

"I'm sorry."

"Yes, you told me. You're sorry. I know that. But I don't know anything else about you."

"Wait. Wait and see."

"Wait and see what? You turned up from nowhere. You're just as likely to disappear in the same way. The March Hare."

"Oh, I've come from somewhere, all right. And if I disappear I won't know any more than you about it, I can tell you. I'm in the dark as much as you are. I'm not the conjuror in all this. I told you; I'm just the trick."

She believed me. It wasn't difficult. "Jesus God. I'd sooner you weren't. Tricks, games—I'd sooner we were all out of that and could find some living to do."

"Yes."

Her face had become drawn. Nothing stirred in it, asleep, apart from the open eyes. I could sense very well her trouble. I was the false Prince Charming who could not kiss her back to life. George Graham had been that figure, the key to her bright future. I had set her adrift in the dark, far from land, and delivered her over to all the old dooms. I had condemned her to sudden age in the middle of a perfect maturity.

She left me outside the restaurant and took a cab crosstown to see some friends. And it was then, just afterward, that I saw the man on the other side of the avenue trying too eagerly to hail a cab going in the same direction. He had stepped a yard off the pavement into the cross street, with the lights green behind his back. The cab driver, shooting along with his foot down, didn't give him a chance. The near fender hit the man in the legs, spinning him over like a tenpin.

I ran across to the accident, the taxi stalled in the middle of the crossroads, the body lying at the corner a few yards from the gutter—a tall fellow in a dark mackintosh, hatless, fair-haired. And the first thing I saw, before I'd even noticed the twisted leg tucked in behind him, was the moustache, the fair-haired Pancho Villa whiskers. It was the man who had bumped into us two hours before, forty blocks uptown, as we left the church.

Coincidence? I hardly considered this after my conversation with Helen Jackson ten minutes before. The man had been following us all morning. And there must almost certainly be two men involved, I thought, if it was a proper surveillance: one for each of us in case we separated, or just a second man to relieve the first. We'd been about the city now for nearly five hours.

I could have lost him in the crowd that had gathered on the sidewalk. But I wanted to see if I could identify any second pursuer. He'd surely come, if he existed, to help his colleague, I thought. Or would he have tried to follow Helen Jackson uptown? A difficult decision. But I thought he'd have realized it was too late to go after her. If there was a second man, he'd soon be here, somewhere in the crowd.

So I hadn't long. I bent over the figure in the road, pulled his wallet out and emptied the contents over his chest. Then I started to pick all the pieces of paper up

again and put them back. Halfway through, I found his
card: James Moloney, with the address and phone number
of a New York private detective agency. I pushed it up my
sleeve just as another man joined me, a man with tufts of
white hair sticking out from beneath a small black homburg
and carrying a pack of sandwiches. And then the cab driver
came over. The three of us leaned over the body. Pancho
Villa was unconscious. There was a graze on the side of his
head, but no bleeding. No more than a broken leg perhaps.

"Jesus, that guy is lucky to be alive," the cab driver
said. "Don't move him. What are you doing?"

The homburg man had seen the half-filled wallet on
his chest and was looking through it. "Just checking his
name and address," he replied, "and his Blue Shield card.
He's going to need it. Go phone a hospital. Where's the
nearest?"

"Hell, I don't know," the driver said. "Roosevelt, I
guess, up on Fifty-ninth. OK, you stay with him."

A police car had stopped over by the restaurant and
two patrolmen walked casually across the avenue towards
us. The cab was still in the middle of the crossroads.

"Where's the driver of that cab?" the first patrolman
shouted. "Let's get it the hell out of here."

"He's gone to phone the hospital," the homburg man
said. The first patrolman went to move the cab while the
second bent over the body. "Who is he? What's his name?"
He took his wallet and started shuffling through the papers
and a few folded bills inside.

I eased my way out of the crowd, hurried across the
avenue, and went back inside the restaurant. There was a
piece of clear glass in the center of the door and through it
I saw the homburg man in a moment, clear of the bunch of
people now, sandwiches still gripped in his hand, looking
wildly about for me. He was the second tail.

"Yes, sir?" The headwaiter came up behind me. "Did
you leave something?"

I patted my pockets. "Yes, I think I had a pack of cigarettes, I wonder if. . . ." I turned back and saw the homburg man running across the flow of cars on the avenue,
coming toward the restaurant.

But one of the policemen had seen him too, and now he was yelling across the avenue at the homburg man, waving a notebook. He followed him and stopped him just in front of the restaurant door. "Hey fella, you a friend of his?" The two men started to talk about the accident. "You know anything about him? They say you and another fellow saw it all happen—you were there from the start, the cabbie says. . . ."

The two men recrossed the avenue. I let them get back to the crush of people before going to the telephone booth at the back of the restaurant. "This is Moloney," I said, when I got through. "There's been some trouble on the Jackson job. The fella who ordered the surveillance—the husband isn't it, what's his name? Tall English fella. . . ."

"Yeah, it's the husband, sure it is," the other voice broke in. "Come on, Moloney, what's up?"

I started talking again but almost immediately cut myself off, letting a finger dance rapidly on the handset cradle.

5

"Who are they, then, if you say that our British SIS people over here aren't tailing me?"

"I don't know. I'll have one of our men try and check the man out at St. Luke's Hospital, if you like."

Guy Jackson fiddled with his big brassy wedding ring as we sat in his office. I could hardly keep my eyes off the nervous performance in a man otherwise so bland and cool.

"They may have someone following you," he said. "On orders from London, direct. But I've heard nothing about it. My instructions were simply to liaise with you, wait for information, if and when this Stayer chap made contact and gave you the names of the KGB men Moscow wants to check on."

"But you know all about me as well, don't you?" Not

George Graham, but Peter Marlow. I've just been let out of Durham jail."

"Yes. I know. Of course." He seemed puzzled for a moment, looking at me carefully as though the implications of this double identity had struck him for the first time only now.

"Had you ever heard of George Graham before?" I asked, "*The* George Graham. He spent a lot of time in East Africa. In Nairobi and round about."

"No. Why should I have? Why do you ask? It's a big place—East Africa."

"Small enough, too, for white people now. He was working over there quite a lot. Radio programs, documentary films, for the COI. A government department. You were in the Foreign Office. I thought you might easily have run across him."

"I was on an attachment in Nairobi—to the Kenyan government. I wasn't with the FO then."

"Yes, of course." The charade had gone far enough.

"Look," I said. "I'm sorry. I know who was tailing us this morning. Some New York private eye business. I found their card on the man, phoned them after the accident. Now governments don't hire private detectives agencies to do their surveillance for them." I paused. Jackson had stopped fiddling with his wedding ring. "But husbands do. Why don't you tell me? What were you having us tailed for?"

Guy Jackson smiled. He seemed as inappropriately suited to the role of jealous husband as to that of spy—his self-assurance so visible, like a silver spoon in his mouth.

"Jealousy is a terrible thing," he said flatly. He might have been describing the British weather.

"I know. She told me."

"You haven't wasted much time, have you?" He was suddenly brisk, affronted.

"Listen, I only met your wife yesterday. You don't think—"

"Oh, it can happen in far less time than that, Marlow," he broke in. "My wife can be in bed with someone within an hour of meeting them," he went on eagerly, as though commending one of her virtues.

"Women *can*, but seldom *do*." I laughed slightly. But he didn't take it well. I could see he was badly smitten. "It usually takes longer than that, even these days," I added, trying to placate him. But this idea of sex delayed pleased him no more than the idea of a quick bang, and he said almost angrily: "But in any case, it wasn't you. It was the real George Graham they were following."

I smiled again. How quickly this haughty man had tumbled into a world of bedroom farce—of sleuths, French maids, and trousers falling down—drawn to these mockeries of eavesdropping and double identity to avoid the tragedy of it all. And he was right: farce makes infidelity bearable; cauterizes it, cheapens it, brings a belly laugh to kill it. Guy Jackson had found the Iago he needed in the squalid truths of a private eye.

"But," I said, "you knew the real George Graham had been taken, two weeks ago in London, that I'd replaced him. London explained all that to you."

"I was still interested. It's become a habit."

"When did you first know about it, about him?"

"Six years ago, just after she first met him, on one of our leaves in London. And afterward in Nairobi, when we separated."

"You mean—you sent someone after them on that trip they made around East Africa?" I was really surprised.

"Yes, as far as anybody could follow them in the circumstances. It's pretty open country."

To say the least, I thought. Taking the territorial imperative too far altogether.

"God, what a habit," I said.

"A habit of our trade, Marlow, or just—a bad habit?" Jackson asked easily.

"Neither," I lied. "I understand the professional habit and the personal temptation well enough. I meant, what a habit in the circumstances. Your wife has been running around with a senior KGB officer for six years, and your private eyes never got that information for you."

"No, never. Just the evidence of personal, not a political infidelity," he said unctuously.

"And what do you think now? Don't you think she's involved politically with him as well?"

"No," he said firmly. "There's never been any evidence. Absolutely none. Just coincidence. Pure coincidence."

"I wish I could be as sure. I don't trust coincidence in this business. It was just a 'coincidence'—my own wife turning up in Moscow by chance one day—that sent me down for twenty-eight years."

Light pierced the gaps in the tall buildings to the west, bright crystal knives of afternoon sun. The air-conditioning sighed from grills beneath the sealed windows. I was tired again, suffocating in the false climate.

"I'm sorry," he said, perceiving my discomfort, "the windows don't open. Need a special key." He got up and turned the machinery down, then he came back toward me, clasping his hands piously. "If you want to be sure, why don't you try and find out yourself? You're in a much better position, after all, than any agency, government or private. You're George Graham, her lover." He paused, as if considering the excitement of the idea. "It must have been a cruel surprise when you turned up here and not him. She must be curious, to say the least, about your provenance, about what's happened to him. Doesn't that give you quite a lever with her?"

"Yes, I'd thought of that." What I really thought was that he wanted me to pimp for him now, to feed his jealous obsessions. "You forget, though, that's not what I'm here for—to carry on your private eyeing for you."

"Oh, I don't know—since you mention the political factor; this could be relevant to your job here: as well as being lovers she *might* just have been one of Graham's KGB contacts. Even the Stayer we're all looking for. It's worth a try —looking at the whole thing in that way," he said.

"You want it 'that way'? That she should turn out to be a KGB agent?"

"Of course not." He was suddenly backtracking. "We've children, a family. I've a career. All that would be ruined."

He sat down at his desk, picking up an FAO report, returning to his role as guardian of the world's conscience. "Well, she shouldn't know of all this in any case," he said.

"I'm sure she's never been politically involved with him. There's no need to chase after that hare. It was a bizarre thought, that's all. You understand—living with a woman who—" he paused, at a loss.

"Has so many other lives?"

"Yes," he nodded. "Exactly. One becomes prey to the worst emotions." He spoke like a Victorian paterfamilias tempted by a shop girl in the Bayswater Road. "And of course there's another point, Marlow. Without ever having been politically involved with him, she may, unwittingly, have passed on information about my work with the Foreign Office and so on. He may have used her."

"Nothing of that emerged when they interrogated him in London. I was told, specifically, that he wasn't involved with any women. Besides, London would have been on to you at once, surely, if he'd told them about her?"

"Yes, they would. I'd thought of that. I'm sure it was nothing more than a genuine relationship. All the worse, in one way, all the better in another. But we should keep it to ourselves in any case, and I'll call the man off. Forget the whole business."

He and I were joined in a conspiracy now, for of course London ought to have been informed of this development at once, whether it was pure coincidence or not. But that was his decision. He was the liaison officer; I was just the stalking horse. And how, I wondered, should anyone ever know the truth of their relationship? If London, with all their tortuous tricks, had failed even to extract the fact of her existence from Graham, how should Jackson and I ever expect to discover whether they had ever been anything more than lovers? Or find out, which we seemed to want even more, the exact nature and emotional weight of their love? That part of her was surely safe from all our prying eyes, an affair securely locked in time, as it was distant in Africa. She had lost that love herself; how should we ever find it?

I felt this so clearly then that she was safely beyond our grasp, saying good-bye to Jackson in his grand office—like a solicitor and client who have completed the sad formalities relevant to a dead friend's lost estate. And yet a week later a process started which was to lead me into Helen Jackson's old life; which was to animate her past as sharply as though someone had filmed it all—or at least written a script of it.

6

I had been asked to a reception for new members of the Secretariat given jointly by the U.S. government and the City of New York. The party was held on the top floor of the U.S. delegation's office opposite the UN building on First Avenue, a long room with a dreadfully slippery floor filled with a lot of awkward foreigners sliding about the place with tumblers of orange or tomato juice. It was an appalling occasion of well-meant hospitality and formal speeches, which instead of all being delivered at once, which might have saved matters, came in fits and starts throughout the hour.

Between one of these kindly homilies on our expected participation in the social delights of New York, Wheel, who had come with me, introduced me to an African girl. She was beautiful in an un-African way: tall and skinny, everything about her—face, lips, legs—long and thin; Semitic-looking, Arab blood from somewhere, a color like a gray-blue dust powdered over her skin; and large oval eyes, tremendous pools, with circles of dark water in the middle.

She was from Ethiopia, distantly connected with the royal family there. Recently, she had joined the UN as a guide—a princess, no less. She was with her younger brother that evening, and he looked just like her. He was in movies, a producer in a company recently formed to make African films. And that was where the script began.

Michael and Margaret Takazze. I suppose he was in his mid- and she in her late-twenties. They had the air of two successful, vivacious, very confident orphans. There was about them the stamp of a long-isolated warrior civilization, a temperament, I felt, at once intensely civilized and savage.

We talked a little about nothing, about my work in the UN among other things. And then she said, "Are you the George Graham that made that documentary on Uganda, that won a prize; what was it called, Michael?"

"*The Mountains of the Moon.*"

"Yes, that's the one. It was good. Fine. It was shown here a few months ago, on the educational channel."

I laughed, agreed that I was the man, and wished that there'd been some real drink about. It was one of Graham's COI films about the Ruwenzori Mountains in the Western Province of the country, which I'd seen hurriedly before leaving London. But I'd never been to Uganda.

"You must know Uganda well," she said. "Have you been back recently? I was at Makarare University there, before I went to the Sorbonne."

"No, I've not been back, I'm afraid. All that was some time ago. I've rather forgotten it all," I said quickly, thinking wildly.

Then Wheel said, turning to the boy: "Have you found any good stories yet—for one of your African productions, Michael?"

"Yes," he answered with almost tired assurance. "We're working on it at the moment. An extraordinary story by a Kenyan writer, Ole Timbutu. Have you heard of him, Mr. Graham?"

"No, I—I don't think so."

"Yes, he's written a novel about it: *White Savages.* It came out here a few months ago. He's adapting it."

"Oh yes? I didn't see it. I'd like to."

"It's a mad book," the princess put in, smiling. "I *hope* you'd like it. It's none too kind to the English."

"I hold no brief for the British in East Africa," I said. "What's it all about?"

"It's the story behind Obote's *coup de palais,* among other things," the prince explained. "Two English people, a man and his mistress—she's married to someone else—both working for British Intelligence traveling around East Africa.

A love affair. And then how they bring about the fall of King Freddie, betraying him."

"And it's true," his sister added, "There *were* these two people. Ole Timbutu got it all from a journalist working on the *Kenya Standard*."

"A sort of spy story?" I asked her carefully.

"Yes, that's the basis—but there's the allegory, "White Savages," the two people regress into savagery by the end."

"They eat each other?" Wheel asked hopefully.

"Metaphorically," agreed the prince.

"Quite a story," Wheel went on. "Full color, wide screen."

"I'd certainly like to read the book," I said. "Do you know where I can get a copy?"

"I've got several, I'll lend you one. Be glad to hear what you thought of it," the princess said graciously.

7

The novel arrived on my desk some weeks later, dropped by messenger from the princess. On the same day, I received a note from Guy Jackson asking if I'd like to spend the following weekend with the Jacksons upstate at his father-in-law's house. They'd be traveling there by car on Friday afternoon and there'd be a place for me. I called Jackson at his office to thank him, but he wasn't in.

Wheel and I had a drink together in the Delegates' Lounge before lunch that day. "How are things going?" he asked.

"Coming along."

"What about your domestic arrangements, the apartment you were looking for with Mrs. Jackson?"

"Nothing came of it. I'm all right at the Tudor for the time being. They've moved me to a larger room at the back, away from the traffic. And the Jacksons have asked me up to their place in the country next weekend."

"Oh, yes? Belmont—I don't know it."

"But you know the Jacksons pretty well?" I asked Wheel. "How did you happen across them in the UN? It's a big place."

"No, not that well." Wheel sounded anxious to assure me, as though I'd accused him of social climbing. "I met him here at the bar. You may have noticed, very few Secretariat people come into the North Lounge at all. We're a sort of Club, anyone who uses the place regularly. Guy is usually here every day—has two religious martinis, then lunch."

It seemed a fair explanation. Yet I thought what unlikely friends they were: the meticulous, rather withdrawn Englishman and the gregarious, talkative Midwestern American; the bald and big-boned Wheel and this finicky, discreet Foreign Office figure whose hobby lay in the careful investigation of his cuckoldry. Unusual companions, as different from each other as a rodeo rider and a butterfly collector.

I went back to my office after lunch, closed the door, put aside a two-volume FAO report entitled *Implementation of Agraraian and Riparian Information for Small Farmers in South East Asia*, and took a look at *White Savages* by Ole Timbutu. It was a short book, told in the first person by an unnamed narrator, a kind of God-like omnipresence, who, it seemed, had in part actually observed the activities of the two main characters (a man and a woman described simply as "He" and "She") and had filled in the rest from memory or imagination, one couldn't be sure which.

With this mysterious, sexless narrator; with its accent on minute physical detail, unnamed people, and equally un-determined African settings; and with its lack of every sort of formal designation—the book was like a *nouveau roman* of the Robbe-Grillet school. The prose moved slowly over the surface of things like an insect for long unparagraphed pages, followed by bouts of nervous, often inconsequential, and always inconclusive dialogue, as though in a badly tran-scribed tape-recording, succeeded finally by passages of bleak psychological and sexual description, flat as a medical manual.

Ole Timbutu. A Kenyan. I was curious about him, and his biography on the back flap was as vague as anything in his book. Kenya has very little modern literature in English, to say the least, and none at all, I was sure, in the style of the *nouveau roman*. Ole Timbutu seemed an unlikely figure, and *White Savages* an unlikely novel, to emerge from a decade of African *Uhuru*, from the extroverted, beer-laden social temper of Nairobi. The book, despite its savage themes, used forms and made assumptions which were sophisticated and civilized to a degree. It smelled of the Left Bank, not the African plainslands. There was some innate contradiction in all this which I couldn't fathom.

> The town was surrounded by clumps of shimmering, bluish trees—behind the airport and running up the hills and through the suburbs of straw and tin shacks—and their scent was everywhere in the air, a tangy smell, far from romance, like part of a cold cure. The porter carrying their bags wheezed heavily and hoarsely. Asthmatic. Eucalyptus. The smell was everywhere, everyone permanently out of breath. The sign at the airport, giving the name of the town they had come to, said "8,159 feet above sea level."

What country? It could only be Ethiopia, the capital Addis Ababa, 8,000 feet up, the start of the trip which Helen Jackson and George Graham had made through East Africa in 1966. But subsequently, such easy interpretation became more difficult: the action of the characters more vague, their dialogue more allusive. The two people, the two "White Savages," and their bleak love-making seemed to fade into the groves of eucalyptus around the town like figures in a Douanier Rousseau painting. But then, forty pages in, I came to a passage which reminded me of something I couldn't at once place.

> "Africa," she said, "is not all fat-lipped. The man we spoke to last night at the Peroquet had very thin lips."
>
> "He was not Bantu. These people are Semitic. Africa south of here is fat-lipped. The people here regard all other Africans as slaves. This is an old kingdom cut off from the world on top of a mountain where everyone is thin and proud."
>
> "They have almond eyes in faces from a Byzantine fresco," she said. "I should like to look like them." She stirred the tall glass of white rum.

"It is fairy story here," he said, "that is ending. The old men with sticks and lanterns against the night are dying. The frescos are fading."

And then I knew what it was: these descriptions of Ethiopians in their isolated Christian kingdom almost exactly described the physical characteristics of the princess. I saw her face quite clearly with these identical attributes: the almond eyes, huge pools in the thin face from some Coptic Church painting.

And then it struck me: whoever had written these precise physical descriptions must have actually been to or lived in Ethiopia. The novel was far too detailed to have been worked up by Ole Timbutu from the journalist. And who the hell was Ole Timbutu? He was beginning to seem less and less a real figure—his authorship a pure fiction. So who had written the novel?

The woman with almond eyes, I thought, and a face from a Byzantine fresco. The woman who had studied in Paris, who had an air at once intensely civilized and savage. Margaret Takazze had most of the necessary attributes for authorship of this tale, just as her sex would have made it easy for her to go undetected. She could have very well met and talked with the two protagonists of the story, without their being the least suspicious of her.

Was it possible? If it was, there was an uncomfortable corollary to her story: she had been pursuing someone called George Graham; she must have known his name. And I was George Graham. But we were two different people, as she must so readily have confirmed at the reception when we had met a week before. She had asked me just that, to be sure: "Are you George Graham, the one that had made the film?" And yes, I'd said, I was. I was.

And then I began to think that there was just too much convenient and inconvenient fate in the whole business, so that it wasn't long before I discounted the idea of her authorship and her involvement with these two figures lost in time. It was too long a shot by far.

But I was wrong.

I called her at the UN guides center, but she was out

with a group. So, taking *White Savages* with me, I went downstairs to the conference building to see if I could find her. It didn't take long. She was at the top of the escalator on the fourth floor, standing beside a model of the UN building, explaining the various departments and their functions to twenty or so speechless, middle-aged visitors. I joined them casually, watching her. She was dressed now in something native to her kingdom, sarilike, in green silk, sparkling in stripes and patterns of gold. She recognized me at once with a brief smile, as though I was expected, just a taste of conspiracy in her expression, I thought.

"Hello?" A question as well as a greeting.

"I like the book, what I've read of it. Are you free at all later? Could we talk?"

"Yes," she said without any surprise. "This is my last tour. Meet me in the coffee shop on the ground floor in the UN Plaza apartments at five o'clock. Go out the visitors' entrance here, up First Avenue, right on Forty-eighth, and you can't miss the building on your left—a great big phallus. The coffee shop's at the bottom." She was precise as she was outspoken.

"Fine. I'll bring the book," I said brightly. Then I added: "I'd like you to autograph it for me." But she didn't reply, her head half turned away toward her flock. Just her eyes came back to me, swinging around, fixing me with their dark beams, briefly pondering.

Guy Jackson was back in his office when I called to thank him for his weekend invitation. He was in cooler form.

"Fine then. Meet me here at three o'clock next Friday and we may avoid the rush hour out of town. We don't want to be late. It's the twins' birthday. Helen's organized a tea party for them with their grandfather." It was as if we had never spoken of his jealousy, of his wife's infidelity; or at least as if these were not his problems, but simply part of an interesting movie we had both recently seen and discussed. But I had to draw him back to the plot.

"I'm sorry to drag it up again, but what sort of detective

agency did you use in Nairobi six years ago? Who was it? Who did the actual following?"

Jackson sighed. "I don't know who it was. It was part of a security company out there, supplying guards for banks and so on. The man I dealt with was a Rhodesian. He gave me the reports. That's all I ever saw."

"You never heard of an African involved in it all, a man or a woman?"

"No. Why?"

"I was just thinking. Curious. I couldn't imagine there being any private detective agencies in a place like Nairobi. I thought gossip would do all that kind of work for you out there. Did you keep the reports; were they very complete?"

"No, I burnt them. And yes, they were fairly complete. And there was no gossip. The two of them were extremely discreet. She went around the place with him as his secretary-assistant on the COI program he was filming."

"Didn't you find it surprising that someone could follow the pair of them so closely, across the breadth of Africa in all those open spaces, without being noticed?"

"Yes, I did. But that was what I was paying for. That was their job."

"They did it well."

"Yes," he said, the sadder and wiser man, "they did. It's a long, dull story. Forget about it."

"I will, but I'm a little uneasy about the weekend. That's really why I brought it up. I want to know as much as possible. You see my position, don't you? It's rather an awkward threesome, isn't it? She knows, you know, and I know. But we don't all three know the same things together. With her I'm Mr. X, impersonating her lover, about whom you know nothing. But in fact you do know about him; you know everything. I'm in the middle and I know very little." Jackson nodded his agreement.

"Of course, she's been asking you where he is?" he asked.

"To say the least."

"It was her suggestion—that you come up for the weekend."

"I've told her nothing."

"Of course."

"Except asking her to say nothing about it all—my impersonating Graham—to you or anyone until I finish my work here. But how long can this go on for, this charade?"

"I should tell her I've had her followed you mean, that I know all about George Graham?"

"I don't know."

"Look, it's simply a personal business, all this with Graham. We've agreed on that. There's no political connection. So why upset our present situation?"

"She wanted a divorce."

"Yes, I knew that. She can have it now."

"Now that he's gone?"

"Yes."

"Now that you won't be bruised by knowing and thinking of the man she's leaving for you? Now that there's no one for her?"

"Yes. Is that unreasonable?"

"Fairly."

"Then I'm unreasonable. Where does that leave you for your weekend? You can get out of it easily enough."

But why in the circumstances, I thought, had Jackson not got me out of the invitation before? I was a potential risk to him, both professionally and personally, in any association I might have with his wife. I might give any number of games away. Yet it seemed he wanted me to see as much as possible of her—he had encouraged me to go flat-hunting with her in the first place—in circumstances which he could control and oversee. He would lose his private eyes and replace them with mine. I would spy on his wife for him and make my reports, perhaps that was what he hoped. Sensing my interest in her he had the opportunity now of hearing of her flaws and infidelities direct from a surrogate lover—or perhaps as her real lover, for such seemed the role he was tacitly encouraging me in. Yet, though I was not interested in satisfying his voyeurism, I was interested in his wife. I felt sure that somewhere in her past with Graham lay the key to my own immediate future. There was something I didn't know, which she would never tell me; something which had happened between them, a plan, a future arrangement, which could only now have an outcome in me. I needed to know about her now for reasons quite beyond affection or sex.

So I said: "No, I'd like to come up for the weekend. It sounds a marvelous place. Wheel was telling me about it."

"Yes, he knows it. Good then, just a family weekend. And the rest—let it drop. I've had them call the man off. We'll forget that."

"*The* man? But there were two men. I told you. There was a second man, with sandwiches and a homburg, deep-set eyes, and white hair around his ears."

"Must just have been a bystander. I checked; the agency had only one man on the job—Moloney—the man you impersonated."

"There were two of them, I know. The other fellow tried to go on following me afterward, when I'd slipped back into the restaurant."

"Not from the agency, there wasn't. There was someone else following you—if you're sure. That's all."

"That's *all*? Well, who? If there wasn't anyone sent after me from London."

"Your KGB contact perhaps. The Stayer. That was the plan, wasn't it? He was going to check you out, make sure you were really George Graham, before passing on the information about KGB unreliables over here. No doubt he'll be in touch with you now, give you those names, and we can wrap all this up and send you home."

"I doubt it," I said, while doubting just as much Jackson's glib idea of "home." Where was that? A small flat I'd had in Doughty Street near the office in Holborn, before the years in Durham jail. And I doubted Jackson himself now as well. Or rather Wheel and Jackson together, for hadn't he just said that Wheel knew the house upstate in the Catskills? Yet Wheel at lunchtime had said equally clearly that he didn't know it. That he had never been there. Someone else was following me. And someone was lying.

As I left Guy's office I bumped into Wheel just about to enter it, carrying a sheaf of papers.

"Hi!" he said, flourishing that badge of permanent good humor which was his face. But I wasn't entirely convinced by it now. The two of them didn't just meet in the Delegates'

Lounge for two religious martinis before lunch. They shared some business together as well.

"Yes," she said in the Coffee Shoppe, where everything had an "e" at the end of it, the decor and furniture all folksy and ye olde from an England that never was, paneled in synthetic fumed oak with black plastic beams overhead. "Yes," she said, sitting on a milkmaid's stool, dressed now in a rust-colored Pringle sweater, the same shade in slightly flared corduroys and a leather belt, "I wrote the book. How did you guess?"

I just said I'd guessed, and she licked her lips gently.

"How did you come to be playing the detective?" I went on.

"I wasn't. We were all there together, staying at the same hotel in Addis. George Graham was a friend, my English professor at Makarere University in the early sixties."

What was she saying? Already I was on the defensive.

"Is that what you do to old friends? Write novels about their private lives, their mistresses?"

"What do you do with *my* old friends, Mr. Graham? Kill them? Your story is surely better than mine. Though I don't suppose you'll ever publish it. I used a pseudonym. You've stolen his real name, his body, his life." She played with a sachet of sugar, tore it open, dipped a finger in, and then sucked it.

"How did you manage to follow them around East Africa without being noticed?"

"How do you mean? That was part of the job." She was properly surprised. "Didn't anyone tell you when you took him over? We were filming together, a documentary about an African girl visiting other African countries: I was the girl. Didn't you see the film?"

"No. One of his I didn't see. There wasn't a lot of time before—before I came over here."

"I used to think that George was involved in something more than just public relations for the British government."

"Think? You surely must have actually known—from what you've written in your book."

"No, I didn't know exactly. That was an invention of mine in the novel. Now I see that I was right. You've taken his place. And I shouldn't know about it," she went on. "Should I? Such bad luck—our running into each other the other night. Your 'cover' is broken. Isn't that the word?" Now she laughed outright. "Just like the spy novels. I have you in my grasp, at my mercy—Grrrrr!" She leaned across the table toward me over the sour coffee, mimicking a tiger. I drew back involuntarily, alarmed. "It's all right. I'm not going to tell anyone." She rested her hand on my arm for an instant. "I've nothing to do with that world, I promise," she said, the animal tamed in her now, meek and mild, still lightly amused. "This is my world. New York this month. This here, this now. My apartment upstairs. That book was a long time ago. Written and finished with. I'm not going to use it against you."

She started one of her long smiles, a rising beam of fun coming over her face, like sunlight emerging, drifting slowly into a blaze from behind a dark cloud. She was one of those women who, in an instant, can fill themselves with happiness, as if she had a tap in her soul, a confident fountain of truth and trust which bubbled immediately for everyone at her request.

"I'd like to hear more about it. The novel. . . ."

"Why don't you tell *me* first?" She leaned back, withdrawing her favors for a moment, bargaining gently. "You're going to *have* to trust me, aren't you? I know too much already. Or are you thinking of knocking me off? That's how it works isn't it, in the stories? Hitchcock and James Bond. I have to be 'liquidated.'"

More laughter, more happiness. It was as though I were the feed in a comic act she had hired me for. "Anyway, why the novel, why the past? Why not things *now*? About you. About me. Isn't there always time later for the past?"

She semed to be propositioning me.

"I'm fascinated," she said, suddenly, sharply, apropos of nothing, like one of her characters in *White Savages*.

"About?"

"Having coffee with a spy." In a deep, funny voice, she asked: "Do you carry a revolver?"

"No, as a matter of fact. No guns, no golden Dunhills, no dark glasses."

"No vodka martinis either—very dry, stirred and not shaken. Or is it the other way around?"

I felt the skin on my face move awkwardly, creases rising inexplicably over my cheeks. Then I realized I was smiling.

"Yes, I drink. Sometimes. Bottles of light ale, though. I'm a spy from one of those seedier thrillers, I'm afraid."

"Let's have a drink then."

"Here?"

"God no. Upstairs."

I looked at her blandly.

"Women are out too, are they? Not even 'sometimes'? What a very dull book you are."

"I disappoint you."

"Not yet."

She stood up and tightened her belt a notch. She was already pretty thin.

Her apartment was on the tenth floor of the UN Plaza building. It had almost the same view of the East River as my office had, except that we were further upstream now, and closer to the ground: she saw less of the huge northern horizon than I did but she was closer to the boats. A big silver motor cruiser, rigged out for deep-sea fishing, moved down the current in the last of the sunlight, a burly figure with a beard and a baseball cap at the helm.

It was one of those very modern, expensively decorated New York Design Center apartments made for money to live in, not people.

She fiddled with a bottle of Fleischmann's gin, vermouth, lemon, and a bowl of ice which she'd brought in from the kitchen, handling the component parts smartly, like a nurse with a hypodermic tray in her long, clever fingers.

"Well, what about the book then? What do you want to know?"

"I was interested in the woman he was with."

"Miss Jackson?"

"Mrs."

She came over with the drink and sat down on the floor opposite me. But this wasn't comfortable, so she sat bolt upright instead, like an idol, cross-legged, leaning forward, as thin as the stem of the martini glass.

"Yes, she wasn't just his secretary. I knew that. Well, what about her—you've finished the book?"

"No. What happens?"

She leaned toward me, arching her narrow back between her legs as though starting something in yoga, putting her glass on the floor between us.

"Why you? Who are you?"

I had postponed the decision. But now I made it willingly; I would tell her the truth, or some of it anyway. I felt perfectly confident of her discretion. Talking with her I had sensed almost immediately a quality that I had missed with everyone else since I'd left prison, with the Jacksons, with Wheel, and with all the men in London: the sense of rational life in a real world. With this woman there were no flaws; no lost affairs, no unsatisfied obsessions, no old wound, no guilt that would warp the future. I could see now how, by comparison with those others, she was quite free of that air of impending calamity which marked them and which I had not recognized before.

She had come out of Africa and into the white man's world and had gone beyond the diseases of both. She had left the savagery and the cleverness equally—a person, one felt, who had thrown doubt and enmity and jealousy right away. She was dark from the Dark Continent but her vision was completely bright, an astonishingly clear heart in the darkness. It was a simple thing to tell the truth with her.

So I said, "I was never a spy. I was just in Information and Library. But now I'm involved. In that stupid game, for boys with guns, and I don't play it well. British Security is using me as a stalking horse. George Graham, the real one, has been working for the Russians for years. They caught him in London a few weeks ago and replaced him with me— we share a similar sort of background—and I've been sent over here to wait for some of his Russian colleagues in a KGB network to contact me, and then hand over their names. There's more to it. But that's the essence, and I'm liable to get my head knocked off if the KGB or anyone else finds out." I looked at her seriously.

She laughed. "That's the corniest story." But she believed me. "My God!" She paused, considering, I suppose, the guns and golden Dunhills and all the rest of the childish impedimenta which my words must have conjured up for her—a world as unreal to her, I was sure, as it was to me. "Why risk telling me?" she said.

"You asked. And I need to know. I need to know as much as possible about Graham and his past, which is partly this woman."

"Your 'life depends on it.' "

"Perhaps. Insofar as my successful impersonation depends on it."

"Why? You're not likely to run into this woman in New York are you?"

It was my turn to laugh. "She would have said just the same of you, if she'd known. I 'ran into' Mrs. Jackson on my first day here, just as I did with you that evening a few weeks ago."

"What a lot of accident." She turned her glass slowly between her fingers, elbows leaning on either knee. Then she went on, even more precise in her words than before. "Yes, I know about them. Apart from what I saw of them myself when we were filming in Ethiopia, what's in my book. My brother was the 'detective' you spoke of—or one of them, they used several. That's how I filled in a lot of my story."

"But how? He can't have been much more than a child at the time."

"So much the better; he may have looked that way, but he wasn't. The whole thing appealed to him. Childish, I suppose. I never followed the reason behind it all. Now I see it—it wasn't a private inquiry this, but a government one."

"Apparently not. It was entirely private. Her husband had an obsession about her being with older men—and knowing all about it."

"An expensive sort of pornography. But the material we gathered wasn't like that at all, not much sex: it was political."

"You mean they were *both* talking politics?"

"Of course. That was in most of the reports I saw. A lot of it's in the book: Maoism and the political future of Africa; Nyerere's Chinese policy. They were both extremely left-wing about it all—not the doctrinaire, hardline stuff but a 'new Marxist interpretation for new conditions,' you know; they were very keen on Nyerere's self-help program, small autonomous communities and not big industries. Of course all this was a surprise, coming from her. She didn't seem that sort at all; much more the high flyer, the jet set girl in dark glasses with that butter-wouldn't-melt-in-my-mouth American face."

"Yes, that's her all right. You had the impression they were working together in some way—professionally?"

"Yes. Well, I assumed so."

"And the KGB, was that ever mentioned, that they were involved in that together?"

"Not that we ever heard. But whatever he was up to, she was too. That's certain."

She got up to refill our glasses. "But it's all years ago. How can it have to do with you now? Her husband, or who-ever had those reports, must know all this too. It can't be much of a secret somewhere. Where is the husband? Are they still married?"

"Her husband's here. With British Intelligence, like me. He's my 'control,' in fact. You'll know the term—it goes with these martinis, 'stirred and not shaken.' "

I received my glass from her, stood up, and went over to the windows. The big Pepsi-Cola sign had come on above a warehouse on the opposite bank, a colored gash against the dust-filled, leaden sky. Other lights appeared as I watched, spreading over Queens and lighting the river, lights every-where rising across the suburbs as darkness came. Helen and Graham's association, I reflected, had taken on now an added dimension which affected me. Here was another vital facet, a link between their past and my future: Margaret Takazze had just made clear to me that Guy Jackson must have known all about his wife's political involvement. But that morning he had denied just this.

What on earth was he up to? Had he, in fact, been pursuing his wife, not for himself, but on behalf of British Intelligence—McCoy, Harper, and the others in London knowing of her real involvement with Graham all the time, and sending me to New York to meet her, to sound her out in some way, to trap her? And if this was so, why had I not been told?

I had trusted Guy Jackson too as my only sure liaison in the whole matter: this Jackson, with his Foreign Office robes, old-boy's tie, and high purposes, who now appeared as trustworthy as a ferret, who held truth like a collander; this Jackson, who knew far more about his wife than just the fact that she was unfaithful to him, but had said nothing, who perhaps had no jealous obsessions about her at all, but was simply hunting her down and using me as the pointer. And then there was Wheel, who had introduced me to them both, that first day at the UN, so conveniently as it now appeared. Wheel, who had never been upstate in Belmont. . . . Indeed, indeed. Where did the expansive Wheel fit in? The decent, funny man from the Midwest; the big man from an older, more confident America.

The princess's eyes were so deep, I noticed, when I turned away from the window, seeing her standing behind me in the darkness which had come over the room: eyes buried away in her skull, the huge whites visible like light behind a mask.

"What do you want to do?" she said, walking slowly toward me. And then a different question, remembering my professional predicament as well as my presence with her: "What are you going to do?"

But she was in my arms before I could reply and by then my answer had become a question: "Are you sure you want this?" Always the procrastinator, I thought; the pretended diffidence—as if I'd not wanted it myself after so long.

I could feel her smiling, her cheek crinkling next to my ear. She smelled of wool, freshly washed, the smell of a warm linen cupboard where someone had buried a bar of sweet soap deep in the clothes. We stood there easily, lightly pressed together.

"You've surely better things to do."

"I have. Not better, but other. I'm going out in an hour."

I did nothing—and suddenly felt I could do nothing. Now that it was possible, the years of abstinence in Durham jail and all the abandoned imaginings of those years were the only things that rose in me then. So I procrastinated once more.

"Why me?" I really believed the question. She didn't reply. "You're bleak about this in your novel. Is that why? A bleak thing . . . ?"

She moved her head around to the other side of my face, her lips brushing my chin. "Not bleak, no. I was exact about it, I hope. We should be more exact."

She lifted one of her long legs off the floor and, standing like a heron, she wound it slowly around behind the back of my thighs.

"You mistrust it when it's easy, don't you?"

She let her leg slide to the floor.

"It's simply that I'm not used to it," I said.

"Of course, you're Mrs. Jackson's lover," she said. "I hadn't quite realized all that that must mean for you both—in the way of mistaken identity, sexual disappointment, diminished performance."

She rolled her pullover up her midriff toward her chest, one rusty skin peeling off to reveal another. Her small conical breasts rose with it, caught tightly by the fabric, before they fell outward suddenly like pips from a squeezed fruit.

"That doesn't inhibit me."

"No." She paused, holding the jumper up, turning it the right way out again, shaking it.

"No. It's decisions that inhibit you," she went on. "I thought that was the basis of your kind of job—the quick decision."

"I've been out of my 'job' for a long time. Anyway I'm sorry. Go ahead, don't let me hold you up. You want to go out."

She bent down, slipping her briefs off with one hand. "I want you to come in."

She was right. I'd always been held up by the trappings of sex, the preludes, the difficulties. And no doubt that was why Helen Jackson, with her copious old wounds and blocks, appealed to me.

I stood in the dark room as if anchored to it, held fast by these dull speculations, and I would not have thrown off this mood of flatulent disengagement if the telephone hadn't rung at that moment on one of the low tables in the main room.

She knelt on the floor beside it: pressed her knees together, thighs running in a smooth dark line to a small triangle of hair, her back rising upward, arched slightly, the tummy rounded, pushing outward, her waist narrowing dramatically, and then the abrupt conical breasts. She was like an art deco design, a sculptured bookend, a copper-plated Diana from some suburban household between the wars.

"Yes? Hello! Yes, fine—in an hour. Eight. No, there's no need. As we arranged. I'll meet you there. Fine. Bye."

"Who was that?" The words were out of my mouth before I could stop myself. The enquiries, the doubts, were under way. She stood up and gripped my wrist sharply, gazing at me.

"The man I'm going out with tonight."

And then it was all right, when she came into my arms. I could feel her now for the first time—warm and electric. For she was not mine now, not my responsibility, my script. She was the object of someone else's designs. And it was an easy thing then, playing the robber right under this man's nose.

Her leg came up once more like the heron's, and this time I wanted her without hesitation as she wrapped it around me, and we made love that way, standing like birds, almost motionless.

8

Belmont House lay at the foot of the Catskills in New York's Ulster County, two hours' drive up the Hudson Valley along the New York Thruway, then westward along roads that became narrower and less frequented as they ran towards the hills.

The valley was a busy place, with its six-lane highway running straight through to Chicago, and its supermarkets as big as villages on the outskirts of towns. But once off this main artery the countryside changed character gradually as it rose from the valley until an almost primeval America took over: a landscape of rugged woodlands, forested hills, high bluffs, ravines, great boulders, and torrents of water; inhabited only at the edges of the small roads, elderly people living in straggling villages with frame houses, all alike with screened front porches and miniature lawns, and chickens wandering disconsolately in steep back patches.

Belmont House lay ten miles or so beneath the highest of the Catskill peaks, on a ridge of land, once an Indian trail, bordering what was now the Catskill Forest Preserve. There was a village which we passed through a mile from it. Stonestead, a single street with a pretty white clapboard church, a general store, a liquor store, and the district headquarters of the American Legion. We turned off the main road here and followed what would have been no more than a lane if it hadn't been paved.

The house itself was lost among huge elms and horse chestnuts at the end of a long curved drive, so that one came on it suddenly in a clearing of spreading lawns, dotted with maple groves and flowering shrubs. It was a long, two-story, yellow clapboard mansion with a steep hipped roof over the central block and green louvered shutters on either side of the tall windows: classic American colonial, with a Greek revival portico—huge white columns and a triangular pediment—a transplantation from the Old South. Its proportions were solid and dignified without being heavy; the landscaping carefully premeditated yet the effects informal; the views of the Catskill and Shawangunk mountains precisely commanding. Love and thought had had an outing here—and money too—an old-fashioned American capitalism still buoyantly evident. That didn't surprise me, for Helen Jackson's grandfather, she'd told me on the drive up, who had created the place in the 1890s, had been a New York broker, a friend of Carnegie and Rockefeller, a vital cog in that huge monopolistic machine that had come to control America by the turn of the century.

And indeed if one takes account of familial opposition, the sometimes violent reaction between successive generations, Helen Jackson's Marxist apostasy, if such it was, was quite conceivable: she had found distress in all this unearned bounty, fled the rich hearth for the hovels of the poor, left the castle for the cabin as princesses do in fairy stories. Seeing her in front of the great house, confidently stepping into her heritage, the idea of her hidden nature, of revolution beneath the eye shadow—this seemed so unlikely a thought, so bizarre, that one felt it must be true.

Harold Perkins laid aside a book he'd been reading and came running down the porch steps to greet us— a small, compactly built, bubbling man with white hair cut en brosse, in a yachting pullover and plimsolls. He looked like a retired tennis coach and not the son of a millionaire broker. And it was obvious almost immediately that he had reacted against the influence of his father not just by taking up the academic career, which Helen had told me about, but by retaining, as he did now in his mid-sixties, the dress, the air of a college freshman, running down the library steps, breathlessly anxious for a game before sunset.

Yet there was just beneath his friendly ebullience something else that I noticed in that first moment and was later to confirm in strength: a diffidence, an excuse in his approach to us all on the gravel surround, as if he were butting in on a party he'd not been invited to; the marks on his small face —a shriven quality—of something which had hurt all his life; a disappointment in the mild blue eyes.

Inside the porch was a large, octagonally shaped hall, darkly paneled, with a chandelier dropping from the high ceiling, which ran across the width of the house to a veranda looking westward down a sloping lawn and beyond that a meadow which the sun was beginning to leave, the sky above now pale blue and pink and a cold haze above the grass.

The tea had been laid out on a round table in the middle of the hall, with the red birthday poppers piled up on the circle of white linen, and balloons laid along a wide

Carrara marble mantelpiece, the colored skins gently expanding above a grate of smoldering logs.

A middle-aged woman was introduced to me—the housekeeper, I understood. In addition to the twins, there were two other children already there, a boy and a girl from a neighboring family who had come to make up the party. It was very much a family occasion and, of course, I felt outside it: there was the sense, all the more clear now, that I'd been asked up here too precipitately, for reasons that were not entirely to do with hospitality or friendship. I felt uncomfortably close to the fiction of *The Man Who Knew Too Much*.

Guy Jackson took me up to my bedroom at the end of the house facing out over the lawn and the meadow. The branches of a tree, I noticed, almost touched the window and when I looked out I saw in the fading light that it was a huge chestnut. About the inside of the tree twining itself among the branches, a wooden balustraded walkway had been built, leading to a thatched tree house, a little conical pavilion, at the far end. How wrong the phrase "idle rich" was, I thought.

When I came down the party was under way with the ticklish, sweet smell of mild explosive in the air over the wood smoke as the children pulled the poppers with faces savagely taut for a moment as they tugged—screwed up and frightened before the snap and the short sparks of light in the firelit room. Helen Jackson moved around the table supervising the party, watching her children, Sarah and Sheila. She was close to them now, so obviously tending, watching them: reason enough for not leaving her husband, I thought. That seemed so clear now, and I was surprised that I had ever thought otherwise.

They were not identical twins, though identically dressed in brown corduroy dungarees and white pullovers, with straight fair hair with fringes like the spokes of a rake down about their noses. I watched her watch them, and it was as if her life with George Graham, all the past she had written and we had spoken about, the places where she had lived, no longer existed in her; that it had been completely erased in this linkage she had made again with her roots in this house in the woods. This was where she really belonged, where her natural affinities lay, and what had happened in all those other foreign places were no more than visits of a rich man's daughter, a grand tour made by a woman essentially domestic, calm, and full of her children.

The hall had become warm with the roused fire, the excited breath and movement of the children, and with an impalpable warmth of family community, the present re-union merely one more play in the long repertory of meeting and departure that had taken place in the room over the years—a warm confirmation, for the moment, of continuity, of a heritage willingly accepted.

I stood with my back to the grate next to Mr. Perkins with a cup of tea in my hand, and he said, "It was good that you could get up here. Very good." But he said nothing else, looking away abstractly. The children now put on paper hats and there was some squabbling over the peanut butter sandwiches before they settled into them, hurrying over the plainer food, eyes fixed on the two birthday cakes in the middle of the table, iced in pink and blue, with sugar animals and five candles apiece.

Finally Harold Perkins was called to the table and two small circles of flame lit up four pink faces and fired the chandelier above with diamonds.

After tea they opened their presents. I had brought them a pair of Babar books: *The Travels of Babar* and *Babar and Zephir*. And of course the first thing they noticed on the second page of the Zephir book was the double-page spread of Monkeysville, the city with its shops and rope ladders built in the trees. "Like us," they shouted. "The tree houses—like ours!" They were children for whom even the most inventive art naturally imitates life.

"They can change them, if they have them already. I asked at the shop," I said to Helen.

"No," she smiled. "Not these. They have the earlier ones. Thank you. And this is surely from Alice in France," she went on, turning again to the children, helping them open a flat, well-packed parcel. Inside was a selection of children's records, small forty-fives, French nursery rhymes, folk songs, and fables, and also a larger record: "Alice Per-

kins à La Porte de Lilas." There was a glossy photograph
of her on the sleeve, a girl with glasses and short dark hair,
bobbed and fringed, cradling a guitar. She had at the moment the features of a beautiful but severe schoolmarm. "I
may be a popular singer," the photograph suggested, "but
that's not the point; that's neither here nor there. I have
serious work to do"—an impression which Helen immediately confirmed for me.

"That's Alice, my runaway younger sister. Lives in
Paris. She's the revolutionary for you. Every cause you can
think of, from Vietnam to the battle of Wounded Knee.
She got herself locked up in Paris with the students, May
sixty-eight. Do you remember the song 'This City Never
Was For Lovers'? She's very serious."

"I've heard of her, not the song. I'd no idea—"

"Oh yes. She's the famous sister. Guy and I don't see
much of her. Thinks we're outrageously bourgeois and
right-wing. Almost fascist pigs. Father, do you want to hear
Alice's latest?" She turned to him, waving the sleeve in the
air like a flag.

"What is it this time? 'Wrap The Red Flag Around Me'?
Let's hear it. I like her."

Helen put the record on in the next room—a dark
drawing room with heavy leather furniture I could just see
through a doorway off the hall. And the sound of a sharp,
classic guitar emerged through the stereo equipment, a decisively fingered, lilting introduction, followed by a surprisingly deep, almost male voice—ringingly vibrant, slowly
rising into the music, becoming passionately modulated,
Piaf-like, whenever the words offered the chance:

> Si je n'avais plus
> plus qu'un heure a vivre,
> je le voudrais vivre
> au pres de ton lit—
> sur un lit d'amour. . . .

"That's not altogether revolutionary," I said when Helen
returned.

"I'm sure there's something in it, some hidden political
thing," she said, picking up the sleeve. "It's by someone

called Moulouji, 'Algerian musician and singer.' The Arab cause. It's that, don't you think? That's it."

Helen seemed strangely anxious to cast her sister in the role of musical agitator, as someone who, in her rather mocking tones, she viewed as politically irresponsible. Yet her father's politics, as I was to learn later that evening, had been very similar—as were her own, I knew, despite the pains she took to disguise this. The three of them had taken from this rich estate not the autocratic bounty that was their inheritance but a deep sense of shame in the injustice of that gift. Their history in this house had somehow led them all to a shared political cause: the concerns of an imperiled world that lay beyond its gates.

. . . He remembers Alice so affectionately, Helen thought, as she listened to her sister's voice, a radiant presence about the hall. He thinks of her so much as a continuation of his own philosophies, as someone making up for his own political failure. I'm the older, safer, drearier daughter, the Manhattan socialite who married a dull diplomat, a stuffed shirt from the British Foreign Office. I've taken after mother, an old Daughter of the American Revolution, while Alice is a daughter of the proper revolution. That's what he thinks. But that's how I wanted it, exactly how. That was the cover. And now the point of it all? It's gone. I needn't have bothered—all the lies, the distances I've made with my family. I could have been true in the open and sung rebelly songs like Alice and had a good time with her and father and shocked my husband. Although Guy wouldn't have married that me, the real one. Not a chance. So that marriage was a lie I could have avoided too.

I shouldn't have taken it all so seriously. It could have been something you sung about when you were young, talked about in college, argued about in bars and cafes, a dream you shouted from the rooftops while the pigs were letting off gas grenades at you: kidnapping the dean, burning the draft cards, and blowing up the computer building. I could have done it that way—the way you grow out of it, like Paris in the spring, because you weren't ever really go-

ing to see it come about, were you? The revolution or whatever you called your hope. Sing about it passionately, yes,
like Alice; that was very much part of the scenario, because
it was going to fail. That was always in the last reel, wasn't
it? The riot police, gas masks, rubber bullets, then real ones,
then tanks, finally the rigged trial and the ten-year sentence.
And then you spent the rest of your life making up sad
songs about it all, commemorating the failure.

But oh no, not that. That's why I took it seriously. I
didn't want that. I saw that from the beginning. Alexei
showed me, and George too: the students' phase, the amateur revolution of the privileged. I took it seriously. Serious.
That had been the key word in everything. "If you *are* serious about it," she remembered Alexei saying, "you will
put up with every setback. And they'll come, be sure of that
—the public disappointments, and much worse, the personal
loss of faith. And when they do, remember the choice, the
decision you make now: that you believe these ideas we've
talked about are *right*. And nothing should really change
that."

And yes, she thought, I still believe those ideas to be
right. But it's a dry belief, without feeling. And I must suffer that. I must go on. That was part of Alexei's whole
scheme, that whatever happened there would still be people
outside to carry the business through. The person next to
me—George, who shared and warmed my belief—is gone,
that is all. And someone has taken his place. He smokes
his pipe, wears his watch, carries his old fountain pen. But
it is not him. I have not properly understood all that yet—
looking at these objects that once touched the body
I touched.

The children can have their story now. He can read it
to them, this man, whoever he is. And I shall find out who
—that, and what has happened to him, that other. He will
tell me.

The party finished and the children went to bed. "Will
you read them one of your Babar stories, George?" Helen
asked me, something unexpressed in her voice and face:

"George." George Graham. I wished I could have told her the truth of it all, my truth and his.

I read to the children in the nursery next to their parents' bedroom where Helen had gone, moving about, unpacking. "The elephants' school at Celesteville is closed for the whole summer," I read. "Zephir, the little monkey, as well as his bigger schoolmates, goes off for the holidays. What fun to go and see his family again! But how sad to leave his friends, King Babar, Queen Celeste, the old lady, his teacher, and his beloved Arthur. . . ."

". . . Queen Celeste, the old lady, his teacher, and his beloved Arthur! All four have promised to come to the river near the bridge to see him off and bid him a last fond farewell. . . ."

Helen listened to his voice in the next room, quietly assured, as if he'd been used to reading bedtime stories all his life. Had he children of his own from his failed marriage, she wondered? Had she asked him? She'd forgotten. There was nothing she knew about him. And worse, there was nothing she could remember in him, as there had been with the other men. He stood up for her in the guise of someone deeply loved, as a memorial to him, and thus he constantly provoked her memory of the real man. And so, in the days since she had met him, she had started to remember, involuntarily at first, the past cascading back to her—odd, very clear incidents at odd moments.

"They have to use a rope ladder to climb up to the house perched there in the treetops. Zephir scrambles up easily, but laughs as he says to himself 'This wouldn't do for my friends the Elephants. . . .' "

Elephants. She closed the drawer she had filled with the twins' clothes. After the filming in Ethiopia, she and Graham had gone on alone, southward to Kenya, to Tsavo National Park to look at the elephants. George had been researching another TV story, the College of African Wildlife on the slopes of Mount Kilimanjaro. And from there

they'd gone out on a training safari with the college in-
structors and students, careening across the open plainsland
of the huge park in open lorries.

That first morning had always been a clear enough
thing to hold. It hardly took the form of memory, but lived
safely, ever available in the grammar of the historic present:
that first time properly alone with him, believing so surely
then in the next few weeks—a happy stretch of certain days
ahead of them. Confident with him, yet not grasping; a reasonable happiness, no more than that. And surely that would
come in this empty world, this plainsland which human dissension had not yet marked?

And loving him too. That as well. But love was an easy
thing now, something you could stop thinking about if you
wanted to.

. . . The first night out we camped, not in tents, but
in the crumbling manager's house in a ruined mining village at the center of the park with the students bedding
down in the old labor lines. And it was creepy and far more
strange than tents under the stars. There was no electricity
in the house, yet the bulbs were still there and the electric
fires had never been taken away, and I found an old hair
dryer in a cupboard of the manager's bedroom where we'd
been put to sleep with our bags. Mr. and Mrs. Graham. . . .

That evening when it turned cold and pitch dark within
half an hour of sunset, great blocks of cedar from a ruined
tree in the garden roared in the living room grate, the Tilley lamps hissed like snakes as they were pumped up in the
kitchen, and people chatted and laughed over their beers
and before dinner.

And that night up in the manager's old bedroom getting undressed, talking to George, watching him, standing
with one hand against the chimney breast, warm from the
huge fire that had blazed all evening in the grate immediately below, and thinking him somehow uneasy now that
we were alone.

"Do you like it here?" I asked. "Or loathe it? Honestly.

You're so wary of liking things. Or just wary of running around East Africa with someone else's wife?"

"No, it's not that. It's what you might, or might not, do with me in the future that worries me."

"This is just a prolonged one-night stand?"

"Not for me."

"Nor me."

"There's the problem, then."

"What about living *now*?" I asked. "What about that great old idea? Let's leave the words for later, when we've lost this, if we do. That's what words are for."

He got into his sleeping bag in the narrow camp bed beside mine—the two beds like two separate valleys with an iron ridge between them. It was ridiculous. We took the sleeping bags off and put them down next to the grate, where the floor was warm from the fire below, and made love and slept there, very warm in the cold night, a broken window pane rattling, sleeping and doing it again, waking when the wind had gone very early before dawn, and feeling entirely alone stretched out naked in the middle of Africa.

". . . Zephir falls asleep almost as soon as his head touches the pillow. But in the middle of the night, the nightingale wakes him with his song: 'Trou la la-tiou; tiou-tiou! Tidi-Tidi.' . . ."

The twins had fidgeted during the story, unable to relax after the excitement of the day. But now, quite suddenly, they were still, their eyelids wavering. And by the next page, with Zephir pushing his little rowboat out into the lake, they were both fast asleep. "Oh, what a daredevil that fellow Zephir is," I read to the sleeping, silent room, closing the book.

Helen had come in and was standing behind me. "You don't have children, do you?" She asked, turning off the main light and standing now in the half darkness, a small bedside lamp with a decorated shade illuminating the room faintly with the colors of some nursery fable. "I don't remember; you told me you were married to someone in the same business, in British Intelligence."

"No. None." I stood up. She was carrying some of the twins' clothes and had started to put them away in a small chest of drawers.

"Did you know about her from the beginning—I mean, that she was in the same business?"

"No. I only found out in the end. Almost the very end. She'd been in the business as a colleague, and more, of a number of other men, in other organizations."

Helen looked up at me, with compassion or derision, I couldn't say in the darkness.

"But don't worry," I went on. "It didn't matter by the time I found out. We were coming apart anyway. The usual things. Nothing exciting—like finding out she worked for the KGB. Nothing like that."

"I'd better change," Helen said, quickly finishing with the twins' clothes. "Thank you for the story. Dinner's quite soon. Help yourself to drinks downstairs if there's no one about."

She turned and left the nursery, loosening her blouse at the waist as she walked back along the corridor to her bedroom.

. . . The KGB, she thought, closing the door of her room, opening her blouse, starting the zip on her skirt. At first she thought with alarm: Has he found out? Does he know anything? What does he know? And then she realized that if he had discovered her, it was because all the time she had somehow wanted him to, that she had unconsciously left a transparent area in herself for him to see through. She had—now she knew—from their first meeting trusted him, for himself alone and because of that other he person-ified.

"The usual things. Nothing exciting—like finding out she worked for the KGB. Nothing like that." His pointed voice and look reminded her so much of her own confusions when she had found out about Graham's involvement with the same organization when their few weeks in East Africa had started to go wrong. . . .

. . . At the end of the safari we went back to the College of African Wildlife near Moshi, winding up the little road from the town through green coffee plantations and lush farms, with the mountain and its great collar of snow always in front of us, glistening through the tall green forest which covered its middle slopes. The air was crisp there, at 10,000 feet around the college, huge trees and bougainvillea blowing their rusty purplish leaves over the basketball courts—the place like a marvelous Swiss health resort in the fall.

He phoned Nairobi several times for messages just after we got back. "I have to go back to Ethiopia," he said. "A project way down in the Awash Valley the office wants me to check on before we go on to Uganda. A new cotton plantation, and the Russians are building a road. They're making a small plane available to us, direct from Addis."

It was stiflingly hot after we landed on the cracked sandy soil of the Awash Valley and the Danakil all rushed out from their low grass huts to see us. The older men of the settlement stood a little apart, their women behind them, but the children—the child brides totting babies on their backs and the boys—all clustered around the small plane in a frenzy. "They want to be the ones to guard it," the pilot said. "It's a great privilege to guard the bird. It's a bird to them, of course."

Two Israeli members of the UN cotton-growing team met us; we drove back to their camp which they'd built beneath a glade of thorn trees by the river.

"Until they finish the road, we're two days from any civilization out here," the project supervisor, Mr. Calman, said. "We were the first Europeans many of these people had ever seen."

The chief engineer of the Russian project, Leonid somebody, joined us for lunch in the tin shack. He was a small yet burly fair-haired man in shorts, with a rather Aryan face, young-looking and high-spirited. He talked a lot in good English—talked too much, I thought, for an engineer; more like a teacher or an actor.

That afternoon we drove with him to his road works, about five miles away upstream, where they were finishing the last stretch to the new agricultural settlement for the whole area.

With the heat at more than a hundred and thirty degrees, the billowing clouds of dust, the screeching roar of the huge graders and scrapers and trucks, the site was an impossible place for any sustained conversation. Yet I noticed that this was exactly what George and the Russian were doing. Sweating terribly, walking away from the rest of us, they were pointing out things to each other, their mouths moving rapidly in what must have been shouts, though we could hear nothing of it at all.

Of course it all looked so perfectly natural and appropriate—the two of them wandering off like that, dodging between the huge machines, dwarfs beside the ten-foot tires. George had made the trip to do just this, get information about the road and the cotton crop. What was it that made me certain that he was getting quite a different sort of information altogether, that the two of them weren't talking about gradients and gravel at all?

I said something about this when we got back to the hotel in Addis that evening, in the mid-thirties cocktail bar, the Ritz, full of angular mirrors, wicker chairs, and a eucalyptus fire in one corner. We were sitting on high cane stools by the counter, sipping lagers from tall glasses like a pair from an advertisement in an old *Vogue* magazine.

"You are an ass, Helen," George replied calmly, kindly, still so much at ease, happy in the long hot day with lagers at the end of it, food and sleep yet to come. "The heat's gone to your head. What on earth *could* I have been talking to that Russian about—if not his bloody road?" He laughed.

"You went to get some sort of message from him: 'instructions.' That's why we had to come all the way back here."

"Look, I had to go off with him, you idiot. How else would I have found out about his work? It's absolute nonsense, your 'intuition.' You watching the two of us shouting and feel 'left out,' and therefore there was something 'clandestine' between us; that I'm a KGB agent. That's the worst sort of woman's magazine stuff. How on earth did you get hold of that idea?"

"I felt it, that's all. And you're quite right to deny it. But not my feeling. That happened."

"Very well then, we're both right. And I'm sorry. I accept your intuition; you must accept my facts. We've misunderstood each other, that's all." He paused. "But Helen, what an extraordinary thing to think about me. I might just as well say that you were a Russian agent. It's as likely."

She heard a floorboard in the corridor creak, a long succession of knuckles breaking as the joists in the old house cooled after the heat of the day. A door opened and closed, one of the bedrooms along the passage. But she knew exactly which one and knew at once: the Tree Room, looking out over the deformed chestnut on the front lawn. She recognized all the sounds in the old house, could put a name to them all and a reason behind each of them. She had at one time or other slept in all these bedrooms: the Tree Room, where he had been put for the weekend; the Boston Room, with her grandmother's collection of rocking chairs; the Blue Room; and all the others. The sound of a door slamming—any door—its particular resonance, could remind her at once of the drama and the disappointments of her childhood here. One sound—a door closing—was in sure memory of her mother's frustrated affection for her; another sound was an exact memorial to her father's preoccupied indifference. She had never had any trouble in finding out where it had all begun, nor in knowing what a bore it all was—so much unnecessary enmity toward decent life.

She got undressed and ran a bath in the small room attached to their bedroom where the fittings had never been changed; the huge brass taps, golden, top heavy; the wash basin grossly substantial like the bath itself. Yes, she had wanted a father, she thought, as she got into the sweet water, smiling. And had been given a mother instead.

She sank in the water, feeling the small buoyancy in her body each time she breathed, and thought then of that night in the thirties hotel in Addis, long after they'd gone to bed, when she had woken up suddenly from a deep sleep of sex, and looked across at George, and seen a man writing, dreaming, talking—a man she'd never met.

Guy was by himself when I got downstairs, sitting in an armchair by the fire, his long legs stretched out like trip-wires across the sheepskin rug. He had dozed off in the heat. A book he'd been reading lay on the floor beside him. I could see the cover in the lamplight: *White Savages* by Ole Timbutu.

By then I had really given up surprise, so I was able to say to him quite easily when he woke: "What's the book?" And he replied just as easily: "New novel about East Africa I brought up for the weekend. Rather like books about the place."

"Good?"

"Not very. Haven't got far but it's too complicated. Don't know who anyone is, sort of intellectual thriller. I prefer the straightforward stuff. Have you read *The Day of the Jackal?*"

"No."

Could he really be unaware of the real nature of the book, of the identity of the two main characters? I decided to say nothing about it.

He started to read from the blurb: " '. . . frighteningly recreates the obsessive quality of a jealous vision—an out-sider's view of other people's happiness. . . .' What on earth is that supposed to mean?"

It seemed to me that he was being intentionally ob-tuse. He stood up, a puzzled look on his thin face, all the signs of a mystified family man confronted with some psy-chological aberration totally unknown to him.

"Drink? Over here. What would you like?"

We walked over to a table in the corner by the veranda windows. There was the Fleischmann's gin again, I noticed. He poured out two deep measures and added a froth of White Rock tonic to each. Then he said quietly, finger-ing the long dark-blue velvet curtains, pulling them gently across the darker night outside: "That's why I bought the book, Marlow. East Africa first—but then I read that on the blurb. It's funny—how one wants to talk about it. And besides, you. . . ."

"I know."

"You're right in the middle of it. Part of it."

"I'm not her lover. I told you. For God's sake."

"You are in one way: the image of him. And therefore the reality is not impossible. You must see that."

"That's a very long shot indeed. But—all right, tell me about it."

We walked slowly around the large octagonal hall, drinks in our hands.

"You were in prison. So you'll know the feeling: you are inside and excluded; she is outside and included. You are looking on, powerless: you want to put her in the prison with you. That was really why you married her: to hold her completely supine, making your presence—your rather heartless presence—unique and indispensable to her. And when you begin to fail in this—as you will, for she is far from supine—when she begins to move away from you, back into life, then comes the other things, the thing you really wanted, the punishment: you start to follow her with a magnifying glass, a telescope. Because if you can't have her on your own narrow terms, you must see how she deals with other men on *her* terms. That's what you really wanted all along—for her to *make* that move so that you could find out the exact emotional weight of her privacy with someone else; the precise shape of her fantasy and invention with him —conversationally, emotionally, sexually. Above all you must *see*; this is the obsession: you want to see her eyes, their shared regard. One must see *exactly*; nothing less will do— to map out precisely the free flow of all her imprecisions: capture her emotion. Then there is the release."

I was astonished. "What was *your* prison—that brought you to all this?"

"It's usually failure, isn't it? A deep sense of that in oneself."

"Why? Since you aren't. Not conventionally—"

But he didn't answer, so caught was he in the excitement of his words; words, for that moment, exactly mirroring and releasing his obsession.

"One wants to see someone else's success, don't you see? Where you have failed. If love is not mutual, then certainly the punishment will be. I know all that—dreary business of destruction. It's not as if I didn't know *what it was*." He turned away, almost shouting, shaking, maddened like a rejected lover.

"But you don't know where it began—why it's there? I'm sure a psychi—"

"Of *course* he would," Guy came back vehemently. "He could tell me at once—what I know myself. And together we'd paper the whole thing over for a while with convenient friendly words. But how do you cure it? I don't think you do. I don't really think one can. And do you know why? Because you are not to be cured of your pleasure. One forgets that, that it isn't finally a pain."

"Pleasure unto destruction, though, which is the same thing."

"The ideal combination, isn't it? What I've been looking for all along."

"Of course—if you don't want the help: there isn't any. That's an intellectual decision. I didn't think you lacked that ability."

"I've made that decision many times, only to find it overridden."

We both drank heavily from our glasses, both shaken now. I well understood his sense of incurability, the weight of guilt he carried from something far back: something he said he knew about. What was it?

"What was it?" I asked, the two of us passing the heavy double hall doors, drawing near the fire again. "Where do you drag up all this sense of failure from? As a child?"

"I was happy then. Or reasonably. Never remember thinking myself unduly unhappy, anyway. No, it was marriage, I think. Marrying the wrong person—or for the wrong reasons; both of us. Somebody else might have stood my failings better—or needed to depend on me more deeply; either way, someone not so full of life, so many lives, as she is. You see, I was too taken with her ease of living, far too much, her natural capacity for everything *now*. I started to bear down on her for that: a net on a butterfly. I suppose I should have had a duller marriage, something cosy. I couldn't understand her—her volatile—well, a sort of secret energy in her life, a sheer determination to be happy, to rise above. There always seemed something hidden in her happiness, some reason for it that wasn't me, and which I had to find out about."

"And then you found it was another man?"

He nodded. "And still I wasn't satisfied."

"There were others?"

"None that I ever found out about. But by then one imagined there were. One always imagined there was something else with her—because one *felt* it: a thought, a secret, a man—it didn't matter what. But whatever it was, I never felt completely alone with her; you know, possessing each other fully. Always something between us."

He hadn't been wrecked entirely on the shoals of his own obsessions, I thought. He was right: there had always been "something" between them: her Marxism. Not just a lover but her politics, which he pretended to be ignorant of. Yet, if he had read those African detective reports properly, how could he have been? That was the thing that had surely destroyed their marriage as much as anything, which he must have known about, but wasn't telling.

But what about her? With such beliefs, why had she married him, why had she led him on, lied to him? Why take up with this pillar of the establishment, this man of property and capital? Why should a woman searching for revolution fall in with a man dedicated to preventing it: a British Intelligence officer? She must have had some guilt too, and for the first time I felt sympathy for her husband. What had her marriage been for her? A way of extracting secret information from him, a liaison of sheer political convenience?

Suddenly, for all her charming energy, her happy commitments to life, I found it easy to dislike her. And I did so for a moment, thought her a proper bitch, before I realized I might not be justified, that I didn't really know. After all, why shouldn't she have loved him to begin with, whatever the difference of their political beliefs? She had the capacity for love as well as social theory; why shouldn't she be given the benefit of the doubt?

We had come back to the fire. He took a lone, colored match from the mantelpiece, bent down, and lit it from the flame. Then he lit a cigarette.

"In the beginning," I asked, "was it all right? What happened?"

"Yes," he said slowly, calmer now, dousing the match. "Oh, yes. Twelve years ago. My family was farming in Northern Rhodesia; in the beginning it was fine."

"What was she doing out there?"

"Teaching. In an American mission school in the Highlands. Quite near us."

"*Mission* school?"

"Well, it was some Quaker foundation, actually. American-backed. No proselytizing. Self-help, all that. She'd taken a degree at the American University in Beirut where her father worked. But she didn't much like the school. She was just leaving when I met her."

"How?"

"Horses." He laughed, a little quick, snorting laugh. "My parents ran a riding school as a sideline. She came to ride. It's really too much isn't it? The Quaker girl, the mission school, a lot of pickininnies; then the Big House, the young master, riding together; the colonial highlands, the huge skies, sundowners on cane chairs, flame trees over the veranda, and a lot of decent old black retainers moving at the double. God, it had everything for *Woman's Own*. Absolutely everything, but it worked." He stood up from the fire, his face and voice easier now, the light thin body of a man hopefully passing into a period of convalescence after a bad illness.

"A romantic novel. That's exactly what it was to begin with. And I suppose that was wrong too. We didn't think. We didn't have to. It was a perfectly mindless, completely happy time. All of it. And you know—I was wrong: it did work then, the reciprocal thing. There were no doubts. Once I understood her unhappiness she came to me completely. That's very much part of the romantic thing too, isn't it? Coming to someone on the rebound, finding each other through that."

"The rebound? I didn't know."

"Another drink before they come down? I think that must be Harold." I heard a door open upstairs above the stairway; and then close: a strange sound like a bellows sighing.

"Yes," he said, as if he'd told me before. "Some student infatuation in Beirut. One of her professors. Nothing to it. He was much older. But one's very hurt at that age. Very easily. It means a lot. She'd gone and buried herself in Rhodesia. No—we were very happy. That fellow made us very happy—some Armenian-American: brought us together; she needed me then."

He went to the drinks table again. And I thought, well, I'd been wrong about that: she hadn't married him for any bad reason. She had loved him.

And then, thinking of this correspondence, and the weeks before in London in Graham's apartment when I'd read it, I remembered briefly all the work I'd done at the same time on Graham's dossier, his curriculum vitae, the reports and transcripts which Croxley and his men had extracted from him.

And something worried me in all this information I'd absorbed and partly forgotten, something which Guy had just now hinted at: some vital connection between his words and Graham's file. What was it? Quaker girls, mission school? No. Beirut? Yes, something there. And then I had it: some "Armenian-American" she'd been infatuated with. Those words. That was it. And now it came back to me clearly, urgently, my stomach turning: George Graham had been recruited into the KGB in 1952 by Alexei Flitlianov—Croxley had told me all about him—the local Beirut Resident. And Flitlianov at the time had been "posing as an Armenian-American teaching at the American University."

The chain was now suddenly clear, though the links weren't; several years after Graham's recruitment by Flitlianov, Helen had had an affair with Flitlianov in Beirut, and several more years after that she had done the same thing with George Graham. But did all three know that this had happened?

The water was cooling in the big bath upstairs. Helen pushed the hot tap with her toes, moving her foot quickly away from the sudden gush of very hot water, bending her knee upward sharply, legs apart, twisting her body out of the way of the fiery current. . . .

Twisting, dreaming, talking. . . .

She had woken very early that morning in the hotel in Addis, sweating in the small double bed, and had looked across at George. She had thought him awake too, for though he had his back toward her, he was writhing about, struggling restlessly. But when she leaned over him, the sheet thrown far down his body, she saw that his eyes were closed, tightly closed, with crow's-feet wrinkling away from them on either side. His face had the tense disappointment of someone trying not to cry. His normally relaxed body, his limbs which flowed so readily in any kind of movement, now seemed animated by some awkward, kicking demon. His hand came down searching for the sheet, trying to pull it up over him: to hide, to bury himself in it, legs drawn up all ready for the womb.

She took the sheet herself and drew it up over him gently, her hand touching his chest. But he pushed her away, struggling, mumbling incoherently in a resentful tongue.

An anguish seemed to be filling his sleeping mind, transmitting itself to her urgently but indistinctly, an SOS from someone sinking far down over the horizon, the desperate intention lost in the static of a nightmare.

But she thought she knew what the message was. She had touched his real life with her words in the bar downstairs the previous evening, found his most secret place. She had been right. He was with Moscow.

She left the bed silently and turned on the tepid shower in the small cubicle at the end of the room. And then he woke, turning quickly on his back and lying quite still after the torment of his sleep, propped up a little, arms arched behind his head, blinking at her in the shower, a happy form again in the early morning light listening to the trickle of water on the tiles.

"I thought it was raining. A shower," he said.

She smiled, feeling within her the hardening excitement of desire and sure reward, the same sense of imminent pleasure that she had felt at the Whitehall party after she'd first met him, seeing him walk across the room toward her, rescuing her from the Belafonte man from the Voice of Kenya Radio. And just as they had come together physically so quickly and easily after that, so she felt now a certainty that they could share each other in another way, a mental release as sharply pleasurable as the sexual.

"I'm sweating," he said.

"Were you dreaming? A nightmare? You were pushing and shoving about—possessed. I've never seen you like that."

"No. No dream I can remember." He looked at the sheets about him, rumpled and tossed in the shapes of an arctic landscape, his knees rising steeply in the middle of it. "Just very hot for some reason."

The water danced on her shoulder, catching the bottom of her hair, turning the ends of it into a lot of black eels trying to swim down her back in the rush of water.

"You were killing yourself, darling. Because you won't say. But you mustn't. Because you *can* say. Now."

"What?" He wiped his eyes, starting to move again restlessly in the bed, "What was I saying? Was I talking in my sleep?"

"Nothing I could follow. But I know. I'm sure I do."

"Not that again. Not the bloody Russian."

She moved her head around the flow of water, letting it come over the front of her body, looking at him through the rainfall. "I work with them too."

"You have such fantasies." He relaxed again, taking the sheet up and flapping it several times, aerating the bed. "But go on then," he continued, amusing himself with the conspiracy. "Which Directorate of the KGB? Who is your control? isn't that what it's called? And what's your target? And your poison pill when they get you—you've got that, I hope?" He paused, looking at her happily, and then with annoyance when she didn't reply. "What are you doing to me? What game are you trying to play? It's bloody stupid."

She dried herself at the end of the bed and then came forward, pushing down his knees, lying on top of him with the sheet between them.

"Why a game?" Then she considered her question, arching her body against his. "Well, all right, a game in the sense that we shouldn't get all dreary and upset about it." She didn't kiss him.

She wanted to look at him, every moment. So she moved her body to and fro over him, coming to him with her eyes, then drifting away again.

"Listen," he said, "this is quite crazy, if I did work for the Russians—your lying on top of me like this, quizzing me. That's real Mata Hari. I wouldn't tell you a word, would I?"

He touched her shoulder, then ran one finger down judiciously to the point of her breast as she leaned away from him. The sun had burst on the 'window, a streak of gold across the curtain.

"You don't have to tell me. Let me tell you," she said.

"Why should I believe you?"

"You think I really have such fantasies—as *that*?"

"No, funnily enough, you're rather serious. That's what worries me."

"You *really* think I'm a plant—from the other side?"

"It's not unknown, is it?"

She pushed herself up from him for an instant with one arm and pulled the sheet down from between them with the other.

"And this is the seduction scene?" He went on looking at her with interest, with a calm surprise. "This is where I 'tell all.' "

"No. This is just the seduction scene."

He was hard then beneath her, his skin damp and warm against hers, her body bruised with cold water. She touched him and it was hers, an object as freely available, as openly acknowledged as his index finger might have been. It had been like that from the beginning—always like that, making love, as easy as falling off a hundred logs together. They

loved very openly, happy with every skill, without secrets or
stress. And so, just as surely, she thought, his other life could
now be brought into the light with loving.

He put his finger on the tip of her nose, pushing it
gently upward. "I don't believe it. You know I don't. An
all-American girl, bright wide face, long mouth, smile like
a toothpaste—"

"Advertisement—you bastard!" She clutched his shoulders and lowered herself onto him. There was soap there
too, which had not all come away in the shower, so that he
came into her without any effort.

"Married to a Whitehall diplomat, too. You really expect me to believe you work for the Russians? You work
for the British. You've been sent to seduce me. Well, I'm
not telling. So there."

She glided on him now, his head sliding down the pillow, his eyes closing.

"You have no evidence. And I have no evidence," he
said happily, turning his head away. "So what's it all about?
Want to play at being spies? Is that it? Some frustrated sense
of adventure? All right, then, if that's what you want. Who
recruited you, where?"

She pushed on him harder, more urgently. "The KGB
Resident. In Beruit."

"When?"

"1957."

He opened his eyes, but didn't turn around. She stopped
moving. She was excited, close to the end.

"What was his name?"

She lifted herself up from him and looked with fascination down along his body to where they were together,
her hair falling damply on his shoulder.

"Alexei Flitlianov," she said, her throat constricting,
her stomach beginning to rise in her body. And then suddenly the tension broke far inside her, and she had to come
—falling down on him, pushing him into her deeply and
violently, until her body seemed to run inside out and tip
upside down, a steep plunge that lasted for a long time and
no time at all. There was no measure she could give to it,
it was so full, so spinning, so draining.

"Alexei Flitlianov." She said again, "Alexei—" letting all the tension flow from her as the truth emerged, like a birth, so that the name rose up for her, a repeated affirmation, a new sound, a new life in the sunlit room, as sharp and real as the physical truth she had just experienced; and thus, so linked with it, something which could not now ever be doubted, or denied.

He turned around now, amazed, gripping her, head straining backward, his whole body beginning to tremble against hers, arching himself, then coming—at last, she felt, responding to her truth, sharing her spirit.

But what he said as the long spasm died in him surprised her. "Not him, surely. Surely not—no, no."

Then they lay together, absolutely still, without speaking, knowing the truth though they had spoken nothing of it yet; listening to the rising voices on the street outside, the porters and taxi drivers outside the hotel arguing on the new day, the clip-clop tympany of many hooves going to market.

At breakfast that morning, at a corner table over milky bitter coffee, the men clearing out the ashes of the eucalyptus fire in the Ritz bar next door, he asked her in tired astonishment: "How did it all begin? Alexei Flitlianov and you? You of all people. What made you believe in this, in all this—that world? Moscow." He stopped, lost for a moment in the enormous implications. "In something people don't really believe in any more."

She started to tell him, shielding the morning sun from her eyes.

Harold Perkins drank three martinis quietly but quickly before dinner and by midway through the meal, his hand beginning to slide clumsily around his claret glass on the long polished dining table, he was studiously, carefully drunk.

It had been a beautifully laid table: English silver, red Bohemian glass finger bowls, tall clear celery glasses, Waterford decanters, a big spreading vase of wildflowers in the middle. And to begin with, Harold had presided·over it all with happy regality. But now he seemed small and beaten, his white crewcut head swaying low over the half-eaten remains of his food, delving into unhappy memory.

"Marshall aid gave us ideas above our station," he said with sad venom. "That was where it began; we couldn't stop at the soup kitchen, had to police the charity as well. . . . Suddenly, there was a 'moral responsibility' that went with the handout. . . . The next thing we were the defenders of the 'Free World and guns replaced the butter."

He had been talking of the Middle East, of his life in Beirut, but now he had brought his frustrations into a global context.

"You know, I'm not too old. But I've seen all I want to see—so I'm old that way—McCarthy, McCarran, Nixon, and the rest. When you start to police the world there's something rotten under the carpet at home. And so you have to have a moral justification to support your guilt—encourage hysterical grass-roots self-righteousness. . . . And that brings out your witch hunters, and all the other two-bit men suddenly stricken by high principle, my God." He tailed off, wiping his chin.

"Yes, indeed," Guy murmured. "Indeed."

"And as for your United Nations," Harold got onto his high horse again, looking hard at Guy. "That collection of . . . of . . . the 'underdeveloped' world, indeed. What cheek!"

"The less developed, we call it—"

"Sitting on their asses in six hundred committees, singing while the world burns. Why in hell should they want our development? What's it really done for us?"

"Coffee?" Helen stood up. Harold continued to browbeat Guy.

"Yes," I said, getting up and following her into the kitchen. The housekeeper had disappeared, leaving the coffee cups on a tray and a big dishwasher warbling in the corner.

"He lost his job you see," Helen said quite suddenly, putting the kettle on. She opened a fresh tin of coffee and sniffed it. "His opinions. Those ones. He was in Washington. An undersecretary in the State Department's Middle East Bureau, Eisenhower's first administration. A little left in the thirties, communist friends then, though he was never in the party. But McCarthy got onto him, dragged it all up in a congressional committee; wanted him to name his friends. He took the Fifth, refused. And he was ruined, fired, *caput*. No one here would give him another job; nothing in Washington, nothing academic. Finally, he got a post at the American University in Beirut and we all went out there. It wasn't the money. He just wanted the work—the position to work for those opinions. He was no communist, but he might just as well have been—he'd have suffered no more. He might as well have gone the whole way."

And I thought I saw it then: the beginning—or perhaps just the final confirmation—of her beliefs; she had taken up her father's failure, fifteen years before in Beirut, and made a success of it. Senator McCarthy had ruined her father's career, but made hers, delivering her into the hands of Moscow while attempting to save his country from the same scourge.

"What an awful business," I said, trying to get through one of those moments when there is really nothing to say.

She turned. "Yes. You probably knew all about it anyway." The kettle boiled, and she made the coffee. "Knew about me, about father, about everything."

"Why do you say that?"

"I feel it. Felt it all along. You know everything about Graham—you've taken him apart and put on all the bits and pieces yourself—so you *must* know about me. How could you not?"

Suddenly she was slack, empty, the coffee brewing on the table between us, all the social energy gone, her face tired, troubled—the one where she put on experience and knowledge and was no longer an advertisement for success and innocence. "Why have I been pretending with you all this time? You *must* know, mustn't you? And I'm tired, really tired."

"Know what?"

She was tired beyond anger, which would have been there otherwise. "Why don't you tell them, your own people, and have them tell the Americans? Isn't that your real job over here? To check me out, to find all Graham's contacts, the people he would have dealt with over here, who wouldn't know what he looked like?"

"And you're one of them?"

"What do you think?"

"I thought you were just his mistress."

"Nothing more?"

"Yes. I've begun to think something more. But you knew what he looked like; you couldn't have been one of my contacts."

"I wasn't supposed to know Graham at all. That was just sheer chance."

"You're telling me you were an agent with him—you realize that?—with the KGB?"

"You knew it," she said, gazing down at the coffeepot. Then she pulled her hair to either side of her ears and looked up at me, standing terribly straight, with an expression of royalty taking the salute on a parade ground. "Why carry on this farce, the pretense? You knew, either from Graham himself when they caught him in London, or some other way."

"Some other way. I told you, Graham never mentioned any women. I heard nothing about you in England. I explained all that to you as well."

"Yes, I believed you—that, and the fact that you wanted none of the whole business. It struck me all along, that you were some kind of fall guy, forced into the whole thing."

"Maybe. But why do you tell me that you're a KGB agent? That's more important. Why not get hold of your Russian contacts here, and tell them *about* me: that I'm impersonating a KGB officer? They'd be interested in that."

"I don't have any contacts here. That's why."

"Funny kind of agent."

"Yes." She stopped dead, passing the ball to me.

"Well, there you are. That's just it: you've confirmed something I suspected. But there must be so much more—"

"Oh, the CIA could get the rest out of me. No trouble, don't you think?"

"Exactly. So *why* tell me? Without any prompting. No agent ever does that. I'm on the other side, even as a fall guy, you knew that. It doesn't make sense. You trusted me. Why? That you never do in our business. Never."

"You trusted me, didn't you? Not telling them, or Guy, about Graham and me. And saying nothing about the letters. It's quite simple. And that meal we had, watching you, watching you eat as if it hadn't been for years. Looking at you. Talking with you." Then she came back and leaned over the table, looking at me carefully. "About Rip Van Winkle, and my marriage, remember? And Women's Lib. And before lunch, drinking, that Pernod or whatever, munching olives. It was pretty easy to trust you. And even easier, remembering you were George Graham. And wanting him."

I remembered Guy's talk about how she had married him on the rebound. And it was the same with me, finding me that way as well. And I thought then that it was all too neat, too convenient: she's only playing, pretending trust; she wants to find out more about me before telling her Russian contacts, before turning me over.

She took up the coffee tray. "I can see you don't believe it all; you're looking for the flaw. But there isn't any. Not for us. There needn't be because neither of us is playing that game—not involved in the big league. You've something else on your mind altogether and I've very little left to do now. So don't you see? If we trust each other we'll both get out of it in one piece."

"Why—why that trust in me?"

"We're both more or less transparent to the other, don't you see that? That's why."

I half saw. . . . "All right," I said, "I'm no professional. But I know one thing about the business: they don't let you out of it once you're in. Least of all the KGB. Besides, to be with them in the first place, for them to have taken you on— you of all people—you must have believed in everything, hook, line, and sinker. You surely don't give all that up so easily, least of all just because your lover has disappeared. It couldn't have been so weak a thing with you—so lightly to throw it away now."

She moved toward the door. I could hear footsteps coming toward the kitchen. "We can talk," she said. "There's the whole weekend." She left the room.

Yes, she thought that night in bed, he was right: it was no weak thing and I cannot, will not, lightly throw it all away. But I must get out of this—not lose the belief, but the hell of believing and not being able to live or share it any-more.

Her two lives—political and emotional, both secret—now had no reality for her, were dead. With George, for more than six years, she had shared them both and could well have lived with him that way in the future. But there was no one now. He was gone. And her position with Alexei Flitlianov, whom she saw very rarely, was no more than that of post-mistress for his organization, a safe repository for the letters that came to her private mailbox which she held under an-other name at Grand Central Post Office in New York; letters with envelopes inside which contained the coded names of the recruits for his clandestine agency within the KGB, in which George had been his principal overseas deputy.

She had been nowhere near the mailbox in New York since the day she'd met Graham's double at the UN, for she had to assume the worst—that they had found out about this poste restante address from Graham in London, which he had used in writing to her—and would be watching it now, waiting to see who picked the mail up. And she had no way of contacting Alexei in Moscow. That contact was always one way, a marked envelope in the box which she then opened. There was no other contact; George had been her only un-official connection with Flitlianov's group, a connection which Alexei had never known about.

Thus she held the key, the master plan to the whole secret organization within the KGB. And the group had now been penetrated by the British, of all people, and she was quite helpless to do anything about it, to warn anybody, for that had never been an expected part of her job since, apart from Alexei, she was never supposed to know the identity of anyone else involved in it. And she never would have, except for the chance of meeting Graham six years before in London.

Of course, she should never have confided in George Graham. They should have stayed just lovers. Why had love made her so sure—and so stupid? Alexei had left her, almost fifteen years before in Beirut, with clear instructions: tell no one, ever, of her position; do nothing, ever, which might draw attention to her real beliefs. If anything ever went wrong in picking up the letters from Alexei she would have to deal with it herself; she was never to try and contact him. He had told her quite clearly that afternoon nearly fifteen years ago when they had driven round the hills above Beirut; warned her that she would take no risk at all in the work she wanted to do other than one major risk: immediate and complete exposure which she would have no warning of if the KGB, or anyone else, discovered her poste restante address. Did she realize that? Was she so sure she wanted the task?

Yes, she realized all that; she wanted the task.

She and Alexei had been talking on the way to Bhamdoun, circling up the hill roads from the coast, the car windows all wide open, gradually feeling the increasing sharpness of the spring air as they rose higher toward the mountains. Beirut had been damply hot with the onset of summer, people oppressed and sweating already at ten o'clock in the café on Hamra where they had met that morning in the city.

They drove for an hour and when they were high enough from the sea, where the air was warm without damp or chill and there was a sudden view down a small rocky valley—a ruined orchard, it seemed, of feathery scrub and old olive trees—they stopped, parking, just off the road.

"It mustn't be a strain for you. I'd hate that," he said later.

"Hate to be saddled with me, you mean, the object of a hopeless longing?" She laughed. "No. Not that. We've talked that out, haven't we? You're older—one foot in the grave—that's the only difference."

"It's quite a lot. Not just fifteen years; a totally different past—and a different future."

"We talked that one out too. We agreed on that: just to have now."

He threw away the cigarette he had been smoking. "You have it all so well organized in your mind, Helen. You set all your feelings out so clearly, like things on a tray, all in order. As if you were older than I was, had lived it all, and found just these few really valuable things—got rid of all the rest, the bad feelings, disappointment, being hurt. I've always been amazed by the clarity of your vision."

"You've just an old-fashioned idea about women, that's all—you old Georgian peasant."

He paused, looking at her carefully. "It makes me frightened of leaving you, that's all, that's what worries me. Missing your temperament. It's something very important to me: your balance, yet your full love; the uncomplicated way you express your feelings, yet the depths you show as well but never talk about. One wants that all one's life—passion and reason. One wants the same thing politically, after all."

She looked at his unbalanced face and thought how much his lack of symmetry appealed to her: the chipped front tooth; hair dark and slightly coarse at the top, fine and going white at the sides; the eyes set a bit too close and too deep; the long arms a little too long and the torso a little too short. And she thought: We do not love human perfection. Have we come to that simply through long disappointment, or is it a quality in our nature, a natural truth, an essential factor in the preservation of the world? And if so, why should we hold out such hopes for any political ideal? Why should she? As an antidote to human failure, perhaps—hers as a child, and her father's now, both of them searching for an outside order, like a child in a huge candy shop craving the satisfaction of all that ordered sweetness. Yes, that had been the original impetus in her case, however much she had rationalized her beliefs afterward. She might just as well have taken to God and all the hands of Providence, she thought.

They went a little way down the valley toward the vision of sea, pushing through the dry underbrush beneath the old trees, slipping on loose stones, frightening salamanders, treading on clumps of lemon thyme, running their nails along the stalks of other herbs as they passed, collecting dry balls of leaves, a pungent potpourri, pushed up into the palm of their hands as if by machine as they moved along, which they smelled before throwing them away behind them.

And it was a bit of one of these leaves, thrown over his shoulder, that caught her in the eye, and his hands smelled incredible as looked for it, the skin dry and the ribs on his fingers a little coarse like fine sandpaper.

The hands of care about her face, without invitation or suggestion. They had not come here to do that. They had come out for the day to walk and talk and look: two ordinary people, she thought, ordinarily involved in the most casual pursuits, not bent on any sexual gratification, not grasping for emotional success. All that they knew they possessed in any case. And even though time was running out, that did not matter either. Well, yes, it might matter a little. And she would get over it. For surely there was that balance, that complete understanding between them that must include a palliative against any real future hardship?

Yet now he said he was going to miss something—her, it, everything. . . . It seemed a contradiction of all the terms in their association. Now he was setting up the loss, the hurt; assembling the bridges that she had never thought to cross, suggesting pain, and therefore creating a future that had never existed before—a time of empty, unhappy consideration and memory for both of them. It annoyed her.

She said, angrily, "Why tempt me, tempt yourself, with a future between us, Alexei, sad or happy? Why do that with talk of missing me?"

And she was surprised at the small, measured anger of his return: "You can easily think of now. There's lots of it for you, even if it wasn't a quality you possessed so fully anyway—living now, with reason, curiosity, passion, all that. But perhaps without too much reflection, the need for hope. And we need both: ironic reflection as well as the singing and dancing."

"Listen, what sort of hope can you suggest for us? If you had, I would have thought about it, I can tell you. Shall we go and live in Moscow? Or back in the States? Or anywhere—I don't mind. But there isn't that hope, there never was."

Anguish rose from somewhere strange inside her and blew up in her mind, a bitter explosion, and with it came a rush of violent needs, an uncontrollable desire to demean their whole shared experience, to cut it all down to size.

"Words, you have the words, Alexei, all as neatly arranged as you said my feelings were. And just because you put it into words, you think it's all explained—and therefore all over and all right. You've justified yourself. *But not me.* Not my feelings. I can't argue myself into that kind of happy good-bye anymore. I could, but not now. Now *you're* more or less saying it: 'Cheerio, and toodle-oo, and good-bye, and wasn't it wonderful? Absolutely great. Oh yes, and we shouldn't worry about anything else, no, not at all, absolutely nothing. Because it's been great. And hasn't it been great in bed too? Hasn't it? Smashing. And that's all there ever really was, all we really wanted: the now business, and doing it first thing in the morning as well. And thanks very much and we can both of us reflect on it ironically now.' 'Ironic reflection,' that's just what I needed, that makes it all absolutely wonderful. But I can't fucking well reflect on it all *ironically*. Not *now*."

"I didn't say any of that, Helen. I said I'd *miss* your future; that's what I said."

"That's what kills me, because I'd never seen us missing each other until you mentioned it."

Tears came, unnoticed, her face angled from him, her vision clouding.

"What you're angry at, Helen, is my loving you," he said. "I'm sorry. I know the feeling, how much easier without that, with just the fun and the affectionate thing between us. And not the tense business under it all. I know that: the wasting sense when you're thought of, not with me, which isn't a feeling to live at all comfortably with, which is always pushing you to all sorts of desperation, which is not loving but more destroying, so that you would do anything to turn the tap off—but can't. You're sorry for that, Helen, those sorts of feelings in each of us that we don't talk about because there isn't a future in it. I know. All we can do is live it now, and not think about it too much. And that's marvelous. But it's also very little."

And she didn't feel like crying then. The tears had drained away, while he talked, without ever falling, leaving her eyes sore and dry. And she could look at him now, and she did, without any more anger. And she said, "Where shall we have our picnic?"

9

The sign above the side door of the liquor store at the end of the single village street of Stonestead said "Rooms—Vacancies." But the door was locked, so Alexei Flitlianov came around to the front, stepped up onto the small veranda that gave out onto the hot asphalt, and came into the shop. There was no one there either.

It was hot in the small quiet room, full of the long afternoon's heat, with the quick "flap-flap-flap" of tires on huge trucks as they passed over the soft tar every few minutes outside. But outside there had been a breeze and on it now, coming from an open doorway at the back of the building, he smelled meat burning, the air singed with fat falling on charcoal, a dry smoky breath that he could almost taste in his mouth as it flowed through the room and out of the mosquito-wired front door.

A woman appeared in the corridor, passing from the kitchen to the garden in the rear, wiping her hands vigorously on a meat-stained apron. But she saw him. She was small, delicate, spinsterish, shy-looking woman with glasses, wearing very new, colored sneakers. Yes, she had a room: $2.50 by the night, or $14.00 the week. He took it for two nights, paying in advance.

"Put your car out back," she said, not at all shy. "Down the side. There's a lot at the end."

"Grigorian," he said, though he'd not been asked to sign anything and she seemed quite incurious about him. "Mr. Grigorian. I'm from overseas. Come to look up some of my relatives around here."

"Oh yes? Not a name I've heard around these parts. But we're new here. Only a couple of years. They'll most ways know in the store down the street." She showed him up to his room.

He had followed the Jacksons and the Englishman up from New York that same afternoon, an hour behind them, in a hired Avis, for he'd known exactly where they were going. He'd seen Helen and the children, with their summer gear, piling into the car outside their apartment in the East Fifties and had followed them down to the UN building where she'd picked up her husband and the other man, and he'd known the destination must be the house at Belmont.

He'd been nowhere near her mailbox at Grand Central Post Office, of course, and had sent nothing to it. Nor could he risk telephoning her; the phone would surely be tapped. She was almost certainly being followed by someone from the CIA or British Intelligence, as well as by Graham's double, so that any direct approach to her in New York had been out of the question too. The only chance of making a safe contact with her, he felt, was in the country, in the house upstate which she'd talked to him about in the past. There was plenty of cover there, and he might get a message to her. There was a fair chance, too, that any secondary surveillance might be dropped for the weekend. In any case, in those open spaces, he could *see* who might be following her, besides the other man, which he could not do in New York.

The other man, the man the British had put in Graham's shoes. How had he got onto Helen, he wondered? Simply through her poste restante address in New York? They'd got that information out of Graham in London of course, watched the mailbox, and seen her pick something up from it quite recently, then followed her back home and identified her. The man couldn't have found her any other way. And now they'd be looking for all that coded information which she possessed, were closing in for it. Where did she keep it? Whatever happened he would have to get that correspondence first.

But the other man—he, him, the unknown, rather uncertain-looking Englishman wearing Graham's clothes whom he'd followed all across the Atlantic—there was something strange there, beyond the man's impersonation, that worried him. How had Helen become so immediately friendly with him? How had he picked up with her so soon, so easily, so conveniently?

He remembered the lunch the two of them had had together in the Breton restaurant on the West Side—a long meal of close chatter within a few days of meeting the woman —and the street accident afterward where he'd nearly been caught with the other man who'd been trailing her. Was it all just sheer chance? Or had the man some other personal or previous relationship with her? And in any case why had the British chosen the same man to replace Graham *and* to follow her? Sheer administrative convenience perhaps? He could think of no other reason.

He unpacked his small suitcase, looked over the new Zeiss pocket binoculars, cleaned the lenses gently, and thought of Helen. He remembered being with her in Beirut simply as a man and not a KGB agent, when a person obsessed him and not an idea. And the temptation there'd been to follow that emotion through and not the dry toil of political theory. Of course with her he might have had both, the first nurturing the second: the salami curling in the sunshine of that olive-filled valley and the long haul of revolutionary change. But that would have all have had to take place in the West, as a defector, as an academic somewhere perhaps, as an outsider in any case, as one of so many dispossessed Marxists, intellectual agitators whose work could never be more than a frustrating, masturbatory itch, an idealistic commentary or forecast on a movement which you had to be inside ever to influence. A man thinking as he did, at the very center of the KGB, was worth a thousand hopeful books from sympathizers in the West.

And so he had stayed in Russia—and left her outside in the world for other men to have lunch with, and long talks in small Breton restaurants on the West Side.

What had they talked about? He wished his long training could have told him what; that his profession as spy could have done this one thing for him, more important than all the other things at that moment: the words, the tone of voice, the angle of her face, the statements and hesitations—the tempting magic of two people at the start of even the most casual relationship. The spoken thought, and the unspoken one behind that; the present fact between them; the next one already forming, jointly proposed, immediately agreed upon and defined; and the limitless variety of future moments. That was what lunch with her had been like in Beirut, the meetings in the early days. And he realized that he was thinking of Helen and this other man as poten-

tial lovers, not as quarry and hound. Or old lovers? The
thought suddenly struck him. He sensed—or did he imagine?
—this extremity of familiarity between them, thought he saw
in their behavior not the beginning of something but the
happy renewal of an old habit.

10

In London that Saturday morning Harper had come in specially for a meeting with McCoy in their Holborn office, an
empty glass honeycomb, shot through from wall to wall with
bright July sunshine. Middle East espionage and Navy Recruitment were both closed down for the weekend. The duty
security officer let them into McCoy's office on the eighth
floor in the northern wing and a smell of sun-warmed disinfectant greeted them, a disgusting mixture of synthetic lavender and carbolic.

McCoy studied the text of the message which had come
up overnight from Government Communication H.Q. in
Cheltenham, rustling the flimsy, heavily typed orange paper,
the letters pierced through to the other side like Braille.

"Well, Marlow's had nearly two months—and no joy."
He looked up at Harper, passing him the message. "Nothing.
No approach to him. And no approach to the mailbox at
Grand Central. And nothing sent to the box either. We've
no idea who the person is who's getting all this stuff—the
names of all these people. They must be onto us. Someone's
seen through Marlow."

"Of course we don't know how often these communications take place," Harper said seriously, trying to give his
hope weight. "Or how often the letters are picked up. They
may let it pile up; or the recipient may be away."

"It's no good, Harper. Something should have come
through that mailbox by now. It's the only dead letter drop
for this KGB internal security division in America. There
must have been messages to send. That's what Graham was

going to do in the States after all, be given a batch of names from that box and check their security out."

"Well, we know it's a woman." Harper pressed his optimism. "The Post Office authorities in New York told us that. It was a woman who rented the box in the first place."

"Yes, three years ago. And the clerk fellow had no exact memory of what she looked like."

"Said she was American, quite young and pretty."

"Even in America there are quite a few women who fit that description." McCoy was sour and depressed. His scheme was falling apart, the trail had died: the CIA would soon cease to collaborate with them on it, and he didn't want that. He wanted something to take out of it all, even if only the smell of success which he could waft in the faces of his superiors. And Harper knew this. McCoy's vanity was really the only card he held.

So he said, "We've not had Marlow on it long enough surely? You were more than eight weeks before you pulled in Graham."

"Exactly, and no one contacted him either."

"Can't always hurry these things."

"I know that. But we've lost this hand. I feel it. We've got all the information we're going to get on this KGB secret security service—from Graham himself. Special Branch are still working on him. Perhaps they'll get some more from him. We might as well leave it at that."

"Why?" Harper asked. "After all there's no urgency, no deadline. Marlow appears quite happy. Why not leave him there for the moment? And we're not paying for him after all, the UN is. And the surveillance on that mailbox is costing very little. And there's one other thing: I don't think this fellow Jackson has run Marlow as well as he might, not got enough out of him. I'd like to talk to Marlow. You see I'm sure that this KGB Security Officer—this Stayer woman in New York—must have sounded Marlow out already. Someone in the UN maybe—she *must* have made some sort of tentative approach to him, either socially or professionally, and Marlow's thought nothing of it, not seen the approach as at all important. And Jackson is not trained as an interrogation officer. He doesn't know the right lines with him, how to run back through each and every person Marlow's met since he arrived in New York. Probably has his mind on his next posting. Moving to Cheltenham, isn't he, in August? Some new course in communications there?"

"Yes. He said something about that. Couldn't go on liaising with Marlow."

"I think I'd find something out if I spoke to him. I'm sure I would."

"I'm sure you wouldn't," McCoy retorted. "The trail's dead. They've packed up."

Harper's spiel had been frustrated at its climax and he was annoyed. But he showed nothing. The humps and hollows, the switchbacks of skin about his pockmarked face, remained quite stationary. Had he been pressing too hard? He tried the opposite approach as a last chance.

"Maybe you're right. Just thought we might rescue something from it all. But it's too long a shot, I agree. Not worth it," he said, crossing his fingers in his mind. He got up and looked out the side window onto Red Lion Street. Then Harper's stomach turned and he smiled as he heard McCoy say: "Well—perhaps. Yes. Yes—if you like, why not try it, Harper? Last chance for a feather in our caps."

And they agreed then and there that Harper should leave for New York on the following day.

"Thank you, sir," Harper said as they left the office, blowing their noses against the fearful smell. "I think I may find this woman: 'American, quite young and pretty.' I think I will." And he really hoped he would, for Moscow wanted nothing less.

11

"Yes, take him riding, Helen." Guy Jackson got up and went to the dining room window, sipping his coffee. Hair too neatly brushed, dressed in a polka-dot Sulka dressing gown, framed in the grand casements, he had the air of someone testing for the part Cary Grant got in the original

High Society. There was something insincere in his suggestion. He looked out over the terraces of sloping lawn, past
the meadow to the trees and mountains rising beyond, with
too eager an expression, as if contemplating a bed and not
a landscape. "We can swim later. Or take a picnic lunch to
Flatrock."

The twins were in the kitchen, being fed by the housekeeper. Harold Perkins had not appeared for breakfast; no
reasons offered, and none needed.

"But I *don't* ride. I've never ridden," I said, lying. I'd
been around the pyramids several times years before—the
sand made it easy falling—and as a child I'd been thrown
twice by an old pony, suddenly come young again, passing
other horses on the road. "Well, I've fallen off more times
than I've ridden," I added.

But it was no use. Guy wanted me off riding with her,
getting his generous obsessions to work again first thing,
gathering fodder for his morning fantasies. By lunchtime,
no doubt, he'd have organized some other little scheme for
our exciting togetherness and his absent delectation.

The stables and other yard buildings were quite a distance down from the side of the house, behind a big patch of
chestnut trees with a grand arched gateway leading into them.

There were two big bay hunters which we looked at,
eighteen hands or whatever, fierce in the eye and quite frisky
too, one of them bowing and pawing the ground ominously.
And I said at once, there and then, that I wouldn't think of
riding either of them. Suicidal.

"No. Not these. There's another horse over that way, an
old thing that barely moves. You'll be all right."

Helen hadn't gone in for the riding garb, I was glad to
see—the dreadful black boots and jodhpurs business, the whip
and saucy cap: just in Levi's and a shirt, as I was myself. But
she was very professional about all the rest of the mysterious
business: testing the girths, adjusting bridles, dispensing
with martingales.

My horse indeed was quite an old thing, with a downy
sheen of white the length of its nose, something like a small
cart horse, with tufty hair around its hooves and the melan-
choly expression of a seasoned drinker. But it had a powerful-

looking rump and was in no way decrepit. I was prepared to believe in its age but not therefore in any serious mechanical failure—slightly less horsepower, simply, by comparison with Helen's supercharger.

But there was no way out now. Guy's ridiculous idea had become a fact, with the groom busying himself with my stir-rups, Helen telling me how to sit, and Guy himself ponder-ing the whole scene with silent approval. What a bore his fantasies were, I thought, a dangerous bore.

And yet there was a feeling of sharp enjoyment: getting up on the beast and sitting in the saddle before anything happened: smelling the saddle-soaped leather and the damp cheesy smell of horse; my head ten feet up, looking down at the smooth crown of Guy's head, and finding Helen parallel to me, and the two of us suddenly in a quite unexpected position, strangely suspended above the ground. And I'd have been perfectly happy to have stayed that way and just walked around the yard for a bit and then got off and gone home. But of course that wasn't the idea at all, and off we went, out the archway and along the back drive that led through neatly planted maples and old elms down toward the farm.

It was magnificent, untouched country, rich in foliage, color, form—rampant in everything. It was as if a classic English parkland had exploded and run wild over a thousand acres: a world unfound, it seemed, where people had not come.

I said, "Guy seems terribly concerned to get us off alone together."

"Yes—pimping for me. One of his problems."

My horse was falling behind. "What do you do to make it go faster?"

"Kick it, gently."

I kicked. Nothing happened. She looked back. "Harder."

I kicked it harder. Nothing.

"Knows you don't know how to ride. They sense it at once."

"Thanks."

She reined in, waiting for me.

"Isn't that rather uncomfortable?" I asked.

"What? You've got to sit up straight, not slouch. Keep your knees in line with your toes."

"No, I meant the pimping."

"Yes. But there's always got to be something in some-one, hasn't there? Some flaw. Better to have it in the open. He really does it quite openly. That's something."

She looked over at me, questioningly, perfectly upright yet relaxed, as if I was the only person now who was hiding anything. And of course that was true. She pressed the ad-vantage.

"How is your work going? Think you'll soon be able to finish it and get back home?"

"No. Nothing's happened."

"We agreed—you remember, at the Guggenheim Mu-seum—to work together so that *both* of us might get out of this business: 'in one piece' you said, you with your work done and me with—I don't know what now. Have you for-gotten? That's what I was saying last night too. Don't let the reins slack; hold them firmly, hands just above the withers."

We moved off the back drive toward the hills to the north along a narrow, heavily overgrown lane, a rutted old cart track with rotten branches and sometimes whole tree trunks fallen along our path, and elders and a great deal of tangle from other trees above us.

"No, I remember." I sighed mentally. The fine day seemed less good and the air was dank and almost wintery and rotten-smelling in the covered laneway. "You want a progress report, you and the KGB. For me to hand you on a plate all my stupid arrangements. That's ridiculous."

She bent away a large briar, then held it back for me as I passed. Her shirt was dotted with some kind of green fly and they must have got into her hair too for she started to scratch it. "Look, you could have gone back to New York last night and told your people about me," she said. "But you didn't. And neither will I. I promise, even if I had someone to tell."

Well, why not this conspiracy, I thought? It was as good as any. Just she and I. I knew a great deal about her now—and felt no more need to tell them about it in London than I had at the beginning when I'd read her letters. And as for her betraying me, that was a hurdle of trust I had to take blindly or not at all. I didn't go on her looks or her words. They meant very little in the decision. It was a matter of simple choice on my part and nothing else, a gamble one way or the other, something for life or against it.

So I told her. And it was quite easy once I started—very easy, really, telling this second woman all about myself. I suppose I must have a penchant for that sort of confidence.

I told her about Durham Jail, coming to London, being forced into Graham's shoes and being packed off to New York to wait for the contact, the Stayer, with the names of suspect KGB agents. I told her the whole thing, and it sounded a wonderfully stupid charade in the telling.

"Graham was going to set up a KGB satellite circle over here, part of their internal security division," I said. "I suppose that's what you're in too? You're the Stayer surely?"

"No. Absolutely not."

"You've got all the qualifications they told me to expect: someone quite *un*expected, outside all the usual grubby circles, not active in any way, just a postbox, with a practically unbreakable cover: Manhattan socialite, yet Marxist—that's all of you."

"It's not. I'm not your contact. I promise!"

"No." And I believed her words and her face then. "No, I suppose not. That would be too easy; you could give me the names I need, then, couldn't you, and I could go home with them and get a medal."

"I've nothing to do with that KGB security circle."

"But Graham had. And you were linked with him—and don't tell me you neither of you knew the other was in the KGB."

Either her face was coloring or the green light was getting darker. She didn't answer my point and I let it be. The answer was obvious: her silence confirmed it. Instead she asked: "And Graham—what will they do with him?"

"If no one contacts me they'll try him and put him away —and use him as a future bargaining counter with Moscow if one of our men gets picked up there. That's what they usually do."

"That's what you call my 'getting out in one piece' is it?"

"What do you expect? I'm amazed you're still here, that they didn't manage to get your name from him in the first place. They seem to have got everything else out of him."

So he was gone, dead for her now; she knew it at last, without doubts anymore. And I thought her face showed some relief in this knowledge finally accepted, so that the tense expectancy in her expression that had hovered there from the beginning disappeared and the lines in her face became molded in a calm way, like a child asleep after a long and boisterous party. She got off her horse and led it around a dead tree trunk, which had fallen diagonally along our path. I did the same. And now there was a lot of dead timber in front of us, whitened where it faced the air in jagged ribs and covered in moss, and deep grass underfoot. We picked our way along through the ruined path leading the horses through the olive light.

"Where does this lead to?"

"Edge of the Catskill Preserve—there's a good ride there."

Something cracked in the thick underbrush to our left.

"Deer," she said. "Or something." She was thinking of something else, still picking at the green flies.

"Not bears, I hope. People are always getting munched up by grizzlies out here, aren't they?"

"In Yellowstone. Not the Catskills. Why don't you run? I would."

"I'd thought of that. But I want to live for a change. In the world, drinking the wine. Not scurrying about or locked up. Surely you've got *some* names you could give me—just a few suspect KGB fellows? Then I could take home the bacon and spend the rest of my life in the Cumberland Hotel."

Her face woke up a little, first with surprise, and then, seeing my smile, with one of her own: a little wan, it's true, but she was trying.

"Listen, what are you called? I never thought—"

"Marlow . . . Peter. . . ."

"Well, listen Peter, I've not told you everything. I can't.

But it's nothing to do with your job, I promise, no danger to you—"

"Don't worry." I was suddenly angry at her reticence after my own confession. "I know, it's to do with Graham. And with his boss in Moscow. The man who recruited him in Beirut: Alexei Flitlianov, isn't it? Because you were in Beirut when he was, just after Graham had been there. And that makes three of you. And you're all linked in some way— isn't that it?—and it's not to do with this KGB internal security organization, is it? Or so you say. Then what is it? You tell me."

She stopped the horse and looked at me wildly. If she'd had a stick with her I'm sure she'd have come at me with it.

"Come on," I said. "Don't make a scene. It's the holy hour, time for confession. Why not do it properly?"

"The British knew all along, then—about the three of us?"

"No. They can't have linked you with any of this. They'd have told me. I got it from Guy last night: an infatuation you had with a professor in Beirut—an 'Armenian-American,' he said. Well, of course, that was Flitlianov's cover then. They got that out of Graham. I knew that. I just put the two together."

"And what else have you put together?" Her horse started to nibble at her elbow. She pushed it away.

"Well, since you ask. . . ." We were getting dramatic, but I didn't want it that way, so I changed course. "No, I'm sorry. But he knows about you and George Graham too."

"Christ. Just that we were together, or the political thing as well?"

"Both, I think. He had a lot of private eyes out after the two of you on that trip you had together in East Africa. And here in New York."

"I don't believe it."

"So he says. And I think it's true. I saw one of them that day we had a meal on the West Side. From a detective agency here. Not a government man. But Guy said not to tell you, so you'd better forget all about it. He's stopped it now."

She was shaking in the green chill, the sun no more than

an odd bright dazzle between the leaves. We had no coats. I put my hands high up on both her arms and pressed them together, and then shook her body gently, as though rubbing a fire stick.

"But how can he know this—and not tell your people in London? He works for them after all"

"Yes, but you're his wife. It's quite natural, isn't it? He doesn't want to turn you in. It would ruin his own career too—quite apart from whatever he feels for you."

"I'll take your first suggestion. And it's not altogether natural; he feels for me—in this way: you with your arms around me. That's the only way he feels for me."

"Yes. He told me all about that too. You shouldn't be too hard on him."

Another stick snapped somewhere behind us. "Think he's out after us here as well?" I asked. "With a spyglass, foaming at the mouth?"

She laughed then, and came for a moment completely in my arms. But without anything else. There was no need in us for that. We had no freedom to come into our own, both of us still tied to others, halfway through a puzzle.

"I wonder why we haven't both been picked up long ago," I said, "with everyone knowing so much."

"I don't think we've started knowing," she said. But her horse seemed restless over something, dipping his head and pricking his ears and smelling the dank air, so we moved on.

Alexei Flitlianov had been some distance behind them all the while, moving parallel to the lane through the thick bushes and scrub that bordered it. Twice he'd stumbled on hidden branches and stopped, the horses' footsteps disappearing into the sunlit green silence ahead of him. But he wasn't too worried. There were animals about, chipmunks and squirrels and others he couldn't see, making odd starts and forays, crackling the undergrowth just as he had done. Besides, in the few glimpses he'd had of the couple he'd seen how completely preoccupied they were with each other, deep in talk, quite unsuspecting.

They'd dismounted and finally stopped, and he'd been a little above them then, on a slight rise over the lane, and he'd been able to watch them for a minute with his binoculars through a gap in the trees; he watched him hold her first, shaking her a little, and then the two of them together in each other's arms.

Their words were lost to him, just odd murmurs, but the message was clear enough: she had taken up with this plant from British Intelligence just as he had suspected—some sort of affair, old or new he didn't know. But did *she* know what the man's real job was? That was the point. And if she knew who he was, that he was no UN pen-pusher, what had she told him? When you were close to someone like that, he thought wearily, you told them everything, didn't you?

Had she betrayed him or not? That was what it all boiled down to.

And because he had so clearly seen them close together in the attitudes of potential infidelity—to her husband in one way and to him in another—he found himself believing that she had told the man everything, that the years had been too long for her, exposed and isolated, and that her faith in him and all his doings had waned or died.

And he knew so well how that could happen; nothing dramatic, no overnight recantation, but a gradual erosion through absence from the center of things: not an end of belief necessarily, but a terrible weakness in it. A woman, he knew, with a failing marriage, may take up something illicit and passionate with another man for a while, and so regain, and even find, a fuller love for her husband when she returns to him. But in his politics, once you had left you could not come back again to any stronger or more appropriate belief. And so he saw in their acts at the end of his binoculars the breaking out of individual happiness and the dissolution of a political ideal. And most people would have said that was fair enough; the two things couldn't go together; it was a hopeless task to try and link them, and he had simply been very lucky once. But now he saw how every ideal begins and ends in the realization of eccentric self-will.

He watched them disappear from the space in the trees, saw their heads bobbing up and down among the leaves further along the lane. They were like a cigarette commercial, he thought: happy but dangerous.

Helen was riding ten yards ahead of me as we reached the end of the dark lane. We could see open, rising country beyond, a heath with lines of elm and big blocks of forest higher up. And her horse saw all the pleasant invitation too. The big powerful animal had been constrained too long. And she couldn't hold him properly when he reared and made for this delightful vision of space. And my own horse followed it, its rear legs stuttering for a moment as they found a grip. And then it lunged forward, veering awkwardly to one side as it stepped in one of the ruts. And I was off its back then, like a shot, as cleanly as a champagne cork, and into the ditch at the end of the lane. I hit the bushes and seemed to keep on falling into them, deeper and deeper into the moist grass, my head and shoulder hitting something on the way. And then the piercing shot of pain.

After a minute, I suppose, lying there invisible and insensible, my head cleared and I tried to move. And I was surprised that I could, propping myself up into a kneeling position, my head just above the undergrowth.

And then I saw the man, on the far side of the lane just out of the bushes, about fifty yards back, in a green jacket and faded slacks and field boots looking down past me onto the heath with a pair of binoculars. I couldn't see much of the face under his canvas hat, just something of white hair over the ears and deep-set eyes. I ducked back into the grass as he moved forward slightly to get a better view down on the heath. And when I looked up again he was gone.

I didn't tell Helen when she came back for me. I felt some obscure need to possess a secret myself, as a bargaining counter to hers, perhaps—for she'd not told me everything yet. And I wanted time to think. Had I seen the man somewhere before? I thought perhaps I had. And what possible agency, or combination of agencies, private or national, did he represent? Perhaps he was just someone working on Perkins's estate or a forest preserve warden. But his covert behavior made this seem unlikely; and Guy had said he'd called off his Peeping Toms. So who was he?

I was suddenly very angry at this endless hide-and-seek. And that must have had a lot to do with my drinking too much at lunch when we got back to the house. First it had been a medicinal brandy, but with the taste in my mouth and the pain in my shoulder melting, I found a psychological easement in the brandy and then other beverages. And Harold Perkins was a willing ally, taking up again over the long dining table his own liquid crusade against the failure of all right thinking in the world. A liquid lunch and I liked it. And I liked him, the open old man beaten before his time. And I thought: the hell with them, Mr. and Mrs. Jackson and all their crooked past and knavish tricks. And the hell with their bloody horses as well. I was truculent and I liked that too.

"Can we play in the rooms?" the twins asked later that afternoon when we'd got back from a picnic at somewhere called Flatrock, a small steeply wooded canyon several miles away, where a river flooded through a gorge. Their hair was still wet from the spirals of haze that had come over them as they'd played in the fine spume.

"Can they, Father?" Helen asked Perkins. She spoke as if these rooms were his toys.

"A little late isn't it? But it's O.K. by me if you go with them."

"Let's get you dried first. And a bath. Then come on up in your robes for a bit before you go to bed. Anna?" She turned to the housekeeper standing by the kitchen door. "Will you look after them and bring them up?" And then to me: "Like to see the rooms?"

"Yes. Show him the rooms, Helen," Guy put in quickly, always the perfect host, generously self-seeking.

"Rooms?" I asked.

"Yes," she said. "Rooms. But curious."

And they were. They were up in the long attic of the

house, built in under the eaves: an extraordinary adult fantasy, a child's dream. There was a miniature cobbled street down the middle, with sidewalks, gas lamps, and a dog cart at one end. Along either side were a short row of New York brownstone houses with steps up to the four-foot-high front doors. Inside, the rooms were not built to the same scale, each side of the street making up the lower floor of one complete house—with a drawing room, nursery, and kitchen, all perfectly furnished to scale in the late Victorian period: a velvet-covered and tasseled chaise longue, rocking chairs, a minute Persian carpet, an upright satinwood piano in the drawing room; a child's cot, a high feeding chair, oleographs of Little Red Riding Hood in the nursery; and a kitchen equipped with a miniature coal stove, tongs, poker, a brass grocer's scale, and a line of little pots and pans, each one bigger than the next, hanging from a dresser, with a series of painted wooden plates above, depicting the life and times of a family of rabbits: a Mrs. Tiggy Winkle's kitchen—the whole mood close to Beatrix Potter, yet twenty years before her time.

"Grandfather had the place built for his children. Got the idea from the dwarf family—the Kellys—in Barnum's Circus. They had something of the same thing as part of their act."

Helen bent down and got into one of the houses—the lights were on in the rooms already—and I climbed into the one opposite. The ceilings inside were about five feet high. She opened the street window and waved.

"Hi!"

I opened mine.

"Hello," I said less easily. The scale of everything was very strange and unsettling: neither dolls' houses nor real ones. And I felt neither adult nor child myself but a trespasser of a quite indefinite age and nature. Someone, appropriately small and almost certainly malevolent—a dwarf—would at any moment, I felt, come through the little hall door and command me to get out of his house. It was the confusion of Alice after the magic potion, when she grew bigger instead of smaller in the rooms of Wonderland.

Helen disappeared from the window opposite and the

little piano began to tinkle: *Boys and girls come out to play*. . . .

Then she stopped and reappeared at the window, her face very bright and young-looking.

"The thing I like best is the street," she said. "More than the houses."

I looked out my window, past the dog cart on the cobbles, at the attic wall at the far end where the rows of brownstones disappeared in a painted perspective. She put the lights out in the rooms and turned the street lights on and we both looked out our windows. And now I could see the curved metal girders of a bridge on the skyline in the distance, past ghostly four-wheelers and horse trams.

"Brooklyn Bridge," she said. "They'd just finished it. One Christmas I remember we put salt all over the street and holy garlands on the doors and had a party up here with the windows frosted and lit up. And I liked best being out on the street and looking up at the bridge and in through the windows. Especially that for some reason. Being *out*side, not in."

"Hardly as a result of a deprived childhood," I said in the soft darkness, the place smelling of old candle wax and long-warmed pine from the rafters above us. "This and the tree house on the lawn." The very front part of her face— eyes, nose, and mouth—were just visible in the faint light: a huge ghost in the middle of the small window frame. I looked up at the street again. "And that's not exactly the expected road to Moscow. I find all that difficult to follow."

"That was later. You'd have found it easy enough to follow then."

"You remember wanting to look *in*; not to *be* inside?"

"Yes. That's what I felt—outside my parents, outside all their concerns, the real life that mattered."

"Should get a little couch up here and a miniature trick cyclist and open a clinic."

"Trick cyclist?"

"Psychiatrist."

We had learned to laugh together now in this magic settlement under the eaves, drawn by its conceits, as children after the Pied Piper, into the inventions of a happy childishness. But how could it last? We were so obviously not fitted for that world, tall people in dolls' houses, simply eavesdropping on that music. So I said, as the water suddenly started to rumble in the cisterns for the children's bath downstairs: "It worries me. All three of us here held together in a cat's cradle. All knowing, but not all knowing together: each of us having a better reason than the other for keeping quiet. You won't tell the KGB about me, because you've got something else more important to do. Guy won't tell because he somehow thrives on the exciting secrecy of it all. And I won't tell my people—"

"Why?" She sat down on the floor of the front room, leaning on the windowsill. "It's not really because you trust me."

"The British have fucked me about for far too long. That's the main reason why. And I feel safer with your secrets than with theirs. But what I want to know is how long do all these pieces of string stay up? How long before someone outside this triangle steps in and cuts it to pieces? Because we're not living all this out in a vacuum; there are others, and they don't share our manners. And Guy—how long to go there? He's living on hot bricks. He won't tell them in London about you and Graham—all that he knows about you, the politics as well. Yet of course he should. They'll put him away for ten years if they ever find out he knew about that. And then he has this running sore with you, this obsessive thing. And that's explosive. All the more so, since I'm here now, filling Graham's role."

"But you haven't."

"Exactly. And that's the danger. He's pushing it all the time. It's the potential that attracts in these circumstances; not the reality. That kills the obsession."

"You mean we should climb into bed together in front of him. And then live in peace?"

"No. I meant that Guy is the loose end between us. Whatever we have to complete he may—"

"Screw it up?"

I thought for a second that it was Helen who had spoken. And I looked across to her. But she was looking the other way. And then I saw Guy.

He was standing in the shadows at the end of the street, at the far end of the attic just above the stairway, towering over the first of the gas lamps, a tall leggy figure changed now incongruously into his pinstripe suit for dinner, a distinguished monster making an entry in some horror movie.

And now Helen turned on him in a vicious way, a ruthless manner I'd not seen in her before, poking her head out of the window and hitting him with words, bitter accents, a loathing that seemed far too strong for the little houses, a fury that would split them open like an earthquake. All the years of her marriage seemed to explode inside her now, the first words a gaudy rocket signaling the start of a violent carnival.

"Bastard. Mother fucker. Aren't you? *Say* so, for God's sake. No life of my own—without you. Anywhere. Always creeping up behind me—looking, listening, peeping. Trying to run my life for me—what I should do, and think, and who I should meet. All the time, forever. And all over Africa too. Even there, I hear. In a million miles of space you still have to live off me like a vegetable. Everywhere. And now in the attic. It's what you wanted; wasn't it? All along. Getting us up here somewhere quiet so as you could spy on us. All right then: I can do it here with him now, right now here in front of you—that's what you want. And maybe then you'll leave me in peace and go away."

She had lost control, ruled now by a terrible flirtatious rage, imperious and wanton—her face sparkling, a bright offering, looking at me with an absolutely determined desire. She stood up in the little room, began to unbutton her blouse and take off her skirt.

"For God's sake, Helen, stop it," I shouted across the road above the noise of the cistern.

Guy had come forward now. "You're mad," he said. "I simply came up to join you both." He knelt down on the sidewalk so that he could look in the window and try to calm her. She bent down to meet him with her blouse half open and hit him on the face—two, three times. He took it and then hit her back just as hard. I tried to get out of my house to separate them but it wasn't easy with the small door opening inward, my pocket catching on it, and by the time I was out on the street they were at it hammer and tongs. Or rather poker. She had picked up the small metal poker that went with the drawing room grate and was trying to get at him with it through the window, the two of them playing Punch and Judy. But Guy had leaned back now and the bludgeon played wildly in the air in front of his nose.

Then she stopped. It was the moment for collapse or tears. But neither came from her. Instead she put the poker down and looked at the two of us bitterly: Anna Magnani at the end of a fight with her lover—blouse awry, hair tossed about, red welts rising on her cheeks. But they were not acting. This was terribly real. It was also quite ludicrous in the miniature setting, but they neither of them seemed in the least aware of it: the two of them shaking, still locked in the horrific surprise of their acts, contemplating their violence now, unfulfilled by it, wondering how to extend it.

"You've owned me for too long, Guy," she said, making his name an insult. "I'll do *what* I want, *where*ever, with *who*ever."

He laughed without humor. "You've always done that, Helen. Think of something new. This is certainly a waste of time. I told you, I just came up the stairs. I'd no idea—"

She aimed to hit him again.

"Look, not this—stop it," I said. But they weren't listening. I had come to that country in a marriage where an outsider, no matter how understanding or sympathetic, has no visa and where he can really only do the inhabitants a disservice with advice. I could only look on as they fought it out. They could never meet again now in any fair balance, I thought, he trying so hard to find her and she fleeing from him—lost to each other in a dreadful game of mental hide-and-seek.

"It's your life, Helen," Guy went on in a reasonable tone. He could afford it. He was in the driver's seat for the moment. "Has been for years. I've had little to do with it. I've told you: settle up about the children and leave any time you want. I *don't* own you. That's terribly obvious. And, yes, I tried to. But that's over. You wanted it once, remember? But for a long time you've wanted both—security and freedom. And we've not had the patience or the temperament to manage both, have we? But you'll have to choose now."

"You've spied on me," she said with wide eyes, staring at him, pouring an intense hatred into him. "And had your fill. And now I can go, can I? I've performed for you, fulfilled your dirty fantasies. And now I can just fuck off? Well I won't. This is my house, *our* house. The fucking off is for you Guy. Not me."

"Is it? You really think so? Use your head, Helen. *Reason*. Or you won't survive anything. This will be the last of your nine lives. I *am* the 'loose end' between you two. It's not just our marriage we're talking about or the children: it's our separate professions. Don't forget that."

"Blackmailer as well as voyeur."

"And you're a promiscuous cheat, Helen. And a traitor."

She was terribly pained, as if an all-absorbing illness had reached a terminal stage in her; and his frail poise was foundering in the tide of a returning jealous mania—each of them gouging out the carcass of the other, knowing exactly where the maggots lay.

"You knew all about her politics?" I put in, trying to divert them, sitting down on the steps of my brownstone. "Why didn't you ever say anything about it?"

"All the rope I needed to hang myself, that's why," Helen said. "That would have been the final thrill for him: seeing me put away for ten years—the climax of his joyous punishment."

"I would have gone as well," Guy said, edging back into calmer water.

"Why should you?" I asked.

"Besides," he went on, "I'd never have wanted to see you in prison. Never. You forget that, Helen—there was always love enough for that. And it's not blackmail. I want to see us all out of this safely, if it's possible. That's why you must reason, Helen, not fight. It's not just us. There are others."

"Fine," she said, still fighting. "And all these years you've just sat and watched me—me and the real George Graham.

And never told me. That was very reasonable, wasn't it?"

"What else? I should have told my department about your political affiliations with Graham? Or simply stopped you sleeping with him? I couldn't do either."

"You got *pleasure* in doing neither. That's what I can't stand. You *lower* everything, make everything stink."

"Of course you were so fine with your infidelities, weren't you? Perfectly marvelous. It was such a good, proud thing, wasn't it? Deceiving me. And your country. You had it both ways, of course, didn't you? There was idealism too —sucking him off for the good of the party."

I listened to them, tearing each other apart, both right and both wrong, both stamping the seals of irretrievable failure on their marriage.

"Look," I said, standing up and putting my hand on the roof of the brownstone. "What does it matter? We have to understand *now*, not yesterday. And Guy does. He's here and has heard—"

"'Promiscuous cheat and traitor' indeed," Helen interrupted. "It was simply living a life that you denied me—"

"Is that it? Going off with other men behind my back and working for the Russians—I *denied* you that? Well, why shouldn't I?"

"All right—I'm a whore and a traitor," Helen said quietly. "OK. But it wasn't like that at all."

"Of course not—all for the purest motives: the great God Lenin and so it was perfectly all right for you to hop into bed with the whole Communist Party if you wanted." Guy smiled, almost laughed. "It's laughable. Farcical. No one would believe it. And to suggest that I drove you to it —well, that's just cloud-cuckoo-land. What are you doing for them anyway? Not pumping me, as I remember. So what else? Sleeping around with diplomats, colleagues of mine? You're not trained for much else, are you?"

"You're not going to know."

"Has she told you?" Guy turned to me. "Or are you really working for the KGB as well?"

"No. And I'm not."

"Think she's the person we're looking for by any chance? The Stayer?"

"No. She says not. And I believe her." I looked over at Helen. Her face was taut and creased, all the easy curves gone, showing her age at last in the dull light. The beaten look of a slave up for auction. She was frightened, frightened of losing. And it did look bad against her.

"You've told her, have you, about what you're here for, who you are?"

"There seemed no point not to. She knew from the beginning I wasn't George Graham."

"That's wonderful. Now she just tells her KGB contacts here all about it, if she hasn't done it already. And that's the end—of you particularly."

"She says she isn't going to. She has some other work to do. She's not interested."

"And you *believe* her? Do you know anything about the KGB? They don't hire that kind of charity, I can assure you."

"Yes, I do believe her. And it *is* wonderful, isn't it? Our business is all a lot of nonsense anyway, and it's a good thing that two of us at least seem to realize that—that the personal commitment is far more important. And you're in it too, Guy. You knew about her, and you didn't tell."

"I don't put much store by us three against the Russian, British, and American intelligence services."

"Why not? If we do keep our mouths shut. That's the last thing they can expect—trust in such circumstances. So now that each of us knows all about the other, why don't we all get on with our various jobs? And live our lives. And maybe one day we can just do the living and throw the other rot over—the dark-glasses game. Any other ideas?" I looked at both of them.

"It's crazy," Guy said. "Mad."

"Why? Any alternative is going to mean a long time down for all of us. And that's not fun. I know."

But Guy wasn't convinced. "Crazy." He repeated the word to himself, walking up and down between us. "Mad."

Yet he must have seen that mine was the only course: we had to trust each other. But I felt something else was worrying him—something still on his mind, unexpressed and therefore dangerous. But of course there were so many things that could go wrong, even with trust, and I supposed he must just be thinking of this.

A moment later the twins charged up the narrow stairway in dressing gowns, two round, blond-fringed faces exploding with excitement. They ran along the cobbled street between us toward their father shouting.

"Daddy! Play us the fiddle, will you? Will you do that dance with us? Will he, Mommy?" They turned toward her. "And you do the piano—please! Let's do that, can't we? *Yes!* The Flibbertygibbit—that one. Can't we?"

They jumped into our bitter atmosphere and made it plain and sweet almost in a moment: an irrepressible demand for now, a stinging comment on the folly of our ways —if proof were needed, I thought. All such thoughts: the inventions of a happy childishness. And how dull we three were, infantile, unliving adults: what fatuous toils we were engaged in, what sour intellects and dry ideals, flesh withering on three old sticks.

Guy opened a small fiddle case that had been stored among the rafters. Helen was persuaded back to the piano in the miniature drawing room. And then the two children and their father began to hop about the street with strange bouncy steps to a scratchy jig. It was something the family had obviously worked up before, steps of their own invention, awkward and unbalanced, from no book of the dance, yet polished in their own way, and well remembered: an almost tuneless music, yet a perfectly shared harmony, unique to these four people—a family now quite without dissidence, generations firmly locked, the drawbridge up, secure in their own imaginative country, distant from me, inhabiting themselves properly at last. Where are we, I thought? And what on earth have we all been talking about? And I felt, looking at their unfathomable gyrations, that perhaps all of us were going to have some luck after all.

12

Harper arrived at the East Side Airlines Terminal in Manhattan sour and unkempt after the long flight from London. He took a cab to the Hilton on the Avenue of the Americas, and signed in. His room was 2057. He didn't bother to unpack or wash, just took his shaving things with him in his pocket, came down two flights on the stairs, then walked toward the elevator banks. A maid came toward him with a trolley of linen just as he came to Room 1819. He continued down the hall, then doubled back after she had gone, slapping his pockets as if he'd forgotten something. The door of 1819 was unlocked. He went straight in through the narrow hall. Andrei Popovic was lying back, feet up on the big bed, watching Ronald Colman in *Random Harvest* on a big TV set.

The two men watched the film for a moment without saying anything. Then Harper looked up at the ceiling questioningly, cupping a hand over one ear. Popovic got up, nodding his head. He spoke to Harper very quietly, a whisper almost completely drowned in the noise from the TV. "Yes. There's a Russian agricultural delegation buying wheat on the thirtieth floor. But I'll tell you about it. Come into the bathroom."

"I've got to shave anyway," Harper said. Popovic went ahead of him into the cubicle, ran the bath taps gently and after that those in the wash basin. Harper got his kit out, took off his shirt, doused his face, and started to work up a good lather.

Andrei Popovic was a small, dapper man, in the trousers of a tightly fitting navy-blue synthetic fiber suit; a firm, broad-boned, high-cheeked, Slavonic face; fiftyish, but looking younger with dark sparse hair standing up a little and then running straight back—thin strands with a lot of empty space underneath so that one could quite clearly see most of his scalp. He was compact, sure of himself, yet without any air of command or superiority, like an accountant at the back of a board meeting who knows the company figures better than any of the directors and will quite soon be taking over from them. The eyes were faint blue and very steady, the nose, chin, and everything else about him neatly and inconspicuously formed. He looked entirely the busy, anonymous Russian bureaucrat he was, one of half a dozen attachés at the Soviet consulate in New York.

In his communication with Harper, he displayed one individual trait: the sense of a mother conducting a good-humored game with a fretful child, a playful femininity, which Harper, who had dealt with him before, disliked considerably. He might have been flirting with him, Harper thought, but he could never be sure, for Popovic was never blunt about it. It was a gossamer-thin quality in the Russian —this knowing sensuousness—a hint like very faint perfume in the air: a twinkle in the blue eyes, a sudden gentle but unexpected movement, a minute roll of the lips, a quick softness in his perfect English pronunciation. And it kept Harper uneasy with him whenever they had met. The man swelled with a quality of secret, ultimate knowledge—easily borne, temptingly hinted at to favorites, potentially dangerous. And Harper could never decide if there were any sexual overtones in these marks of a hidden character, or if, as was quite logical, they were simply the fruit of his position as the most senior KGB officer in America.

"Good," Popovic said firmly, watching Harper intently as he started to shave. "Good, good."

Harper looked at him curiously in the mirror. "Good what?" he asked above the soft rush of bath water. Popovic was standing very close to him now, hardly two feet away from his face, so that his voice could be heard. But was that the only reason for his proximity, Harper wondered?

"Everything is good. But we must not rush it."

"Where is he then?" Harper finished lathering his beard. But Popovic delayed. He kept looking at Harper, smiling.

"Flitlianov? Or your man Marlow?" he said at length. "They are both upstate in New York at this moment. Our men are there. They are both together."

"*Together?*"

Again Popovic paused, twinkling. "No, not together. In the same place."

Harper frowned, and turned with his razor to consider a suitable route through his stubbled pockmarks. "And what about the letter drop in Grand Central?" he asked. "Anything there. The woman? Have you any lead on her?"

"We have her too. She is there as well. All three of them," Popovic said neatly.

"Christ!" Harper turned halfway through a scrape. "The *three* of them. I needn't have bothered to come then. Are you sure it's the right woman?"

"Yes. As soon as Flitlianov followed them up to the country last Friday. Why else would he go? And he's been tailing her before."

"What woman? Who?"

"Mrs. Jackson."

"Mrs. *who*?" Harper stopped everything.

"The wife of your SIS Liaison Officer here, Guy Jackson."

"No." Harper showed an awful dismay through the white streaks of lather.

"Yes, yes, Harper. We've checked her out. She lived in Beirut when Flitlianov was there in the mid-fifties. And of course George Graham was there before that. It all fits. That mail, the names we want, must be somewhere up in their house in the country. Mrs. Jackson is the end of the letter drop, all right."

Harper felt real disappointment. His own plans for getting Marlow to New York had been quite incidental to the main action, he realized now. He was redundant: of course Guy Jackson had been useless—the contact with Marlow which they had wanted him to pinpoint had been his wife.

"It's all over then," Harper said, thinking of Holborn again, and failure, and McCoy. "You just wait till she hands the stuff over to Flitlianov. And take him. It's all over, really."

"Just beginning, I think, Harper. No despair. It's starting—just *starting*." He repeated the word softly, solicitously, as if to encourage. Then he opened the top of Harper's aftershave lotion and smelled it. "Good, very nice," he said.

"How? It's all wrapped up. Apart from Jackson," Harper said petulantly. "Jackson's a whole new script. I'd never have thought he was working for us—or her."

"He's not," Popovic said, putting a dab of the undistinguished pine cologne on his fingertips. "That's where it begins: Guy Jackson is working for the Americans, the CIA."

Harper had just finished shaving and now he turned and looked at Popovic angrily. "May I?" He took his lotion back and put it on the shelf without using it. "Thanks—well, that'll be your affair, won't it. I can start packing again."

"Don't be difficult, Harper." Popovic was suddenly very calm, staring at him. Then he relaxed, his serious message received and understood. "You'll be needed. I want you to know all about it. We'll need you back in England. I'll tell you: there are two points here, both connected, and you'll be able to help, you'll be very necessary indeed, when the time comes. One—we've no idea where these papers she has are hidden. And no idea when or how she'll hand them over. It's all sheer chance there. Open to any bad luck. Very difficult. And secondly, Guy Jackson: he's been given a very interesting assignment by the CIA. He's being posted back to England in a month, to Cheltenham—"

"I knew that," Harper put in casually, trying to rescue something for himself from the whole business. "That he was going—"

"You *don't* know. Listen and I'll tell you." Popovic moved away.

Harper put away his shaving gear and they went back into the bedroom where *Random Harvest* was coming to an end. Popovic turned the channel selector on the TV set and at once a picture of the front lobby of the hotel appeared. Another twist displayed the side entrance on Fifty-third Street. A third movement gave only a dark screen but with voices over it in Russian, a spirited conversation full of facts and figures on wheat tonnages and prices. A fourth time—and they heard the drawl of American voices, then a long pause. Then: "O.K., this is the deal again. Get Adam back, will you? He's in the lobby. He wants to have it all first-hand."

Popovic turned the volume down. "We've adapted this set for ourselves," he said very softly. "And we've had a little help on the other side from one of their electronics people. You see what we're into here? All the private circuits in the building: the hotel's closed-circuit TV system, the FBI bugging lines, and also a return line to a hidden micro in their central recording rooms in the basement. We can play it all back through this set, if we keep the volume low enough. So there's no feedback."

Popovic moved the selector again. They were back on the main lobby downstairs. "Now watch, you're in luck," he said. "Watch who they get. They've just called for him in the recording room. He's in the lounge—there, to the left."

Harper watched carefully. A man crossed the screen, went off it, and came back on a moment later with another American—a big, tall, bald-headed man, genial in a creased Cabot Lodge tropical outfit, abundantly American, folding up the Leisure and Arts section of the Sunday New York *Times*.

"There he is. That's him. Adam Wheel."

"So?" Harper was completely at sea.

"He's Guy Jackson's CIA Control. Works with him at the UN. Russian specialist. That's why he's here. Listening in on this wheat deal we're fixing with the Americans. Well, he's the fellow that's set up this plan with Jackson in England. And that's what we want, really as much as we want Flitlianov. And I think we can get both together: two birds, one stone. Put on your shirt and I'll tell you about it."

"What deal? What deal in Cheltenham?"

"Communications. A new system they have working at the Foreign Office Communications headquarters there. Pulsed code modulation. So far an unbreakable system of satellite-directed radio transmissions. The Americans want it; that's why they got Jackson on it. They found out he was being posted there. And we want it, too, of course. That's where you come in. And Mr. Marlow."

"How did they get Jackson?"

"The oldest way. The oldest profession. Blackmail, call girls in New York. Jackson has some very peculiar habits.

They photographed him, taped him, the usual things. He was very susceptible."

"Photographed him *with* them?"

"Well, that and *looking* at them."

"Is that a crime?"

"He thought so."

"How did you come on all this?" Harper asked.

"You don't really need to know, Harper. But—through this." Popovic tapped the television set. "Here in the hotel, this is where they set the whole thing up. Call girls, photographs, everything. We listened in."

Harper turned his collar down, straightened his tie, and looked out at the patch of leaden summer sky. "Something is wrong." He turned to Popovic. "An experienced officer like Jackson would never have fallen for that old trick in the first place. And if he had, he'd have told us in London. There must have been something else."

"There was. The CIA told him they'd found out his wife worked for the KGB, that they'd get him as an accessory on that if he didn't cooperate."

"How did they find that out?"

"I don't think they did. They invented it."

"Come on. She *does* work for the KGB. It couldn't be coincidence. And in any case, when you heard that, why didn't you close with her sooner?"

"We did, Harper. We checked her out completely. But we'd nothing on her in Moscow—no traces, no associations with us. We went right through her. It wasn't until Flitlianov arrived here and started to follow her that we started to add things up. Until then we assumed that the CIA was bluffing, or had cooked up some evidence. You see, they wanted Jackson badly: the British aren't sharing this information with anyone. And Jackson, they knew, was going back to England—the one man who could get them into the center of this business."

"Well how in hell do we get the information? Turn Jackson a second time?"

"He wouldn't buy it a second time. But that's beside the point—which is that I don't think for a moment that Jackson is going to go along with the Americans anyway.

He'll drop them, but not until he's clear of them, out of America and back home. He *is* far too experienced an operator. On the other hand, that's just the quality which your man Marlow lacks, from what you've told us. There's where we can bring pressure, with twenty years jail hanging over him."

Harper looked numb, quite distant.

"They're really quite like each other, too," Popovic went on. "Not that it matters. But it helps." He went over to his coat and produced two photographs, New York street shots, of Marlow and Jackson. He gave them to Harper.

"Well, the same height—" Harper said.

"Same age, build, weight, thinning hair, rather English-looking," Popovic continued.

"I don't see it." Harper paused. Then it hit him. "You're not thinking of—"

"Yes. Yes, of course I am. They switched him for George Graham; we'll switch him for Jackson."

Harper laughed. "Not in a million years! It won't work. They must know the man they're getting in Cheltenham, know what he looks like. And you forget, Jackson's married; he'll be going back with his wife and family. What are they going to say about taking a new husband back with them?"

"We've checked, Harper," Popovic said, calm again now, quietly hard. "And you'll do some more for us, personnel details and so on in Cheltenham—and as far as we know they *don't* know anything about Jackson in Cheltenham. His work with British Intelligence has been entirely in Africa, a few months in London, and here with the UN. And as for his wife, well she's with us, isn't she? She can be *made* to respond. Of course it's a big risk. Someone *may* know Jackson in Cheltenham. Or they may check Marlow against a photograph of Jackson when he arrives. He may never get beyond the front gate. But it's no more of a risk than the British took in substituting Marlow for Graham in the first place. In this business small risks never pay. Big ones sometimes do."

"And Flitlianov? The names of his group? I thought that was the most important thing."

"Well, he fits in with this too. Think about it: How

can we move on those letters? Force her now? No. The Jackson deal would fall through. Force Flitlianov? How? We've no idea when he's going to get them from her. Go through the house upstate? Or her apartment here? Impossible. So what? Well, there's one time we *know* she'll have those papers: when she moves back to England—to some empty house or apartment in Cheltenham. That's certain. She'll take them with her. And that's when we can get them. And take Flitlianov as well. Since of course he'll follow her back there."

"What if Flitlianov gets the letters from her *before* she leaves? He may even have had them off her already, if he's up there now."

"No. Not on our information. Our men say he's just sounding the ground out this weekend. And he won't have the time to get them before she leaves; she's leaving next week, getting out of the summer here, going ahead to England with the children. Her husband is not joining her for several weeks."

"The whole thing seems risky and unlikely to me, Andrei." Harper moved away a little, but Popovic drew up with him at once, gesturing toward the bathroom. They ran the taps again and Popovic took the opportunity of brushing his teeth. "First of all," Harper went on, "Flitlianov can still get these letters over here—"

"We're onto him all the time. If he does, we'll take them off him here. And go ahead with Marlow and the Cheltenham deal as planned."

"What is this deal? What are you after there?"

"You don't need to know, Harper—just that it's the crucial data on this new electronic one-time pad they've developed there. And if we get it, it's the Rosetta stone for us."

"A needle in a heavily guarded haystack, Andrei."

"Of course. But that's the luck of Jackson. He was going back to learn about this very process in Cheltenham."

"*Was* going back?

"Yes. Marlow will be taking his place."

"And Jackson? What'll become of . . . ?"

"We'll arrange all that. Nothing for you to do there." Popovic looked at Harper carefully. "You just talk to Mar-

low as arranged when you see him. Then go back to London.
And wait. We're going to need you back in England when
the whole thing starts moving." Popovic finished with his
teeth, rinsed out his toothbrush, and spat vigorously into the
flow of water.

"And what about Marlow?" Harper asked. "How will
you persuade him?"

"I think he will be persuaded. By Jackson's future,"
Popovic said neatly.

"I see." And Harper did see now, and he sighed.

"Good." Popovic replaced the toothbrush on the rack
above the basin. "Good, good, good." Then he looked at his
face studiously in the mirror, rubbing his chin gently. He
turned to Harper invitingly. "I like that aftershave. What's
it called? I must try and get some."

13

It all happened very quickly—that evening in the UN building a few weeks later, late summer, the sun still blazing
damply everywhere outside, but cool as ever in the false
weather of our huge aluminum shrine.

Helen had left several weeks previously with the children, with nothing of my business with her resolved. I had
seen her only once more alone after our weekend upstate,
and that only for ten minutes in the Delegates' Lounge before Guy had joined us. And though I took the address she
was going to, a rented house somewhere outside Cheltenham,
and said I would look them both up if and when I got back
to England myself, I didn't really expect to see her again.
Graham was dead to her, and, I inferred, I would be too, as
far as keeping quiet about her real work was concerned.
Hopefully, indeed, after my talk with Harper when he'd suddenly turned up to quiz me a month before, I was to be out
of the whole business by the end of August, if no one in New
York contacted me, and back to London to some undecided
future.

Helen Jackson was out of my life, and in our last conversation I'd simply feared for her future with Guy—the long days, coming to them both, full of enmity and hopeless disgust. Why didn't they separate or divorce, I asked her again?

"The children," she said, without conviction.

"But if you go on destroying each other like this; what use will either of you be to them?"

"Yes, I know. Maybe a month apart will help."

She was postponing. She said, "It's difficult—you wouldn't know—to throw everything of a family away, a relationship, even when it's been as bad as ours. It's really difficult."

And yet I knew that in the days when Graham had stood happily on her horizon, she had wanted just that, was willing to lose everything in the way of family mementoes. It was simply that now she had full knowledge of her isolation, and this was why she would stay with Guy. She had no one to go to. And she was a woman, I had recognized, who moved always toward people, who fulfilled herself with them more than with ideas or things. And then, too, she was very tired, at that moment, of stage-managing her life, and I think she felt the need for fate to take a hand in her affairs for a while.

On that last evening the offices were nearly all empty on my floor. But I'd stayed behind, having had a message left on my desk—from Guy's secretary, as I thought—saying that Guy would like to see me before he left and would come by around six o'clock.

It was Guy's very last moment with the UN. There'd been a small cocktail party for him the previous evening. And that day he'd simply come in to tidy up, get his papers, and sign off. He was flying back to London first thing next morning. The rest of his furniture and effects were coming over by ship later.

But when he came into my office he was with two other men, right behind him, pushing him into the room quickly and then locking the door. They were both in smart dark suits, very properly dressed, one of them carrying a brief case, the other with very long, sinewy arms, long almost to the point of deformity, like those of a nineteenth-century prizefighter. Their faces were anonymous, bureaucratic, perfectly part of the building—calm and without any expression: two government servants from one of the "Great Powers" holding their cards close to their chests before the 1,014th meeting of the Decolonization Committee. And I thought for a moment, as they locked the door, that they must be colleagues of Jackson's from Intelligence in London come to question me again about my nonexistent progress in New York.

I thought this, at least, until one of them drew a gun and pointed it at me and the other started to undress Jackson. He began with the suit coat—Guy was in one of his finest pinstripes—and the moment he laid his hands on the lapels Guy started to protest, quietly and politely at first, as though making a small but important criticism to the secretary of his London club.

"No. No, *please!*" Now he was utterly shocked by the effrontery of this initial touch: this touching him, this intimate proximity without so much as by-your-leave. He didn't seem to mind the rest of the disrobing so much.

But it was quite terrible to watch, this indignity in this formal man who had so carefully dressed himself that morning, as he did every morning; terrible to see this sartorial destruction, for clothes were something that Guy had put a lot of his life into: Savile Row coat, waistcoat and trousers, the pale blue Sea-Island cotton shirt, the fine silk old-boys' tie, gold cuff links, the handmade dimpled leather shoes— they all piled up on my desk against his intermittent, pleading voice: "No. No! For God's sake, what are you doing?"— as if he thought he was going to be raped by them. And indeed at that point I had no idea what they were up to. Yet, in some sense I knew, seeing Guy being stripped, for I had watched the destruction of a man long before the real end, the desecration of life before life in the flesh was gone.

When he was finally nude, a lifeless skeleton, he was six feet of naked emptiness, his neatly groomed hair tossed around, the elegant face disrupted fearfully, fallen, as though bones had been broken in it, and red: the whole of his face from the neck upward turned a bright, blushing red. All his lanky poise was utterly destroyed as he looked around him with a sort of terrified prudery, as though a matron had suddenly come up on him in the shower after cricket thirty years before.

I saw all this and was so saddened by it that I hardly noticed when the other man with the awful gangly arms came over and started to undress me. But I'd had the message by then and did it for him. It never occurred to me to make any struggle. I suppose that was wrong.

"Get into his clothes," he said when I'd finished, Guy and I both naked now, the two men facing each of us, all of us standing for a moment like statues in some obscene ballet, two nude and two blue-suited dancers.

We changed clothes. And I realized then what was happening to me, simply a more violent change of role, from George Graham into Guy Jackson now. But what was happening to Jackson? I put on all his things, and he mine. And they fitted both of us surprisingly well. Except for the smell—the faint odor in Guy's clothes; his hair, his skin, his sweat mixed with the rumor of some old-fashioned hair oil. There was something awfully unreal about that for a moment—his shirt and underclothes warm about me, still warm from his warmth: a properly stolen life, this time; violently robbed in front of me, so that I felt I was part of the crime.

They had taken his wedding ring off him last thing, the brassy signet ring that he wore like a memento of failure, and I put it on, the prizefighter handing it to me, poking it up toward my face, like the best man in a nightmare wedding. And Guy, I saw, had everything of me—or rather of George Graham: his old black Mentmore fountain pen, the gold squared-faced Hamilton watch, the long-stemmed briar pipe, and the aromatic Dutch tobacco. Guy became George Graham in front of my eyes, the lover replacing the husband, who in turn was replaced by me. Three men had gone into two; and one of us was going to be caught without an identity when the music stopped.

Finally, they checked everything, went through all our pockets, to see that Guy had all my papers, my wallet and UN identification and so on, and that I had all his. Then the prizefighter said to me, "Now watch. Watch this carefully."

And there is that moment now which one doesn't care to remember. One of the men took a key and opened the aluminum casement looking out over the East River, and a muggy breath streamed in from outside as if a furnace door

had opened. And sudenly then, at the same instant, Guy and
I both knew what the whole thing was all about, when the
prizefighter took him by the shoulders, turned him round,
and faced him toward the window. We both knew it all then,
very quickly and completely—when I looked at Guy, when
he knew he was dying, was going to die; when he crumpled
up on the floor; when they picked him up and I shouted, and
the other man gagged me and held me from behind; when
Guy was dragged over to the window, and started to cry, a
great sobbing cry, a desperate anguish on his face; when
he clung to everything on the way, every bit of furniture,
being dragged now, feet first across the room; and finally—his
head out in space, yet still, like a trapeze artist, trying to hold
on frantically to the metal window ledge until his fingers
were prised up—when he gave the faint squeak as he fell away.

We both knew everything as it was happening, shared
everything as the men intended, Guy's eyes fixed to mine
during all that awful passage across the room—outraged eyes.
And yet somehow there was something like an unseemly
gentleness glowing through his normally austere and cynical
features, a statement of love and redemption that had only
now suddenly become clear to him at this last moment, and
which he wanted to pass on to me before he died, in a great
hurry to get rid of it before the music stopped and he went.
He was pulled across the office floor, a dead man, yet full of
life. Exactly as they had intended, the two men left me with
a unique taste of death in my mouth—not only his death, any
death, but my own as well.

And then we were away, one of the men on either side
of me, pushing me down the empty corridor toward the elevator banks in the middle of the building, where a third man
was waiting for us, holding the doors apart by the controls
inside, and the four of us went down without stopping to the
underground car park giving out on to the East River side.

They had a car there next to the elevator ramp. There
were several other groups of people around, getting their
keys and cars out, going home, and I shouted and tried to
run. But they had me in the back of the car before I got any-

where, hitting me with something over the ear as I was being pushed in. And when someone came over toward us I could hear the prizefighter speaking as I drifted into a dark world of ringing stars: "He'll be all right. Had a few too many. We'll get him home."

Home, I realized when I regained consciousness going up First Avenue, would of course be the Jacksons' modern apartment at East Fifty-seventh Street and Second.

"Ah, Jackson," the little man said, welcoming me into the Jacksons' large but now almost empty apartment six floors up in a modern cooperative block looking down Second Avenue. "Good evening, Mr. Jackson."

He was standing in half shadow over by a drinks tray in the corner of the main room just off the hall. The carpet had been taken up and most of the furniture pushed into another corner waiting to be crated. The floor was of blocked pine and slippery. A stack of pictures, Redouté rose prints for the most part, had been piled up on a huge oatmeal-colored sofa in the middle of the room. On one arm of it were a number of Jackson's overcoats and mackintoshes, all the perfectly tailored summer and winter protection that Guy had acquired against the varying rigors of the New York climate. What a careful man he'd been, I thought, prepared for every sartorial eventuality—except changing clothes with me.

The only light in the room was from a floor lamp with a huge pumpkinlike Chinese paper lantern on top, and this had been placed in front of the sofa, between me and the small blue-suited fellow fiddling with the drinks, so that I could make out hardly anything of his features. He spoke in Russian and the prizefighter cleared the Redouté roses off the sofa and moved me over toward it.

"Sit down, Mr. Jackson. Relax," the voice said from behind the lamp. Ice fell into a glass. "Whiskey? Or Cognac? All there is, I'm afraid."

I didn't reply. The prizefighter left me and returned with a glass of amber liquid. "Take it. Have some," the voice advised. "You need it. It's not an easy business this, I know. And yet," he added carefully, turning toward me in the shadows, a strange, soft, sympathetic tone coming into his voice, "you'll have to admit you do have some experience of it all—this changing roles, characters. It's not the first time, is it? So this shouldn't be too difficult."

I sat down and at once I started to shake. My stomach and the inside of my arms seemed to vibrate together, and then my shoulders, and I felt a violent nausea rise inside me, a long-delayed sickness now come to full term. I leaned my head back, hoping to stay it. But the first spurt of vomit rose up anyway and lay in my mouth, a lumpy bitter fluid. And then I couldn't help myself with it and I bent forward hopelessly. But they'd seen what was happening, and as I retched I found the prizefighter holding one of the deep-framed Redouté roses in front of me like a tray, and I came on it, puking violently, sweating, my stomach going inside out, seeing the stream of seedy yellow fluid covering all the red flower. I slipped off the sofa then and was down on my hands and knees on the blocked pine floor, and another print was pushed in front of me, a fine sprig, some golden thorny species, and in a moment it too was like a dog's breakfast.

"This is a farce," I said when the sickness was over and they were helping me back on the sofa, one of them sponging my forehead with a damp cloth. "Utterly stupid, impossible. I'm sorry." Suddenly, I found myself addressing these thugs quite openly, in almost a friendly way, as if they were colleagues. It seemed I wanted to thank them for their help in my sudden travail: I had done something stupid, taken too much drink at a party. I was not angry; I was apologetic.

I felt very weak and I had forgotten why I was here or who I was. Marlow, Graham, Jackson? The names ran vaguely and unimportantly around my head, like children in a playground being watched by a mysterious anonymous presence. It simply wasn't important. As long as the three children were happy. Someone else was responsible for them. The person I had been or might become had been wiped clean away, purged out of me with the sickness. And what was left of me at that moment, was nothing, nobody, void.

So that when the man beyond the lamp eventually began to speak I grasped his words willingly, as a thread back to life—any conscious life, which I suddenly craved, just as I had in Durham Jail months before, when McCoy had first voiced his mean proposals.

I could live Jackson's life as a recompense, I thought, for his failure and mine, in such a way that would vindicate both of us and destroy them. So instead of arguing when I'd recovered, I said calmly: "What is it? Tell me what you want of Jackson?"

"I have a plan," the man said in the shadows, speaking the words slowly, almost in a lilt, like a singer taking the first words of a song alone, without the accompaniment, "a plan for all of us—"

"An offer I can't refuse," I broke in, taking the advantage. And I could feel them looking at me in some surprise.

And when I heard what the plan was, I was happy in a way, a hard and brutal way perhaps, but one needed something of that—for the first thing I thought now, after he had given me the outlines of it all, was that now I was Helen Jackson's husband. My association with her had been licensed here at last, a wedding by proxy. I was her husband and her lover all in one. And thus surely, I felt, when we met again, I could not help but find out all about her. Surely, I thought, she could not deny me that knowledge any longer.

That night I slept in the Jacksons' big double bed, his fine black-leather suitcases half packed all around me, all the bits and pieces of his departure scattered about the room waiting to come together in me.

We had spent the hours before going through all Guy's effects, his papers from Cheltenham, his new identity card with my photograph on it now, his passport which had been changed in the same way. Another man had arrived with these halfway through the evening, some kind of electronics expert, and he spent a long time familiarizing me, as far as he could, with the job Guy was to have done back in England.

I had told the blue-suited man that I thought his plan would fail very early on, that the communications experts in Cheltenham would surely see through my lack of expertise at once. But he disagreed, and the man who had briefed me said, "If you memorize these basic details we've gone over—

here in these papers—and say nothing else, don't attempt to offer any thoughts of your own, you'll be all right. In any case, we know that Jackson would have been given a two-week induction course with this new system. So they'll be *teaching* you the business. They won't *expect* you to know anything about it. As to the general procedure in this building—codes, ciphers, cryptanalysis—you should have nothing to do with this at all: you're being specially posted as a trainee to this electronic one-time pad unit."

"And you really think no one in this place is going to know me?" I'd said at the time, talking across to the little man, still in the shadows. "Nobody from personnel in Cheltenham? Surely Guy Jackson must have been interviewed by someone down there?"

"No. He was interviewed and cleared for the posting by the Foreign Office Communications section in London when he was last on leave there. And he's since been checked up again, and debriefed on his New York posting by your friend Harper when he was over here. Jackson has no unfinished business in London or New York. He's completely cleared to start the course."

"All right. But what about my 'wife'? Have you thought about her? How's she going to react to my sudden presence and her husband's death? Take it all quite calmly, you suppose? She may do something quite wild. And what about my 'suicide' here in New York this evening? The section in London is going to want to check Jackson out on that when he gets back. He was my Control, remember. Or someone here in New York, now. The UN people will have been onto the British Consulate already."

"I'm sure they have. But as far as they're concerned you're just an ordinary British citizen. Jackson was the only person in America who really knew what you were doing here. The Consulate will make the usual investigations—with your hotel, a report to your bogus address in London. It will be some time before anyone in your London section knows you've killed yourself. And when they do, and want to talk to you about your 'death,' we have means of ensuring that the enquiry will amount to nothing."

"How?" The first person they'll send down to Cheltenham to see Jackson will be my section chief, McCoy—or more likely his deputy, Harper. And Harper is certainly going to know that I'm not Jackson."

"Don't worry about that. Leave it to us."

And I said then, I remember, looking along every avenue while I had the chance: "What happens if I don't go along with you? How can you kill me if I tell them everything when I get back—and they put me in a top-security prison again where I came from? What then?"

"We'll kill Mrs. Jackson instead," the man said carefully. "And surely you can't let her die, can you? With no husband and two young children to look after. I'm sure you'll see that. And remember there will be people of ours with you both, all the time in Cheltenham, waiting and watching, all that kind of business. We've not gone into this lightly. Any ideas you have about getting out of this on your own will result in certain disaster for Mrs. Jackson and her children. And the same applies if you try and run together. Try running with two small children; you won't get far. Leave them behind anywhere, and we will find out where they are—and their lives will be held against your return, and carrying out the job, Mr. Marlow. It is as simple as that. Overdramatic, you may think, but as far as we are concerned an absolutely precise intention. You were meant to see clearly what happened to Mr. Jackson this evening. Just remember what you saw."

"And if I succeed?" I asked. "If I get you what you want?"

"You'll be free then, won't you? Perhaps you'll find you like the work in Cheltenham. Or like being Mrs. Jackson's husband. Who knows?"

Of course I knew he was lying. For the information to be of any use to the Russians it would have to be extracted from Cheltenham without the people there ever knowing it was gone. And the only way of making sure they never did know would be to get rid of me and Helen afterward in any case; kill us in some way made to seem an accident, a car crash, a fire, or some such. Our deaths would have to be part of any successful deal.

"Perhaps you fancy Mrs. Jackson already," the little man

continued. "She seems to have been quite free with her favors."

"How do you know?" I turned to him, very surprised at this sudden revival of Helen's infidelities, this intimacy with her affairs in the words of a total stranger who, he seemed to suggest, had long ago known more about her than I ever had.

"We have evidence. Some reports we found in his suitcase." He spoke to one of the other men in Russian and I was brought back a green folder with a number of typewritten, yellowing sheets inside.

They were the reports the detectives in East Africa had made out for Guy on his wife's affair with Graham six years before, the reports which Guy had told me he had destroyed but hadn't. I glanced through them. They seemed all the shabbier now, the hard, businesslike words describing a passion fulfilled between two people for the delectation of a third. And I saw them as Guy's death warrant somehow: it was this obsession that no one could live with, but which he had been unable to lose, which had killed him. Spying on real life, and not his official espionage, had led to his end.

I glanced at one of the reports, dated "Nairobi, 17th September, 1965."

. . . he signed the register at the Tsavo National Park game-lodge as "Mr. and Mrs. Graham" at 4:35 P.M. on September 10th. The two parties then went immediately to cabin number 27 at the end of the northern spur. They returned to the lounge of the main building at 6:05 P.M. where they ordered drinks—two local Crown lagers for him and two whiskey-waters for her. Afterward they had the set dinner on the terrace, with a single flask of Chianti. They adjourned to their cabin at 10:25 P.M. Our man was unable to. . . .

How prosaic. Yet Guy's jealous obsession had thrived on just this sort of thing, I thought, since before we can properly imagine any act of infidelity we must have the precise bricks and mortar of the setting.

And in this way Helen's past rose up for me again in these reports, as it must have done for Guy. Here was an outline of all those mysterious intentions in her life, a rough map of the forces which had ruined him and whose effects I was now to inherit. Somewhere behind these bleak pages, as beyond the arid descriptions of Margaret Takazze's novel, lay the real woman, untouched.

"Read it all," the little man advised. "Carefully. On your journey. They give great insight into the woman you're married to, the woman you're seeing tomorrow. Tomorrow afternoon. Your wife."

14

It was an absolutely still and fine afternoon when I got to England next day, watching the manicured land run away from the train I'd picked up at Reading for Cheltenham, sitting in an empty first-class compartment in one of Guy's Savile Row pinstripes, wearing a striped old-boys' tie. There was an endless hazy blue sky over the neat green pastures and gentle tree-filled rises of the Thames Valley. The corn had run to a final blackened gold and was ready to burst; the leaves of huge chestnuts by the river were a dusty, pendulous green.

We got to Cheltenham in two hours. I had heard about Regency Cheltenham, the spa town, the Promenade, the fine trees and gracious terraces, but had never been there. And it was a place I saw from the taxi on my way from the station, which still just—but only just—retained an air of Georgian grandeur, aristocratic conceits, the graceful and decorative arts of a pleasure-filled era, a hundred and fifty years before.

Presently we emerged from the town center, past a garden pub at a busy crossroads, a children's hospital, a straggle of ugly pebble-dashed suburban villas which gradually died out as the road went higher. And then quite suddenly the buildings ended, and we were in the country, with a farm and fields with a herd of Frisians away to our left. And now, about half a mile away, near a reservoir and a large cemetery, I saw something I thought I recognized from a series of photographs I'd been shown by the Russians in New York: a group of wartime Nissen huts surrounded by a high fence, a large car

park, and in the center, a long, three-story red-brick building
with a lot of glass windows and a tall power station chimney
at one end. The building looked like a strange ship. It was
far away from the roads of the town, tucked into the side of
the chalk escarpment. I thought of asking the driver what it
was. But there was no need. It could only be the Government
Communications Headquarters in Oakley Park. The Russians
had carefully pointed it out on a map they'd shown me in
New York—an expanse of anonymous buildings on the outer
suburbs of the town, between the reservoir and the cemetery.

And now I knew too how far we'd got on our journey,
for they'd shown me, on the same map, where the house in
the hills was which the Jacksons had taken, about three miles
above the town. It would have to be there, up in front of us,
in the ridge of thick trees that lay on the horizon, and it
would have a perfect view, I realized, not only of the town
but also of my future office.

And then, as I realized how close I must be now to
Helen, I was suddenly terrified. The whole perfect landscape
threatened me, and I knew that the coming words could only
be words of pain.

The road narrowed and twisted and became very steep.
We passed into the tree belt I'd seen from below: at first,
immediately beside the road, a long line of ancient, twisted
copper beeches, and beyond them a mixture of woods, decid-
uous and conifer, old ruined copses, and a new forest, a plantation of fir that seemed to run over most of the brow of the
hill. It was a strangely deserted area for somewhere so close
to town, without farms or habitation, almost dark in the
failing light. And dead still. The driver paused at a small
crossroads near the top. Ahead of us was open common, but
we were still in the trees, their shadows casting long marks
on the road beyond. He wound down the window. A bird
twittered suddenly. And I could hear it, quite clearly, running away into the woods over the dry mold of leaves.

"It must be down there," he said, looking along a stony
track that led off to our left, gradually sloping down the hill
again.

"Yes," I said. "I'm sure."

He drove down into the woods again and after about a

quarter of a mile I saw the house to our right in a clearing of old trees, a fenced paddock in front, with the fir plantation rising immediately behind it.

It was set back about a hundred yards above the road, with a pathway leading up to it between two rows of crab apple trees. It was a long, low, converted Cotswold barn, covered at one end with a brilliant, coppery red Virginia Creeper, with windows all along its length. It had a wooden terrace giving out over the town and a small lawn at one end, where the front door was, with a lot of roses and glowing autumn shrubs bordering what I could see of the turf. A drift of gray smoke rose from some hidden fire at the far end of the lawn, barely moving against the late sky, pale blue above the horizon of firs. And now, with the noise of our arrival, an extraordinary cackling broke out in the orchard and paddock which surrounded the house, and I saw a flock of handsome plump white geese, suddenly roused and strident, craning their necks and tilting their beaks in outrage, looking at us with deeply offended eyes, complaining bitterly at our intrusion in a long, rising cacophony of alarm.

I got out of the car and helped with my luggage. I was shaking now and my hands were trembling as I paid the man. He offered to help me up the steep pathway but I said no. And he turned in the garageway and drove off back along the dusty road, the exhaust dying, the smell of burned petrol rising in the still air.

And then I heard the cries that I had not wanted to hear —the beginning of what for another man would have been the first notes in a singing homecoming—the first words, in happier circumstances, that begin every book of family reunion.

"Daddy! Daddy! It's Daddy—he's here, Daddy!"

The twins were standing at the top of the pathway undecided for a moment, in their brown corduroy dungarees I remembered from upstate New York, topped off with big round faces and fair-fringed, rakish hair. Then seeing my dark suit for the first time, they both moved at once, quickly, anxiously, tumbling down the shallow rough steps to meet me. And I moved toward them.

I suppose they were about five yards away from me before

they realized I wasn't their father, merely the image of him. But they didn't really stop. They paused for an instant in their rush, and looked at me quizzically, fiddling with their thumbs, suddenly sucking them. Then they recognized me, as the bedtime-story man from that weekend upstate, for they came on quite happily, one of them saying "Have you brought another Babar book?" And the other said, "Yes—have you?" And now they were both very close, looking up at me—bronzed, wide American faces, eyes as clear as water, noses turned up; and one of them—I couldn't tell which—touched my suit. "You're in Daddy's clothes, aren't you?" she said knowingly, stroking the cuff. "They're fine aren't they?" She smiled, looking all over me now. "And his tie, and his shoes, and his bags," she went on in wondrous appraisal. "And you've got his ring as well!" She was particularly intrigued by this fact, touching the brassy metal very delicately. And then the other child looked at me, much more seriously and questioningly, unable for a moment to make any sense of this mysterious transformation. And then, finding the answer she needed, she turned to her sister.

"He isn't Daddy. But he is. He's another Daddy. Our Daddy must be wearing *his* clothes. Don't you see?" And she looked behind me, peering between the crab apple trees. "He's hiding someplace I bet. We're going to have a game."

"Yes," I said quickly. "That's it. But he's not here just yet. I came first to start it off."

And with this answer they were quite happy, and they jumped up at me and clutched at my arms. And I lifted them off the ground, the two of them together, riding one on each arm, and I held them to me and bounced them a little. And then Helen appeared at the top of the pathway, without recognizing who it was, I think, for my face was hidden by the movements of the children. I left my luggage where it was and walked up toward her.

For the first few minutes we behaved in a trance of awful formality.

"Hello."

"Hello. How are you?"

Apart from this we were speechless, looking at each other

with only the vaguest interest, unfocused, unconcerned, the twins running around us shouting eagerly.

She had been gardening or raking, with rubber gloves on, rusty cord jeans, and a white Aran knit pullover spotted with leaves and mold. She took the gloves off and brushed herself down and pushed her dark hair back behind her ears, her face pale in the light, all its questing incisiveness gone. And we just stood there on the paved terrace with aubretia growing out between the cracks, between the lawn and the small churchlike porch and double hall door, the sun low now, but still brilliant away to the west over the town, with a pale blue sky running down toward the horizon, melting into pink and then gold. I looked around at the wide view, and frowned and was almost pompous when I spoke to her.

"It really is a splendid place you've got here," I said, like an auctioneer. "Marvelous. How did you get it?"

"Yes, isn't it?" She looked over the town, pursing her lips, frowning herself now, as if trying to remember something. Then, after a long pause: "Oh, how did we get it? Yes—well, they told us about it. Someone—Mr. Nichols in the housing section at Oakley Park. He wrote to Guy about it in New York."

She turned now and began to look at me clearly for the first time, as if the mention of Guy's name had given her a first clue to present reality. She looked at me with an amazed intensity, an expression that carried no other emotion. Something started to burn behind the skin of her face, a gradually rising heat in her skull which put a fire in her eyes, colored her cheeks, and seemed to fill out her whole being with flame, with a questioning wordless force. So that I said, feeling she was accusing me unjustly and wishing to retaliate: "I thought you might have met me at the station."

"I'm sorry," she said quickly, almost apologetic. "I've never met Guy at stations or airports. It was something we agreed on years ago. You know—not unless I had to. I'm very bad at comings and goings like that."

And there was a tinge of exclusion then, even then: one among a thousand small things between them which I knew nothing about: all the minutiae of their life together, the details they had shared without enmity, the little agreements

which at one time they had made with so easy an acceptance
and understanding.

She had a basket with her on the ground full of freshly
picked lavender and another basket full of crab apples. I
picked them up and sniffed at them both; the first sweet and
dry, the other moist and tart.

"I was getting bunches for the bedroom," she said. "And
Mrs. Grace is going to make some crab jelly with me."

"Who?"

"The lady we have helping."

"Oh. I'll get my bags."

They were halfway down the path and as I turned to
get them I saw someone in the shadow of the hall beyond the
porch.

"Mrs. Grace, this is my husband, Guy," Helen said
when I got back and had put my bags down in the hall. We
shook hands. She was a large, middle-aged, yet clearly very
alert woman who moved quickly on her feet; a good face,
strong and full of character, intent eyes, well-kept fluffy dark
hair, a fine aquiline nose. There was something obscurely
passionate and unfulfilled about her, a mood of poetry almost,
which she wished to communicate, and had failed only for
lack of an understanding audience. She had obvious finesse
and intelligence, and long, unmarked fingers, one with a gold
cameo ring on it. She was like no daily help I'd even seen.

"I'm very pleased to meet you Mr. Jackson," she said.
"I've been looking forward to meeting Helen's husband very
much." She turned to Helen with a friendly, tender look.
"We have got on so well together."

Helen came upstairs with me. There was a landing to
the side of the building, with a run of small windows looking
out on the fir plantation up the hill to our right, and four
bedroom doors in a line to our left. She paused for a moment,
between the first two doors—undecided for an instant. Then
she opened the one nearest the staircase and we went in. It
was a spare room, very neat with a dark-blue fitted carpet
and two single beds with patterned blue-and-white coverlets,
curtains to match, a steeply slanting ceiling and a dormer

window looking down on the valley. I could just see the top floor and the tall chimney of the Government Communications building, the red brick lit by the dying sun.

"I suppose you'd better use—here?" She turned, perplexed, uncertain as I was of my role and placing in the house. "Mrs. Grace goes home. But there are the children."

"Of course."

I put my luggage down. Where could I begin, I wondered? How did one start? What were the right words? I started to fiddle with the locks on the cases, and she went over to a dresser beneath the window and started to arrange the lavender stalks in a roughly glazed Italian jug. She seemed completely her old competent self now, the sophisticated Manhattan socialite, adept in all the social virtues, every nuance of formal greeting: a friend had come to stay for a few days, and all the hospitality would be gracious and perfectly ordered.

"I. . . ."

"I. . . ."

We both spoke at once. She turned from the window and came toward me—and then, very formally with a hint of annoyance, she said: "Where is Guy? What stupid game are you both up to now?"

"I . . . we. . . ." I stammered. I was intimidated by the sudden schoolmistress in her. "Look, could we talk about this later, when the children are in bed? It's very serious. There's no game."

"All right, but roughly what? Where is he? What are you doing in his clothes? What are you *doing*"—her voice rose suddenly with incredulous anger—"in his suit, his shirt, his shoes? *And* his wedding ring?" She grabbed the lapels on the coat and pulled them, shaking me. "What in God's name are you up to?"

I felt she'd be hitting me in a second. "Now? You're sure you want it now?" She nodded. I took the ring off and gave it to her.

"Guy is dead." And then I rushed on before she had time to say anything. "He was pushed out of the window in my office in the UN yesterday evening in New York. By your organization, the KGB. In *my* bloody clothes. And that's why

I'm wearing his. It's up thirty-two floors, you know, my room; and I'm supposed to have killed myself: a pulpy mess filleted through the grating on the cafeteria roof. But that was Guy, I'm afraid, though they wouldn't have recognized either of us after that tumble. They want me for his job—to get some information for them, in that building. *Down there*."

And now I was angry too—at the inescapable hurt that I was causing her, though she didn't show it.

"They put me into his clothes, dragged him to the window, made me watch everything, then took me back to your apartment, briefed me, and I took over everything of Guy from there." I paused. She said nothing. She held his ring, turning it over slowly in her hand, her face perfectly composed, expressionless, her eyes on mine but unfocused, looking through me.

I was shaking now again—and suddenly completely exhausted, a shivering overwhelming nauseous fatigue. I lit a cigarette.

"You need a drink," she said. "You must. I'll go get something."

When she got back with a bottle of whiskey from somewhere, and two toothbrush glasses from the bathroom, she said, "I'm sorry." I was sitting on the bed, my head in my hands, barely able to move. I tried to smile.

"*You're* sorry? It's the other way around, Helen."

"No. I couldn't have seen him killed, couldn't have stood that. Not the actual sight of it, that would have killed me. You had to see all that."

"Yes. He looked at me. . . ." But I didn't go on.

"Exactly," she said. I could hear the sound of the children downstairs, shouting over their tea. "There would have been such pain in that look for me, as if I'd killed the marriage and he was being sacrificed into the bargain; as if I were physically killing him as well. You know the feelings sometimes in a bad marriage, actually wishing the other person were dead. Well, it would have been that, going through that in reality, seeing it happen. And you know, it might have been me who had to watch that, they might have wanted to use me in the same way. Instead, you were the one."

She sat down on the bed opposite, and drank with me,

and she was warmer now, and still extraordinarily composed.

"Times when you wanted him dead. Yes, I suppose so."

"Yes, there were. But not real death. I wanted some act, some action in our relationship, some decision for good or bad: a development of the marriage or an ending to it—not just tagging along together, unfriendly, as strangers, for the sake of the children. And that's happened now. *Something's* happened."

"The most appalling sort of action though, isn't it?"

Then she smiled, fingering the ring. And I couldn't help recoiling, seeing this smile and remembering Guy's very different expression as he went to the window, the always disdainful, isolated face so suddenly flooded at the last with all the essential warmth of life.

"I was thinking about irony," she said at last, slowly. "I have to smile—looking at you in Guy's clothes, and seeing, thinking, how you've come from being my lover to being my husband, without ever having been either: yet still the image of the two people I shared most with—but without our knowing anything about each other, or even having really touched in any way. You see? What kind of reality is it that makes such things happen? I don't know. It's not real. Yet."

She put her hand across the space between the beds and touched mine.

"Come on," she said. "Let's see how Mrs. Grace does her apple jelly."

We went downstairs to the kitchen. In a muslin bag that Mrs. Grace had slung between two chairs, the first cooking of crab apple jelly dripped slowly into a big pan: an hour glass containing an essence of ordinary life, a perfect domestic calendar counterpointing all our terrible deceits.

Afterward, when the sun finally went and Mrs. Grace drove off into the twilit woods and I'd read the twins another bedtime story, Helen and I went into the garden to talk. We piled leaves on the remains of the fire she had built earlier, and, as the flames grew, I told her all the other details of my own tale, which she then accepted as completely real. There were no smiles.

We came in and out of the drawing room several times during the evening, fetching drinks. It was a comfortable split-level room with a bookcase full of the owner's military memoirs dividing it, a brown carpet, russet curtains, a green sofa and a big open hearth, a roughly cut Cotswold stone fireplace with a vase of bracken in it: a slightly cluttered, homely, intimate room, made for winter evenings, for talk and drink and people together high on the hill, hidden in the trees, away from the world.

But now as we talked, whispering in the house for fear that it was wired, with barely louder voices outside, the wretched details of my story poisoned the mood: soured everything of the cosy architecture and the yellow rose bushes —strangely luminous now in the half light. And we drank: drank fast and badly. And it didn't calm us, simply sharpened our nerves, so that we moved all the more distractedly from the garden to the house and back again. Helen pacing to and fro from the drinks table: Helen thinking of lighting a fire, of phoning someone in America, of cooking supper. But she did none of these things, trying through all these mundane actions to escape back into ordinary life, away from this increasing horror. But there was no escape that I could see yet, and I told her.

"They're here somewhere—around us, bugging us, following us, all the time," I said. "And we're down a lane, miles from anywhere. They can cut us off completely, watch our comings and goings, every move. There'll be somebody watching the house—now, this moment."

And then I suddenly remembered Mrs. Grace.

"The woman, for example, what do you know of her? Where is she from? Her accent . . . ?"

"Has she? I thought it was an English accent."

"No. From Europe somewhere."

"She's a dancing teacher in the town. Ballroom dancing. She has a studio somewhere. But it's doing rather badly. No one wants to learn the old-fashioned steps anymore."

"One of them? A KGB appointee?"

"How could she be? She told me she's been living here for years, since the war."

"They have stringers in a place like this where there

are important government departments. A permanent KGB Resident. They could have placed her here years ago."

"But surely . . . ? No, she's not the sort, she's so nice."

"Why not? A lot of communists are nice." I looked at Helen. "And are even good at making crab apple jelly. And the foxtrot."

"But I got her from the government people here."

"How?"

"She'd given her name to them as someone willing to do housekeeping and baby sitting during the day. So how could she be with them?"

"Simply turning down other jobs she was offered, and waiting for you to arrive; then saying she was available for work, and did they have any—knowing you'd need someone. They're not fools. They're doing everything on this job very thoroughly."

"We have a week to think before you start your job. You're on leave, remember." She drank some more whiskey.

"A holiday! Marvelous." I smiled. "They'll follow us anywhere we go. You and I could lose them, maybe. But with the two children it's not very likely. And you've no one here in England you could leave them with. And anyway, go where? And into what future? Family life on the run? Or you could go back to America on your own. But they'd find you there easily enough. They have the ends all tied up. And yet, as I told you, we have to get out. Even if I succeed in getting them this tape machine they are still going to have to get rid of us afterward: the information would be no use to them otherwise. So we *have* to lose them. And I'm no good at guns or fast cars. Are you?"

"No. Surely we have to tell your people here? That's a way out. They can help us."

"Yes. I'd thought of that. Dump ourselves on them, all four of us. It would have to be that. We can't phone. That's surely tapped. I might be able to get down there and tell them," I said, looking at the Government Communications H.Q. beyond the reservoir. "But that place has nothing to do with counterespionage. They'd laugh at me. It would have to be London, my old section there. McCoy, or a fellow called Harper, my immediate Control. I could contact them somehow. And maybe have them turn the whole KGB plan around—get their men. Play along with the KGB."

"But they'll have thought of that." Helen waved a hand slowly through the curl of smoke and then smelled her fingers. The lights of the town were more visible now, a hazy glow beginning to form in the dusk of the valley beneath us. "That's just what they'll be expecting. They know we can't run. So they must assume we'll try and tell."

"How can they stop it? I know we can't phone from here. But I can surely get to someone long enough to make a call without their knowing."

"Yes, of course. But that's just it—it doesn't make sense." She turned to me urgently. "Why did they go ahead with the plan, knowing, as they must have done, of that one obvious loophole: that you would tell your people in London, and that then there would be a good chance of their having their whole scheme played back to them? What makes them so confident with that huge crack in their plan?"

"I don't know. They said they'd kill us—you and me or both—if anything went wrong. I suppose they were relying on that: It's quite an effective lever, don't you think? That's why they got me to watch them killing Guy."

"Yes, but you only have to make one phone call. And make sure you're not seen—a shop or hotel in town, or some house over the hill here. That can't be impossible."

"Why not?" I suddenly thought of something. "They may intend keeping all of us in the house locked up, prisoners, from now until I have the job done. Block the road. Someone with a gun. Have Mrs. Grace bring the food. Very easy. They've probably got some sort of lookout post up there in the plantation. And the telephone wires go along the edge of the trees by the road. They could be monitoring it. Or even simpler, just cut the thing off now that I've arrived. Have you tried the phone recently?"

"Yes. This morning."

"Let's try it now."

We went inside and when she picked up the handset it was quite dead.

*   *   *

"I wonder when they'll show their hand?" I said.

We went out into the garden again and looked around: the lights bright over the town now in the full night, the dark plantation above us, the shadowy rows of apple trees in the paddock, the end of summer, a hint of fine sharpness in the air, and a lot of stars cluttering the sky. Someone, somewhere, was watching.

And as we listened, the air was suddenly pierced with a sharp crackle of alarm: the geese below the house had been roused by something. Their cries rose, then wavered and died.

We were both frightened now, moving over to the flower-border looking down on the road, a rose bush just in front of us, a strong, infinitely sweet smell on still air. Then we moved to the other side of the lawn and peered up through the long lines of dark fir.

And it was this simple, sudden feeling of fear which we shared then, I think, which finally confirmed for both of us all the other details of my story—which at times, in the telling, had seemed fantastic to me as it must have done for Helen. But now we both knew the full truth of the whole business, knew it before it happened: we were trapped.

"Of course the phone could just be out of order," Helen said. "That's always happening in England."

"Yes, it could be just that."

But neither of us believed it. We were trying to support ourselves with words, avoiding the issue, postponing the truth, weary with drink and with my terrible traveler's tales. And it was this feeling of being caught, yet not admitting it, that brought us together in the darkness. Already feeling ourselves victims of some outrage to come in the morning—the arrival of a new and treacherous Mrs. Grace and God knows who else—we both of us must have decided to combat this evil rising about us with some shared action: a statement that would assert, whatever happened later, that we two, at least, knew the strength of affection.

I turned to Helen, seeing her outlined vaguely against the faint light of the fire, the white face with its dark frame of falling hair, the rough white pullover. And wordlessly, with so much ease, we took each other in our arms, ears side

by side, and stayed that way, strange at first with the feeling
of being close, but growing quickly familiar with the idea
as we gave it flesh.

After a time, we sat close to each other on the ground
by the fire, Helen with her knees drawn up, resting her arms
and head on them, her long thighs rising almost vertically,
the rusty cord trousers golden against the dying flames.

"Guy was right about one thing," she said quietly, not
looking at me. "There *was* something hidden in me. I
shouldn't have married him, knowing I couldn't share that
with him."

" 'Something hidden' in you?" I said. "Alexei Flitlianov?"

She turned toward me and said quickly. "Yes. Yes, Alexei." And she kept on looking at me questioningly, as if
in her use of his Christian name alone, in her giving me
this personal clue, I would be able to reach back into her
past and immediately re-create all the facts and nuances of
her relationship with him. But I couldn't.

And I didn't really want to know, having tried to do
that for so long. I wanted to let Helen be, as she was, the
full person then, at that instant, when she contained everything of any importance. Her past, which had so absorbed
us both, was not available to me; she would tell me all about
it if I asked her. And so I no longer felt the need for it.
Curiosity dies completely in the sense of sure possession. And
I must have felt that, then, with Helen: a pact arrived at
wordlessly.

"Well," I said, "I was sure Flitlianov must have been
involved with you, and with Graham; I told you that evening upstate—that he'd probably recruited you both in
Beirut. But apart from that, I don't know. . . ."

"Yes, you're right," she interrupted urgently as if she
had at last found the right audience for a speech she had
suppressed for years. "Yes, it was Alexei, when I was at the
university there. And it doesn't matter now, that you should
know."

"That you and he were. . . ."

"Yes. Him. Before anyone."

"It wasn't just political?"

"No. It was both."

"As with Graham. You've been lucky."

"As lucky as a woman in a story. But it was true. You believe that?"

"Yes, I do. Why not? But what happened?"

"I went on working for Alexei."

"For the KGB?"

"For a part of the KGB. None you've ever heard about."

"The thing you said you couldn't tell me about—the work you had to complete in America, which had nothing to do with me?"

"Yes."

"Well, what is it?"

She didn't reply. And then I remembered the man I'd seen in the dank, overgrown laneway upstate in New York when I'd fallen off my horse, the man in the green jacket with binoculars, staring after us, but not seeing me in the ditch.

I said: "What does Flitlianov look like? Short, fiftyish, hollow-eyed, tufts of white hair over the ears?"

"Yes." She spoke softly. "You've seen him?"

And then I remembered. "Twice. The first time, the day we lunched together in New York. And then that day we were riding. Each time he was following us."

I told her what had happened when I'd fallen off the horse in the laneway.

And then she told me the whole of her story: the story of a dissident group within the KGB, which Flitlianov headed, which George Graham had been a deputy in, and whose total complement of names were known only to her. She said, finishing: "And Alexei's being there—upstate, hiding—can only mean they've found out about him in Moscow, that he's on the run and wants those names, wants them before the others get them."

"The KGB knows you have them?"

"How can they? Alexei was the only one who knew I was the post box. And he can't have told them, if he's escaped. George knew the address of the mailbox in Grand Central, but he never knew it was me behind it."

"My London section could have got the number out

of him when they grilled him, watched the box, and seen you going to it—before I got to New York."

"Possibly. But how could the KGB get to know that?"

"Someone in London, working for them. It's happened before."

"Well, if either the British or the KGB knew I had those names why didn't they go for me in upstate, or the apartment in New York? They've had plenty of opportunity and time."

"Yes, but would they have found it? Belmont's a big place and how could they rifle through your apartment?" And then it struck me. "Of course, they were *waiting* for you to leave America, to come into an empty house over here before they moved on you. They could find those papers easily enough here, take the place apart if you didn't tell them. And they'd know for certain that you'd have brought them with you. And you have taken them, haven't you—those names? They're here, aren't they?"

She nodded.

"Well, if that's so, then Flitlianov must be somewhere around here as well. He'd certainly have followed you over, not having made contact in America. He must be here. As well as the KGB and British Intelligence. They're all after the same thing. And why not? You're sitting on history— the most explosive sort of information. Nothing like it can ever have got out of Russia before. It could alter the future of the whole country. How many names? Hundreds, thousands?"

"They're in code. So I don't know. But there are plenty of them. So hundreds at least, yes."

"Of dissident KGB men—and others, no doubt, in the political hierarchy: the Central Committee, the armed forces."

"I should think so. It's certainly a movement quite outside the acknowledged dissidents, *The Chronicle of Current Events* people."

"If they know you've got those names they'll do anything to get them from you, you know."

"Yes, of course they will."

"And exactly the same goes for my section, here in London."

"Yes."

"Of course, it's up to you what you do with them. But don't tell me where they are."

"No. All I want to do is give them to Alexei, if he's here."

"You may not get the chance. The KGB are probably expecting just that—for him to make contact with you over here. Then get rid of you both when they've got the names. Perhaps you should destroy them. Those people's lives won't be worth much if the KGB gets hold of that list."

"If I do, no one can ever start the movement again. It can only be linked together through me."

"It's up to you," I said hopelessly.

"I'll wait. Alexei might still get through to us. But what about this tape business here, your taking Guy's job?"

"A sideshow, an excuse. Or else two birds with one stone."

It was getting late. We looked around at the woods again, looking for, and thinking of, another person now— an old love returned, perhaps watching us at that moment as he had upstate, hating me, anxious for Helen's renewed attention. She was in an impossible situation.

I wanted to make love with Helen that night. But I was too tired, completely finished, so that we just kissed indecisively on the landing, and I fell asleep almost as soon as I got into bed.

And then, for some reason, I woke. It was nearly one o'clock. My bedroom door was open, the landing light on: I could hear a tap running somewhere. I got up, walked along the passageway, and found Helen in the bathroom, cleaning her teeth.

She turned, wearing a long blue-and-white-striped cotton nightdress, crisp and collarless. "I'm sorry," she said. "I didn't mean to wake you. I looked in. You were fast asleep."

"That's all right."

"I couldn't sleep."

"Yes."

She finished rinsing her mouth.

"Do you want to sleep with me?"

"Yes, of course," I said.

She put the toothbrush back in the rack.

We made love with the children's door open next to her bedroom, listening for cries that never came. It was no great lovemaking, more a succession of tired questions and responses, but the nervousness, the desperation drained from us.

And I felt as we did it that, for her, I was not now in any sense a replacement for her lover or her husband. For she looked at me openly all the while, her face clear in the landing light, with an expression of great novelty, finding something quite new in the experience, something which she had not touched before. Here she was not casting her mind back or forward as she held me. She was in no trouble with memory or expectation. It was now, and now only once, and that was everything.

A key which she had, she used then, which made her lovemaking for me a strange act in a sweet place, far from disruption or tragedy—and removed, even, from sexual desire. She seemed pressed by something else. Our bodies locked together didn't matter. There was some greater pleasure beyond that which she found, and held, and gave.

When we lay apart, I looked at her—one leg, so long in the bed, lying diagonally across it, the other crooked up like a cyclist's against the sheet, arms behind her head so that her breasts became long slopes, the flesh at her waist tightening as she twisted, a bone appearing, as she reached for a towel on the bedside table. Words were no good. I said: "I love you."

I'd been avoiding that. But it had been there quite some while.

And there was no need to say anything else, for she turned back to me, doing nothing with the towel, and looked at me very carefully.

*   *   *

They came next morning, Mrs. Grace and a man with a gun.

We'd had breakfast, happily eating cornflakes and looking out over the sun filled valley, the twins worrying us with plans to fill the marvelous day: a walk over the hill, toy shops in the town, a visit to a zoo. And we'd said yes, if possible, perhaps. And then she and I were unhappy, wondering what other overriding duties the day might bring that would deny every happy plan.

The phone was still dead.

The twins playing outside on the lawn saw them first, and started shouting. When I went out the twins were halfway down the steps toward them. And the four of them came back together, two shining and two rather somber faces, the twins dancing round Mrs. Grace and pointing out the other man to me. "Look!" they said. "Another Daddy."

Mrs. Grace was visibly upset for a moment, though I noticed she took care to hide the fact from the man, looking at Helen for an instant with great feeling, an expression of resignation and sadness, as if she were about to be made prisoner and not us.

He was tall and blue-eyed, fresh-faced, in his mid-thirties, Nordic-looking and extremely polite, his thin fair hair blowing slightly in the hill breeze as he stood by the porch carrying a box of groceries. He looked like a figure in a romantic winter holiday skiing poster. I thought of going for him there and then, while his arms were full. But he looked at me as I thought of this, an easy, understanding expression crossing his face—almost a smile, as if to say: "Do you really want a fight in front of the children? And if you did overpower me, which is very unlikely, there are others—believe me, all around you. So why bother? It would be inadvisable and above all, impolite."

"May we go inside?" he asked. How well he spoke English, formally, deprecatingly, without trace of accent. He was like an evil but very well brought up child who hides his real nature in placatory, conventional phrases, his vicious potential perfectly camouflaged.

He talked to us in the drawing room, while Mrs. Grace busied herself in the kitchen with the twins. Helen and I stood by the fireplace while he stayed by the closed door, leaning against it at first, then pacing around the end of the room slowly.

"You don't really think you can keep all four of us cooped up here for a week, do you?" Helen said at once. "Like chickens?"

"No, of course not," he said evenly, not at all surprised by her deductions. "Your children may go out with Mrs. Grace. You may do the same, while your children stay here with Mr. Marlow. And Mr. Marlow may come out with me, if he chooses."

"And you'll be here all the time?" I asked.

"I'll be around."

"Of course," I said.

"Of course *nothing*!" Helen suddenly shouted. "Of course I'll do nothing of the sort. We were going out this morning. And I'm going."

The man turned to her in surprise, and his reply was genuinely solicitous. "I am very sorry." He looked over the town from the big windows. "Separately, yes. Together, no."

Helen moved toward him. "We're not going to run away—with two young children. You can follow us. We won't telephone."

She was lying. She was suddenly desperate.

The man saw this, as I did, and he said again, with real courtesy: "I am not responsible for the orders, Mrs. Jackson. You will know that. Let us get on together as well as we can. I know that it is not pleasant. Obviously. But it must be finished."

"All right," I said. "Let's finish with this. We're trapped until I start my job down there. Mrs. Grace will feed us. And you'll stop us from doing anything stupid. You and your friends. We understand, it's perfectly simple. Let's leave it at that."

"Thank you, Mr. Marlow," he said, with meaning. "I will make everything as easy and pleasant as I can for you." And I felt he meant that too.

"Would it be of use if Mrs. Grace took the children out now? A walk, a zoo perhaps? And you both—will you let me know of anything, anything you want at all, which we can get you in the town?"

We said nothing. His pleasant, accommodating tones were too much like those of a warden recommending to the condemned man that he eat a hearty breakfast.

Mrs. Grace took the children out and the man took a book of military memoirs into the garden and sat in the sun reading it on a seat by the steps. We could see him from the corner of the kitchen window. Helen was making coffee.

"So," I said, "a plan of campaign?"

We laughed. The situation was so peaceful, so ludicrous; it was unreal.

"How many men do you suppose they have here?" she asked.

"They must be using outsiders from another country, or deep-cover illegals in England, like Mrs. Grace. They'd avoid sending anyone from the Embassy or trade missions, who could be followed down here. Though there may be one or two of them organizing it: Cheltenham is a big town, a holiday place, lots of hotels, quite a few tourists still. Easy to place strangers here. I should say they have at least a dozen people on it. Probably in three groups, with cars, and some central liaison point—a hotel where they can leave messages. What about the area round here—the laneway, where does it lead up to?"

"A common on top of the hill, with a golf course: the twelfth green."

"And the plantation?"

"It must lead back to the common as well—further up."

"And in front?"

"You can see yourself—just fields, hedges, cows, then the reservoir, then the government buildings, about two miles away, and open ground most of the way."

As we looked I saw a tractor with a circular-saw attachment trimming the hedges, about half a mile away. We could just hear the sharp intermittent whine as it bit into the wood. In a long field next to it a combine harvester was moving ponderously, spewing a hazy white dust into the air around it.

"Binoculars, or a telescope, would be useful."

"There might be something in the attic. The people locked away a lot of things there. We could look. What about a mirror? You could signal down to the government buildings?"

"I don't know Morse. What about the postman?"

"Mail comes in a box at the end of the lane, by a main road. Mrs. Grace picks it up when she comes, with the papers."

"It all fits. The KGB might have chosen the place for you." I drank the coffee. "They must have someone above us in the woods, in a logger's hut or something, where they can look over the house, the lane, and the fields in front of us. And someone patrolling the main road end of the lane and the golf course end as well—all linked by radio. But what do they do at night? If we decided to run then, taking the children with us."

"I suppose they think that's very unlikely, with children, in the darkness. Or else they're going to have him here at night, or on the laneway, in a car by the garage."

"Completely geared to stopping us getting out. But how about someone getting in—Alexei Flitlianov, for example? That could be easier. If he's here he'll be doing the same thing as he did in New York: checking the ground out before making a move. And if he's doing that, he must have seen all these people and cars around us. He can't get through as yet; he's blocked."

"If he got out of Russia and hasn't been picked up in America," she said, "he should be able to get into here, or meet us somehow. There must be a way. Look at the place, so easy, so open." She looked down again on the town baking in the light, the sun shimmering on the uncut corn beyond the laneway.

"Is there? I don't see it."

I opened the local paper that had come that morning. I glanced at the editorial, a desperately equivocal piece about a new ring road inside the Georgian town, trying to please the motorists and the conservationists at the same time. And then I saw it, a notice in the entertainment column next to the editorial: the Kirov Dance Troupe and Balalaika Ensemble was coming for a night to the Town Hall next Sunday evening.

"I don't believe it," Helen looked at me.

"It's a coincidence," I said. "It must be. Must have been arranged months ago."

"All right. But it means they can have many more than a dozen men around here, all with perfect cover: a whole company, the KGB orchestra no doubt, with a few heavy secret police dancers thrown in."

We laughed, with a strange feeling of genuine elation.

"What do you think his name is?" I said, looking out at the man lolling in the chair.

"Ask him, why don't you? Bring him a cup of coffee."

She smiled, touched my arm; we were happy. For this future musical event, though in one way possibly making our prison more secure, nonetheless suggested hope: it was a vivacious message, confirmation of plans and activities in a real world that we had lost, and through this music we might regain it.

We waited. One day, two days, Thursday, Friday. We talked and we waited. The sun shone and the colors in the landscape began to turn a little, hints of yellow and red creeping over the trees on the hill. And for part of each night we slept together, came to know each other in that way, carefully and without stress, giving to this part of our relationship a substance, a reality which we could give to little else in our routine.

The man came each morning, saying little to us, but ever helpful and considerate. With Mrs. Grace we had an equally formal relationship, though this became slightly warmer because of her great goodwill toward us. I was surprised at the efforts she made in this way: they were so obviously genuine, as if she really valued our friendship, and was appalled at the turn events had taken.

Helen, who had remarked on this same fragile regret and had continued therefore to trust her, let the twins go

out with her. And the two children were perfectly happy in
what they considered a marvelously continuing game.

At night a car came and parked next to the garage in
the laneway. We watched the news on television, which told
us nothing. We listened to some records; a military march
which Helen somehow liked. I skipped through a biography of Earl Alexander of Tunis and made ever shorter work
of one of Montgomery. The photographs were interesting:
I liked the guns especially. We had Campari-sodas in the
heat before lunch and at six o'clock. The man had got the
bottle in the town for us.

We lit a fire on the second evening, just to see what
it was like, and watched the seasoned beechwood flame and
crackle, and ate next to it with a bottle of wine. The man
got that for us too, half a case: Chambolle Musigny, '66.
Obviously expense was no object in this KGB operation.

We had time—and nothing to do but occupy and entertain each other in it. And wait. And I thought how, if I
had tried to prepare such a situation—with any woman—
how very difficult it would have been: and how practically
impossible, these happy arrangements in an isolated hide-
away, with another man's wife and children. And it was
good to be so lucky—at least in this—that I had Helen, and
that we could share each other so sharply and well, as if in
the last days of an affair, for we didn't and couldn't think
of any future.

The affection and the love between us was, no doubt,
all too easily nurtured, for it was contrived, a creation quite
outside the dictates of ordinary life. As it had been for her
with Flitlianov, and Graham, so it was now with me. And
I regretted that inevitable equation: the excitement of the
intermittent or the absent, the illicit or stolen, and all the
little deaths that come with long familiarity between two
people.

In what was in one way a brief and perfect situation,
with wife and family, I saw very clearly how this perfection
might have continued in a future I couldn't think about.
I experienced in those days all the vitality of love in an
affair that had no future, and all the familial gifts of a marriage that had no existence. As we did things together—

played with the children, read them stories, handled objects about the house, listened to the march, drank wine, made love—I felt myself feeding on a precisely limited number of iron rations which, when finished, would result in our deaths.

On the third morning, Mrs. Grace spoke to us.

The weather had held marvelously, an Indian summer. The children were on the swings, the man pushing them. Afterward, he'd taken off his coat and wandered around the garden, head in air, hands on hips, savoring the world.

We were in the kitchen, tidying up after breakfast, Mrs. Grace pondering the larder cupboard.

"Don't bother cooking anything," Helen said. "We'll have a salad for lunch."

"Yes. I brought some tomatoes."

"Do you want to take the children out this morning?"

Mrs. Grace turned with a tin of vichyssoise in her hand, put it down by the sink, then went to the window. While she was still looking out at the man she said: "I can take them away altogether, if you like."

I looked up from the paper—they were still arguing about the ring road. "You can't do anything with them here," Mrs. Grace went on. "And you're going to have to get away, aren't you?" She turned toward us, her big, fine face at ease now, as it had been when I'd first met her. We said nothing, spellbound, waiting for some truth, or a trap, not knowing which.

"You may not believe me, but I don't want to be part of this."

"But you are," I said, annoyed, interrupting her, choosing the trap rather than the truth. "You're the stringer here, must have been for years. You're not going to throw all that up. What would they do to you? Do you really expect us to believe—"

She interrupted me, "No, I don't. But I've made my mind up."

"Why don't you get out on your own then?" Helen asked in a much easier voice.

"Because I can help. I don't know all the details of this plan, and I don't want to. But I do know that if I don't take the children away, they will: and hold them as hostages in case you don't do exactly as you've been told. They spoke to me last night. They want to take them next time I bring them out, sometime over the weekend, just before you start your job on Monday in Oakley Park."

"What about *your* job?" I asked. "The cause. You've not been sitting here in Cheltenham for thirty years without some sort of belief in it all."

"I've plenty of belief in it all. But not in using children. Belief stops there."

"I thought the end always justified the means?"

She laughed. "Not in this case."

"How do you know? This 'case' might be the most important ever—for you people."

"Perhaps. But I don't know that. I've not been told."

"Need you have been? I thought communism was a dictatorial creed. You did what you were told."

"Yes, I used to do as I was told—until yesterday."

"Now you've set yourself above the Party?"

"Yes," she said quite simply, staring at me coldly. "Yes, I have."

Helen and I were silent, looking at each other. The cries of the children were suddenly loud in the garden, and we heard them well, and then Helen said, "I believe you. What do you want to do? You must be protected as much as the twins."

"Well, I'll take them out tomorrow afternoon—but not to the rendezvous we've arranged. I'll take them to a hotel I know, just outside the town. And wait for you. I'm not going to take any messages to your people in Intelligence here. Not that. You must do all that when you get out."

"How?" I asked. "As soon as you miss your appointment with them tomorrow they'll be down on us like a ton of bricks."

"You must get out of here before that, before three o'clock. It shouldn't be too difficult. They won't be expecting you to run—without the children. They'll be completely off guard."

"But the man?"

"Yes, he's armed. And there's a car always somewhere in the laneway or up on the common—two men, also armed. And people above the house, in the woods."

"So?"

"Well hit this man over the head or something—and run straight down over the fields. Your people are down there, aren't they? You can almost see them from here."

"Yes," I said with a touch of uncertainty. "Of course, I see them."

Mrs. Grace took me up at once. "They're not 'your people' then?" She looked at me.

"It's complicated. Not exactly."

"You're with the Americans?"

"No. Not at all. My 'people,' such as they are, are in London. At headquarters. I have to get out and contact them. And on a Sunday it may not be easy. But that's our problem. And yes, we can try getting over the fields and contact London from there."

"If you can't, or have any difficulty and have to hide out overnight, use my dance studio in Pitville. There's a telephone—and a room above it which no one knows of: in the attic; I prepared it myself. It's quite comfortable, with a way out over the roofs into another side street."

"That's the first place they'll make for when you don't turn up," I said. "After they've been to your house."

"Unlikely. But if they do, the studio will be full of people all tomorrow evening: Western Area Ballroom Dancing Certificate Examinations. I'm not involved. If they come, they won't stay, not with fifty people bouncing about the place."

"All right," I said, "that could be useful. How do you get in, where is it?"

She told us and gave us a spare key to the place. And then she gave us the name of the hotel where she'd meet us on Monday, or whenever we could make it: The Moorlawn Park, a mile out of town just off the main Cheltenham-Swindon road.

"Well, what do you think?" she said when she was finished. The man had gone back and was playing with the twins

again. But now we could see in his playing the real end of
the game.

"Yes," Helen said. "Yes. It's wonderfully generous of
you. But what about you afterward—your job, your family?"

"I haven't any. My husband died. My parents killed in
the siege of Leningrad. I was away at the time—in Intelligence. Afterward the KGB placed me as a DP in a POW
camp in Germany, then I came on here after the war."

"And all that thrown away, just at the drop of a hat?" I
asked. "All gone. You'll be much more a displaced person. I
find that difficult to—"

"I was sent to get information here. Not to kidnap children."

"We can surely get some sort of protection or asylum for
you afterward," Helen said.

"More likely prison." Mrs. Grace laughed. "No, it's best
to say nothing until I'm out of the way. I'll move on. I've
money. Perhaps America. This is not my kind of London
anymore." She stopped.

The man had left the swing and was walking toward the
house. We separated. And I thought, looking at the town
below us in the sunlight: Is this really true? Are we going to
be there tomorrow?

That evening, when Helen and I were alone and had
talked the plan over, I said to her: "There's only one thing:
What about Alexei? All those names you have. What do you
do with them—and him?"

She got up to play a phonograph record: a march. "He
isn't coming. He can't. I've no idea what to do with them—or
him. I'll just have to take them with me, that's all."

Then the needle hit the disc and the military band
blazed into haughty life, a bouncy martial tune of brass and
drums and cymbals, heralding some kind of war after all this
peace.

It went like clockwork next afternoon to begin with. Mrs.
Grace took the children out at 2:30. And at 2:35 I hit the
blond young man over the head—over an ear rather, not being
used to it. He'd just come back from his car by the garage,

reporting the twins' safe departure on the radio to his colleagues at the end of the lane. I got him with the drawing room poker from behind the front door as he came into the house, Helen having called him into the house from the kitchen. We were getting on well with him at that point. He went down very quickly. Helen told me to hit him again. But there was no need. I stood there, annoyed somehow. I'd wanted to knock him out but not to hurt him. And he was obviously hurt. I took his gun off him and locked him in the downstairs lavatory, leaving a half bottle of brandy and some cigarettes inside for his recovery.

And then we were off, running down the steps between the crab apples, onto the dazzling sunlit laneway and into the first field of corn stubble, dodging around the bales of straw, for we were in full view by now of anyone in the fir plantation watching the house. But as we went the geese in the paddock, shocked and annoyed at this sudden impudence in their domain, set up a frantic cackling, awful cries of alarm all over the quiet hills. And then we heard the crack of a rifle shot behind us.

But we still would have made it, the long line of straw bales shielding us, if it hadn't been for the hedge-trimming tractor with the circular saw.

We'd forgotten about that—no, we'd never thought about it—and then there it was as we went through a gap in the ditch into the second field, making for us fast, about two hundred yards away, speeding across the field to a point where it would cut us off before we could get to the only exit, a gateway in a thick bramble hedge in front of us.

The saw was spinning fast at the end of a long articulated hydraulic arm, a crablike pincer whining bitterly on the air. The man inside the cab was practically invisible, protected by a wire mesh, a gray shape bearing down on us from the right. We were gaining on him, but only just, the gate still a hundred yards away. Then he suddenly turned, and instead of trying to cut us off, made straight for the gateway himself. And now he gained on us.

We slowed up. It was no use. He slewed the tractor about in front of the gate and faced us again, pulling the arm around so that the saw spun right in front of us, just above our heads. Then he began to move forward, very gradually, driving us back toward the house like a sheepherder. I got the revolver out and fired. But the thing jerked up in my hand, the bullet going off high above him somewhere in the direction of the Malvern Hills. A second shot was nearer, hitting the spinning saw and ricocheting away. I didn't have time for a third. By then we were moving backward, dodging the blade. And each way we turned, he turned with us, manipulating the arm and tractor together with easy skill.

The cows saved us, a herd of young Frisian bullocks. They had been curious at first, on our run down the field, and had followed us. But now, as we were driven back together, they began to stampede, kicking their hind legs up in retreat, and we found cover among them. And then the tractor stalled, trying—literally—to hack its way through them. It was pure Hitchcock.

"The golf course," Helen shouted, pointing up the hill to our left, away from the laneway and a car which had just arrived in front of the house. There was a line of old trees, I saw, beyond the next field, and then a young fir plantation on the lower slopes of the hill beneath the laneway. We made for that, keeping our heads low along the ditches.

And we made it—getting into the cover of a beechwood, resting a moment before running on along the side of the hill, which rose slightly now, until we reached the new fir trees where we could go faster, moving through the green alleys over a sun-speckled carpet of moss and old fir needles.

We came out of the woods near the clubhouse of the golf course. Outside the staff entrance to the clubhouse I saw two bicycles. The road from here, I knew, was downhill all the way to the town. Besides, it was an afternoon for cycling: soft and fresh and sunny. The drive gave out onto a main road very nearly at the apex of the hill. We turned left, pedaled upward a bit, and it was brakes from then on, seeing the town around a bend three or four miles away in the valley, rushing toward it, past spacious Victorian villas on the left, the Malvern Hills across the hazy distances away to our right.

We forgot pursuit and future then, forgot everything.

We flew, or seemed to fly, adrenalin running as we dived on the town.

There was a phone box at the foot of the hill and I got through to my section in Holborn, reversing the charges, speaking to the duty officer. But McCoy was away, he said, on leave.

"Let me speak to Harper, then," I said. "John Harper, his deputy."

"I can't do that, sir," the bland voice said. "Can't give you his private number."

"Then get him to phone me, for God's sake. At this number. It's urgent."

We hung about, trying to keep out of sight behind the kiosk until the phone rang behind the glass five minutes later.

"Harper here. Who's that?" The Australian voice was impertinent and harsh, ringing down the line at me, looking for a fight.

"Marlow. Peter Marlow."

"Oh yes—*who*? *Marlow*? But we heard you were dead— last week in New York."

"That was Guy Jackson." I began to explain what had happened, that the KGB was after me. But after a minute he interrupted.

"Look this is an open line. I'll get down there with some men right away. Are you on your own?"

"No, with Mrs. Jackson. I told you."

"Right, well stay with her. Keep off the streets, out of sight. Where will you be?"

"A police station—or the Communications H.Q. here."

"Your KGB people will have thought just the same thing. You'll find them there before you, waiting. Go anywhere else. It'll be a couple of hours before we can get down, even if I can lay on a plane. You'll have to wait somewhere— hidden."

I gave him the address of Mrs. Grace's dancing academy in Pitville and told him about the Western Area Ballroom Dancing Certificate Examinations that evening.

"That sounds fine," he said, and he really seemed pleased. "We'll be there as soon as we can. At any rate before they start dancing. And keep *together*," he added. I didn't quite follow him. Did he think Helen and I were going to part? That might have been the case. But he knew nothing of her activities with the KGB: I hadn't told him. Solicitude perhaps? I couldn't expect that of Harper. It worried me a little. But as I came out of the box I said to Helen. "I think it's going to be all right."

The studio was in Pitville Mews and it took us some time to find it. It lay behind one of the few restored terraces in the inner town, a narrow, empty cul-de-sac, which we cycled past several times before going down. Mrs. Grace's business was in the middle of it: "The Pitville Dancing Academy" in Festival of Britain lettering on a long board above the doorway: a smart black door with brass fittings. Three or four garages had been run together and converted, we saw when we'd let ourselves in, into one long studio, with a hall, reception area, and changing rooms at one end.

There was a smell of floor polish and French chalk and some other sweeter smell, a combination of various old and cheap perfumes, lying on the air. The light was very pale and unexacting in the narrow mews, giving the long studio with its white pine polished floor, lemon-colored walls and mirrors, a submarine quality, a sense of fragile, colorless space.

We stepped on the shiny floor for a moment, very quietly. But even so delicate a movement reverberated about the room on the sprung boards. There was an old colored photograph of the Queen at one end of the room, next to a record player with a lot of Victor Sylvester numbers stacked beside it.

"Did you ever dance?" Helen asked.

"We were taught in my prep school. Every Saturday morning. Girls came. It was very popular."

"I like it. I used to."

"I've forgotten the steps though."

"Afterward, perhaps?"

I smiled, "After what?"

She turned to me. "If we get out of this, what will you do?"

"If. God knows. Back in jail probably."

"You could still get away now—on your own."

I laughed. "It's too much like *The Thirty-nine Steps* already. And I'm tired of running. We're together. Let's see how long we can stay that way. With these names you have—the British might do some sort of deal with you, give you anonymous asylum."

"If I do that, won't they think you've done something of your original job for them as well: not the names of the real KGB people in America—but this dissident group? They could be far more important to the West: to know who these people are, to help them."

"Maybe. Do you want to do that. Are you sure?"

"Yes. What else can I do? Alexei's not going to get to us now. They'll be here in a couple of hours. So why don't we work on the idea together—give them the names?"

She looked at me carefully, suggesting a future, all that future that she had once been so ready with.

"All right, we could do that. If you're sure."

"Yes."

There was silence. She kissed me briefly, stood close to me, quite still. We were waiting for the music, about to dance. We might have been. And I saw the two of us, and the two children, living somewhere in London—a terrace house in Regent's Park would have suited—with Mrs. Grace as housekeeper. And all of us happy, of course.

"Well, it might work," I said, letting this crazy vision grow in my mind, burgeon irresponsibly, seeing the red sailing boats on the lake in the park, and the zoo the other side of it, myself the recovered paterfamilias taking the twins for summer walks up Primrose Hill, skating on the lake over icy winter weekends. Yes, I would buy a pair of skates in Lillywhite's, the assistant suitably deferential, and learn the skimming business, awkward at first, but soon finding the knack, the balance, moving smoothly into a happy and responsible middle life. And I thought it's never what we are but what we never could be that keeps us going.

There was a hot cupboard in the lavatory of the gents' changing room, and we climbed the shelves past the cistern, pushing out a panel above it, pulled ourselves up, then screwed the shutter down again from the top.

A rough room had been laid out under the rafters, with

boards on the ceiling joists, a camp bed, books, tins of food, a big polyethylene jerry can of water, an electric ring with a tin kettle on it, and a single forty-amp bedside light.

At the far end of the attic a small curtained window had been let into one side of the wall. Opening it slightly, I looked out onto a wide lead gutter with a steeply slated roof immediately beyond which would shield any exit from the view of the rear windows of the big terrace houses to the left on the far side of the mews. To the right I could see the small backyard of a pub, with the ladies' and gents' lavatories to either side of it, and a lot of aluminum beer casks and wooden cider crates in the middle: everything as Mrs. Grace had described. A man came out as I was watching, a big farmer chap with a peaked tweed cap, just his head visible as he went for a leak, but I had to duck down all the same. Our cosy retreat was somewhere to leave in the dark rather than the light.

"Did you tell Harper that we were going to be up here?" Helen asked when I got back. She was picking through Mrs. Grace's reading matter: a number of old copies of the *National Geographic* magazine and an early text by Victor Sylvester: *First Steps in Ballroom Dancing.*

"Yes."

"And what about the twins? Did you tell him where they'd gone—about Mrs. Grace?"

"No. Just that they'd gone with someone to a hotel outside town."

"What did he say?"

"To keep off the streets. Oh, and to keep together. We'll pick up the children as soon as he comes. Don't worry." She looked at me doubtfully in the hot gloom. The slates above us were still hot to touch after the brilliant day. "They'll be there," I went on. "They weren't going to follow Mrs. Grace to the hotel. That car we saw—after the tractor, in front of the house—that was the one they kept at the end of the lane for us. Not the children. And we'll hear Harper downstairs as soon as he comes. We're only up here in case the KGB calls by."

*   *   *

They called an hour later. It was 6:30—half an hour to go before the dancing started. First we heard several successive keys groping the hall-door lock, then quiet footsteps in the reception area, then—nothing. I was tempted to call out, fearing it was Harper and his men and that now they would leave without knowing we were there. A minute passed. I looked at Helen, whispering, "Shall I call?" And if she had nodded a second sooner than she did I would have. My mouth was just opening. And then her hand was across it in the same instant, gagging me desperately, as the voice rose clear as a bell from the studio immediately beneath us.

"Nichevo. . . ." Then two more voices in Russian, talking. And now the three of them were walking about the place, moving things, looking. One of them came into the gents' changing room, then the lavatory. Silence. Then the hot cupboard door opened.

Helen's arm lay across my chest. I started to push her away, trying to get at the revolver. But the footsteps went back into the hallway, then into the studio where the voices started again.

"Nichevo. . . ." Followed by a lot more in the same vein. And then the word appeared, the name, emerging from the Russian dialogue as clearly as if the man concerned was being introduced at the Kremlin.

". . . Harper . . ."

And just after that the other name, less well accented, but clear enough: ". . . Moorlawn Park Hotel . . ." Then they left, the hall door closing softly, footsteps dying away down the mews.

Helen's arm dropped away from me and I found I was holding the revolver after all, but had no memory of how it had got there.

"Christ. It was Harper. With the KGB. All along. I'm sorry."

She said nothing, looking at me in the gloom; she turned away, went over to the trapdoor, and started to undo the screws.

"Wait. It's no use. They'll have someone at the hotel already, if they know about it. Harper must have had them check all the hotels on the outskirts of the town. But the twins will be all right. They won't move on them—"

"Of course they will. They probably have. Hostages. We'll find a note when we get there."

"All right. But let's think. You still have those names. And that's what they want. The twins will be safe for the moment, as long as you have them. I can get somebody else down from London—now that I know it's Harper—"

"Yes—and have a shooting match somewhere. With the twins in between."

"All right, but—"

"Well, we can't simply stay here. We must *do* something. Anything. Telephone. Come on."

It was cool outside on the roof where we crouched until the light began to fade. And then it was safe to move and we were down the short drop into the pub yard and lurking among the cider crates in the half light.

The back door opened. Two men came out, slightly tipsy. There was music inside, a piano being hammered, people singing, a lot of chatter and laughter, with broken bursts of huge gaiety in the steady hum, as if everyone inside were being systematically tickled.

We went through into the crowded saloon bar. It was an old provincial city pub, a small Victorian alehouse happily forgotten in these narrow streets in the inner town, with the original porcelain-handled beerpulls, curved mahogany counter, and a series of dirty seaside postcards pinned up next to the dartboard. And it was packed tight with elderly folk, part of some group it seemed, very merry, the men in their best dark, crumpled Sunday suits holding straight glass pints of bitters, and the women, squat, with bright-hued mackintoshes and unsuitable hats, full of Guinness. A seedy, narrow-faced man, cigarette ash trickling over his double-breasted suit—a caricature piano player—was playing the piano, thumping out a fifties Jimmy Young number.

The crinkled faces beamed, sang, swallowed, belched, and swayed.

We pushed through this happy alcoholic euphoria, this

old England briefly revitalized in merry song and strong ale at the end of a Sunday charabanc outing to Weston-super-Mare, into the public bar which gave out onto the street. And this was crowded too, with quieter regulars and with a group of men in smart blue suits drinking at the end of the bar by the doorway. The suits, I thought. Suits. What are they doing here?

But by then it was too late.

The first man at the counter had turned and was looking at me. It was Harper, the pockmarked face expanding in astonishment, a glass of gin and tonic raised to his lips. The second man looked up over a glass of light ale. It was Croxley. Detective Chief Superintendent Croxley of the Special Branch. And beyond him there was a third figure, tough, well-built, who wasn't drinking and had obviously just arrived in the bar.

"Marlow!" Harper almost shouted, like a bully, putting a hand on me. "How in God's name did you get here?" He took no notice of Helen. I was suddenly angry.

"Harper," I said, "you little—" But I stopped. "You tell me—how did *you* get here? Why didn't you pick us up?"

The tune had changed next door. They were singing "Good-bye Dolly Gray."

"Good-bye Dolly, I must leave you. . . ." The piano going very strongly.

"We couldn't get down the mews. They were there before us, saw them go down as we arrived. We got them as they came out, end of the street in their car. But you weren't with them. Or back at the studio."

I looked at Croxley. He smiled. "What's this, then?" I asked him. "The Last Round-up?" He nodded, deprecatingly.

"How are you Mr. Marlow? We'd heard you were dead."

"I'm fine. Or I hope I am. This is Mrs. Jackson."

But Harper broke in suddenly, appraising her like a barfly muscling in on interesting company. "Hello, how are you, Mrs. Jackson?" He might have gone on: And the children—keeping well?

"And your children," he said. "Where are they?"

"A hotel outside town," I interrupted. "I told you."

I stared at him. He sipped his gin.

"Yes, of course. But *which* hotel? Where?"

"What are you up to Harper?" I asked. "What are you going to do?"

"Do?" He turned and looked over into the saloon bar, listening to the music wistfully for a moment, as though the tune had stirred some old colonial memory in him, tales of derring-do: the Boer War, Anzac Day, of times when the far-flung Empire had saved the sceptered Isle.

". . . Good-bye DOLLY GRAY! . . ."

They ended it with cheers, roused old voices.

"Do?" He turned back. "Round up these KGB operatives you've put us onto. That's the first thing—now you're safe. We've taken three of them. But there must be a crowd of them in town. There's a show on tonight in the Town Hall, some Russian guitar stuff. So God knows how many men they may have here. We were just considering it, making plans."

The young Special Branch man broke in to Croxley. "Yes, sir. The extra men are on their way, got it on the radio. Coming through Northleach now. Should be here in twenty minutes. And the caravan has been set up behind the Town Hall."

"What are you going to do?" I asked. "Storm the building? Very good for Anglo-Russian relations."

Croxley smiled again, his little sweet weary smile. "Not exactly." A man of few words. I remembered that. Except when they were needed.

Harper said, "We were going over there now; thought they might have taken you there somehow. We have the place surrounded: the plan was to make a few 'inquiries' among the cast after the show. Cleared at the highest level, this. The P.M. You won't have heard, but there's a bit of a purge in the works with these KGB fellows." He turned to Helen. "Anyway, your children are just as important. We should make sure they're safe first. So let's pick them up at that hotel now."

I could see what Harper wanted: to play a double game right to the end: arresting a few KGB men for the sake of a far grander design—getting the names of all their dissident members from Helen. Obviously he must have known about them, known she was the woman behind the mailbox in Grand Central. He'd been part—the English part—of this whole KGB plan for me all along. Now he was closing in, making sure of the kill, part of a pincers movement: if the KGB men already in Cheltenham didn't get the papers off Helen, he would, which would amount to just the same thing. And if I'd said to Croxley that Harper was a KGB man himself, he wouldn't believe me. No one would. They never did. There could be no help from that quarter. So Harper was heading us both now toward some other plan, a situation somewhere in the city where Helen would be confronted with the deal: the names she held in exchange for her children.

They were onto another song in the saloon—the mood besotted and elegaic: "Roses are Blooo-ming in Picardy. . . ."

"Come on," Harper said. "Let's go. We've no time. Where are the children?" He was threatening now. And there wasn't much time.

"All right," I said. "But just a quick one. I need it."

"Brandy?" Harper turned away to order, and when he turned back I had the revolver out, pointing at him. Croxley looked at the weapon with great boredom, as if it was a dirty postcard I was trying to sell him. But he put his hand out, restraining the young policeman who had made a slight move forward. I liked Croxley. He'd always made the effort to try and see my point of view.

"Thank you, Croxley. Get him to give me the keys of the car he came here in please."

Croxley complied. So did the young policeman.

"Stay here till you've finished your drinks," I said. "Don't hurry."

The car had only gone halfway down the narrow street when the engine suddenly stalled, then stopped. I tried the starter once, twice, but nothing. Yet there couldn't have been anything wrong with it. There must have been some antitheft device, an automatic cutout on the ignition, some technical precondition which I had omitted to fulfill. And there was no time now to try again.

The door of the pub opened a hundred yards behind us. And in front, at the end of the street, a Panda police car appeared.

We were out of the car and running. There was a narrow alleyway twenty yards ahead of us to the right and we made for it. It led between two back-garden walls to a piece of open wasteland, the site of some fine old urban estate now razed, with piles of brick and broken masonry everywhere.

We could hear them clearly now behind us. And then suddenly, looming up in the soft darkness in front of us was the shell of a whole house, still standing, a white-stuccoed Italianate villa that had not yet come under the hammer.

At the side were steps leading down to the basement area and a door hanging drunkenly forward out of the deep shadows. Inside it was totally dark with a strong smell of fungus and old damp, and a more recent odor, dry and peppery, of lime dust and plaster rubble. We crouched just inside, backs against the wall, not daring to move further in or strike a light.

And now we could hear them running forward all around us, on either side of the house. But for some reason they had no flashlights and must have been as blind as we were. Someone stopped at the top of the basement steps. But then his footsteps moved away with the sound of half a dozen other running feet and we breathed again.

"Where do you think the Moorlawn Park Hotel is?" I asked. "To the east of the town, off the Swindon road, Mrs. Grace said. We're heading westward. We'll have to double back. The hotel is the first thing. And the second is to get rid of that packet of names, drop it somewhere. And pick it up again afterward. What do you think?"

"I don't know. Are you sure this is right at all?"

"What else? Harper is *with* the KGB, not against them. He would have pushed us into their hands somehow; then 'rescued' us and the children when they'd got those names off you."

"Listen, why don't we give it up? I can't risk the twins like this. Let's give the KGB the names—and get the children back. There's no alternative really."

I paused, thinking: the children versus hundreds of

lives in Russia. But of course she was right. There was no alternative.

"There isn't anything else, is there?" she asked, a strangely conversational, easy voice coming from a black void, a hole in the air. And suddenly I felt the need to confirm her physical existence and I put my hand out and it touched her breast for an instant and then I found her arm and squeezed it.

"No, of course not. There's nothing else, Helen. Come on."

And I felt we'd come to the end then, given up the battle, that the story was over: I trusted her completely at that moment, was completely convinced that she was right. How right and true she was, I thought. We could find the children and give the names up and then we could stop running forever. And perhaps we would live together. Or perhaps we wouldn't. That didn't matter. But at least we would never do this again. Let them have their world of politics and spies, their long battles of belief. We would belong to ourselves from now on, lose the horrors that are due to great ideas: we would take the little roads that led somewhere.

So we went back the way we'd come, creeping through the alleyway, and there, in front of us, where we'd left it, was the police car. Empty. And I suddenly thought: What if I turn the ignition key counterclockwise first, then in the normal direction? I got in and tried this and the engine fired and kept on running.

We came to the High Street, were forced right on a one-way system, then left up the long Promenade of the town, the lamps bright all along its sloping length under the huge canopy of chestnuts. But where to? Which way now?

There was a uniformed policeman on the curb halfway up by a set of traffic lights. I took the chance. Our car was unmarked. He gave us very precise directions to the hotel.

We went left off the Promenade and to our right we saw the floodlit Town Hall, a great Edwardian rump of blackened stone standing back from the road, with a poster outside: "The Kirov Dance Troupe and Balalaika Ensemble." Harper had said the place was surrounded, but no one stopped us or followed us as we passed it.

The hotel was a mile or two further on, a strange two-story Chinese-styled building with a pagodalike roof and delicately carved wooden eaves, just off a byroad, behind a row of new pseudo-Georgian villas.

The receptionist was very helpful. Yes, a woman and the two children were in Number 14, at the end of a ground-floor corridor. At least they weren't in the lounge in front of us. Of course they might be eating: the dining room was on the left just before the bedrooms.

We looked in the dining room—full of quiet, elderly people murmuring over Dover sole and roast chicken—then we moved on toward some French windows at the end of the corridor. Number 14 was the last bedroom on the right. Helen gestured me to go in first.

I knocked. Nothing. I tried the handle and went in.

The bedside light was on and a man was standing next it, behind the bed, facing me with a revolver, a silencer at the end of it: a small, intelligent-faced man with deep-set eyes, in his fifties with ruffs of white hair about his ears. He saw Helen, immediately behind me, and he began to move his gun about, looking at her, waving her out of the way. Then he fired. I heard a slight "Pop" the same moment as the bullet hit me somewhere in the thigh. There was no pain at first, just a quick stab like a syringe needle going in. And I was down on the floor, writhing, yet still there wasn't pain; one was waiting for it somehow. And then it came, as if another bullet had hit me—a sharp and colossal pain, a succession of jabs, as though my whole thigh were being pressed down into a row of knives.

Harper was leaning over me when I came to. I was lying on the bed of the same room. Croxley was standing behind him, and there was a doctor there, packing up his bag.

"What happened?" I asked after a minute. My mouth tasted of some kind of disinfectant. My trousers had been cut and my thigh was bandaged and numb.

"Happened?" Harper said pityingly. "You madman. You walked straight into it. I'd have told you if you'd given me half a chance, without the woman, if you hadn't jumped us in the pub; your friend Helen Jackson is with the KGB. She was using you all down the line, stringing you along. And you fell for it. If you'd stayed with us in the pub we'd have had them both, her and the other fellow she was meeting here."

"What other fellow?"

"The man who shot you—Alexei Flitlianov, head of the KGB's Second Directorate, on the run. That's who she was making for all the time. She works with him. She has some names for him. We've known for some time. That's why I told you to stick with her."

"And her children—the woman they were with?"

"Well, they're not here are they?" Harper asked, looking around the room. "They've all gone. You one-man army. Never mind. All the roads out of the town are blocked. We'll have them. They can't get far with two children in tow."

Croxley left the room with the doctor.

I said, "You're lying, Harper. You're making it up."

He managed a look of very genuine astonishment. "Am I? Then that's an imaginary bullet the doctor took out of your leg." He picked up a smudge of lead from the bedside table. "All right, then, if I'm wrong, you tell me what happened."

"I came into the room. And he shot me—"

"Yes? You had your own gun out, of course?"

"No. I wasn't expecting—"

"Of course you weren't. But he was. Got you first time around. It was all fixed. You walked into the room first, didn't you—because she asked you to, didn't she?"

And she had, I remembered. I nodded.

"Look," he said, like a teacher spelling it out for a dunderhead. "you've been living in the Jacksons' house above the town, haven't you? And the place has been surrounded by the KGB. They got rid of Jackson in New York and put you in his place to get hold of this new code process here. That's the gist of what you told me on the phone. But the real thing they wanted was a collection of names from Mrs. Jackson—unreliable KGB operatives all over the world—which she'd been keeping for Flitlianov. And all she wanted was to get these to him; and get herself and her children safely out of the place at the same time if possible. You were the means. How did she do it? What happened?"

Harper was lying. He must have been. Hadn't she said. . . . No, not that. We'd said very little up in the hills. Much more, hadn't we completely trusted and understood each other? Of course it could all have been counterfeit.

"She *must* have used you, Marlow," Harper went on; the clever Iago, I thought at first, until I began to wonder. If I didn't believe him, I'd begun to doubt Helen. "Can't you see?" He was studious now, an earnest commentator on the arts of betrayal. And then I remembered Mrs. Grace, that sweet smile full of some shared confidence which she had given Helen on my first day in the hills and her subsequent— and to me, almost unbelievable—recantation of her faith. Harper's theory fitted there all right: she had been in league with Helen all along. She was a member of Flitlianov's dissident group. That would fit her very well. She had been in contact with him on the outside; they had arranged the whole escape together, all three of them: she would take the children out and I would take Helen, for we would never have made it altogether. And afterward I would have to be dispensed with. With a bullet. It seemed unfair. Yet it had been a bullet. There was no doubt about that. I didn't trust Harper. But, yes, I had begun to distrust Helen; and, yes, she *had* gestured me into the room first, then got out of the way as he fired. That was certain too.

"Well, so she used me. So what?" I said brashly. And then I thought of the few days on the hill together, the easy things we'd done, the brilliant light and the leaves turning: all that sanity, affection, and fun up there in the woods and the fire in the evening. And I thought, no, it couldn't be. How could she fake all that?

And then I thought, why not? She could. Hadn't she spent a lifetime faking things with people? A fake marriage with her husband. And in her belief a whole faked face to all the world. Hadn't she always inhabited permanent cover, absolutely according to the book, lied convincingly about everything? About her politics as about her lovers?

Her belief, which was no doubt genuine, and the secrecy with which she'd had to hold it, had led her to infect and destroy every close relationship with the same illicit urges—to sacrifice any present truth, a happy body or thought, for a clandestine political ideal. Things had to be secret for her before they could be real and so she could not sustain love in any open reality. She was a woman who thrived on the intermittent and clandestine in any affair, who required eventual failure and betrayal in love as others seek orgasm as a culmination.

Or perhaps, simply, she had just wanted to be with Flitlianov again. Perhaps it had really worked only with him: a father, a body, and a belief all wrapped up in one; and everything in her life since had simply been done in memory of him. Graham, Guy, and I, we had simply been bystanders, stepping stones to that end, to that eventual reconciliation with the one man who had really mattered to her. These were theories. And Harper could have been bluffing and lying. But whatever her motives there was no doubt that I'd been shot, that she'd left me and gone off with Flitlianov. That was no theory.

"She used you good, Marlow," Harper went on, anxious and concerned for me now, and not dismissive. "Cut you up into little pieces. Couldn't you have guessed? Seen it coming?"

I couldn't look at him. My thigh was numb but lower down in the calf something had begun to throb. "Maybe," I said.

"Tell me," Harper asked, with one of his crumpled smiles, "you weren't just pretending to be man and wife up there? You slept with her I hope."

"What's that got to do with anything?"

"You did, didn't you?"

"Why not?" I asked angrily, as though I'd simply forced her to share a physical whim with me.

"You liked her a little too, though. I can see it in you, Marlow." I looked at him with distaste. "That's why you won't accept it, that she pushed you down the river. The facts speak for themselves. Shouldn't get involved that way with Russian agents, Marlow. That's Rule One. But how should you have known? You've no experience in this business."

And then I was really angry—at him or Helen, I didn't know which. At both of them, I thought: angry at the truth.

"Yes, but why shoot him, Alexei? Why?" Helen asked.

"I had to. How could you trust him?" He looked at her in astonishment.

I did, she thought, I did.

"He'd have ditched you at the end, after they'd got the names from you and taken me. I had to get him out of the way at once, without his having a chance to offer talk or arguments, to hold us up. He was a double agent all along. And would have been at the end too, for all he's fooled you in the meanwhile. Couldn't you have seen it coming, Helen? I've been following him for weeks, months—since he left London—while I was trying to get in touch with you. I saw you both upstate in New York one morning riding. I followed you there. I wondered how in hell he'd got into your family circle so quickly, and then in a flash you were in his arms."

"That didn't mean anything. I was worried, that's all."

"Of course you've been too long in the open, without anybody, any links with us that would have kept you going. I understand that. But falling for a British agent; that's too much. That's Rule One: not to."

"I didn't know he was a double agent," she said. "I just believed the KGB was using him to get the technical information here, as I told you."

"That was one line, yes. But the British were using him as well, all the time: to get you and me together when you handed over the names. That's obvious."

Was it? She wondered. Had Marlow lied to her? Had there been nothing true in him during those days in the hills—and before in America when they had talked for so long, in Central Park, the Breton restaurant, and upstate? Had his whole bearing toward her, from the beginning, been a crucial degree out of true, driving her toward the rocks, to this betrayal which Alexei had just prevented?

She was totally confused.

She had trusted and loved both these men. And now

Alexei was killing Marlow in her mind, just as he had tried to kill him in reality. Was it jealousy or truth? Surely, after so long apart, Alexei could not have been jealous of her? He'd never been that sort of man. And there were no grounds for that now: the whole business for him with these names was a matter, precisely, of life and death for many people, including himself. Besides, he was vastly experienced in the business of subterfuge. And so she began to think that perhaps he was right. Or, at least, if he were not exactly right, she had begun to doubt Marlow. What she had seen as his naïveté, his inexperience in the work, his being framed by British Intelligence and forced into the New York job, as a tool—all this bruised innocence had been a very clever front, perhaps.

And then she remembered the extraordinary coincidence of their first meeting, the moment he'd got to New York, in the guise of George Graham. He'd said the British had never known anything about her, that they'd never picked up that information from Graham. But of course, they had. And her meeting with Marlow had been no coincidence at all. It had all been arranged. He'd been planted on her—to get the names and, in the event, Alexei as well. Marlow was really as clever an operator as Alexei. And now that she was with Alexei she felt the truth of all this kindle in her and burst into flame in the suddenly renewed warmth of his presence.

In the hotel, fifteen minutes before, she had tried to do something for Marlow, struggling on the floor, before he passed out. But Alexei had pulled her away. They'd left the place by the French windows at the end of the corridor, hurried across the dark lawn under the huge ilex tree, and now they were walking along the small suburban road back toward town, to a church by the traffic lights further up where they were to meet Mrs. Grace and the two children.

He'd told her about Mrs. Grace: how, when he'd been unable to get through the KGB cordon at the house in the hills, he'd followed the woman back one evening, found out where she lived, studied her carefully, and then taken the decision to approach her. And he'd been right. She was a member of his dissident group, recruited years before by one of his deputies in Russia. And the rest had been easy; the woman had no taste for kidnapping in any case. The only problem had been getting Helen out, for they couldn't have all escaped together with Mrs. Grace. But Marlow had done the trick there. After all, he'd been as anxious as anyone for her to get out so that the British could take her and the names and himself—in the clear, without a shooting match, a diplomatic incident, up in the hills. And wasn't that just what Marlow had done, Alexei had asked Helen, the moment he'd found a telephone box? Phoned up H.Q. in London and told them everything was ready and given them the address of the studio hideout in the town.

"But why did he bolt from the pub then?" Helen had asked.

"Another bluff. What kind, I don't know. Don't you see it, Helen? He double-crossed you all the way along. You *must* see it."

She believed him now.

Trees hung deeply over a high stone wall all along one side of the road, and the street lamps were hazy yellow globes, strung up high at intervals in the leaves—dark, heart-shaped patterns waving slightly in the warm air, moving over this abrupt, awkward, angular face which she had not seen in years. Yet it was the same face, exactly so, as in those previous times, which had survived and was an indubitable presence, here in this suddenly glum autumn evening on this suburban road.

His face. A good face. Its lack of conventional symmetry had so affected her in the past, had made the matrix of her love for him so much more precise, that now, as she looked at it closely again, she was able to trace and renew those old emotions for him in herself instantly, as though she had found in his physiognomy a long-lost map describing the treasures of her life and could now at last resurrect them.

An earlobe still curled outward in a minute, strange way; the wrinkles on his forehead were deeper but not more numerous; a front tooth was still chipped: she had traveled intimately about this body once. And then she had come to think, in his long absences, that these physical characteristics didn't matter: you could forget them. You had to. Affection lived in the spirit, not in fact. But now she realized how the spirit was so often dependent on the unique configurations of flesh and bone: a precise reality, a moment when you looked at, touched, a living, present face—and knew it was yours. And such loss—the touch of someone's hair—could well be the only real loss, she thought.

She felt her stomach move with this sudden renewal of emotion—at this realization, which she had suppressed, of how imperative immediate presence was in love; of how, just as it often started with a shared look across a room, so it survived, or could be regained in a moment, long afterward, with this same simplicity of an intense regard.

So her affection died for Marlow as it rose for Alexei: Marlow began to disappear and Alexei swung toward her, like the wooden figures on a miniature Swiss chalet that came out for sun or rain. And the articles of trust were transferred from one to the other, as the deeds of a dead man's estate are passed to a living heir.

The church was coming up on their left, Catholic, a long, modern building, characterless, in reconstituted Cotswold stone, the Christian vernacular of the seventies, where the setting had to be as bland and undisturbing as the new liturgy.

As they got to the gateway of the church, a police car swung around the traffic lights ahead of them and stopped on the corner. Two plainclothesmen got out. Alexei and Helen could see Mrs. Grace and the two children sitting in her car, parked on the far side of the chapel next to the rectory.

Alexei looked up the road. The men hadn't seen them yet but they would at any moment.

"Go inside, Helen. Quick. I'll bring the others."

In a minute the five people, a perfect Sunday family, with Auntie, were sitting in one of the back rows. The Mass had already begun. The children sniffed the air appreciatively, their eyes fixed on the altar and the movements of the priest as on some charade, a dumb show whose meaning would at any moment become clear to them, when they could then laugh and cheer.

Helen and Alexei were at the end of the row, by the windows, in a distant hollow of the chapel. The congregation knelt in front of them for the consecration. But the children stayed on their feet, happy infidels, peering intently over the edge of the pew.

"Where are we going?" Helen whispered to Alexei, their heads bowed, close together.

He shook his head, without saying anything. The priest prepared the Host. At last he whispered back, "Out of here. You have the names."

"We're not all going to get away. The roads will be blocked. The children. We can't run forever. Couldn't you give the names to the British? Get them to help in the future?"

"No. They wouldn't believe it."

The priest lifted the Host above the altar. A bell tinkled quickly—and then again.

"You're beginning to believe like they do." He tilted his head briefly in the direction of the altar. "In failure. But we *know* all about that. That's obvious everywhere. You don't have to come to *believe* in it. You do something about it. I told you years ago. I said 'You believe in these political facts now; remember that, when you begin to despair of them— as you will.' As you have."

"I still believe in those facts. But children are facts too. And so are roadblocks."

"We'll have to get out. The names you have—we're responsible for hundreds of people: that's a whole world in our hands."

"And so is this—us, here, now. That's a world as well."

"Yes, of course," he said with tiredness. The little bell rang again, insistently. "And you'll lose it, if you stay."

"I'll lose it either way, Alexei. We were lucky, sharing each other as well as a belief. But they don't often go together. And not now. You go on your own with the names." She took out the plastic envelope tucked in behind her trouser belt, and passed it to him. "They can't do much to me."

"They can. Prison. You'll lose your children. And haven't you lost enough already?"

"Yes. But I knew the risks when I started. Be realistic: those names are more important than me. You know that, Alexei."

"Yes, I know that."

"I want to go with you. But it wouldn't work. I want to very much. But you must go on your own."

She smiled—a rapid, intense smile, compacting the message, making it a sudden, boundless gift, through which she could tell him that she felt hope, and was not sad, in this divided future: a smile that would confirm her renewal with him as much as their imminent separation; that would tell him, without doubts, that she had reachieved all the forward parts in her nature, that she had found again—here with him at this moment—the world, that proper world, which they had both sought for so long, where charity and affection ruled, where prayer was continuous and not distantly intermittent. And to find that world you had to lose it first. Wasn't that what they said?

"You *must* go, Alexei," she said quite simply.

Harper traveled with me inside in the ambulance from the hotel. He didn't want to let me out of his sight, I thought: I was the one man who might know too much. I wondered if he'd try and kill me. We drove to the side of the Town Hall to a police caravan hidden in the trees, a temporary command post. There he got out to see how the roadblocks were getting on.

And now I could hear the balalaikas quite clearly on the still air, coming from the Town Hall beside us, a restrained vibrato, then the tune.

"Nothing," Harper said when he got back into the ambulance, sitting on the bunk opposite me. "Nothing yet." His face began to crinkle, filling up with a sly smile. "But they'll come. We'll get them." He was so happy.

I said, "Now there's only me to worry about."

"You?" He reached out his arm and fingered the tape on an oxygen cylinder strapped to the partition at the end of the ambulance. He lifted the mask up and put it against his own face and stared at me, unblinking, like some fearful prehistoric fish revived from the depths.

"One can die of too much oxygen, I suppose," he said, dropping the mask, "as well as too little."

"Might be tricky at the postmortem though."

"Would it—in your case? Delayed shock, a sudden seizure. I had to give you oxygen quickly. . . . Would it?"

We looked at each other carefully, like boxers between rounds.

Harper put the mask back. "I don't have to run the risk. I know what you think about me, Marlow. But it's just your word against mine. And after I've shopped hundreds of KGB men tonight, who is going to believe you then? No one."

"How are you going to get those names?" I asked. "They're not going to leave the town all together. They'll separate. And in any case they're not going to give the names to you, of all people, whatever happens."

"I'll get them."

I wanted to keep Harper talking. He was too confident. He was bound to relax—for an instant, at the wrong moment. Then I might get him. He thought I was an invalid. But I hadn't been that badly wounded. I could move, I was sure, move fast for a few seconds at least.

"They'll give themselves up—the women and children. But he won't. And it's quite a big town, inside your road-blocks."

"He can't hang around in someone's back garden forever."

"And you can't stop every car leaving town forever either."

"No."

"It may not be that easy, Harper. You may never get those names. I hope you don't."

"Ah, Marlow, I should never have suggested you for this job in the first place." Harper shook his head in mock despair. "You believe in it all. In the rights and the wrongs. But there aren't any in this business. It's fatal to believe anything about it. You get your head chopped off."

Flitlianov moved carefully through the municipal gardens that lay at the back of the Town Hall, around a fountain, along neat paths, beside a succession of wilting herbaceous borders. Clouds had come in with the evening and for the first time in a week the night was dark.

Ahead of him, between clumps of evergreens, he could see the stage door, to the right of the building, with a man posted outside. But to the left, on the other side of the hall, was another doorway with a pile of beer crates stacked beside it. A man came out, pushing a trolley of empty bottles. Flitlianov cut across the grass toward the catering entrance.

Once inside the building, he walked through a pantry, across a corridor, and up some steps to a door which led backstage. He opened it and the music hit him, flowing over him, a Georgian peasant dance he remembered well, a bright and stormy affair, where two circles merged and then flowed away from each other, the men moving outward, stamping their feet, the girls clustering in the center clapping their hands. He knew the shapes of it all exactly without seeing anything behind the back curtain. A Russian approached him. Flitlianov showed him his card. "Embassy Security. I've come down from London. Just a checkup. I'll be leaving with you after the show." The man nodded blankly. Flitlianov listened happily to the music. He was home again.

The next time Harper left the ambulance I reached up for the small brass fire extinguisher above my head and hid it beneath the blanket, holding the plunger tap firmly, and pointing the thing to where Harper had been sitting opposite me.

And when he came back he was sitting comfortably and had lit a cigarette, had talked some more, and was saying, "No, you've had a lot of bad breaks, Marlow—" I emptied the canister of foam straight into his face. And then I was up, hovering on my good leg, falling toward him, the canister raised until I cracked him over the head with it. I was getting quite good at chopping people's heads off.

As soon as I was finished with Harper the back doors of the ambulance flew open and Croxley was there with two plainclothesmen. They looked disappointed, I remember. One man stayed behind with Harper, while the other two carried me across to the police caravan. All three of them had been waiting just outside I realized. They must have been there all the time.

"Harper is with them, Croxley. With the KGB." I said when they'd got me on a chair in the caravan. Croxley looked embarrassed.

"Yes, Marlow," he sighed, politely. "We knew that. We—"

The skin at the back of my neck and in the small of my back pimpled in an instant and my stomach turned violently.

"Well, what the fucking hell have you been doing then?"

"It wasn't my—" Croxley stopped and shrugged his shoulders. "The idea was that he'd hang himself, if we gave him enough rope. We—"

"What rope? How?" Croxley looked over my shoulder.

"You were the rope, Marlow," a voice said.

I turned. McCoy was standing in the doorway, his puffy face gleaming from some exertion, folds of skin seeping out over his starched collar and tightly knotted old-boys' tie. He came in and looked at my leg with distaste. "We knew about Harper. But couldn't really prove anything." McCoy was suddenly an awful version of Hercule Poirot, assembling the candidates for murder in the library, about to superintend the final denouement. We had moved from Hitchcock and *The Thirty-nine Steps* to Agatha Christie. It was all still so unreal, still a fiction to me. But not for much longer, I thought. The fiction was running out fast.

"So?" I asked, working now for the truth.

"We'd been watching him quite a while, tapping his phone. And when you called him this afternoon telling him about Guy Jackson in New York and how you'd got away from the KGB—out of that house in the hills—we thought he'd probably try and get rid of you then. You were screwing all their plans up. But once you ran from the pub, we were sure he'd go for you. Because somehow you knew about him then, didn't you? That he was a double with the KGB. And he knew that you knew. So we gave him his head with you after that—left you alone together—in the hotel room, in the ambulance. And hoped he'd get on with it. Instead you bungled it—tried to kill him. If only you'd let him do it, then we'd have had cast-iron evidence."

"Thanks."

McCoy took no notice. He moved over to the sergeant on the radio desk. Some information was coming in, a voice crackling on the receiver. McCoy listened carefully.

"We'd have stopped him actually killing you," Croxley put in, by way of mitigation. "We were just outside."

"Thanks again."

McCoy came back.

"Well, you have Harper now," I said. "A week with Croxley here, and he'll spill everything. But what about the others? You know about these names? Flitlianov must have them now—a liberal group within the KGB, dissidents. They're important."

"Yes," McCoy said wearily. "We know about the names. But they're not liberal dissidents, Marlow. Our politicals have checked. They're just unreliable KGB agents, the names we sent you over to New York for in the first place. Nothing to do with liberalism. Mrs. Jackson sold you that idea. I suppose she thought we might take them over and believe we were running them back against Moscow. But it would have been the other way around; we'd have bought ourselves a brigade of double agents, instead of the one or two like Harper we have anyway. 'Liberal dissidents' my foot. I can tell you—when we get those names we'll pack them all out of the country smartish."

"You knew about Mrs. Jackson then—all along?"

"Yes."

"About her and George Graham?"

"Yes. Graham told us about her as well as the names—in the end. And of course we'd read her letter to Graham that morning in Marylebone before you did."

"So I was planted on her—from the start? You knew she was with the KGB?"

"Well, obviously we couldn't have told you, Marlow. We had to get you to trust each other, so that we could keep tabs on her, through you. Guy Jackson was no use. We knew that. He was working for the Americans. So you were the crucial link there. And it would have gone fine; we'd have had all the information about her out of you, and got those names a lot earlier, if the KGB hadn't decided to switch you and Jackson in New York and start this Cheltenham deal."

"You knew about that too?"

"Yes. And we decided to ride with it. Jackson was no loss. And it looked like an interesting situation, full of possibilities from our point of view: whatever happened when you got back to England, we were going to lay our hands on a lot of KGB men in this country—legals and illegals. To handle you they were going to have to come out of their holes and be counted. And they have, Marlow, they have: half a dozen so far, and more to come, many more, before the night is out. So you've done all right, Marlow. Even though you did your best to screw it all up. Don't despair."

"I don't, McCoy. Only of you."

McCoy got out a handkerchief and began to wipe his hands with it carefully. "Don't be like that. We have to do a job. And you're here—alive, in one piece."

"No thanks to you."

"One doesn't thank anyone in this business. It's quite thankless."

"So you knew everything, all along," I said. My leg had begun to throb and ache.

"We had to, didn't we? That's what it's all about. Sometimes people are used in the process. But that's just as true of ordinary life. You'll see—if you get back into it."

"If?"

"Who knows?" McCoy finished his toilet. "If we get these names tonight they may consider your slate clean, Marlow; that you've worked your passage. A free pardon, even compensation."

Compensation. I remembered my tirade against McCoy in Durham Jail months before, my anger at four years lost behind those granite walls. What would compensate me for this, these months as a patsy on everyone's behalf: Helen's, McCoy's, the KGB's?

But no, I didn't need any compensation for it now, I thought. The hell with it. It hadn't been funny. But it wasn't really tragic either. A bad tragicomedy. I had been forced into a number of roles and now I could drop them. It hadn't been a good production; it was folding. The audience had only been mildly amused. The backers were withdrawing their money. It was time to wipe the greasepaint off, tip the stage doorman, and make my way quietly home. There certainly wasn't going to be any party.

I said, "Well, there's time yet, isn't there? Flitlianov may get away. You may never get those names."

And I hoped that he would get away, that someone would come out of it all clutching something decent, the deeds of a worthwhile future. For I believed Helen at least in that: that these names represented something valuable in Russia: a force against the indifference and brutality of that world. And I believed what she'd said about Flitlianov too, that he had something vital to offer, something sane and passionate to invest in the confused affairs of men.

And what did it matter if Helen had used me to escape back into this hopelessly optimistic adventure? She would pay more than I would in the end for her daring.

I said, "Flitlianov may still screw it all up for you, McCoy. And I hope he does."

McCoy nodded his head several times, as if at last confirming something long suspected. "You're a good fellow, Marlow. You really ought to have got a job with Oxfam or Shelter. Out of harm's way. We've got Flitlianov already, or as near as makes no difference. He's in the Town Hall at the moment. Just had it from one of our men backstage. Last thing I thought Flitlianov would do. But I see it now. He must have thought he could have got away with the dancers and musicians—they wouldn't know anything about him—in the coach after the show. And even if we'd spotted him he'd know we couldn't touch him among that lot— cause a terrible political rumpus. And the P.M. wants all this kept completely under wraps for the moment, till we get those names."

"So?"

"So—we're going to have to separate them, aren't we? Before they leave the hall and hop on the coach. Not too difficult. We've a lot of men in there. The finale could be the moment." McCoy got his glasses out and consulted a program with distaste. "The finale, yes. 'Gopak Dance,' whatever that might be. The whole company is on stage then. And Flitlianov will be somewhere alone behind the scenes. Just a matter of timing. I'll tell the men." McCoy stood up. "Now there's only your other friends to worry about, Marlow. Your wife and children, I should say. That must have been a lark." He smiled at me like a man on a winning streak at the races. "And you think *we* used you. But don't worry; they'll come safely home, wagging their tails behind them."

Ten minutes later they brought Helen, Mrs. Grace, and the children into the caravan. They sat up at one end, next to the door, a woman police officer tending them. I was up at the other end, on a bunk, by the radio equipment, immobilized, or I should have got out of the place at once. The police doctor was giving me a sedative. And of course, it must have seemed to Helen as if I was very much with the police: the *agent provocateur* come home to roost.

Helen's hair was wet, though there had been no rain—dark and glistening, as if she'd just come out of a shower. The policewoman gave her a towel. There were cups of tea. And silence. Helen looked at me briefly with indifference. Not hate, that would have been better. That would have meant something, that I existed for her still, as I didn't any longer in this empty regard. I thought of saying something. But I knew it would do no good now. Excuses, she would have thought. Lies and excuses. I was the little robber, her look said, a cheat from the beginning, who had wormed my way into her trust and then sold her down the river, or tried to.

I looked at her, and she was still so fine, so clear a person, that I began to doubt that she had ever intentionally betrayed me. I should like to have talked to her about that. But, my God, hadn't we talked enough? And it had got us nowhere but here—to this huge division, where any words said would be the wrong ones. We had been driven into an implacable enmity toward each other.

We had no reserves in our relationship, which might have saved things. Trust, which needed time, hadn't had a minute. She and I had traveled across the whole spectrum of an affair in a matter of a few days, even hours; had experienced the happiness and the pain, the beginning and the end, almost simultaneously, without ever having had the chance to live things in between, to save ourselves from a bad end. But could we have done that in reality, I wondered, if there'd been the chance, even in Regent's Park with Mrs. Grace as housekeeper and the children boating on the lake? Could we have saved each other from the familiarity and boredom that eat away the poetry of even the happiest association? An end had overtaken all our surprises. Expectation had been killed; all the mechanics of happiness had been smashed. "Shall we do this tomorrow, next week, or next year? Or shall we do that? Will you phone me? Shall we meet?" The mundane arrangements that are yet so bright, so imperative in love had been struck off the calendar. The future had shut up shop and sane adventure had been locked away for the duration.

She had written to Graham, I remembered, how we think we have experienced the past, because we have lived it, willy-nilly. But how there were so many turnings off it which we knew about but had never traveled—the little roads that went somewhere; and how she had wanted to live now, with him, all that was unlived then. And that she felt she had the gifts for this. And she had. She might have done it with me.

And I was angry then—not at her, but at the loss of this. And I looked at her with this anger, which she could not have understood. She could only have taken it as evidence of a mutual disgust. And perhaps that pleased her, thinking my enmity as great as hers, that our disgust balanced out—so to end things neatly, which is the last ambition of two people who have come apart: to leave something neat and tidy between them, even if only hatred.

So there was silence, an empty space, where words had died and anger bloomed; and where that fabulous regard which two people can share, that calm offering of self, so unmistakable in promise and beyond all language, had gone too. That vision between us had become despicable. The radio behind me crackled and perhaps the wind changed, for I could hear the balalaikas from the hall again now, rising and falling sweetly. But neither message pleased—the words and music from a cooling, sour world.

The twins had been looking at me, I suddenly noticed. And of course I realized I was still in their father's clothes—his shirt and old school tie and coat and ruined trousers.

They tried to walk over to me but Helen and the policewoman held them back. They were tired and the pain of all these confused events was beginning to show in their faces. The game was wearing thin. But they had recognized me—brightly and eagerly—and were sorry now that they couldn't come over to me.

"But that's the daddy we play with," one of them said. "The one that tells us stories, Mummy. Can't we have a story?"

"No, not now," Helen said, smiling at them, touching their hair, stroking their cheeks, intensely familiar, in these last moments. "Later perhaps. When we get home."

And that was the saddest story I ever heard.

I hobbled over to the doorway of the caravan, but of course could see nothing of the real action inside the huge building. I don't know exactly how they got Flitlianov. But they got him, of course. And they got the names, for by the end of the month the whole thing blew up and more than a hundred Russian diplomats and trade officials were expelled from the country.

I tried to imagine Flitlianov's last moments. Like something from a film, I supposed: the men creeping up through the audience, along the aisles, and the others coming in by the stage door at the back. Perhaps he'd hidden in a lavatory and had tried to flush the names away? Perhaps he'd put up a fight—fisticuffs or guns? One wouldn't have heard anything above the din on stage. It was ludicrous, I thought, a man being trapped like this. It always was. Sheer fantasy. Perhaps it had happened like the Marx Brothers in *A Night at the Opera*—Flitlianov swinging across the stage on a chandelier, losing himself among the players, then a frantic chase about and behind the stage. The comedy of this idea appealed to me. And I longed for a comic life.

They brought him out through a side door quite close to the caravan—while the applause for the end of the show was at its height—so that it seemed that Flitlianov was the reason for the frenzied appreciation, a hero being hurried away from the field of his glory.

Helen and the others had been taken out of the caravan just before. And now I saw her and Flitlianov for an instant before they were put into separate cars, and though I couldn't make out anything in their faces, I saw them wave to each other before the cars drove off and turned into the lights under the huge chestnut trees along the Promenade.

McCoy came back into the caravan to pick up his things —happy, savoring already a tremendous future: the bureaucratic commendations, possibly a medal from the Queen.

"All over, Marlow. Finished. Safe and sound. And you've helped. At least, I'll say you did. A week in hospital and then I'm sure we can let you out to grass."

I looked at McCoy, the puffy, ruined face proud now and full of all the silly rewards he worked for.

"We've got them all together, now. Everyone. All happily resolved. Don't you see?" he said, as though he was offering me at last the incontrovertible evidence, the veracity of faith I had long denied.

I smiled at McCoy then. The only thing that had been resolved was our absence from each other.

"All together, McCoy, of course," I said, "as it was in the beginning, is now, and ever shall be, world without end. Fucking Amen."

McCoy looked at me curiously.

"Don't be like that Marlow," he said.